Sincerely yours

Anne B. Fisher

Cathedral
in the
Sun

ANNE B. FISHER

STANFORD UNIVERSITY, CALIFORNIA

JAMES LADD DELKIN

To

THE MEMORY OF ISABELLA MEADOWS

who held high the torch to light the way

for those who follow her

Books by ANNE B. FISHER

WIDE ROAD AHEAD

LIVE WITH A MAN AND LOVE IT

BRIDES ARE LIKE NEW SHOES

THE SALINAS

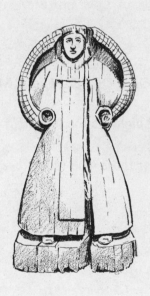

CONTENTS

Book One

JUAN THE MISSION BUILDER

CONTENTS

Book Two
LORETA OF CARMELO

Book One

JUAN THE MISSION BUILDER

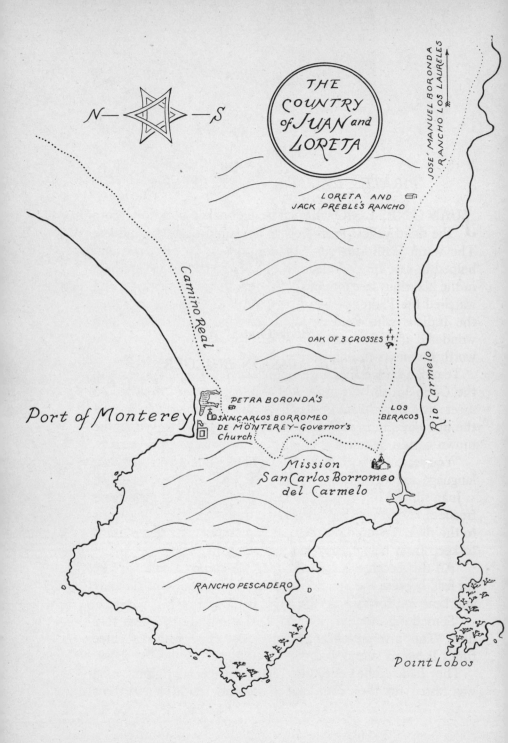

N — ✶ — S

THE
COUNTRY
of JUAN and
LORETA

JOSÉ MANUEL BORONDA
RANCHO LOS LAURELES

LORETA AND
JACK PREBLE'S RANCHO

Camino Real

OAK OF 3 CROSSES ††

Rio Carmelo

Port of Monterey

PETRA BORONDA'S
SAN CARLOS BORROMEO
DE MONTEREY — Governor's
Church

LOS
BERACOS

Mission
San Carlos Borromeo
del Carmelo

RANCHO PESCADERO

Point Lobos

Chapter I

PIRATES, CALIFORNIA STYLE: 1818

JUAN O-NES-E-MO wriggled his half-naked body lower into the dried yellow grass so that he would be better hidden. The warm California sun was comforting on his back, and helped to ease his conscience a bit. Somehow, as he lay there in the luxurious freedom of the golden November hillside, and watched the Padres of San Carlos de Borromeo move among the Indians who were grinding corn for the Mission, Juan wondered if the meals and the saints and the chants were worth the never-ending work of being a Christian Indian.

Te-mo, a savage Indian from the rancheria a mile or two up the Carmelo, slid down beside Juan. They had promised to meet and fish for trout under the sycamores along the river, on the first day the fog lifted. Te-mo grunted and picked at the brown cotton pantaloons that the Padres made Juan wear.

"You scare fish with these," he said in Room-se-en. His own language sounded good to Juan's ears after Mission Spanish.

Juan slipped out of the Christian lowers, and felt even more freedom. Together they crawled through the tall yellow grass to the river. Te-mo didn't like sliding on his belly like a lizard to keep from being seen, and he told Juan so.

"All this because you like saints," he chided, "and can't go for fish, because the Spanish soldiers will find out you are away and beat you for missing the work."

"Something more at the Mission besides saints," Juan told him. "They give presents to Room-se-ens there, and food three times between sunup and dark."

They had reached the tules in the river bottom, and going was faster, for they could move forward on their feet now

3

without danger of being seen by soldiers.

"They give you food that is hot and burns the stomach," Te-mo grunted. "You work too much. See how you carried rocks to build the Mission, on your back in thongs, from a place a whole day away. You sweated and pulled at your bowels along with seven other young saint-loving Room-se-ens, to bring the cypress beam all the way from Point Lobos. A beam to hold up adobe and make a Mission door to open for Spaniards! All Indians get is food and songs for work!" Te-mo sniffed, and his fingers were soon busy weaving a net from willow branches. "I don't like saints. The carrying thongs cut on the backs of Indians and make blood come."

Te-mo was like the Satan Padre Amores talked about. Te-mo was trying to make things seem better away from the Mission. It was true about the work. Padres made Indians work very hard building the Mission of San Carlos. Many a time Juan's bones ached with weariness, and great swellings came where raw-hide thongs pressed deep into the flesh of his back. But not even Te-mo or Satan himself could take from an old man the memory of his youth, of building a church. He remembered the beginning of San Carlos as if it had been only a full moon back.

First Padre Junipero Serra had blessed the bare yellow earth. He made Indians keep eyes looking down while he talked to God and the saints. Another brown-robed Padre passed among Indians, and gently pressed his hand on the head of Juan, who looked up to watch a gull flying high against the wind. After the head bowing, Indians had smoothed and flattened the earth with sticks, and then a Padre went with them to bring rocks from the hill across the river.

Many moons they worked, through rain and sun, from sunup to dark, until at last Mission walls were up and a beautiful tower, that was taller than any tree, stood against the blue sky. Te-mo could never know the happy feeling inside that O-nes-e-mo knew, when he climbed up and put the cross on top of the tower, while Padres and Indians sang the chant!

4

Backaches, beatings, nothing could take that happiness away from an old man.

Junipero Serra and the other Padres had given their humble Indians their cathedral in the sun.

"The church bells are beautiful when they ring, and corn is better than acorns for meal," Juan managed at last.

"I can lie on my back in the sun all day," Te-mo said, "and snare rabbits with grass, or catch lizards for supper, or fish in the Carmelo for trout." He let down the coarse net made of laced twigs. "My woman grinds acorns for flour, and I get no saints or bells, and no whipping posts with Spanish soldiers to lay on the whip."

Juan knew better than to make a fish trap of his own, for trapping was Te-mo's pride. Instead he broke up bits of dry willow and soon had a tiny smokeless fire started. He was very careful not to put on too many sticks at once, for if the soldiers saw smoke they were sure to come.

"Padre Amores tries to keep soldiers from beating," Juan said after a while. "The Padres are good."

Te-mo lifted up his net and removed five big speckled trout by their gills to the grass. "You have no more chance to miss a flogging than these have to miss being eaten, when the soldiers at the Mission *rancheria* cry out 'Indian hunt' and start running. I know. I watch."

Juan slipped a fish on a willow stick and started toasting it over the fire he had made. It was good to have food away from the Mission. In many ways this Satan Te-mo was right. Once, long ago, Juan too had spent the days naked, snaring lizards, and toasting them, and had been able to lie in the sun and be waited on, and given herb tea each time his woman was to drop a baby. He took a long breath. But that was long ago, before the earthshake sent down earth and fastened his woman and children up in a cave until they were dead.

As if to reassure himself about the saints, and the chants that Padre Junipero Serra sang in the tule shelter long ago, Juan spoke his thoughts.

5

"The Mission *rancheria* of San Carlos de Borromeo gave me my fourth woman, and she is dropping a son for me before next moon. Pretty good for a man beginning to shrivel in the arms and behind, Te-mo."

"You could do *that* without the saints and hard work; maybe do even better. I have a child for each toe and finger, and no bells ringing for me to sing before the sun-up. And I keep to Room-se-en talk and Room-se-en name too. Mission Indians lose even their names. The Padres turn everybody into Juan or Thomas, or Pablo." Te-mo boned his fish and ate it in three bites, then shoved another on the toasting stick.

Suddenly the air was filled with shouts. The bell began to ring and it was not time for Mass.

"Pirates coming over the hill to rob us!" Padre Amores shouted. "Quick, gather up altar ornaments, the hides, the corn, and run!"

Juan crawled up the river bank to look. Padres, Indians, Spanish soldiers were running into the church and the store-house.

"Monterey is burning," someone cried. "Come quick, before the pirates get our tallow."

"Soldiers have missed you," Te-mo said as he came up along-side of Juan. "I will kill you. That is better for a Room-se-en than the thong cuts from the soldiers, and to be tied to a post in the sun to feed the flies with your blood." He was breathing fast as he lay on the grass.

"No," Juan said. "They don't want me. If you had heard the Spanish, Te-mo, you would know. Monterey is burning, and thieves are on their way over to rob the Mission of the Carmelo. The Padres are leaving. Monterey is burning up. They tell everybody to run."

Te-mo put his hand on Juan's brown arm. "You will not be flogged then. You can come home to the *rancheria* with me and turn back into just O-nes-e-mo. The Padres are running away. They will never miss you now. Up the Carmelo are mice, little tender ones, to eat instead of hot burning food. Buckeye

6

meal well washed in running water is better for Room-se-en's stomach than Padre corn, and no work, or whipping, or saints to bother you."

Juan realized that now was his chance. "But the son? The boy that is to be dropped? My woman is there with the Padres," he murmured, still watching the furious activity at the Mission compound. Even Ramerez, and the Cornellos, and other Spanish folks were working madly; just as hard as Indians! Usually only Indians did hard work at the Mission.

"Your woman drops the baby alone. The Padres will take care of the boy, never fear. They want him to work. When he is grown large enough, we will make a forage and take him back to the hills," Te-mo said. "Come! Go while they are busy saving the saints and other things except bad Juan O-nes-e-mo."

Freedom to roam. No more dawn to dark at skinning animals and rendering grease for altar candles. No more sitting still in the compound to make shoes for the Spanish Señoritas in Monterey. Shoes that the Padres sold. And no more whippings if he went away to lie in the sun for a day, after a long stretch of foggy weather. Juan lay back for a time, listening to the bustle and excitement at the Mission, and thinking of the new freedom he had, like Te-mo.

Some people were now hurrying toward the San Clemente; toward the hills. They were driving cattle, too. Pablo had the great shining cross from the altar, and Padre Amores was passing not far away, struggling with a bundle, and trying to lead two horses that were heavy with packs. Padre Amores who laughed sometimes, and played the violin so sweetly, and showed Juan how to sew bright bits of red satin on the Señoritas' shoes. This Padre looked young and not so worried in the face as Padre Serra who had come over the hill first, when Juan was young.

Padre Amores thought about other things besides prayers and working Indians. He sometimes stopped to watch the clouds, or to listen to the song of a meadow lark. He always tried to keep beatings away from Indians when they missed

7

Mass. Instead of beating he gave you a stick to put into the ground, and showed you where the shadow would be when it was time to come to church, so there would be no excuses. His eyes always laughed when he showed you.

The line of hurrying figures with their burdens thinned, and Juan saw some of the half-wild yellow dogs sniffing along the dust to catch the scent of missing masters.

Young Padre Amores had a sweet voice, too, and had taught Juan to sing the *Agnus Dei*, and had promised sometime, when work was well done, to teach Juan about the violin he played.

The Padres had been good. He remembered well how he had been lying on his belly eating tender shoots of tules, and watching wasps, when, brown-robed, Padre Serra and two others came over the hill. Afterward he hung strings of sardines to see if the crossed sticks that these new men sang to, would eat. When the God didn't eat, he shot arrows into it, and the Padres came running from the shelter where they camped and sang some more to the sticks. He forgot to shoot arrows while he listened, then Padre Serra gave him food and presents. . . .

A cloud of smoke to the north blackened the sky. Far among the hills someone cried, "Monterey burning!"

Suddenly Junipero Serra's chant rang once more in Juan's ears. There had been no shining cross then, no candles, only a tule shelter, two crossed sticks, and a sweet voice singing in the wilderness. Such singing that O-nes-e-mo was happy inside, or sad even though he couldn't understand the words. He had never been the same again. That voice seemed to sing every San Carlos Day, when the Indians and the Padres made a procession with the statue of the Saint.

Juan looked over at the Mission, gold now in light from the late afternoon sun. Swallows flew toward their nests on the north wall, and the domed tower, that he had helped to build with his own hands, stood strong and fine, against the deep blue sky. Bells pealed every day from that tower—

"No, Te-mo, I can't," he cried. "They'll burn the San Carlos next!"

8

As Juan crawled up the bank and ran toward the Mission, he saw horses and riders coming over the crest of the hill from Monterey. A cloud of yellow dust followed them. Far behind, the sky to the north grew blacker with smoke.

"You'll only get a beating from the soldiers for going back," the angry Te-mo called after him in Room-se-en. "Why do you go to the house of Saints? Even the dogs have gone from the place."

A queer feeling went through Juan when he ran into the deserted compound where just a few minutes ago there had been such feverish activity. No Padres, no Spaniards, no Indians, only a jay bird scolding raucously from the adobe wall.

Swiftly he made his way into the Mission. What disarray! The altar cloth lay rumpled on the floor. Juan picked it up to find under it a rosary, and two books that were used in service. The tall candlesticks at the side of the altar had been forgotten! They were heavy with gold leaf, and the pirates would want those. Hadn't the Padres told Indians how foreign thieves always took gold? He wrapped the candlesticks and books in the cloth, and turned to make his way out of the church. There in the niche by the door was the beloved statue of "Our Lady," the carved wooden one done by Indians. She couldn't be left. How precious she was! She was not beautiful as the pictures were that the Padres had brought from Spain, but it had taken months to carve her, and tears had come to the eyes of the patient Padre Crespi when he saw the reward of his teaching.

Miguel had mixed Indian pigments for "Our Lady's" blue carved veil and painted it early one morning before Mass, to surprise the Padres. Even the good Padre Lasuen, when he came to visit at the Mission, looked kindly on the statue, and forgave Juan's knife slip that made one side of her mouth smile and the other side very sad. He had put his hand on Juan's shoulder and looked with shining eyes. "Never mind the poor mouth, Comero. Your heart meant well as you worked, and often the hands fail us." Then he had turned to another Padre. "Maybe the good God guided this Indian's

9

hand to make the Missionaries remember that sadness and smiles go together to make up life the world over."

Juan dug his toes into the adobe wall, pulled himself up to the niche, then, with one arm around the statue, let himself fall to the ground.

The clatter of horses' hoofs came nearer, and loud voices in Spanish and another language echoed through the silent walls.

Juan raced out of the south door toward the tules, his body bent over the bulky burden. He was afraid they would come around the corner of the Mission and see him before he could manage to hide.

"Heigh! Come here, you savage," a voice called in Spanish. "If you don't come, we'll shoot you. Governor Sola is no longer boss here! Bouchard and Corney the pirates are in charge now, and not even a Spanish governor dares defy us." A horse started down the little hill toward him.

Juan gave a final lunge into the thick tules with his body covering the treasures. He let them go, and with a quick push of his foot, watched them sink into the swamp. Then he turned around to face the horseman.

"What you doing?" The man, by way of greeting, slashed Juan's bare legs with his riata. He was a very white man, whiter even than the Spanish Señoritas in Monterey.

"Seeing if there is frogs to eat," Juan replied.

"You belong here?" The man motioned up to the Mission.

"I ran away." Juan wondered if the Holy Mother would let him get away with this lie and not punish him.

"Where are they? Where are the cattle and the Holy Fathers?"

Juan shrugged his shoulders and put on indifference. "Gone to the hills." He saw a bit of the colored image work up to the surface of the water.

Seven or eight more men came riding down to the marsh. "There's nothing at the Mission but a little ground corn and some pictures and a few hides pegged in the sun to dry. We even dug around in the graves under the altar, and there's nothing left."

"Oh, yes, they left one thing that you will treasure," a young fellow called.

"What is that?" the red haired man asked. "A woman's petticoat, I'll be bound, since it is you that found it."

The young *marinero* held out a paper that Juan had seen the governor's men fasten to the wall near the Mission bell tower.

"This notice says that 'All persons must attend Mass and respond in a loud voice. If they fail to do so, they will be put in stocks four hours.' We thought you ought to be warned, Corney." They all laughed and the young fellow pushed the crumpled notice into the coat-front of the red haired man. He only looked angry and turned to Juan. "Point to where the Fathers and the cattle are now," he demanded.

Juan nodded toward the steep mountains to the south. "Back behind there, a day's ride. You find a trail at the other side of the river." These men couldn't know this was only a hunter's trail, and that everyone who went up there must be ready to meet the fierce grizzlies, or else stay there forever.

A lean man, with a crafty light eye, stared off to the south. "I'm against that, Bouchard," he said firmly. "We've picked off the cream of the loot in Monterey. The rich Spaniards! These savages haven't anything worth real money, and if we go after the Padres, it may take several days, and we can't leave our boats that long without protection. Who knows? The Sandwich Islanders we brought to help us loot might get grand notions now that they've got onto the burning and sacking business. Those fancy Spanish clothes they're wearing have gone to their heads after being naked so long. They may sail off in our ships."

Juan saw the red haired man stiffen. "But the sea otter pelts, Corney. Do you think I worked my bloody head off to learn Spanish, and came all this way to worry over what Sandwich

11

Islanders are doing? I came after sea otter skins. I'm figuring on getting them from the natives before that old salt from Boston arrives here again. He bragged to me that he got five hundred and sixty skins in half a day with goods worth a dollar and a half in Boston. He sold the same things in Canton for twenty-three dollars each—to line mandarin robes." The man with the paunch turned again to Juan, who had squatted on his haunches in the tules to try and hide the telltale bit of wood that stuck up through the water.

"Got any sea otter skins, you?" he roared in Spanish.

"What you mean?" Juan stared past him and thought of the day long ago before sea otters got so scarce and hard to catch, when he and Pablo had traded four hundred skins for a rusty chisel that a *marinero* brought to their *rancheria*.

"Sea otters. Soft fur, from animals that swim out there." The man pointed to the ocean.

Juan shook his head.

"Oh, come on, let's get back to Monterey, Bouchard. The savage don't even know what a sea otter is. Besides, we have our dead to bury, and there's the ships to condition, thanks to the Spaniards and damn their souls." The lean one with the crafty eye started to turn his horse, and then caught sight of the colored wood that was working up through the water.

"What's that?" In an instant he was off his horse and pulling on the top of "Our Lady's" blue carved veil.

"Only my image," Juan said. "Indians carved it. Padres left it. So I bury her."

The thin man pulled "Our Lady" out of the scum. The fat man bent over his paunch to look, but didn't get off his horse.

"She's ugly. She needs to be buried," the man with the light-colored eye said, and with a quick movement of his heavy boot, kicked off the nose of "Our Lady." They all laughed, then turned their horses and rode up the hill toward the Mission. "We'll take the onions and corn meal. They'll help

12

out on the provisions," the fat man said as they entered the compound.

Juan sat for a moment and looked at the statue he had helped carve and color, then carefully he wiped the green slimy water from her poor face, and ran his fingers over the raw wood where her nose had been. Wasn't she the Holy Mother? Somewhere up in the hills with the Padres was his own woman who was to give him a son soon. Maybe the good God would be kinder to that other mother than the pirates had been to the Holy Mother.

The sun was red and angry as it dropped into the sea at the mouth of the Carmelo that night. Juan watched the horsemen go over the hill toward the smoke where Monterey was burning. Each horse had a burden in front of the rider. Hides and corn and onions and fresh fruit from the pear trees of San Carlos de Borromeo by the Carmelo. When the last horse had disappeared, Juan O-nes-e-mo leaned over and groped in the water for the treasures, wrung out the altar cloth and bound the statue in with candlesticks and the wet books. For a moment he looked at what was left of the splintered nose that lay in the tules, then he picked up his burden and followed in the tracks made by the last of the fleeing Spaniards and Indians and sniffing dogs.

Chapter II

"OUR LADY'S" NOSE: 1818

JUAN O-NES-E-MO trudged along the dusty yellow path until nearly dark, before he remembered the brown cotton pantaloons. His body had felt so free and comfortable that the covering of Christianity had never entered his mind again. With a great groan, he set down the bundle and looked back over the darkening hills. He dare not go back to the temporary *rancheria* where the Padre Amores was encamped, without those tight, binding pantaloons, for he would surely be beaten and have no food. Too many Indians had "lost" their lowers, and the Spaniards resented the waste of cloth that was so hard to come by. The soldiers on guard at the Mission begrudged the cloth and food to Indians, and were only waiting for an excuse to beat. Was his empty stomach and the forgetfulness about the pantaloons a punishment that the Saints were sending, because he had been tempted by Te-mo?

Juan tucked the bundle into the chaparral and turned about-face. He ran, then walked, when the pounding inside was too much, but every bit of running made the pantaloons that much nearer, and cut down the time when his stomach would have corn and frijoles, and maybe some rabbit stew that the Padres had taught Indian women to make. He wondered if the son coming would hate to wear pantaloons. Perhaps if the boy was baptized a Christian right from the first he would never know the difference. But if he objected, well, Juan O-nes-e-mo's son would never be beaten by Spanish soldiers. They would run away to the hills first, away from everyone.

At last the Mission hill was reached, and he groped in the grass for the damnable brown cotton nuisances, tied them around his neck, and started back.

14

It was long in the night before Juan finally sighted the red glow of the Padre's fires. His stomach thought his throat was cut. It gnawed. One fish eaten when the sun was high was not much to travel on and carry the heavy bundle. He stopped, removed the pantaloons from around his neck, and put them on, then bravely strode out through the grass toward the encampment under the oaks. Beating or not, he must eat and know about his woman.

Juan crept noiselessly toward the campfire that now spelled home. A curious coyote skittered away into the dark but not even a dog barked. Indians lay everywhere on skins or blankets, sleeping soundly after their hard day of burden bearing. Off to themselves were the soldiers, wrapped in blankets, guns beside them, and caps pulled over their eyes to shut out the flicker of flames.

Padre Amores was the only one awake. He was very close to the fire, on a blanket Juan's woman Polonia had woven. In his hand was the little brown-covered book about saints that he carried about in his habit and read when earthshakes came, or when the Governor sent men to demand more hides as taxes, or times when soldiers beat Indians too long. Juan stood a moment watching the Padre's lips moving, before he went and stood close.

"Juan!" Padre Amores raised himself on his elbow from the pallet beside the fire. "What happened to you? Where have you been? Polonia has a child! We hunted for you—"

Hunger was forgotten. Now his legs forgot to ache. "My son! My son! Where is he?" Juan demanded.

The Padre got up, put a kindly hand on his shoulder. "Hush! Not so much noise. The soldiers missed you. Come—" he sighed, "you will see."

The fire logs burned through and broke, throwing out beautiful sparks before they settled down to a dull red glow. Juan knew this was a good omen for his son! The Saints knew about the boy.

Padre Amores led him past the sleeping Indian children,

15

placed near the fire for extra warmth, to where Polonia lay on a thick rush pallet, the baby beside her.

Padre Amores took up the little brown child, and put it into Juan's arms.

"A girl, Juan. Loreta, we baptized her, because Polonia—." The priest paused. "Polonia is dead. She wanted the baby to be Loreta."

Juan looked at this child of his old age for a time, then handed it back. "You can have her, Padre. She will grow up to help grind corn and sew shoes. She will be a convert for you without knowing it." And he turned to look at Polonia's peaceful face as she lay in the shadow of the fire. Polonia was like the statue of "Our Lady." She had done her best; she couldn't know that the Spaniards' God had thought girls were better than sons.

"Where did you go, Juan? It was bad of you to run away." Padre Amores was close to his shoulder.

For answer, Juan went over and brought the bundle and laid it at the Padre's feet. "There," he pointed. "The altar cloth, and books and a rosary, and the statue of 'Our Lady.' The pirates, white men, that frightened me just to look at them, kicked 'Our Lady' and broke her nose."

"You stayed! You saved these?" The Padre was excited as he picked up one of the books and carefully wiped it off with the bottom of his brown robe. "I told Miguel to see to the altar things, for I had to think of food." He sighed. "Poor Miguel, his heart is willing, but Satan takes happiness in making him excited and forgetful. But tell me about the Mission. What did the pirates do? Was it burned?"

Juan shook his head. "They took the hides that were pegged in the sun to dry, and pears, and the corn and onions that were left." He looked down at the statue with a little resentment. "Perhaps the good God punished Juan for saving the statue instead of hides that can be made into shoes, so he sent only a girl?"

"No—" Amores said quietly. "A little girl, a mother child,

16

to bring many men into the world, Juan, and comfort you in your old age. You did right to save the statue. We shall have more hides, my son."

"But the nose of 'Our Lady'!"

"We shall make her another nose after sunup tomorrow. Now go and eat; you must have hunger." The Padre motioned toward the iron pots near the fire.

But the rabbit stew was tasteless to an old man with only a daughter in place of a son. Life had suddenly lost its importance, for Polonia was gone now, and he had no desire to take another woman. Four times was enough.

"Eat, it will do you good," the Padre said kindly. "You were brave to stay and save the candlesticks and altar cloth."

Juan looked up. He couldn't eat now. "Where is the fiddle?" he asked.

There was a smile, deep with wordless understanding. Padre Amores left the fire, and soon returned with the violin under his arm. He sat down beside Juan, picked at the strings and listened for the tuning, then softly, sweetly, in the light of dying embers, Padre Amores played all the chants Juan loved, until the weary muscles relaxed and sleep came.

Heavy wet drops brought Juan from his sleep. The first rain of the season! More wood was put on the fire, and a Padre murmured a prayer, for the rain was late, and the parched yellow hills gave very little grass to put in the stomachs of cattle that were now too thin for good tallow.

Gusts of south wind rushed through the trees, and embers from the fire moved toward the north, as if to run away. Juan knew how they felt. Soon it rained steadily, as though the drops had decided to come all together like soldiers marching at the Presidio in Monterey. Runnels worked now where there had been only dry, cracked earth, and water music sounded in the canyons that fed the Carmelo.

The next day was very wet and they sat around the fire. Padre Amores showed two Indian women how to sew up a

17

great pocket of hides with the hair inside, to use for Juan's woman Polonia, when she was put away in the earth. Then coyotes would not dig her up and eat her as they did when Indians scratched a hole in the soil and put away dead without pockets to protect them. Each new Padre told the same thing. And Indians waited for the pocket sewing to come. Perhaps the good God treated Indians better when they were put away in hide-pockets like Spaniards.

While the women worked, Miguel told of what he had seen in Monterey before he escaped to run over the hill and warn the Mission. Two ships had anchored, two days before, and fired eight guns. He showed the number by laying out ears of corn. There were too many men for the little handful of soldiers at the Presidio. The white men landed; then, a lot of naked men, dark, and without even the decency of pantaloons. They took things, even to the fine clothes belonging to the señoritas. Sola and the Spanish people ran out of Monterey and the pirates set fire to the houses. It was terrible. He wanted to go back over the hill and look some more at the dreadful happenings; he longed to see if the pirates were still there.

"I was helping Señor Romero gather up things quick, when I heard the pale red-haired man talk to another, that now they would go over to Carmelo and take what was there." Miguel's eyes blazed. "I stopped helping Señor Romero with the food, and ran as hard as I could to tell the Padres. Hypolite, they called the man, Hypolite Bouchard. The dark naked men didn't know that only señoritas wore dresses, and not men! They put on dresses." Miguel looked up at Padre Amores. "Do pirates *like* wearing dresses better than Spanish pantaloons?"

The Padre only sighed, and said that even Satan himself sometimes wore a dress.

When the excitement of Miguel's tale had quieted down, and the rain stopped for a bit, two Padres said prayers for the dead, and made Spanish and Indians, and even soldiers, sing

18

chants. Then they put Polonia away under the trees in the deep hole that the old Padre had had Juan make. The rain was kind and helped him, for it made the ground easier to dig. Afterwards, the Padre put a wooden cross to mark.

Juan watched an Indian woman make a cradle of her arm for his little Loreta.

After the wood was brought, and the women had ground some corn for the day, the Padres went out on the hillside to hold services and ask God to help the people in Monterey who had lost their homes.

Juan's heart wasn't in the prayers he repeated. He had prayed for a son, and had been so sure, and still no son.

The rain started again, and the Carmelo swelled up so that the trees on its banks had their feet in water, and were catching the brush that washed down from above. The oaks dumped rain on the camp when their branches grew too heavy with water. The Padres superintended cutting tules for making shelters before night should come.

Juan saw Miguel run away from his work of driving sticks, and go toward the hills above Monterey. Miguel was too curious for his own good. But Juan hurried a little faster, so that the soldiers wouldn't miss Miguel's work.

The next day was clear, and Miguel came back with news that the powder magazine had been blown up, and Monterey was now only black piles of charcoal, and ashes, with a few wild dogs to keep the pirates company. They had many harmed and sick people, and were pounding at their boats and fixing up the holes in the sides of them. Padre Amores was thankful for the news and told Miguel so.

This meant it was not safe yet to return to the Mission. But the report brought seven lashes on Miguel's back at the hands of the soldiers, because he had run away from the work. The Padre put crushed sage on the bruises to take out pain, and gave Miguel extra rations that day.

The Padres decided that a watch must be posted in the pines on the hill above Monterey, eyes to look down on the bay that curved as prettily as a señorita's ear. They would keep track of the thieves who had taken the little settlement.

Padre Amores came to Juan. "You feel like running away from the Mission rancheria now, because you have no son, but you must not lose your faith, Juan," he said in a low voice, and his eyes were smiling. "How about taking my violin up on the hills behind Monterey? You can play the scales as I taught you, while you watch the pirates."

A great wave of happiness washed away the pain of disappointment from inside Juan. He was to be trusted with the beautiful shining fiddle! How could the Padre read the very thoughts an Indian was thinking?

"Play very softly under the stars, lest the pirates have ears sharp as foxes, and be sure to put the violin in the red velvet bag when the heavy dew comes," Padre Amores said in parting. "And run fast, to tell us if the pirates come again over the hill, for they may decide to search for us, and our hides and tallow."

Juan hurried along the trail toward the hills back of Monterey with the precious fiddle held closely under his arm. He was free from soldiers for a while. He had the fiddle! He could eat a roasted crow and all the berries he wanted! There would be many mushrooms, now, after the rain. Even Te-mo had no such luxury as the Padre's beautiful fiddle. What man could want to leave the Mission with all these blessings? The Saints were indeed good after all. Suddenly he stopped. The nose of "Our Lady!" She was to have a new nose before another dusk. No one had thought of her in the excitement. With a sigh, Juan walked on. After all, being a saint, she didn't need the nose to breathe with, and there was the watch to keep, and the tunes to bring out of the fiddle box. Another time would do, for "Our Lady's" nose.

What freedom! As soon as he found his place of waiting on the hill behind Monterey, Juan took off the hated pantaloons and stuck them in a crotch of an oak. This would keep them safe and clean until he went back to the Padres.

No early morning Mass now, just sleeping and rest, and lizards that he snared with a stem of grass and toasted to a good brown, and mushrooms eaten raw and fresh, as they popped up from the moist earth. He could watch the blue jays busy storing acorns in cracks of trees, for winter, and ants carrying their heavy loads of food to holes. Juan O-nes-e-mo had no work to do, only eating the meal that Padres had given him, already ground, playing bird calls on the fiddle, and watching boats on the white-capped Monterey bay far below.

Two days later, he put down the fiddle and saw the pirate ships sail out of the bay toward the north. He waited until still another dawn to be sure they were not coming back. It was then that he saw the vaqueros and soldiers and Governor Sola make their way from the rancho where they had taken shelter. The governor, too, must have had a pair of eyes to watch the pirates and find out when it was safe to come back.

Satan tempted Juan to play one more tune before he tied the violin into its red bag. Then, slowly, with lagging feet, he walked over the hills toward the camp in the Valley of the Carmelo. Back to work and sweat, and the sadness of giving up the music box to the Padre Amores. Why did he do this? He had the fiddle. He could go to the hills with it.

After all, the Spaniards' God hadn't answered the prayers of an Indian for a son. A girl was nothing to work for at the Mission. He turned and ran fast; away from the direction of the hill where the Padres were waiting for news, and he only slowed down when breathing was too hard and his heart thumped. Finally, he had to stop and snare a rabbit for his stomach, because he had no more corn meal left.

That night, high up on a hill across the river from where the Padres camped, Juan rested in the dark, ate a few raw mushrooms, and played softly the bird calls.

He had been playing a long time, the highest notes his fingers would make, when behind him a twig cracked.

"That is very good, Juan," came the Padre's voice through the bushes. "Before long, you will be able to play at Mass.

21

special Mass, but first you must come back to the *rancheria*, so I can show you how to bring more notes from the box. There are so many notes in there, more than you can count."

Silently they walked together along the trail. "While you were gone, we made a new nose for 'Our Lady,' Juan. That should make you happy."

That was it! "Our Lady" had somehow let the Padre know that Juan had listened to Satan's temptings. She had repaid the Padre for her new nose!

"You shall play music and we'll have a fiesta to celebrate the new nose," Amores went on. "Then little Loreta will have great blessings and so will you, my son. Never will you be sorry that the violin notes told me how to find you."

Already Juan was busy thinking up new bird songs for playing to "Our Lady" in front of all the others. This was a joy Te-mo would never know! After a while he told the Padre of the pirates sailing away.

The next day at dawn, Mass was said, and then oxen, horses, and Indians were loaded with their burdens once more for the return trip to the Mission. Juan led off, and in his pack was the image, her new nose still unpainted. Under his arm, he carried the Padre's fiddle in its red velvet bag.

Not far from him an Indian woman walked. On her back she carried the little Loreta. Juan looked away from the baby and kept his mind on the day when he would play the fiddle in church, for all to see him.

Miguel shuffled up alongside Juan. His eyes were sullen, and Juan saw that the muscles of his face were working in anger. He kept shifting his burden to ease the sores on his back.

"Your back hurts where the lashes were?" Juan asked. "Stop, and I will put more fresh, cool sage on the bruises for you."

"Sage won't reach the bruises inside me. I am flogged for helping the Padres," Miguel mumbled. With a black look he burst into the Room-se-en language. "I will pay back the soldiers where no sage will soothe the hurts."

"And I will help you," Juan said, wondering if "Our Lady"

22

would hear and perhaps keep him from having the violin. "If it is not too bad."

Miguel moved closer, and showed slimy fungus in a cloth. "I won't need help. This will do it. Inside here is something that will make their bowels stand still for a while." He looked off toward the hills.

"But if you kill them, Miguel, the rest will kill you!"

Miguel only cackled. "They won't die. They'll only wish to."

A soldier passed, and Miguel gave attention to his pack. Juan walked on.

Chapter III

SATAN OR THE SPOTTED SNAKE: 1818

THERE was hard work for everybody when they reached the Mission. Even the soldiers had to help by setting to rights their own quarters. The things taken to the hills must be dried quickly or they would soon be green with mildew after so much dampness. Indian women rubbed continually at their *metates*, for most of the grinding stones had been left behind at the Mission, and now the supply of ground corn was almost gone. If only the pirates had left a little in the great bins!

"These hard tasks will make the Saints think well of you," Padre Amores said, when the Indian women stopped to wipe sweat away from their eyes. He was rubbing tallow on the raw places in his hands, where blisters had come from tilling along with the Indians in the field below the Mission. "We will have a big fiesta with sauce and plenty of meat and time to eat it, because the Mission is safe, and in honor of 'Our Lady's' new nose that Miguel carved." He glanced toward Juan, who was cutting shoes from a mildewed hide. "A first fiesta for Juan's little Loreta. She shall be carried around the church on a red pillow with flowers thrown before her."

"Better Indians make fiesta for Mission and 'Our Lady's' nose and no Indian girl on a pillow," Juan told the Padre. "The Saints will like it better that way."

Amores only smiled and went on his way, rubbing his hands together.

When the squeaking sandals and patched brown habit of the Padre had passed by them, Miguel leaned near to Juan. "Each time I cut into wood with the Padre's knife to make that nose for the statue, I wished that the sharpness was going

24

into the throat of a soldier," he mumbled, and his eyes were very shiny.

Juan crossed himself quickly, and said a prayer for the soul that Padres said was inside every Indian. Miguel's soul was very bad, and needed prayers; Juan was sure of that.

"If you slit soldiers' throats, you will only be beaten to death, Miguel. It is better not to think of throats."

"I *like* to think of slit throats," Miguel insisted as he took up his burden of hides and shuffled off, making extra dust.

Indians worked harder now, because of the promised fiesta. Fires were built under the rendering vats, and a Padre watched over the killing and skinning of animals, for a "Boston Ship" was due at Monterey to buy Mission hides and the tallow that was stored in bags made from the dried stomachs of the animals. There was no time to be lost. Without the hides, they could not pay the increasing taxes which Sola demanded.

But the fiesta didn't come, for they were soon very short handed and it was impossible to catch up with work. The governor sent a horseman and soldiers with a message that the Padres were to "let out" Indians to help the Spaniards in Monterey clean up and rebuild their houses, and the governor's orders were law!

Juan wanted to go to Monterey. The work would be heavier. Spaniards never knew when an Indian's back was tired or his feet waiting to rest. Spaniards seemed to have better eyes in the backs of their heads than the beady black ones at either side of their noses. But he would be away from the little Loreta. It was too hard to keep his mind from the son she should have been, when he saw her beside the women as they ground corn.

"No, Juan, we need you here to make saddles and more shoes." The Padre smiled. "Besides, you couldn't take the violin to Monterey. I need it between times for Mass, you know."

That settled everything. The fiddle was more important than being away from Loreta without it.

25

One night just before sundown, when they were sure the pirates wouldn't return, Padre Amores took Miguel and Juan to dig in the sand near the mouth of the river for the golden altar ornaments that he buried when the news of the robbers came. Six paces south from where the Carmelo empties into the sea—that was the landmark. But the river, swelled with sudden downpours and drainage from all the canyons, had changed. The old opening was gone, and a wider, straighter channel cut through the sands.

"Six paces from what?" Amores cried, as he looked at the rushing muddy water. "Holy Mother, my landmark is gone! The treasures! The sand along the beach all looks the same!"

Juan traveled the beach on his hands and knees, looking for the marks of feet, but the tide had been high on those stormy nights; all footprints were washed away. They tried digging several places, but the sands held their secrets.

The Mission bell rang for evening prayers. They turned their back to the waves and walked up the hill. Juan felt sad inside for the Padre's sadness.

"You should have taken an Indian with you," he said gently. "Indians know that the river changes. They take other marks to remember."

"But it has always been the same since I came," Amores cried.

"Indians have lived here longer than Padres, and Spanish—"

"And soldiers!" interrupted Miguel in a surly voice. "Indians had *happiness* before soldiers came."

"I expect it was punishment unto me," Amores murmured, as he lifted up his brown habit and began to climb the steep hill. "I didn't trust an Indian enough to let him know where the treasures were buried. Now they are no more—." He sighed deeply.

Juan hurried and soon was up beside Padre Amores. "Would the punishment feel better if you played an extra chant on the beautiful fiddle at Mass?" he asked as he touched

26

the coarse brown sleeve. "The Saints would know then that you were sorry, and Indians would forgive the Padre for not trusting them." Then he lowered his voice. "Music is needed by Miguel's soul, Padre Amores. Juan has prayed twice today about Miguel and the soldiers."

The Padre only smiled a little with one part of his mouth; not a laughing smile, but Juan knew as he dropped behind again, that there would be extra music that night at Angelus.

When they reached the Mission, the Padre left them and entered by the altar door. Juan and Miguel waited with the rest of the Indians until the Spaniards and soldiers had filed in, then dropped to their knees on the rough, red tiles just inside the door.

It was a rule that after church, Indians should wait until the Spaniards and soldiers had left the church, before they made their way to the door. Juan was horrified to see Miguel hunching along on his knees as the last extra chant was sung and Padre Amores was playing the fiddle. He was out of the door before the Amen. Perhaps the sores on Miguel's back were hurting him, and he was going for more of the sage they had picked on the way home.

Miguel was already rolled up on the floor when Juan came into the long room where Indian men slept. He didn't answer from under his blanket when Juan asked if he was sick. Soon a Padre held high his pine flare, counted the men, and locked the door for the night. Then all was quiet in the compound.

All hands were tired that night from extra work. The five soldiers didn't even talk of the beautiful señoritas they had charmed. Instead, when they reached their quarters, they threw coats and guns on the leather chests that held their dress uniforms, pulled off boots, and rolled up in their blankets.

Private Lopez was wakened suddenly. He pulled up on his elbow and saw a number of white shining spots coming toward him. The breath in him stopped. Large, movable, irregular, shining spots that shone with an uncanny light were coming right toward him from behind his own leather box. He tried to call, to warn the others in the little room, but no sound would come from his lips. The thing moved closer, and then, quick as a wildcat, it landed on his chest and knocked the wind out of him.

"For beating Indians, Satan gives you this," it hissed. Lopez knew no more!

Something knocked against Lieutenant Gonzales. His eyes had just opened to see what it was when a great, unholy spotted snake came toward him hissing. He couldn't move quickly enough to be out of the way in time before the great snake clutched at his neck and pressed. He could feel its body coiling tighter, to keep away his breath and push out his eyes.

"This for beating Indians," it whispered in ungodly hisses.

"Where will I aim to hit?" the newly awakened Escobar cried. "It's coming for me!" But he had no time to grab his gun before he was knocked out.

Pablo Vincente slept on, for he had beaten few Indians, and only when the Padres ordered. He didn't like man hunts.

A kick in the face that mashed his nose was all the punishment the snake gave to Captain Alvarez, for the cruel Lopez was moving to life again. Out of the door the thing went, Gonzales saw it crawling faster than any lizard.

Into their boots with loud cries; then the excited soldiers ran across the compound.

"Toward the church!" roared Gonzales. "I saw it go into the church!"

But the church was peaceful and silent and dark except for the little oil lamp burning near the altar. Hurrying feet of the Padres came. The soldiers told their wild story, and there in the doorway of the church, Lopez and Gonzales started fighting about the creature they had seen.

"It was the devil! He called himself Satan, and said that I was punished for beating Indians!" Lopez roared.

"It was a snake, I tell you, no devil at all, and it hissed and crawled on its belly faster than any lizard when it ran away."

28

Gonzales was furious, and stamped his boots until his loose shirt-tail shook in the wind. "I saw it with my own eyes. Its body coiled tight around my neck to choke me, cold and hard like an iron band."

"And I didn't know where to aim. Such unholy spots of light that shone out through the dark brighter than any candle!"

"It knocked me out," Escobar gasped.

Alvarez was silent, but a bloody nose proved that something had been busy on his anatomy.

Pablo Vincente, the untouched, came and listened while he shivered in the fog.

"Amores, let the Indians out and count them," the old Padre said, and gave the young man the keys. "This is indeed a strange happening; you say the creature went into the church?"

"Yes, we saw it run toward the church." All were agreed on that. "But we looked inside. There is nothing."

"We shall look more carefully, in among the robes at the back." The Padre led the way into the silent church. The long flickering shadows that came from the oil lamp made a restless, eerie pattern on the crude walls.

The soldiers hung back, as the old man crossed himself and knelt for a moment. "Aren't you coming?" he called. "Surely soldiers are brave—"

They knelt, too, and then followed the old man gingerly. There was no stamping of boots now.

Amores opened the locked door of the Indian men's quarters last, for the women had seemed more excited and frightened, and were rushing around the compound now that they were free.

"Pirates again?" Juan asked, as the men crowded around the door to get out.

"No, just soldiers, frightened soldiers," Amores said softly. Juan detected disgust in his voice. "You must get in line. Is

29

everyone here?" With a flare held high he started counting, but Indians were restless and hard to count. "Where's Miguel? What is the matter that he is still sleeping?"

As the Padre started to walk toward the blankets, Miguel called.

"Here I am, Padre, just behind you. Away out of the blankets first!"

Juan stared at Miguel in the smoky, yellow light of the pine torch. Miguel hadn't been in. Something else under the blankets all the time! What had he been doing? Perhaps killed a soldier? Juan muttered a prayer for Miguel's soul, but he had no worried look; he didn't seem to need the prayer at all.

The Indians went to join the search. Soldiers were still arguing about this creature they were hunting. When light came into the sky and not even an animal track was found in the moist earth of the compound, the old Padre grew tired of the nonsense and ordered everybody to Mass and then to work.

Later in the day as they scraped hides with a sharp mussel shell to get off the fat, Juan leaned close to Miguel.

"Where were you in the night, when the Satan was about?" he asked. "Did you see it, Miguel?"

Miguel bent over his work and scraped harder for a time. "I was the Satan, and the snake. Didn't I tell you I would hurt those soldiers where sage would not help them? I made their bowels stop with fright. It will be a long time before they beat an Indian for nothing. You see."

"How could you be Satan, and the snake?" Juan could hardly believe his ears, for such terrible tales of uncanny light, such hissings the soldiers had told about.

"The slimy toadstools I brought from San Clemente, made light. I saw them the night after the rain, and I knew the soldiers were not so brave as the Indians, so I rubbed patches on me to frighten them."

A Spaniard walked by. Juan scraped on the skin for a minute, and then spoke low in Room-se-en language. "But where did you hide? Why didn't they find you?"

"No patches painted on my back. They couldn't see me as I turned and ran with my back to them. I rubbed off the light while I crouched in the bell tower until Padre Amores opened the door. Then I stood behind him quiet until he called my name. He thought I had been there all the time."

"Then Gonzales didn't see the snake run into the church!" Juan laughed. "Soldiers are fools with whips."

Juan and Miguel never looked at each other when the mystery of the spotted snake and Satan was discussed. It was many a long moon before an Indian was beaten, and then only lightly at the command of the Padre when real punishment was needed to keep the body in proper subjection so that the soul could develop.

If Padre Amores wondered how Miguel got behind him that night when he was counting, at least he never asked.

Juan wondered if thoughts inside Padres were different from thoughts inside Indians.

Chapter IV

SOFT AS THE WHISPER OF SATAN: 1819. 1820

THERE was no time to teach an Indian to fiddle in the months that followed the return to the Mission. Every Padre and Indian worked with all his strength to produce the terrific Mission taxes that Spain was constantly demanding. The long rainy season came on, and made Juan's bones sore and stiff. As he sat on the ground under shelter and sewed on shoes, he was thankful for the first time in his life that he was older than some and didn't have to work out in the wet. He was glad that Loreta was so little trouble to the Indian women who looked after her. She did not cry much, or take them too often away from the twisting of wool or knitting socks for Padres. Perhaps she knew that it was good not to make troubles for those who were not bound to love her. Maybe the Holy Mother in Heaven was protecting her, so that she was not old enough to be forced into work before her little legs were strong. Other Indian children had to help carry corn, or tend sheep all day in the cold, and they came in, weary and old in the eyes, as old in the eyes as men with wrinkles.

Juan worked well on shoes for señoritas until the spring sun warmed the moist earth and made a fresh smell to things, and the meadow larks began to sing from posts where soldiers' horses were tied; then, not even prayers were strong enough to make bony old fingers mind! The patches went on wrong and had to be taken off again when Padre Amores came to look at the shoes.

"Why, Juan, what is the matter?" he asked. "Always before you have done the shoes so proudly and so well."

Juan sighed. "Just sewing shoes is bad, now when salmon

32

will be going from the sea up the Carmelo to lay their eggs! Big salmon, fat and shiny, that Juan should be catching for Padre's dinner, and for salting. Te-mo the savage Indian will get the biggest." He looked into the Padre's eyes and saw a brightness there. This was a good sign from heaven. "Spaniards like salted salmon, Padre Amores. They will trade it much better than shoes with red satin. Juan has made so many shoes."

Padre Payeras came up, and Juan heard them talk together. He hoped that the Saints would put it in the heads of Padres to go fishing this warm spring day.

"Juan here, is saying that salted salmon for men's stomachs will bring a better trade than satin-trimmed shoes for women's vanity," Padre Amores said. "I think he is right, just now anyway, for his mind is with the salmon and not with the shoes."

Padre Payeras laughed, the first time in many moons. "What children they are. I suppose it is better to let them fish, or they will find excuses to run away. They will work better, after a day at the river fishing for salmon." He looked at Padre Amores, and Juan saw little wrinkles come around his eyes. "You had better go with the Indians, Amores, lest they stay away too long, and miss evening prayers."

What a day! First they worked hard, and dug from the ground great roots of chilicote to crush and throw into the water, so salmon would be too sleepy to swim away from Indian hands. Then, Juan being older, he led the way to the deep quiet pool that was shaded by willows, where Indians of Carmelo had fished many years before Padres came.

Te-mo was at the fish hole when they arrived, and gave black killing looks to Juan for bringing Christian Indians and a Padre. Soon he disappeared through the branches, and later Juan saw him running away.

Juan walked down through the soft moist mud toward the water, stooping often to miss low willow branches. This was like old free days, to feel the cool mud on the toes. There they were, hundreds of big shining gray creatures, their bodies

33

pressed close together, their heads pointed upstream. Indians ran both ways of the river for a distance to dam up the water. Miguel and Pablo threw in the crushed roots. In less time than it takes a frightened rabbit to reach its hole, the fish came to the top, and Indians were pulling them out with their hands. Juan pulled out plenty of fish, and then listened to birds singing their songs for nest-time. Pablo worked best of all, and Miguel ran around the most of all. They built a fire, wrapped fish in mud to cook, and ate them when the sun was high, then, when little tree frogs in puddles near the river started croaking, and the sun was going down, each Indian was loaded with a heavy burden of shining salmon, to take back to the Mission for salting down and trade—and to eat, Juan hoped.

When they reached the Mission, Padre Payeras was pleased to see so many fish. Juan hoped the Saints would remember that Juan O-nes-e-mo had made them all go fishing to catch so much fish for the Mission, and some day they would give an old Indian a chance to play the shining fiddle. That night Juan prayed for the soul inside of Te-mo; the soul that Padres said was inside even savage Indians, for Te-mo was up to no good when he carried on his face the black looks of killing.

Loreta was just able to toddle around, when one day Governor Sola rode into the Mission compound on his fine brown horse, jumped down, and kicked the baby to one side as he demanded to see the Padre in charge of Indians.

Juan dropped the bundle of hides he was carrying and ran to his little one. The rough kick from a Spaniard's boot had suddenly brought love for his own to Juan O-nes-e-mo. He held the bruised little girl to him, and was never again to be sad over the lack of a son, for Loreta stopped crying, looked into his eyes, and smiled.

In that moment, Juan realized that this little baby was part of his body. Perhaps later she would have O-nes-e-mo thoughts in her head, just like her father. Thoughts of chants, and bird calls, and the low booming song of waves as they broke on the golden beach below the Mission San Carlos. Some day, she would understand about the pealing bell that hung in the tower her father had built; the bell that called Indians to Mass, and let the Saints know that all was well along the Carmelo. Loreta couldn't help it if the Spaniards' God had changed her into a girl.

"The Spanish boat is in, but before you can send hides or tallow away, you must pay more taxes. You must give more ground corn for soldiers' tortillas, more saddles, if you keep the Mission lands," Sola told Padre Payeras who was now the chief missionary of San Carlos. "There is no money from Spain to pay or even feed the soldiers who protect the settlers. They are making trouble. And you are protecting lazy Indians while they live off the fat of the land. Only yourself to blame if the soldiers from the Presidio come and sack the place."

There was such anger in his voice that Juan, clutching the little Loreta, moved away. The governor might kick them again, and there was nothing to do but take it if he did. The governor represented a high chief in Spain, higher even than any Padre, or perhaps the good God.

Padre Payeras kept his voice low. Juan saw that his face was very pale. "But we are paying our taxes. How can we give more ground corn when you take away our Indians to serve the Spanish settlers in Monterey? I have heard they have splendid balls and dinner parties, and the dresses of the señoritas at the bull and bear festivals are dazzling. Why do not these people help feed and pay the soldiers, Your Honor?"

Sola was angered. "Spain has granted the settlers land. They have a right to low taxes for coming." He walked closer to the Padre. "And to Indian servants, too."

"At half the price and harder work than they could get a Spaniard to work." Padre Payeras sighed gently. "May God forgive us for bringing these poor creatures into slavery for the vanities of the Spaniards."

"If you feel so sorry for them, give the savages a bit of land

35

and turn them loose. There will at least be that many less to eat at the vitals of Spain!" Sola cried. "They are always trying to run away."

Padre Payeras put his hand on Sola's shoulder. Juan saw the governor shake it off with a proud twist. "If the cross hadn't braved the wilderness, and been carried by the fearless spirit of a Padre who was zealous for converts, there would never have been a trail for the settlers to follow and gain their free land, my son. Be temperate in your judgments. These people are children. Without the Padres and the Church to guide their footsteps and teach them, they are lost."

"Guide away! Teach away! But give for the soldiers hides, tallow, and wool, or the Mission lands will be taken and sold." Juan saw the governor look around at the great iron pot full of stew that was made from animals whose hides were pegged in the sun to dry.

"The bell will soon ring for dinner, Your Honor. Will you stay?" Payeras asked. "It is not fit food for a governor who is used to the best, but it is what we have. . . . You see, we must use the meat that comes inside the hides we sell, to feed the Indians who raise the cattle." He smiled. "I understand that many Spanish settlers throw away or bury the animals after they have been skinned."

"I don't keep account of what happens to every carcass killed by a colonist," Sola snapped out. "As for your Indians, they look well enough fed." He turned and walked with the Padre to the thatch of tules that made a shade from the sun, where the missionaries' table was set. The midday bell rang, frightening swallows from the tower.

Juan pulled Loreta close while he went with a piece of bark, and held it for a ladle of steaming stew. He saw several old women nod, pleased, when he placed the child by his side on the ground and then lowered his head while Padre Amores blessed the food.

Amores looked worried and sad in the face, but Juan saw a quick smile of understanding in his eyes as he passed on his

36

way to eat under the shelter with Padre Payeras and the governor.

"The little one is beautiful today because of her father's love," he murmured, and tapped Juan kindly on the shoulder.

Sola took no siesta under the thatched tules that day. Dinner was no sooner over than he demanded the hides and tallow.

"I can barter them to get what we need," he said anxiously. "The soldiers must be quieted."

Juan and several other Indians carried out bundle after bundle of the best hides, and they were placed by the adobe wall under a guard of soldiers, until ox carts should arrive from Monterey. Twenty-two bags of tallow came next. Padre Amores looked pained at the tremendous spaces they left in the adobe storeroom. He had so carefully harbored this tallow that was to be traded for the necessary supplies from Spain.

Still the governor was not satisfied. "And thirteen horses!" he cried. "Spanish officers at the Presidio are riding poorer horses than your savages."

There was a sadness in Juan's heart as he saw the little colt he had raised, and carefully broken for Padre Amores, go trotting over the hill toward Monterey with twelve of the finest horses the Mission had produced.

The Padre slowly folded the receipt the governor had signed, and put it in his habit.

Sola's party was hardly out of sight before the Padres were calling every pair of hands to work.

"Quick! A boat in! Get the oxen! Load the carts! Letters, cloth, ornaments from Spain, and more tortilla pans! Maybe there will even be some iron to put bands around the wooden cart wheels and save them from breaking."

By late afternoon, hides, tallow, and wool were loaded, oxen pulled on the leather thongs, and the creaking, wooden-wheeled carts started their trek over the hill to the Spanish capital. Indians walked beside the oxen with soap ready to use on wheels, and Padre Amores rode a horse at the head.

37

For the first time Juan was sorry to go through the gates of the compound. Loreta would be left there. He turned to look at her before he jerked at the oxen; a soldier rode by and gave his ribs a kick.

The trail was slippery from the winter rain, and the oxen were very slow and careful. It was quite dark when they finally descended to the flat just above Monterey. The Padre ordered the animals fed before evening prayers were said, and the tortillas and jerky given out to the Indians. The campfires were comforting, for a cold fog was drifting in from the ocean beyond the rim of the bay.

Lopez and Lieutenant Gonzales were the soldiers sent to guard, but they were impatient to be down where there were señoritas to be eyed, and perhaps companions to share a bottle of wine. Juan and Miguel saw them ride away through the low brush beyond the light of the campfires.

Padre Amores warmed his back, looked over the animals and Indians, and settled for the night on his pallet by the fire. When the Padre's breath came loud, Miguel moved close to Juan. "Soldiers won't beat us, because they have gone to get women," he said. "Monterey is near. Come, Juan, there must be a fiesta tonight on account of the boat. Let us go to see."

There was something startling, wonderful, when they walked past the thick growth of oaks and came upon a knoll where they could see the lights shining from windows of more houses than all the fingers, and perhaps even the toes of one foot also! The town of Monterey!

Miguel was traveled. He had worked in Monterey for the Spaniards. He knew things. "Does the Spaniards' God tell them to light up houses at night like this, and to live so close together?" Juan asked Miguel, for the houses seemed much closer when you weren't looking at them from the top of the hill.

Indians lived far apart, even two days from the nearest family. It made quarrels about fish or aulones or deer to live too close. Juan remembered before Padre Serra came the big fights when two families of Indians came to the good acorn trees. Too many people for one acorn tree. Gentile Indians still had fights over acorn trees, those who did not steal enough corn from the Mission fields to plant for themselves something better than acorns.

Miguel snorted. "The fools of soldiers and Spaniards keep lights because they don't know how to miss from bumping things in the dark, and they have too much in the houses to fall over."

There were pine flares blazing in the dusty winding street; flares that were fastened to the adobe walls of houses. At the Plaza was music, flute playing by Indians, and guitars and violins by Spaniards. The *marineros* and men from the boats and soldiers from the fort danced with señoritas; señoritas in shining, bright-colored dresses that were like Padres' robes on fiesta days! Women's eyes smiled at the men.

Juan and Miguel squeezed themselves into the crowd of Indians pressed against the wall in the shadows. They were close to the beautiful music, and could see the dancers as they turned in the waltz, or did the *jota*.

Across the plaza, lighted by many candles, and strewn with flowers, was a big table spread with food and bottles of wine. The señoritas would go there and hold up glasses and make laughing eyes at their dancing partners as they drank.

Then sometimes they would rub the mouths together and laugh with little bird notes. Juan didn't watch this so much. He liked to see the ones with the violins and guitars, as they made the fast music that the Padres didn't know how to play.

"They are happy and rub mouths like that because they get things written on paper from Spain," Miguel explained. "The boat makes them happy." Suddenly he stopped, grabbed Juan's pantaloons. "Look who is with a señorita!"

Just then Private Lopez whirled by with a girl on his arm. She had very red lips and cheeks deep as a rose, and she was

39

smiling into the ugly face of Lopez. Her dress was shining and greener than the hills in the spring and she had red flowers in her hair.

"He will be good-natured, and dream on his musket for a long time now," Miguel whispered. "She will go into the dark with him to rub mouths. She is one who needs no duenna to watch her. Come, follow me."

Juan was so fascinated by the music that he didn't want to circle around back of the monstrous candle-lit table. But Miguel had worked for Señor Romero who owned one of the big lands that Spain had given. Miguel knew his way among all this brilliance and music.

Girls, with older women close by, sat on benches talking and laughing with men in velvet pantaloons. The duennas just talked to other duennas, and complained of the stiffness of their joints, and how heavy the fog was this year, and why did the young like to dance until light came into the sky, when beds were so comfortable and warming? The old Señora in black, who sat behind the table, bent down to wipe her nose. Quick as a rabbit running for his hole, Miguel left Juan and rushed to the table.

"Tortillas and wine for Señor Romero," he demanded of the serving Indian, and was back with food and wine before the old Señora had adjusted her head shawl and brushed down the folds of black silk across her enormous bosom.

"Drink the wine, and we will put the cups back, then go into the dark of the beach to eat," Miguel whispered.

The wine was good. It made Juan warm inside, and the drink of it had been much bigger than the wine at Carmelo. It was like a campfire burning brightly inside him. He wanted to dance to the fast music. Miguel pushed the food into Juan's hands; then he came back. "To the beach, before they find we don't belong here in the pueblo of Monterey," he whispered.

The enchiladas had many peppers in them, and sweet meat. They were warm. Juan ate in silence as he lay stretched out on the sand. He wished the faraway music would go on forever.

40

"I love you, my brave one," a woman murmured tenderly in the dark behind them.

"I adore you," her companion returned with ardor.

Juan started. This sounded like things he had been taught to say in the church! Miguel put a hand on him.

"Spaniards talk this way to take a woman," he whispered in Room-se-en language. "A *marinero* from the boat. She is a serving woman, without a duenna. Spaniards make a great to-do over duennas."

They sat for a while. There was no further talk from the two behind them. The wine made Juan sleepy. "Come!" Miguel shook him. "We must get back. These people dance until light comes, with music players changing to rest. Padre Amores will miss us, then perhaps a beating if Lopez gets back."

Juan was out of his sleep and onto his feet. He couldn't afford to offend the Padre. There was little Loreta to think about. He wondered if the bruises showed now where the governor had kicked her. Would the women put sage on her?

They hurried through the soft blanket of gray fog, up to the hill. The embers from the fires glowed only faintly when they reached camp. Oxen were chewing in the dark, and Padre Amores was still breathing loudly. Juan and Miguel rolled up on the ground to sleep.

Mass at the first light, on the hillside near the oxen. The tortillas, then off down the hill with the carts. Lopez looked tired and long-faced, as he rode beside the procession. Gonzales had eyes only for the faraway hills across the bay today. He didn't even have energy enough to prod the oxen or call to an Indian to hurry. Miguel looked knowingly at Juan.

Monterey was busy. The crooked, yellow, weed-lined street was alive with vaqueros, and sailors, and Spaniards, in their bright-colored trousers and vests. Indians carried heavy burdens of water from the springs, and one or two black-clothed Señoras dodged in and out between the wooden wheels of the ox carts, on their way to the crowded plaza.

The Padre led his ox carts down to the landing, and the In-

41

dians waited patiently beside the animals while he bargained for things on the ship. Then they were ordered to unload the hides and tallow. Marineros rowed a boatload of supplies from the sailing ship out in the bay.

"Juan! Miguel! Pablo! Load this to the carts," Amores cried, as he checked from a paper the articles that the sailors put down on the landing. It took so much less time to put these strange things into the carts than it had taken to unload the hides. The new load took up little room. Not even one cart was as full as it had been on the way over to Monterey. The oxen wouldn't have to pull hard now.

The Padre had other errands. He sold a string of beautiful shoes with satin trimmings to the Spanish trader, and took cloth. Juan was proud when he saw the exchange. His hands had sewed many pairs of those shoes. Perhaps some day his own little Loreta could have a pair. He would know even better how to make them beautiful. Still, not even once had he seen an Indian woman with beautiful shoes. There were never enough.

"Hurry and get more shoes made," the trader called after the Padre. "We need them. The señoritas of the best families danced away two pairs before dawn this morning at the Governor's ball. I will take all your shoes, but mind they are well made, with trimmings suitable for the foot of a beautiful woman, or they won't sell."

"They will be soft as the whisper of Satan," the Padre replied, and, smiling, he signalled the carts to start over the hill to Carmelo.

Chapter V

THREE OR NOTHING: 1820

TORTILLA pans, lace for the new altar cloth, and full directions for making a great weaving loom! All this, as well as cloth and seeds, came from Spain for the friars of San Carlos de Borromeo. Padre Payeras had letters, too, written in fine black crisscross on the paper, and Padre Amores put strings on the fiddle that had so long been silent. The good God had been kind, for the boat had arrived two whole weeks ahead of San Carlos Day! Juan's heart sang. The great fiesta San Carlos when Indians didn't work, but instead went to extra Mass with music and singing, and marched around the church, proudly carrying the statue of San Carlos de Borromeo under its beautiful satin canopy! There was roasted meat and plenty of it, with sauce made from tomatoes and onions and carefully prepared peppers. Afterwards, came games and happiness until it was time to be locked up for the night, with memories enough to last until another year when San Carlos de Borromeo would be honored for giving his name to the Mission on the Carmelo.

A lot must be done in two weeks. The Spanish ladies in Monterey wanted shoes. There were dresses and pantaloons to be made by the Indian sisters to wear at Mass. This would really surprise and please the Patron Saint when he looked down. Extra corn must be ground so that one day could pass without the sound of a metate at San Carlos de Borromeo. The Mission was very grateful to the Saint this year. Rain had come early, and already hills were showing pricks of fresh green through the yellowed grass. Cattle and sheep would not have to work so hard at nuzzling food from the bare hillsides, and

43

they would make more and better tallow for Mission export.

Loreta grew more beautiful every time Juan looked at her. This year she could walk in the procession on her own feet beside her father.

As he worked sewing bits of color to the shoes he made for Spanish feet, Juan wished that the baby could walk in beautiful shoes, behind the statue of San Carlos. This might attract the blessed Saint's eye to the little girl, and bring her special blessings.

Padre Amores only smiled. "She is more blessed by the Saint if her father is a good worker, and loves her. The Holy Virgin always is the mother to dear children without a mother."

Juan felt better then, for there was no time before dark to make little shoes after the work of the day was done. It was comforting to know that Saints were not deceived by the glorious satin dresses and beautiful shoes worn by rich people. He decided right then, for Loreta's sake, never to be tempted by Te-mo to run away and fish, or hunt, or live in the hills without pantaloons. The baby must have everything her father could do for her, and the Saint's blessing meant a lot.

San Carlos Day was golden; not even a fog bank to mar the deep blue of the sky. Swallows flew excitedly around the bell tower as though to hasten the glad pealing of bells. All the Indians were clean and fresh, and little Loreta had a dress of yellow to wear in the procession. All eyes were eager to see the Padres' new robes that had come from Spain. Indian voices never sang more gloriously or more lovingly than they did that November morn in the little adobe Mission that had been built by the toil of their hands and the ache of their backs.

Juan looked at the pictures on the walls, and Loreta, on her little knees beside him, followed his eyes with her big brown ones. In the niche was "Our Lady," her nose perfect as ever. Her face was serene, as if she had forgotten her adventures and the rainy November night that Polonia had died to bring the little Loreta.

It was time to march with the statue of San Carlos in the

44

center of the procession. This year Miguel was one of the bearers. Maybe next year Juan would do it. Padre Amores' high tenor voice intoned the beginning of the hymn to San Carlos.

> "Thy purity has won for thee
> A crown of fadeless light.
> Oh, may its radiance shine on us
> And cheer the gloom of night."

Then Juan lifted up his voice to join the chorus:

> "Oh, pray for us, San Carlos,
> For dangers hover near;
> Oh, pray that God may give us strength
> To conquer every fear."

Something breathless went on inside Juan O-nes-e-mo as he sang with the others. He was taken back to the old free days, when he had crept near in the tules and listened while the Fra Junípero had lifted up his head and sung alone, to the trees and sky. Serra had known a Saint was listening.

Padre Amores' sweet voice rang clear again:

> "And when we've triumphed over sin
> And death's dread hour is nigh,
> Oh, pray that God may angels send
> To bear our souls on high."

The doorway of the church was reached, and the Indian neophytes went alone to kneel at the altar rail and receive the blessing. Juan had trouble. The little Loreta wouldn't keep still. He hoped San Carlos would remember that she was only an Indian baby, and be patient with her.

Then came the excitement of the races and games, and the good smell of meat cooking. This day an Indian could eat slowly as much as he wanted, because there was no work to go back to. What a day! Even the soft, gray gulls flew over to see

45

and envy the fiesta at San Carlos on the Carmelo. Juan looked at the sea beyond the golden beach. It was green and tender and calm today. Anger and tossing were stopped, out of respect for the Saint.

Loreta ate meat and tortillas, given to her from the hands of a dozen Indians. Her eyes danced as she poked food into her mouth.

Padre Amores called Juan and handed him the fiddle. "Show them, Juan, how you can play and copy all the bird songs."

The good God was indeed kind to Juan O-nes-e-mo. He had dreamed it would be this way, nights when the fleas were biting, and days when the work went hard. As he played, little Loreta stood looking up at him with the tender brown eyes of a baby fawn. She loved music, too, but Indian women knew nothing but work. There would be no violin playing for Loreta.

Three days after San Carlos Day, Juan looked up from his work to see that Miguel had stopped cutting on the wooden plowshare he was making. He looked sick, as he leaned against the adobe wall. Private Lopez had already taken to his bed with a fever. But Miguel had bumps on him! Juan told Padre Payeras.

The Padres looked a long time at Miguel, and then talked together. They looked at other Indians for bumps. Juan was frightened for little Loreta. Never had he seen bumps like this!

By the fifth day a lot of Indians had bumps and were too sick to work or even leave the sleeping place for prayers. The Padres made a great cauldron of herb tea and made Indians who were well enough stand in line to drink of it, and then carry the hot evil-smelling stuff to sick ones. It was on this day that a soldier rode into the compound from Monterey.

"Smallpox came on the boat!" he called. "Several people are dead in Monterey. The mariners were afraid to tell for fear they could not get rid of their goods. The governor says to come and get your Indians if you still want the dead ones

46

that ran away from Spanish masters and tried to wash off the
pimples in the cold water of Monterey Bay!"

Juan watched the Padres. "Smallpox" seemed to be a curse,
a dreadful thing, for they both crossed themselves and made a
prayer.

"I'll take ox carts and Indians and go for them," Padre
Payeras said. "You stay here and care for the sick, Amores. I
shall make the trip to Monterey as quickly as possible. Give
them extreme unction as they need it."

Juan was chosen, because he was an old man, and knew
how to save his strength and make it last, while younger men
threw theirs away in useless motions. Besides, he had no
bumps, nor did his bones ache.

Before he left, he went to the busy Padre Amores. "Will
you ask God to keep bumps from my little Loreta, Padre, until I come back to take care of her?"

Amores lifted his worn, flushed face and looked a long time
at Juan. "God grant that I'll be able to do that, Juan. Pray for
her yourself. Pray to San Carlos as you walk to Monterey for
the dead."

When they reached the top of the hill and could look down
on Monterey Bay, they saw that a ship was in! The Padre
stopped the carts to let the oxen rest for a bit, and Pablo and
Juan watched a small boat leave the vessel and the man in it
row toward shore.

After a while Padre Payeras put away his little brown book
and examined the carts. "Come, Juan, Pablo, we must tighten
the rawhide that holds the cart wheels, and put more soap on
them, and then move on. We have sick ones to think about
and Monterey is still far away."

They met an Indian on the road. He told them that this
boat was a foreign one, *Kutusof*; Russians from across the
world! The Russians had suffered from smallpox not so long
ago, and they scratched with medicine to cure smallpox, and
to keep from getting it! The foreigners had promised to help
the people of Monterey with their great sickness that killed.

47

The governor had changed his mind about taking the dead Indians back to Carmelo. "It is not safe. They must be buried right away, to stop the smallpox from spreading," he told Padre Payeras, while Juan and Pablo waited patiently by the carts, and scratched the flea bites on their bare legs. "The Russians are going to scratch us with medicine, and help us with this great sickness that is killing soldiers and Spaniards—"

"And Indians," Padre Payeras added quickly in a strong voice.

Juan was set to work digging a trench on the hillside not far from the governor's church, while Padre Payeras and Pablo went to get the dead. Services were said, and the soft, moist earth replaced over the bodies. Then Padre Payeras put a cross made of oak branches over the mound, and they turned back to the winding main street of Monterey.

A bell was ringing, and a man called that the governor ordered all to have matter scratched on them!

Padre Payeras hurried toward the plaza, with Juan and Pablo close behind. Soldiers were already being scratched, more soldiers than Juan had toes and fingers. They would not be sick, Spaniards in the crowd were saying. People made way for the governor's lady in a red velvet dress, and some señoritas who were well enough to come and be scratched. After a long time the Padre bared his arm, and had matter put on it, then he pushed Juan and Pablo toward the surgeon of the Russian boat.

"No! No! No Indian, until the Spaniards have all been scratched! There won't be enough!" A Spaniard pushed Juan away and hustled a soldier forward.

"Don't fear, Juan. In no time there will be enough matter from my own arm," the Padre said as he turned away.

"I am an old man, Padre. Old grasses die. But Loreta is young. Can you give to Loreta?"

"We will see, Juan."

The Padre went again to the governor's church to say

48

prayers. Juan and Pablo were left to stay with the oxen, until he returned.

Juan had prayed to San Carlos about Loreta, but even the Spaniards were not depending entirely on prayers. They were using matter from the bump on an arm! He sat on his haunches and thought about it. He wanted someone to talk to about this scratching.

A marinero was stretched out on the beach with a bottle of wine in his hand. He would look toward the boat, and then drink.

"You stay by the oxen," Juan told Pablo. "I will come back before the Padre." He hurried over to the foreign mariner. Pablo didn't mind being alone, for he had real tobacco from the Spaniards to smoke.

Juan dropped on the sand. "You have matter scratched?" he asked in Spanish.

The man stopped drinking his wine and nodded. "Long ago, when the curse first broke out."

"No sickness?"

"Not much."

"The Spaniards say there is not enough scratch for Indians. Have you some?"

"No, but my comrade has a bad arm. He might be willing to trade some." He looked at Juan with sharp eyes. "What do you have?"

Juan thought a minute. "I'm a Mission Indian, and make beautiful shoes for the señoritas. My shoes are the pretty ones. All want them. Maybe three pairs of shoes?"

A pain went through Juan as the man shook his head. "What would I do with shoes? I've no woman."

"But the man with the bad arm. He might use them," Juan insisted.

"He don't give shoes to the women he knows." Again the head shook.

"You sell them."

49

"Too much trouble. Besides, the captain might demand the matter from the arm and we'd get into trouble." He looked off to sea, took another swig from the bottle of wine, and kicked the sand with his boots. "Got any sea-otter skins? We might trade them."

Juan sighed. "Sea otters are hard to find now. Traders take them away." He had no way of getting sea otters. The Gentile Indians went a long way to get them.

The man shrugged, and wiped his mouth with the back of his hand. "The Spaniards will pay through their noses to keep from dying."

Juan thought quickly. Perhaps Te-mo had a sea-otter skin. He could run away and find Te-mo. But then Loreta would be at the Mission! His head whirled with the confusion of thoughts.

"Maybe I can get one—."

"One!" The man shook his head.

"Maybe two?"

"Three or nothing!" The man's eyes were sharp enough to scrape fat from a hide as they met Juan's.

"Three then, but it will take time. How long will the boat be here?" Juan asked sadly.

The sharp-eyed man put up the fingers on both hands.

Pablo gave the call of the jay bird to signal that the Padre was coming. Juan lifted the fingers of one hand, and spread them wide.

"I will come here then, with the skins?" He turned and raced toward the ox cart.

Chapter VI

THE GIFT: 1820

WHEN they reached the Mission, bedlam was loose! Some Indians, frightened because Padre Amores had taken to his bed, ran away to make sweat houses in the hills behind the Mission. Lopez was roaring with fever, and Lieutenant Gonzales couldn't leave him to go after Indians. Miguel was dead, and put in the trench at the north side of the church. More Indians were coming down with the sickness.

Tired as he was from the trip, Padre Payeras rang the bell for Angelus, and afterward went the rounds, attending the sick and giving spiritual comfort to the dying.

Juan watched him take from his own arm some blood at the scratch place and put it into Padre Amores' arm.

Loreta, happy at play with some gourds, was a comforting sight. San Carlos had heard the prayers for an Indian baby! But Padre Amores had said her father must be good and work for the blessings of the Saint.

Juan made fires under the great pots, and fed them constantly to cook broth for the sick ones. Padre Payeras had only to raise a hand, and Juan O-nes-e-mo was there to help. Between times he took a minute to look into the brown eyes of his little daughter to watch for the first blaze of the sickness.

All night the Indians who were well worked, with Padre Payeras to tell them what to do. They carried water and held blankets over the feverish ones to keep the bumps from getting cold and killing them. Every hour or two the Padre went and said prayers by Padre Amores. It was almost morning when Payeras called. "Quick, Juan! The wine!"

Like a flash, Juan ran to the shelter, grabbed the bottle, and hurried to Padre Payeras, who was holding Padre Amores on his arm so he could breathe better.

"Pour some in the cup!" He dumped the water out onto the floor, and held the cup for Juan to fill it.

Padre Amores opened his eyes, smiled at Juan. "The fiddle —it is my own. Give it to Juan—his spirit needs it." He pointed to the red velvet bag hanging on the adobe wall. Murmuring a prayer, he lost consciousness.

Juan stood a moment, waiting, and then silently he turned, took the fiddle from the nail and went out. Only the prayers for the dead sounded in the little cell-like room.

Juan stoked the fire again. San Carlos had not answered a Padre's prayer, a Padre who always sang so sweetly on San Carlos Day! Then surely he would forget a little Indian like Loreta.

Without further thought, Juan gathered up tortillas and meat, wrapped the sleeping baby tightly, and then, picking up the fiddle and the bundle of food, stole out of the compound toward the hills.

He ran until his heart thumped too much so that he had to rest. Little Loreta was heavier than a bundle of hides. But he was away! The sickness would never catch her now. It was too busy at the Mission. And he had the fiddle that the good Amores had given him.

When he had rested in the cool grass of the dark hillside, Juan reached into the velvet bag and drew out the fiddle. He played soft bird calls to the sleeping child beside him, and sent a good thought to the Padre who would never again have to work hard in the sun. How often the poor Padre Amores had wiped the sweat from his brow as he worked with the Indians, and watched over the great rendering vats to make grease for candles and Mission taxes. The violin went lower and lower from Juan's chin as he played. He was too tired to go further now. He put the fiddle to bed in its red velvet bag, pulled the covers closer over Loreta, then curled up beside her and went to sleep.

The next morning at sunup, habit claimed Juan. He knelt with his face toward the Mission, and sent a prayer to the Holy Virgin and San Carlos before he gave tortillas to Loreta and ate a little himself.

What to do with the baby while he hunted for Te-mo? He didn't want her with any other Indians so she would get the sickness. Juan was taking no chances now, since Amores had died. If necessary, he would kill to get skins to trade for scratch stuff to save Loreta!

Te-mo, being a Gentile Indian, would not yet be astir. He would take Loreta and go to Te-mo's shelter by the big acorn tree and see about the skins.

Loreta was cranky. She wouldn't be carried, but insisted on stumbling along beside her father, which made travel over the hills slow. Each time he picked her up she screamed and stiffened her legs in kicks. Finally, Juan saw that they would be hours going a mile or two in the hot sun. His patience came to an end. He picked the baby up, gave her little brown bottom a slap, and raced through the brush in the direction of Te-mo's tule shelter.

But the child was heavy, and the fiddle was hard to hold under the arm that carried the food. It kept slipping down until it almost fell to the ground. He had to stop often, put down the bundle, shove the fiddle up, then grab the yelling Loreta by her naked middle.

Te-mo was not at the hut! His woman shook her head and went on grinding acorns. She had little use for Juan, now he was a Christian. Te-mo's children crowded to look. Juan held Loreta under his arm. She stopped crying to observe all the children around her.

"Where is Te-mo?" Juan asked.

The woman shrugged her shoulders and tilted her head toward the river. "Fishing."

Juan was off again, fiddle, food, and child. Blackberry bushes scratched Loreta's legs as he plunged through them. She whimpered, but he had no time for mere scratches now. He

53

must catch Te-mo away from his woman or there was not even a faint hope of getting the sea-otter skins from him!

Juan made the bird call that was their signal. Far away on a hillside came an answer. Te-mo was not fishing. He was on his stomach at a rabbit hole, snaring little rabbits as they came out. He showed no surprise when Juan came up and deposited his bundles and baby. He just looked at Loreta's body and smiled.

"Only girls come in return for an Indian's hard work at the Mission?"

"She will bring other men into the world, and I like her," Juan said. He reached into the food bundle and gave the child a tortilla to keep her mind from the blackberry scratches on her legs. Then he handed one to Te-mo, who grunted and ate it in one bite.

"Great sickness in Mission San Carlos de Borromeo, and in Monterey, too," Juan said. "Lots die."

"Hot food that burns the stomach," Te-mo mumbled in Room-se-en, and set the snare of grass in the dark of the rabbit hole.

"No, not food. Bumps that won't wash off. Came with the boat." Juan looked off over the hills where in his young days he had hunted deer without wearing pantaloons. "You catch many sea otters, Te-mo?"

"Some."

Loreta had eaten her tortilla, and was working at the knots in the bundle to find more food.

"You let me have three?"

"Go down the coast and get them for yourself." Te-mo pulled the rush snare and caught a rabbit as it popped out of the hole. Juan watched him kill it with a stone and set the snare again.

"I have to take care of my baby. I can't walk so far carrying her."

"Why do you want them?" Te-mo's eyes looked into Juan's with a steady stare. "For Spanish Padres to use?"

54

Juan didn't dare to tell him they were to save Loreta's life, for Te-mo didn't think much of girls. "Not for the Padres. I have left the Mission. For *me!*" He pounded his chest.

"I have none to give away. The Spaniard in Monterey gave a gun and some shots for twelve skins," Te-mo said. "Shots and a gun big enough to kill grizzly bears."

Juan reached into the bundle and brought out Loreta's yellow dress. He held it up. "This?"

Te-mo only smiled and shook his head.

Juan shoved the dress back into the bundle. "I will make beautiful shoes for all your children when I get a hide."

"They walk better without shoes." He looked into the hole at the snare.

Juan was desperate. He slid the fiddle out of the red velvet bag and added the bag to the yellow dress. This was a great mistake! Te-mo didn't look at the bag at all, but fixed his eyes on the shining fiddle of Padre Amores. Loreta, unsuccessful in her efforts to reach the food, started to cry. She cried so much today. At the Mission she never cried. Perhaps the bump sickness was coming to her!

Te-mo pointed to the fiddle. "That—" he said. "For three skins."

"No!" a hurt went through Juan. Te-mo could not make bird notes come out of it. "Not the fiddle."

Te-mo moved away to another rabbit hole. Loreta set up a howl for more food.

"Take the girl away, you squaw," Te-mo grumbled. "She scares away rabbits with her noise."

Juan dug in the bundle and hushed Loreta's mouth by shoving a tortilla into it. He looked at the fiddle, so beautiful in the sun, and thought of the sweet chants that Padre Amores brought from that splendid, shining box. Then he looked across the violin at little Loreta, who smiled. A baby hand offered him a bite of tortilla, but her eyes were too bright, and her face different.

"Give me four skins," Juan murmured.

55

Te-mo shook his head. "Spaniard give me a gun and shot, too, for twelve skins."

There was so little time before the Russian boat would leave. Once the sails were unfurled and it was away, Loreta might be sick with bumps and die. She made a lot of noise, but she was his. She was a part of O-nes-e-mo's body!

"Three, then," he murmured. "But you get them before you have the fiddle. I will wait here."

Te-mo set snares in several rabbit holes, and then went down the hill.

Juan caught up the bow, tuned as the Padre had taught him, and then played frantically as if to extract the last tune from the fiddle's insides before he gave it to Te-mo. A lump came to his heart. He tried to think of Amores in paradise, and asked forgiveness for letting the fiddle go. He was old now, with no woman, and no more chance for a son. An old man alone with no Loreta—surely the good Padre Amores would understand the great need to part with the fiddle. As if to ease him, there came to Juan's rough, brown fingers, the beautiful music that Padre Amores had played in church last San Carlos Day when they were all so happy. Never before had he been able to play that chant! An omen. The Saint had helped him to play. San Carlos had heard and understood.

When Juan finished playing, Te-mo was standing by an oak tree, the sea otter skins over his arm; in his eyes was a hunted look that startled Juan. For a minute neither one of them moved, then Te-mo sat down beside Juan.

"That is a Christian fiddle, not like the ones that play for fiestas in Monterey," he said quietly. "A Padre is inside it!" He handed over the skins. "Take them and your fiddle and get out. The music hurts me in here!" He pressed his middle. "Sickness will come to me from it. I need now the sweat house."

Juan lost no time putting the violin in the bag, and retying the food bundle. The fiddle was sacred; it had performed a miracle right in his hands. Maybe the spirit of Padre Amores

56

had crept inside it, to help Juan now when the good Padre was gone!

"I will give you otter skins back as soon as I can hunt," he promised. "You will not lose these skins. O-nes-e-mo makes a promise." Then, as he picked up his bundle, baby, and fiddle, Juan came closer to the dazed Te-mo. "Otter skins, or something much better, Te-mo, for the San Carlos knows what has happened. The Holy Virgin is looking out for my Loreta as Padre Amores promised she would for all motherless children." Quickly he made his way down the hill and through the blackberry bushes to the river bottom. Loreta didn't whimper now. Perhaps she knew that a miracle had happened to them.

Chapter VII

TORTILLA TROUBLE: 1820. 1821

THE trek over the hills with bundles and Loreta was slow and wearisome, for the baby was cross and twice threw from her stomach the precious tortillas. Could this be the first start of the bump sickness, or had he carried her too much by the middle? There were so many fears now. Indian women just seemed to let children grow like the grass. Why did his Loreta have to be this way? He fed her every time she cried!

It took four days to reach Monterey, for Juan stopped twice to brew balsam tea for tortilla sickness. Then he had to fish. The Mission food, already low, had to be saved for Loreta. He couldn't go where the Spaniards were, for he was afraid of being captured and beaten and sent back to the Mission. He slipped from tree to tree, from sheltering brush to another patch of cover, until at last he could plop Loreta and the bundles down in the sand. He straightened up to ease the muscles of his back. Hides, fiddle, food, and baby were quite a load for a man who had lived as long as Juan O-nes-e-mo. He looked over the sand, and was comforted because the foreign boat was still there. He might be seen by soldiers if he stood up straight like this, but if he didn't do it, the *marinero* wouldn't find him.

There was nothing to do but wait now, and feed Loreta, who was already picking at the knots of the food bundle. He had gathered a supply of balsam in case she needed it. If only he could leave Loreta and the bundles and search for the *marinero*. It would be safer than staying here. Perhaps the man was drinking wine somewhere and had forgotten his bargain.

Juan's eyes grew tired from watching, and the sun went behind the hill back of the fort. His stomach gnawed, but there was so little food left now that he dared not eat. Loreta lay asleep on the bundle of hides. Maybe if he played the fiddle, his stomach would forget hunger.

And then, just before dusk, two men came along the beach toward him. They were not soldiers in uniform. The *marineros!*

There was no greeting. The man Juan had talked to looked at the sleeping baby and pointed. "Those the hides?"

Juan nodded and pulled them out from under Loreta. He waited while the men examined them carefully, and talked together in a language Juan couldn't understand.

"All right," the *marinero* said in Spanish. "Stick out your arm." The second man pulled up his sleeve, and the bargainer took a needle out of his shirt. "Stick out your arm, I said."

Juan pointed to the baby. "For her." He knelt in the sand and bared the little brown arm. The man scratched it, and took some matter from the friend's arm. Loreta pulled away in her sleep.

"That's all," he said. "It'll swell up and be sore like his."

Juan was afraid. There was so little of it to keep away all the bumps on a baby. "Do another," he begged, "on the other arm."

The man only laughed and tapped his head. "You're crazy. No."

"They are good sea-otter hides," the friend with the sore arm said. "Give the old savage a jab, too; I don't mind."

"Stick out your arm, old man, and we will give you a prize." Again the *marinero* took the needle from his shirt, and scratched the matter into the flabby flesh of Juan's arm. Then they picked up the hides and without further talk, walked along the beach toward the Custom House.

For five days, Juan struggled along in the hills above Monterey. He hunted roots and berries, and ground acorns on a

59

rough stone. Loreta cried a lot. She spit out acorn meal, for she was not like Juan. She had been born a Christian Indian with a taste for the Padre's corn. He sighed, laid her down, and went about making a stew of rabbit for her. Her eyes were bright, and her body hot. She would not eat even the stew. There was nothing to do but go to the springs where the women washed and get water and willow leaves to make tea for stopping the fever. Juan took off his pantaloons, put a leg of each of them under each of the baby's arms and tied her to a pine. Then he hid the fiddle under a bush, and slid away toward the spring. His own arm was very sore, and the bump was big and white, with a great, angry red ring around it. He, too, would drink willow water for the fever. He was an old man, and tired. As he stumbled through the brush, he mumbled a prayer to San Carlos.

There were few washing, for the sickness was bad in Monterey, an Indian woman at the spring told him. She sniffed, too, because she saw he had no pantaloons and thought he was a gentile. And then she caught sight of his arm.

"You get a scratch?"

It was Juan's turn to sniff. He looked away from her to the water and gave his attention to dipping it up into the bladder he had brought. Juan was not using his tongue today. Miguel had long ago told him that the washing hole at Monterey was a place of much talking when the women were together, and that Spaniards often found out how to catch thieves from those noisy ones at the spring.

The woman stopped pounding the clothes. She came nearer, wiping her hands on her cloth dress. Juan could feel her eyes boring into the very sore on his arm.

"How did you get scratch? The Governor Sola said there was not scratch for Indians, and they die," she said, dropping to her knees beside Juan.

Juan decided to surprise this sniffy one, who must have been brought by Spaniards from some other Mission.

"San Carlos gave the scratch to O-nes-e-mo by a miracle,"

he told her calmly, and began to gather willow leaves from the tree over his head.

The woman's eyes opened wide; she pulled her heavy body up by a branch, and, still staring at Juan, she crossed herself.

"What did you do for the Saint?" she asked.

"Music."

"Anieta sings chants, too—" she looked at her bared arms. "No scratches come."

Suddenly a beautiful thought took possession of Juan. He turned. "Bring corn to me, and I will give you a scratch. But it must be ground corn." He watched her face. Here was a way to get corn for Loreta. The baby liked to eat corn!

Anieta looked for a long time at the sore, then she nodded. "I will take corn from the Spaniards' bins."

"A big bagful," Juan told her. "I will wait in the willows. You bring a needle and I give you a scratch."

He slid into the cool, leafy green and watched her go at a dog trot toward the houses of Monterey. Her fat behind shook. The wind blew her long cotton dress tight across her body. She would make good tallow! He wished he had a woman to care for Loreta.

Hot pricks soon went through Juan. He hadn't warned the woman that he would give her no scratch if she told! Miguel had talked of the noisy ones who worked their mouths! But she wouldn't talk! If she did, someone else might come first with the corn and there would be no scratch for her! She would be looking out for herself first. He settled back to rest while there was a chance, for Loreta kept an old man busy with her continual fretting noises.

The time that the Padres always rang the bell for eating at midday came and went, and still no woman with the fat behind. Juan's mind was on the little Loreta tied to the tree. The sun had moved now, so that she would be even more hot than the fever made her. But he must wait.

Finally the woman came, a bag of meal on her head. She put it down and wiped the sweat from her forehead with her

61

dress bottom. "I had to wait for taking the corn," she murmured. "The Señora was long before she went to her siesta today." From the ample bosom of her dress she pulled a needle. "Now you give me scratch so I don't die with bump sickness."

Juan took the needle, scratched her arm, then punctured the sore of his own arm and spread matter as the marinero had done to him.

The woman smiled. Willows behind them cracked. Juan turned. He didn't need to lift his head, for his eyes saw the boots of two Spanish soldiers crunching down on the sand near him.

"So! Miracle O-nes-e-mo!" Captain Alverez shouted. "We are hunting Indians like you!"

Juan was furious as he faced the woman. "You worked your mouth! May the San Carlos strike you down dead with the curse for this!"

The woman cringed and crossed herself. "I only told of the miracle to get the corn," she muttered. "I had to tell Paolo, for he has the keys. Paolo is a Spaniard, but he let me have the corn."

"And Paolo goes often to the wine shop!" Alverez laughed bitterly. "We listen at the wine shop for what all the Paolos say!" He gave Juan a kick with his boot. "Come on, waste no more time, Miracle. There is a flogging and work for you at the Mission on the Carmelo."

He turned to the woman. "Take back your corn, before the Señora finds out you have been a thief and has you beaten senseless for your pains."

Juan got up. What would happen to Loreta, up on the hill in the sun? No tortillas, no willow water, and a fever burning at her.

"How did you get the scratch?" Captain Alverez demanded as they walked through the grass to where the soldiers' horses were tied. "No other Indian has it, and few enough Spaniards."

"A miracle!" Juan told him and walked on.

"How?"

"A *marinero* scratched me because of a chant that came unexpectedly from the fiddle that Padre Amores gave me when he was dying." Juan didn't care to explain all the details, especially to Alverez.

"Where is the fiddle?" Pablo Vincente asked kindly. "Did you trade it?"

"No. That would not be a miracle, to trade, Señor. I left the fiddle on the hillside with Loreta while I came for water." Juan looked hopefully into the eyes of the kindly soldier who never laid the whip on hard, and only lashed when he was ordered to do so.

"If you can fiddle up matter, you'd better fiddle hard, for there are many needing it at San Carlos right now," Alverez snorted. "You'll have to run after us. There is no room on the horses for a runaway Indian." He threw a leg over the chestnut mare and dug his heels into her ribs. "Come on, Vincente. We've already spent too much time tracking down one Indian."

"But Loreta! She is on the hill," Juan cried, and looked again into the eyes of Vincente. "I can't leave her with no food, no water. She has scratch, too!" He took a great breath. "And Padre Amores' fiddle!"

Vincente called to Alverez. "The baby, Captain. She is up on the hill, with a vaccination."

"I'll not ride in the hot sun to fetch any savage baby," Alverez said. "He shouldn't have taken her away."

Vincente threw a rawhide length around Juan and then rode to Captain Alverez. Juan had to run to keep the rawhide from pulling on his skin.

"Captain, here is news," Vincente muttered. "The old man says the child has a scratch, too. We better get her, hadn't we? The matter would help Spaniards and soldiers who are not vaccinated at San Carlos de Borromeo."

As he gasped for breath at the end of his rope, Juan was

63

almost afraid to look, afraid to know what the captain would say.

"Right you are," Alverez nodded. "You go, and I'll stay and have a bottle of wine. We'll meet at the fork in the road." He headed his horse toward the street of Monterey.

When Alverez had gone out of sight, Vincente took off the rawhide. "Climb up behind," he ordered. "It will save your feet and my time." Then, two on the black horse, they plunged through the fresh growth of bracken ferns on the hillside.

Loreta had cried herself to sleep. Around her mouth were signs that she had eaten dirt. The arm with the scratch looked red and ugly with a great white patch in the center. When Juan picked her up, she was hot enough to cook with. He ran and brought the fiddle from the shelter of the bush.

"I'll take her while you climb on," Vincente said, and held the baby, not as if she was a snake. "She looks very sick." He turned her over to Juan when he had climbed onto the horse's wide flank. "Here, give me the bundle and the fiddle. They will go on the front of the saddle."

"Loreta has no water to drink," Juan said, as he held the baby close. "I was down for water—"

There was no time to finish, for without a word, Vincente shoved over his canteen. "The wine will have mellowed Captain Alverez by the time we reach the forks. See that you don't irritate him, and I will be able to carry the baby on my horse." The good Vincente didn't even look around as he said these words.

Juan gave the sick Loreta water. It sloshed on her face as he tried to hit her mouth, but that was good, for it cooled her. A wave of happiness and tenderness came over him, for this kindness that San Carlos had put into the heart of Vincente today.

"You are scratched?" he asked. "Soldiers were first."

"I gave mine to—" Vincente's eyes softened, "to a señorita I love in Monterey."

"Stop! I will scratch you. The miracle is for you, too, Corporal Vincente."

64

"I can't, Juan, Captain Alverez will know. I'll have to take my chances that there will be enough after the others at the Mission have been scratched. I had my chance. To die for her would not be too much." He smiled at the thought.

"There will be enough, and without prayers, too," Juan reassured him. "Juan or Loreta will save some for you."

Vincente pulled up in a patch of brush near the fork in the road. "Get down, now," he said, "and give me the baby while you walk. It will make better scenery for the Captain as he rides up."

He untied the bundle and fiddle from the saddle.

"Here, it is better for an Indian to have a burden, too." Then, tenderly, he took Loreta into his arms and pulled a bit of cloth so that the sun would not shine on her sleeping eyes. Vincente threw the rawhide over Juan with his free hand, tightened it only slightly, and then together they went toward the Camino Real.

There was no long wait for the Captain. He was feeling low. Not even the extra wine had taken the soreness out of his heart.

"Women are snakes," he groaned. "They kiss softly in the dark and make a man's lips hungry for more, but they will not even have a glance for him in daylight hours!"

"Then you didn't find the wine you wanted?" Vincente asked good-naturedly. "Never mind. It will be that much sweeter next time you have a draught."

How well Vincente knew Alverez, Juan thought. He kept talking to him of women and love, so that Alverez forgot to hasten his horse, and didn't even notice that Loreta was safe on the arm of Vincente.

"There's excitement along the street in Monterey today," Alverez told Vincente. "Two Englishmen, Hugh McCullough and William Hartnell, are setting out their store of wares from Peru. They represent a firm there."

"This chestnut-haired Hartnell is indeed a fine fellow, with at least five fancy waistcoats to help his looks. They say he is better educated than any around here; a college man, a school-

65

master." Alverez took some snuff. "I suppose he'll be using all his flowing educated language to make love to our women."

Vincente smiled. "I've heard William Hartnell is more interested in wisdom and poetry than in the wiles of women, so you needn't fear him, Captain. He's safe."

Alverez whirled around in his saddle, and Juan saw that his eyes were full of anger.

"Too many Englishmen coming here to trade. There's David Spence, the meat packer, and that golden-haired George Allen. He looks fit to faint from love every time young Señorita Petra Boronda appears at church with her prayer book, and he does favors for her brother José Manuel Boronda without even being asked. *That* for him." Juan saw Alverez spit viciously into the yellow dust of the road. "He claims to be so pious, and has already been baptized Josef Jorge Tomas Allen, and not for the good of his soul, I'll wager that, but so that Señorita Petra will smile on him a little." Captain Alverez sighed. "And now two more Englishmen arrive in Monterey to open up a mercantile shop!"

They rode along in silence for a bit, and Juan had trouble running to keep up. The dust from horses' hoofs made his throat dry, so dry that it was hard to swallow, and the rawhide riata around his skinny middle was cutting into the flabby flesh. He put a thumb between his belly and the rawhide to ease the rub where it hurt worst.

"Vincente, do you think these fine fellows with such white skins, are the reason that certain señoritas are cold toward the brave soldiers who protect them from enemies?" Captain Alverez asked suddenly.

Juan saw Vincente smile, and nod with a knowing look. He was glad when the horses slowed down a little while Vincente thought over the Captain's question.

"So that's the way it is," Vincente said softly. "Captain, why don't you get up in the night and ride over to the governor's church in time for Mass? Maybe the young Petra might have a smile all warmed up and ready for you."

66

"Who said anything about Petra Boronda?" Alverez roared. "I tell you it's no good going to Monterey to Mass. She doesn't even look my way, when I sit near to her. The great beautiful eyes of her never leave prayer book or altar candles." His whip cracked and the chestnut mare broke into a run.

"Be comforted, Captain, the señorita Petra is only eleven. She still has two or three years left to choose a husband," Vincente called. "What woman could bother long with a shopkeeper, when a brave soldier's heart is hers for a few kind looks? You are feeling badly from something you ate. All will be well for you after a dose of physic, Comero."

Captain Alverez stopped, turned his horse a little, and waited for Vincente and Juan to catch up. "It was not what I ate makes me upset. It is memories of a red-lipped girl I kissed in the dark of the governor's garden last night, while the duenna had her back turned to give an Indian serving-maid a tongue-lashing!" Alverez snorted. "Now, today, she glances off to sea when I look up to the balcony where she sews. She doesn't even know I'm there."

"But I thought Petra Boronda was the girl you would die for?" Vincente cried. "And yet you kiss another when the duenna's back is turned! You are a great one to talk of women being fickle."

Alverez pulled at his coat. "A man must have some girl to kiss when he sees the woman he loves deliberately go out of her way to look into eyes of a golden-haired Englishman! A man is still a man."

"But a look, Captain," Vincente laughed. "A look is not too much. I still advise the physic."

"And I still think there are too many English traders and rancheros here," Alverez snapped. "It will take more than a dose of physic to change my mind about that."

Juan was so tired and hungry that the beating he was bound to receive when they reached the Mission didn't seem to matter. He was very glad to see the compound and the swallows flying around the yellowed tower. Women at the Mission

67

knew how to care for the sick little Loreta. A fire was burning under the great iron pot.

Padre Payeras looked up when they came in. "Juan— Juan—" he shook his head sadly. "Why did you leave me when I needed you so much?"

He glanced at Juan's fiddle and the bundle. "And little Loreta, where is she?" He lowered his voice. "Not dead?"

"Here she is, and sick, too," Vincente said as he handed the child down.

The Padre examined her. "Juan, she has been scratched! How does this happen?" Excitedly he looked at Juan, and saw his arm. "And you, too! The governor says no Indians—"

"A miracle—" Juan said, and quick as a humming bird's wings, he thought up an excuse for running away. "San Carlos played a chant on Padre Amores' fiddle, and this made the foreign marinero glad to scratch Loreta and Juan." He came closer. "But we had to run away to get scratch and bring it home to the sick ones we left here at the Mission."

The Padre Payeras didn't seem so sure about the miracle. Juan walked over and showed his sore arm with the large and blooming pustule.

"See? I bring enough for everybody. The San Carlos de Borromeo did this."

"And O-nes-e-mo gets nine lashes on the back for running away," Alverez roared as an Indian took his horse. "We found him at the spring in Monterey, bartering for corn."

Juan faced Padre Payeras. "Loreta wouldn't eat acorns. She is a Christian and needs Padre food," he said.

Payeras looked at the baby again. "She needs willow water to stop the fever." He called an Indian woman and gave the sick little girl into her arms. Alverez sent for his rawhide thongs that were braided into a whip.

"To the post, you!" he cried. "Let's get the work done!"

Padre Payeras clutched Alverez by the shoulder. "Don't be a fool, Alverez. If you whip him and his blood boils, maybe the matter won't work! We need it. Do not risk the lives of many to vent anger on one. That is the way of soldiers the world over—" the old man paused, "and what good comes of it, Captain? Only suffering and death—"

"And the way of Padres is too easy on Indians, and what comes of that, Padre? This may sound impudent for a soldier to ask a Padre, for a soldier already knows the answer." Alverez drew up tall in his uniform and looked toward Juan, who was held hard on the arms by two soldiers. "Juan, here, such a devoted convert, leaves you when you need him most, and cares not a tap of his finger what happens to you, and the sick ones he deserts. He is only back here to work for you because soldiers brought him back by dragging him with a rope around his scrawny middle!"

Padre Payeras looked kindly into Juan's eyes. "Juan is only a child at heart, Captain," he cried, "and he brings help to us on his arm. Do not spoil the help he brings by beating him—"

Alverez motioned the soldiers to free Juan, and then he moved away. There was a black look on his face. This was the first time the Captain had been defeated when there was a beating due an Indian. Juan wished the beautiful Señorita Petra Boronda would look into the eyes of Alverez. Maybe then the Captain would be happy and forget his great longing to beat Indians.

Juan went to the trough made from a hollow log and washed his arms where hands of Spanish soldiers had held him, then he walked into the cool sweet-smelling church to murmur a prayer to San Carlos and to the Holy Virgin who watched over him and had saved him a beating.

Before many moons had come and gone, the time arrived for Spanish soldiers to fight for their beautiful señoritas, and the land too! Hills had just put on the touch of spring green when Mexicans landed soldiers in Monterey. Boatloads of soldiers. Governor Sola sent word for Captain Alverez and his company to come quick over the hill from Carmelo and help fight Mexicans. Lieutenant José Estrada was to lead the battle.

69

CATHEDRAL IN THE SUN

The Indian runner who brought word told Padre Payeras that already Mexican soldiers had burned and sacked some houses and taken away Indian women.

The Padre crossed himself. Juan saw his lips move in prayer, as the soldiers rode out of the compound.

Extra prayers were said at Mass that day, and Padre Payeras was very absent-minded, and didn't even look over the shoes that Juan made.

That night after they were locked up in the sleeping place, Juan took down the fiddle and played softly to Padre Amores, so that he would watch over Corporal Vincente, who had a kind heart for children and runaway Indians, and never liked to beat even when he was told to lay on the whip.

The battle didn't last long. Soldiers were back home in a few days, and Juan was pleased to see Vincente on the white horse.

Padre Payeras ran out to meet them. "What is the news, Captain?" he called as the horses came into the compound. Juan saw that only a few Indians followed the soldiers.

"We lost. The Mexicans took us," Alverez snorted, and swung off his horse. "We were brave soldiers, but how could Sola expect eighty of us, with no ammunition, to fight four hundred Mexicans with plenty of powder?"

"Were many killed?" Padre Sarria asked, and Juan saw him cross himself. "Where are my Indians?"

"Oh, they were too lazy to fight. The Church pampers them and takes the stiffness from their backbones. If the Indians had fought well, we might have saved this country for Spain. You can blame your Indians for our defeat, Padre."

"But you don't tell me about the wounded, or those killed," Payeras asked. "Were many killed?"

"No soldiers, only a few Indians. Estrada led us into battle but when Indians began to fall, he retreated, wise man that he is," Alverez said as he took off his gloves.

Padre Sarria shook his head and sadness was in his face. "I see; when Indians, my children who trusted, fell on the battle

70

JUAN THE MISSION BUILDER

field, then Sola's soldiers retreated and kept their skins whole."
The Padre fingered his cross. "It is all quite plain now. The
underdog must give his blood for others who hold the power
and call themselves his betters."

Juan watched the Padre's lips as they moved in prayer, and
thought of those straight young Indians who would never
again ride into the Mission Compound.

"Now that the Mexican flag flies over Monterey, what will
happen to us? To the Missions?" Padre Payeras asked after
Padre Sarria lifted his head.

"Sola is still Governor." Alverez told them. "We are sent
back to our posts until we hear more. Perhaps Mexicans, now
that they have broken away from Spain, will pay soldiers better
than Spaniards. Some good must come from a battle, even if
it is lost by Spanish soldiers."

"I fear, Payeras, that many changes will come to the Carmelo now that Mexicans are ruling us," Padre Sarria said, and
Juan saw sadness in his eyes, as he looked over the new green
hills.

Chapter VIII

GRINDING STONES: 1823. 1824

WORK went on just the same, in spite of Mexican rule. There were very few changes around the Mission San Carlos. Juan heard from Pablo, who went often to Monterey, that the Mexicans were too busy with more important things to bother the priests and Indians of the Mission, as long as taxes were paid.

"There is excitement plenty in Monterey now. The first banns were read in the governor's church on Sunday for Don Hartnell, the Englishman, to marry Señorita Teresa de la Guerra. You should see the fiesta with plenty to eat, at the de la Guerra house. All the soldiers were there, and señoritas too," Pablo told Juan. "I walked around outside and watched the dancing through the windows, and I heard Captain Cooper tell that he will soon give up being Master of the ship *Rover*, and settle himself down in Monterey, because of the beautiful women." Pablo kicked in the dust and sniffed. "Spanish and English are always thinking of señoritas."

"I used to think of women too, long ago," Juan admitted. "I had four women and that is enough for one Indian man." He thought of the time that Vincente and Alverez had talked about this young Don Hartnell who had so many fancy waistcoats; this schoolmaster who did not have eyes for women. Perhaps the warm climate of Monterey had made the white man like other men so he looked happily on señoritas.

"I never think of women, they make too much noise like jay birds scolding," Pablo said, and shuffled off to ring the bell for Mass.

One day there came a break in the work at San Carlos de

72

Borromeo. The great corn grinding stones, ordered many moons ago, arrived on the boat, and were dragged by oxen to the Mission. They were flat and round and as large as fifty ox cart wheels, and had a hole in the center. Padre Payeras explained to the Indians about them, while they waited for oxen to pull them into place.

"Those great round stones go one on top of the other, and then an iron rod holds them together. See, Juan, that hole at the side?"

Juan nodded.

"Well, a rawhide thong is put in there and fastens to a horse. After corn is put between the stones, the horse goes around and around, and the corn is ground finer than an Indian woman could grind it with long rubbing on her metate."

Juan shook his head. "Too much corn to grind at once, Padre, no good."

"That's just it, Juan, a lot of corn at once. More time for Indian women. It is a new way of grinding for everybody instead of for a few. Your Loreta who is five years old will never have to grind corn on a metate now that the Mission has a better way." The Padre's eyes were bright with excitement, and he went off to order oxen to work.

Loreta stood near the Padre watching the oxen pull on thongs to drag the stones into place, and as she watched, her fingers were busy winding wool. Only five years old and already Loreta O-nes-e-mo could knit coarse socks for the feet of the friars.

Indian sisters of San Carlos de Borromeo were good knitters, and some were dying off from old age of aches in the bones. There was need for young fingers to be ready to take up the work. Wool socks from Carmelo would be expected at every Mission along the coast when the cold and rain came. Besides, taxes were high, and even children must earn their keep at the Mission.

"Pull that way," shouted the Padre. "It must be even or

73

it won't hit the lower stone for grinding." The oxen strained their bodies and the thongs of rawhide tightened. The great stone moved just the width of Loreta's finger.

There was such excitement over the stones! Spanish rancheros from all around had come to see the placing, and they stood in little groups.

Pablo came over to where Juan worked and pointed out the sister of Don José Manuel Boronda, who stood watching, with her duenna near by. "Señorita Petra gave some of the gold that paid for the grinding stones," he whispered. "The saints surely must watch over her bed as she sleeps, for she is so good."

Juan looked a long time at the tiny señorita who was wrapped in a beautiful embroidered shawl that nearly covered her black dress. Her hair was braided around the top of her head like a crown, and there was a gold comb that held her shawl high. On her little feet were beautiful shoes; shoes made by O-nes-e-mo of the Carmelo!

"I have no faith in such great quantities of corn ground at once by horses," José Marquena said in a loud voice to Don Allen, who was not watching the stones; looking instead at Señorita Boronda. "It cannot be so good as that ground by Indian women in metates."

"Padre Sarria is always introducing new methods," Romero grumbled. "Labor-saving, he calls them."

"But there are so many settlers now, so much corn to be ground and Indian labor is of more use in the fields for growing vegetables and fruits to sell to the settlers in Monterey," José Manuel Boronda said, as he filled a pipe. "If horses can do the work of Indians so they can till and weave, so much the better. We will have more hands to hire cheap. That should please you, Marquena."

"You always look well on newfangled contraptions," Marquena sniffed. "For me, I will stick to the old and tried."

"Pull more toward the sea!" the Padre cried. "One more tug and we shall have the stones right."

74

Juan sat in the shade making shoes. He was too old to do heavy work; besides, the years of making shoes had quickened his fingers so that he could put together three pairs in the time it took others to make one pair. They were better made, too. He was the teacher of young fingers now, and he had to be sharp-eyed to see that no knots were hidden that would make lumps for señoritas to complain about when they walked. These young ones were not so painstaking as the old. They were impatient to be finished. Only his Loreta was careful, painstaking. But she was O-nes-e-mo. She was part of his body, and knew that good work was lasting work.

The stones were set! A cry of joy went up from the sweating Indians, and there was a breathless time while horses were harnessed and corn spread on the rocks for grinding.

"It won't work. You see? How can horses do the work of Indians?" Marquena shouted. "They work too fast."

"Give it a chance, will you?" Boronda snapped. "It has worked well in other places."

Padre Payeras went to fetch Fra Sarria, the *presidente* of the Missions, who was here now.

"Start," he called.

Juan's joints cracked and hurt a little as he pulled himself to his feet the better to see the horses as they went around and around, driven by one Indian. There was a terrific sound of grinding like many women at metates, when the great stones moved one over the other. All eyes watched, doubtful of such fast wholesale crushing of corn.

"Stop! We shall see how it looks," Payeras called after a while. "Perhaps it is fine enough." He asked for a handful.

Juan saw the meal. There in the Padre's hand it gleamed, fine and beautiful! Better it was in this short time, than five times as long in metates. These great stones with horses had worked a miracle. Happiness shone in the faces of both Padres.

"We must bless the stones," Sarria said. "The stones that will save the backs and arms of countless Indians in their weary work of grinding. We of San Carlos de Borromeo have much

75

to be thankful for. Herds of sheep for wool, great rains that put tallow on our cattle and grow food in the soil we have tilled—" his voice faltered. "And now God has sent us these great stones so that no Indian will need to grind corn again!" The Padres turned and walked toward the church for robes and holy water to make the blessing.

Juan ran after them. He was breathing hard as if his heart would burst when he finally was able to touch Padre Payeras on the sleeve.

"The chant—" he managed. "Could Juan play a chant on the violin, for Padre Amores in heaven? He will be looking down at us this day in happiness. Juan does not forget Padre Amores."

"Bless you," Payeras said, and his mouth was working in sadness. "Get the fiddle and tune it."

Juan thought the blessings and prayers would never be over. His fingers ached to let Padre Amores hear the chant.

He could not keep his head bent in prayer so long. He looked around the church and saw Don George Allen kneeling behind the beautiful Petra. Just then the golden-haired Englishman touched the shawl with tender fingers, and Juan knew others found it hard to keep the mind on prayers.

Finally the Padre looked up and smiled. He nodded to Juan that it was time to play.

Never had O-nes-e-mo fingers, calloused from sewing shoes, brought forth such music! It was not a chant at all, but a song from the soul of a thankful Indian to the Padre who had given him the notes and the box to make them.

For a time after Juan put down the fiddle there was no sound except a meadow lark's warble. Then Payeras intoned a beautiful Amen and smiled through misty eyes at the player.

"We will have a fiesta," Sarria cried as the people moved away from the stones. "Build up the fires for a barbecue. Make the sauce. A race, after everyone has eaten his fill! The Mission Indians must never forget the day of the great stones!"

The Borondas and the Marquenas and the Romeros and other Spanish settlers stayed for the fiesta.

Juan saw Don Allen move near to Señorita Boronda. She smiled at him as he sat eating on the other side of the duenna. Once there was an exchange of young eyes behind the old lady's back when she leaned over to help herself to another tidbit of meat.

After everyone ate and drank wine, they all added their voices to songs and cheers for the winners of games and races. They asked Juan to play some lively tunes on the fiddle, but he shook his head. Padre Amores' fiddle had sung its song for the day. There were no more tunes inside the box. Finally the settlers hunted out their horses.

"The stones are fine, and always a fiesta is good," Juan heard Marquena say to Boronda. "But something will be wrong with the newfangled things before long, and we'll hear the sound of many metates at the Mission again. I'll stick to the old." And they rode away.

Captain Alverez had been too much in a rage to sing songs, and now Juan saw him send angry looks after the departing Spaniards.

"Did you see the gold-haired Allen making fool's eyes at Petra Boronda?" he cried, as Vincente helped him off with his best boots. "Why didn't her brother or the great flabby duenna stop such a disgusting business?"

"Your eyes must be bad, Captain. Do specks float before them? The liver sometimes plays tricks on the sight." Vincente didn't look up from dusting the boots, and Juan saw a smile come to the face of the Corporal.

"Eyes, nothing! Liver, nothing! It is good we're to be mustered out soon, or I would take it out of your hide for saying such things to me, an officer!" Alverez cried. "I know what I see. Didn't Petra go into the church to lay flowers before the feet of 'Our Lady' before she left?" He paused to look a minute at the toe of his coarse sock. "I had an errand in the church,

77

and when I passed the statue, that Allen was holding Petra's hand, and they were looking into each other's eyes and forgetting all about 'Our Lady.' That is wicked. They will surely be punished!"

For a bit, Juan was afraid for those two young ones who had forgotten the statue, and then he saw Padre Payeras smile and pause beside the soldiers.

"See that you often have errands into the church, Captain, after you leave the Mission San Carlos," the Padre said softly, "and may you learn to forget jealousy, and see holy beauty in the eyes of lovers."

"And may I see fewer schoolmasters making love," Alverez mumbled and turned away.

Loreta came up to Juan as he settled to do more sewing before it was time for evening prayers. She sat beside him under the tule shelter and worked her wool.

Juan looked at her with new eyes. Here was an Indian woman who would have her corn ground for her by horses, a woman who had eaten the acorn meal of her fathers once, and that one time she had thrown it from her mouth. She was a different Indian, who had always had Christian clothes on her body. He sighed. So many changes during the life of one man! There were many settlers in the Carmelo now where there had only been three or four Indians. The Indian rancherias were taken over by outsiders, and the gentile Indians pushed back into the hills. But the Mission Indians were protected by the Padres and San Carlos. They were safe from the crowding Spaniards, and the Mexicans, and had plenty of food to eat.

A soldier messenger rode into the compound. He seemed excited when he asked that his letter be given to Sarria.

While the letter was read, the man walked over to those who were working under the shelter.

"Spanish no longer own this country," he told Juan. "A boat from Mexico has just come in, with word that a new empire of Mexico is formed. That is why Sola sends for the Padre to come to Monterey and give the oath of allegiance to the

78

new Emperor." He came nearer and dropped his voice. "From all I hear, the change may go bad with you Indians. The Padres are afraid, because already there has been talk at the balls and wine suppers, to take away Padres from Mission rancherias."

He flicked a bit of dust from his boots with a handkerchief. "But there is no need for worry now. If the paper is signed at the governor's meeting, a half-Indian, Augustine Iturbide, is to be crowned Emperor with great feasting."

Padre Sarria came out in his good brown habit without patches, and, with a set face, mounted the swiftest horse of the Mission. The soldier had to climb into stirrups and gallop fast to catch up with him.

Juan watched the two horses as they traveled through fields of flowers, belly high. He sighed. Only an hour ago he had thought how beautiful and plentiful the Carmelo was looking. Spring rains had been good, cattle fat, and few troubles. Now this new man called an emperor was to be crowned, and only the good God knew what would happen.

But nothing happened at all. Padre Sarria came back the next day a little sad in the face, quickly changed from his best habit, and made the rounds of inspection. He looked at Juan's shoes, smiled and said they were finer than any before and should bring a good price. He was kind-eyed as he asked Loreta how she was making out with her catechism.

Under the tule shelter during midday meal, Juan heard Padre Sarria talk to Payeras. "It will seem queer to mention His Majesty, the Emperor of New Spain, when we talk now, Payeras." He sighed. "But then, friars and missionaries must be used to almost anything." Juan watched him put more sauce on his tortillas. "I suspect the fight over this new territory with its rich lands and fine climate will be going on when our bodies are moldering."

"Will the new Emperor take away money that is for the Mission?" Payeras asked. "The Pious Fund which seems to bother so many Spanish and Mexican heads right now?"

79

"That is just what we don't know." Sarria didn't look up from his food. "They threatened to close any Mission and turn it into a pueblo after it has been established ten years. That law has been in effect quite a while now—"

"San Carlos was established more than ten years ago," Payeras sighed and looked out over the hills.

"It is only a dream, this idea that the Indians can run themselves without hands to guide them," Sarria said. "The Mexicans and Spaniards will take their land, and steal their cattle if they are left defenseless."

"Aye," Payeras looked thoughtful. "And now that so many English traders are in Monterey, there is more trouble. Hartnell is honest and anxious for schools, though he drives a good bargain with me for hides and tallow from the Mission, and Don Allen is kind, but the old Spaniards do not like the white men coming in."

"The evil Spaniards and Mexicans will take out their anger, Payeras. The strong will overpower the weak. That has always been done since time began. We must fight for our Indians," Sarria said, and nodded his head to make the thankfulness for the food he had eaten.

Chapter IX

THE GOLD NUGGET OF GUADALUPE: 1824

ONE day when Pablo went over the hill with the Padre and a load of cabbages from the Mission garden, he came home with news. At night, after Indians were locked up in the sleeping place, he told Juan that the excitement in Monterey over the marriage of Teresa de la Guerra and Don Hartnell was nothing to the excitement over the marriage of Señorita Petra Boronda to Don Jorge Allen! Why, the whole town of Monterey was up at the adobe on the hill back of the governor's church! Everybody was drinking Boronda wine, and singing songs to the future of the youngest Boronda daughter. "Señorita Petra is to be married next week with big fiesta," Pablo finished breathlessly.

"Did you see Captain Alverez there?" Juan asked, thinking of the ugly talk he had heard Alverez say about Don Allen and the beautiful Petra.

"No, he has gone off on a boat, now that he is out of the army. But everybody around the market place talked about how Alverez stopped Petra Boronda's brother José Canute on the street, and said that he would kill himself for love of Petra."

"What did Don Canute Boronda say?" Juan asked. He crossed himself in the dark, and hoped the Saints could see.

"Oh, he only laughed and told Alverez to have a drink of wine, that he too had thought of killing himself for love once, but the passion soon wore off when another pair of black eyes came around the corner in search of a handsome man."

"It is good that Alverez went away," Juan mumbled.

"Don José Eusebio Boronda, the Señorita's other brother,

81

is in Monterey for the wedding, and rides around in the beautiful saddle you made for him. But you would never know that saddle now, O-nes-e-mo, for Agapito, the silversmith in Monterey, has trimmed it all up with silver. Eusebio Boronda's feet go now into fancy silver stirrups."

"Padre Amores helped Juan to make that saddle," Juan said. "I would like to see it, Pablo."

"You have a good chance to see it, Old One. On the way home, Padre Sarria went to the Boronda adobe to see Don Boronda about Indians to come and work for the wedding fiesta. Señorita Petra asked for Juan to come, and Padre Sarria said Pablo was a good worker too, and didn't just sit in the sun waiting to be told what to do next—so we will *both* go to the fiesta."

"And I will take my fiddle," Juan said.

"Spaniards don't want Indian fiddles, they want Indian backs and Indian hands for hard work." Pablo sniffed. "They will have Mexicans for playing music."

"Padre Amores' fiddle goes to the wedding," Juan said, and turned a back on Pablo and his talk. He wanted to be quiet now, and think of the fiesta for Señorita Petra Boronda. There would be meat and lots of it, and berry *empanada*, and sweet things, and wine that would warm the bowels of an old Indian like a campfire warmed his bones on the outside. The Saints were kind to Juan O-nes-e-mo.

The days of waiting were long. Juan worked hard at his shoes and as he stitched the soles to the tops, and fastened light wooden heels on them, he thought of the chant he would play for Señorita Petra Boronda's wedding. One night he waited until all were asleep in the sleeping place, and making so much snoring that they wouldn't hear, and then he took the fiddle from its velvet bag and played softly, just to try out a few chants and see which sounded most like the beautiful Señorita Petra.

Long before dawn on the day of the wedding, Juan, Pablo, and three Indian women walked along the road toward Mon-

terey. Padre Sarria, in his best habit and sandals, rode behind
them on a white horse. The fog was heavy and made a soft
gray blanket over the country as they neared Monterey, and
the light came on. Juan hoped that the sun would come
through and bring brightness to the little señorita who had
helped to buy the great grinding stones for Indians at San
Carlos de Borromeo.

When it was really light, the Padre discovered the fiddle in
its bag under Juan's arm. "Why did you bring it, Juan?" he
asked, sighing. "This day is for work."

"Padre Amores' fiddle keeps Juan company as he walks, and
will bring happiness if it comes to the wedding of Señorita
Boronda. Padre Amores will be looking down from heaven and
be happy too."

"Very well, but remember, you are going to Don Boronda's
to work, and the fiddle is to be put away." The Padre shook a
head and a finger at Juan.

When they arrived at the long adobe where Don Boronda
lived, fires were already built in the pit on the hillside. Umesia,
a very young Indian girl, was cooking at the oven in back of
the house. Padre Sarria turned Juan, Pablo, and the Indian
women over to Don Boronda's man, and rode away down the
hill to the governor's church. Juan hid his fiddle behind the
great pile of wood when Umesia and the other Boronda Indians were not looking, and then went to help put up long
tables under an oak tree.

Such excitement! Such a singing and a shouting as the Borondas made. The Señoritas Maria Guadalupe and Maria
Teresa and Maria Josefa Boronda were rushing about with
flowers and dresses over their arms, and Indian waiting women
had no time for even a glance at Juan and Pablo, who worked
at the pit where steers were turned by hand on a bar of iron so
they would be roasted to a good brown for the fiesta. The Mission Indian women chopped peppers and tomatoes and onions
for the meat sauce.

The sun felt good on Juan's back, and the fire in the pit

83

warmed his front. It was not bad work, this turning the meat, except that it made an old Indian hungry when he looked at the brown juiciness of it.

The Saints saved Juan just in time from the temptation to cut off a bit when no one was looking, for Guadalupe and Teresa came up the hill. Their arms were loaded with green branches of the bay tree, and blue lupine flowers, and golden yellow poppies. As they worked to decorate the ox cart, and to make a canopy over the top, so that their sister would ride to the church under flowers, they were so beautiful to look at that Juan forgot for a time the brown, roasting meat.

First, the señoritas fastened the poles at four corners with rawhide thongs, then they crossed poles over the top and fastened them to the corner poles. Branches of bright green bay, and dark pine from the hills, were worked into the crossed poles on top, and then Guadalupe tucked flowers all through the green so that they looked like the painted jewels in a saint's crown.

"In front, beside the Indian who drives the oxen, we will have Anzo, the Mexican, with his guitar to play all the way to church, so that Petra will have music," Teresa said, and then turned to tell the Indian boy to rub olive oil on the coats of the oxen so that they would shine in the sun as they pulled Petra to her wedding.

After a while Juan saw a cart come creaking up the hill. The driver stopped the oxen, and went in search of Don Boronda.

Pablo leaned near as he turned his side of the crank with meat on it. "That is wine, and comes a long way from another Boronda rancho. These Borondas have land everywhere."

The sun came out very bright from behind the light clouds of fog, and soon Don Jorge Allen rode up, dressed all fine in black. He jumped off his horse and ran to pound on the door.

"Less noise, you women," he called. "I want to see my wife-to-be."

Juan saw the door open. Guadalupe stuck her head out. "You can't see Petra," she laughed. "You know it's bad luck

84

for the man to look on a girl in her bridal dress before he sees her in the church. You'll have to wait." And she made a little face and closed the door.

Don Allen glanced around, and caught Juan and Pablo and other Indians looking at him, and his face turned red. "Here," he called, "open that door. I have a present."

The door was opened again, this time by Teresa.

Don Allen held out something that gleamed yellow in the sun. "Put these earrings on my beloved Petra and kiss her for me," Don Allen cried. "Agapito, the silversmith, said they would bring luck to her." Then he ran to his horse and galloped off down the hill toward the church.

Juan was away at the back of the house after more wood when Señorita Petra got into the ox cart to go to the church, but he heard the cheering and singing, and laughing, so he knew it was time for Padre Amores' fiddle to sing. Hadn't the Saints sent Juan O-nes-e-mo to the woodpile where the fiddle was hidden, at just the right time for the chant?

Quick as a wood rat, he dropped the sticks and darted for the fiddle. Someone called good luck to the bride, as Juan drew the fiddle from the bag and picked at strings a minute to hear the tone. Then he squatted behind the pile of wood, and played sweetly the *Te Deum* that was Amores' favorite. The good Padre would understand about how an Indian had no better place to play for the beautiful bride because Indians must work. The Saints would understand that good thoughts for the little señorita were going out into the air with each note from Indian fingers.

The songs and laughter died away, and Juan could hear the squeaks from the ox cart wheels as they went down the hill toward the governor's church. He finished his music and then carefully hid the fiddle again.

"That was beautiful," came from behind him, and he looked up into the lovely eyes of Señorita Guadalupe Boronda. "I was the only one who heard it,—you see I came back to get my handkerchief. God sometimes sends a señorita back for a hand-

85

kerchief and she finds a song—or a *husband*—if there is no duenna to bother." The señorita smiled and came toward him in her beautiful blue dress; then, quickly, she pressed a gold nugget into his hand and ran around the house.

The meat was done to a turn, and the table set out and ready when the wedding party came back for the fiesta. The little Señorita Petra with eyes that shone bright as the Christmas star, was now Doña Allen. She came home in the flower-trimmed cart, with Don Allen by her side; Anza, the Mexican, sat beside the driver and strummed softly on his guitar. Father Sarria rode up on his horse, and Don Boronda and the other señoritas came in another ox cart. After that were many horses and ox carts, more than Juan had fingers or toes! Everybody was laughing.

"And Petra nearly forgot to take the pins out of the hem of her wedding dress," Señorita Josefa cried. "She would be running around yet, showing her insteps like a señorita, if it hadn't been for me."

The young Petra looked into the eyes of her husband and smiled, and red colored her cheeks.

Pain went through Juan's heart, and he felt sorry about the red that came into the beautiful Petra's face. When she had gone away he leaned close to Pablo. "Juan is an old man and doesn't see so well, Pablo. Has the Doña Petra gone wrong in the feet, that she should not show them, and must turn red in the face because they are not covered?"

Pablo only put back his head and laughed. "You are used to Padres and Indians and don't know the ways of the Spanish señoras in Monterey," he whispered. "Señoritas show the feet and a bit of ankle to make men look and get prickles in their bellies. Prickles in a man's belly makes him sing serenades under windows at night, Juan. But after the wedding it is wicked for Doñas to show the ankles and bring fast heart beats to other men besides their husbands."

Juan thought about these strange ways of women; he couldn't remember that bare legs of Indian women made

86

prickles in his belly, before Padres made women wear long cotton dresses.

Great pitchers of wine passed along the tables and there was laughing, and then the meat was carved. Doña Petra was everywhere, like a butterfly, in her white flowing dress. She was seeing that people had meat and salza and wine and tortillas. Sometimes she stopped to show the new gold ring on her finger.

Juan had to turn more meat before the afternoon was out, and it was hard work, because his belly was filled with meat and wine and the hot fire made him sleepy. Pablo hardly pulled on his turn of the rod at all. But it would hurt the beautiful Petra if there was not enough meat.

Long after sundown, the second lot of meat was finished. Juan and Pablo went behind the house to get water for their dry throats. Umesia came with wine to drink instead of water, and they both drank deeply, for working near a fire made much sweat come. Soon Juan couldn't see Pablo at all! His legs were like wet stems of tule, and bent so that he could not stand. There was nothing to do but sit down near the woodpile.

It was quite dark when noises wakened Juan.

"But don't scold them, Padre Sarria, for they have worked hard near the fire since early sunrise, and Guadalupe says Juan played a beautiful *Te Deum* on his fiddle as I was riding down to the church. Surely the 'Mother of Sorrows' will forgive a drink or two of wine, to an Indian who plays a *Te Deum* for a bride."

Juan opened one eye, and saw the Doña Petra standing near him, looking like an angel; by her side was Padre Sarria, not like an angel at all, for there was a deep frown on his face, and his mouth was stern. Juan closed the eye again, and didn't move.

"You may be right, Doña Petra, but it was bad of them to drink too much, and I'm afraid I won't be able to trust them again to go out and work."

There was a gay little laugh. "But look at some of the

87

guests! They have had too much wine, but you know, Padre, we will all go on seeing the good in them, and trusting them too, so why blame Indians for doing the same thing?"

"Yes, I suppose you are right, child." The Padre stooped down and shook Juan. Pablo was already sitting up and rubbing his eyes, when Juan sat up.

"Come, where is your fiddle, Juan? It is time we went over the hill to Carmelo. You have made fiesta and taken too much wine, which is bad."

Juan felt for the little gold nugget that Señorita Guadalupe had given him. It was safe in a cloth inside the belt of his pantaloons. He scrambled to his feet and went a bit dizzily to where the fiddle was hidden. He was ashamed that the Doña Petra Allen should find him asleep from wine at her wedding, so he waited on the other side of the house, for Pablo and Padre Sarria and the Indian women.

As Juan sat waiting beside the road, with the fiddle between his legs, Vincente the soldier passed with a beautiful dark woman holding to his arm. Pablo had said that Vincente was just married and had a rancho to the north of Monterey.

"How is Loreta, Juan?" Vincente called. "I wish her well."

"Juan misses the good Corporal Vincente, now. It is not the same at the Mission on the Carmelo without him." Juan called back. "I hope the Saints will send him many sons."

"Not too many—at once," Vincente laughed, and went around the turn of the road.

Juan felt at the nugget nestling near his belly. If the Saints would forgive him for drinking too much wine at Doña Petra's wedding, why, he would give the nugget to the first son of Vincente, who had been so kind to sick little Loreta so long ago.

Padre Sarria came, and Juan followed him along the dusty road. Away from the singing and click of Mexican music, back to shoes and work at the Mission. He hugged the fiddle close, and wished he could be a Mexican with only music to play, instead of just making shoes for señoritas. Anyway, these Mex-

88

icans who caused Spaniards so much trouble had not spoiled the happiness at Señorita Petra's wedding. The Saints and Angels had seen to that. Maybe Padre Amores' fiddle had helped to keep the Mexicans good.

As he trotted along in the dust, Juan felt often of the little nugget. Always it was warm and safe. He hoped that Vincente would not have sons too soon, for it would be nice to look at the bit of gold once in a while.

Maybe the Saints would forget the promise of an Indian, and he could keep the nugget! Saints were very busy now, listening to prayers of Mexicans and Spanish, and these new white English and Americanos. An Indian could easily be forgotten among so many strangers at San Carlos de Borromeo.

Chapter X

FIDDLE STRINGS: 1824. 1825

JUAN wondered why he had ever bothered his head about the Emperor of New Spain. Nothing much changed, except that his joints were not so stiff, and his friend Pablo had been sent to Monterey to work for Señor Soberanes. Many pairs of shoes had been made and sold. The hillside turned yellow, then green again. Loreta was soon to take her first vows as an Indian Sister of San Carlos de Borromeo.

Governor Sola had come to say goodbye before he sailed away and left Monterey to the Mexicans. The governor's eyes were full of anger and he told the Padres that this Mexican Augustine Iturbide would take all Mission land and leave Indians without a single Padre to protect them.

Father Payeras was excited, but Padre Sarria had only smiled and said that there wasn't much difference in them, when rich land was to be had and only Indians without firearms living on it.

Now, after what Padres called a year, but Juan knew to be the time that it took a fawn to grow big enough to make good meat, Iturbide, the Emperor of New Spain, was gone, and a new flag was flying over the Custom House in Monterey. This flag was different. It represented something called a republic, with no one to be called majesty or king. It was the flag of the Republic of Mexico.

Fray Sarria had been threatened with arrest because he would not leave the Indians as these Mexicans demanded. There had been fear in the eyes of Padre Payeras, but Fray Sarria had not been afraid and he was still there, and so were the Indians.

There were lots of white people now, when Juan drove into Monterey behind oxen that pulled loads of green vegetables and pears from the Mission gardens to sell to those in Monterey who would rather sit in the shade than plant their land with growing things. Now that he was old, Juan could ride behind the oxen and do his share, so that younger men could be released for work. He was happy, because there was always the chance of seeing Pablo. Pablo was right in the thick of things and told news.

Pablo told about the fandango houses where games with little cards of paper sometimes made whole rancherias change hands twice in the night! And Indians changed hands, too. An Indian did not always know whom he was working for when he lifted from his knees after morning prayer! The Spaniards and Mexicans were always fighting; hardly a night when some man did not die with his boots on, and no extreme unction from the priest.

Pablo came to the plaza on an errand one morning and lost no time in telling Juan of the agitation of the Spaniards. He spoke low, Room-se-en language, which the Spanish settlers did not bother to try to understand, and he kept his eye out for Padre Payeras who was selling shoes in the trader's store.

"The people are in a rage," he said and stooped close to the squatting Juan and his vegetables. "The new Mexican governor, Don José Mario Echineada, will not come to live in Monterey as Sola did. He likes better the climate at San Diego." Pablo shrugged his shoulders and put his hands in a know-nothing gesture. "Some say it is the eyes of a beautiful señorita keeps him in San Diego. He will send orders from there. The people are very bitter, because there will not be so much business or so many fiestas in Monterey without the governor here. Perhaps all the Boston ships will stop coming here to trade."

"No, no, Pablo," came from behind. "Neither Spaniards nor Americanos will stop coming to Monterey because of the lack of a governor. They do not come to smile on a governor's face.

91

They come for cattle, hides, and tallow, and fur, too." Padre Payeras grinned at the Indians. "You had better be off to your work before you are punished, my son." He tapped Pablo kindly on the shoulder. "We miss you at Carmelo. Don't forget to come over the hill and sing at the Mass when you can. San Carlos will be pleased to hear your voice."

The parish priest from the governor's church in Monterey stopped to talk. He was very happy. John Cooper, the Englishman, and master of the trading ship Rover, had at last decided to desert the sea and settle on his land. And had not only been baptized into-the faith and taken the name Juan Bautista Cooper, but soon he was to marry Señorita Incarnacion Vallejo! The banns had already been read once. Juan Bautista Cooper had done a lot for California. He was honest in his dealings and had brought the first mulley cow from Japan. He even bought his land down the coast instead of settling on it. Señorita Vallejo was only thirteen, but Spanish women knew how to hold men that were older, especially when they had power enough to bring an Englishman into the Catholic faith!

A soldier near by laughed and spoke loud to another soldier so that Juan and the priests could not help hearing.

"David Spence is to be baptized in Santa Cruz. George Allen was baptized Jorje Tomas, and lately married Petra Boronda. Can it be that Spanish and Mexican land grants are making these Englishmen so eager to become Catholics?" Then they laughed some more. Padre Payeras told Juan to pick up the unsold vegetables and they would go back over the hill.

"You must not listen to anything evil said about Juan Bautista Cooper," Payeras told Juan. "He has helped Monterey, and so has Hartnell, the trader. God knows no color. A white Englishman is as good as a Spaniard or a Mexican if there is truth and honesty shining from behind his eyes. Señor Hartnell is trying to arrange a new school so people will not be fooled by lack of learning."

"Cooper is good to Indians," Juan said. "Pablo says he feeds them well, and everyone is asked to eat when he gathers up his cattle and kills them."

"Soldiers' tongues would be improved by a knot of rawhide to bind them. I am thankful that we no longer have soldiers at Carmelo." Padre Payeras opened his prayer book to read, as the oxen walked along the winding yellow road.

Juan watched the bony hind ends of the oxen, and wondered about Corporal Vincente. He felt with his free hand for the little nugget. Could the Saints see gold next to an Indian's belly? If they could, the nugget would surely remind them of the promise he had made about the first son of Vincente, and perhaps they would hurry and send the boy, so that he could have the nugget. It would be safer after this to hide the nugget in the fiddle bag, and then perhaps the Saints wouldn't bother looking there.

Loreta was a quiet girl. She worked at her socks faithfully, and was quicker than most at turning a heel and finishing off a toe. She had learned her catechism, and now, full-bosomed and blooming, she was ready to take her vows as a working sister.

On that beautiful spring morning, she was busy with the rest decorating the church with sprays of blossom and ferns. Juan thought his heart would burst with happiness when he looked at her. Loreta had never even tried to run away from work or prayers. Rarely did she even raise her voice in irritation when the little children turned her drying yarn into a tangled mass. Loreta just spent patient hours putting it straight again.

Juan wondered if that matter scratched into her arm as a little child had taken away anger and hatred, because Padre Amores' fiddle had brought about the scratch. Maybe the good San Carlos loved her more than most folks and made temptations few. Perhaps Polonia looked down from Heaven and sent loving thoughts to the child.

Loreta in her new white dress came over and sat down beside her father. She watched him sew shoes for a few minutes,

93

then put her hand on his arm. "I will be different after to-day," she said quietly. "Will you ask the Padre if you can play the beautiful fiddle after I have taken the vows? I know the Holy Mother, the Lady of Sorrows, will have her heart lightened, and I want it to be so when Loreta takes her vows."

Juan's own heart was squeezed of blood for a bit. He couldn't speak. The fiddle meant something to Loreta even if she was an Indian woman who would never play music. She was O-nes-e-mo even if she was without temptations! She had the soul of his son, even if she didn't have the body of a boy, for she knew the beauty of notes from the fiddle.

"I will ask," he said. "Padre Amores gave that fiddle to me. He played it the night Polonia went away and you came."

Loreta had happiness in her eyes as she got up to join the other sisters.

When Padre Payeras came by on his way to look after the soap vats, Juan stopped him. "Loreta asked me if I would play a chant for the Lady of Sorrows, after her vows are taken. A chant on Padre Amores' fiddle," he said humbly, and watched the Padre's face.

"Of course, Juan. But you haven't played for a long time. Poor Juan! There has been little time for music, except what God puts into our souls."

"My hands are stiff, stiff as the reeds in the river bottom, too old to bend," Juan said. "But Padre Amores will under-stand the notes of an old Indian even if Our Lady of Sorrows thinks it is bad."

Padre Payeras whirled around and put his two hands on Juan's shoulders. "You needn't apologize for fingers stiffened in service," he said hotly. "Your sweat and your back helped to build a church to the glory of God, which is more than can be said of those who criticize the Indians. God forgive them, for they know not what they do!" Then he smiled into Juan's eyes with a twinkle like the one that had so often shone from Padre Amores' eyes. "Play, Juan, with no fear for the saints who hear. They know things that do not come through words."

He started toward the vats and then stopped. "Put by the shoemaking for a bit, and warm up your fiddle against the time to play. Surely we can spare you a few minutes from work for that."

Juan was blinded by the sudden darkness of the adobe room where Indian men slept. He had to grope along the wall for the nail where the red velvet fiddle bag hung. Only Juan knew that it had once been velvet, for now the pile had all worn off and it was merely cotton to the touch.

He sat on his tule mat, and drew the violin out. His eyes grew used to the dim light, and Juan found that there were only three strings. For a moment he dropped the fiddle to his lap in disgust. The day when Loreta was to be a sister and wanted him to play, and only three strings!

Juan was on his way to ask Fray Sarria for strings, and then the black thought came to him that if they knew there were but three strings, the Padres would not let him play at all. He knew full well that no money had been spent for such frivolous things as violin strings, when even necessities were lacking, and the new governor was always crying for money to pay soldiers.

Juan tuned the three strings, and put the shining fiddle under his chin. His fingers were stiff. Padre Amores had never told him one chant that could be played with three strings! Flies crawled on him and were a nuisance. He tried a chant. It would not work. The bell for services rang out clear in the morning air.

As Juan stood waiting for the Spaniards and Mexicans to go into church first, Corporal Vincente and his wife passed, and both smiled. When the fine eyes of Señora Vincente looked into Juan's a feeling hot as a campfire went through his old bones. The wife of Vincente had now the eyes of the Blessed Virgin, and that meant she was to drop a baby before too many moons had gone by. The saints had remembered the promise of an Indian about the gold nugget and were sending Vincente a son to claim the gold!

Then Juan remembered the laugh of Vincente when Juan

95

had wished sons for him. Perhaps the baby had already been started by the Saints then, even before the promise had been made. Did the promise hold then? Juan wondered if he should ask the Padre about such promises to babies, or if it was better for an old Indian to look often at the nugget, and wait to see what God was sending to Vincente.

He followed the others into the church, and dropped to his knees on the rough tiled floor. Loreta, up by the altar, stood straight and beautiful and bright-eyed as she answered the questions. The church was crowded, for many Spaniards had come to see the ceremony. Juan was jammed in near the door, and the long service was hard on his knees, until he looked at Loreta. She was his! Padre Amores had said she would be a comfort to him in his old age. Right now she made him forget his bony knees on that hard floor.

Young voices sang. The Padre intoned. Juan kept his eyes on Padre Payeras to see when to play. At last he could be off his poor stiff knees. Then there was a deep silence, a silence that was waiting for Juan O-nes-e-mo's chant.

He took a breath, thought hard that Amores would understand broken strings, and then through the church a clear note called; a note as high as Juan's fingers could make the violin talk! Highness meant saints. This was the best he could do. A high note on the next string, then a third high note. Like bird calls they went to the ears of Padres, Spaniards, Mexicans, and Englishmen. Juan played every combination of those three high notes that would come from the fiddle. When he finished, people were sobbing, and Payeras intoned the Amen.

Loreta was a sister of San Carlos de Borromeo.

Two days later a horseman rode into the Mission. "The soldiers are revolting in Monterey! Echineada cannot control them! They want their wages."

Padre Payeras came over to the excited vaquero. "Who sent you to tell us this?" he asked.

The cow hand laughed and Juan saw that his swarthy skin was turning red from embarrassment.

96

"Señor Hartnell sent me, Reverend Father," he said quietly, and put his hand in the pocket of his bright leather vest. "And not to tell you that the soldiers were revolting, but to give you this with his compliments, for the Indian who brings tears to the eyes of an Englishman." He handed a small package to Payeras.

In it were half a dozen violin strings.

Chapter XI

SOME LAND FOR EVERY INDIAN: 1828. 1829

JUAN was sewing shoes one day when the sun was hot. Padres and Indians were busy at the regular slaughter. A soldier who had been loitering around the compound strolled over to talk.

"Well, Old Man, you have slaved for the Padres most of your life, haven't you?" he said quietly. "Do you get any money for this?" He pointed to the shoe.

Juan met his black eyes. "The money from these goes to feed soldiers."

"That's what they tell you, these clever Padres." He leaned nearer. "They tell you that to keep you slaving. They take the profits. Many Padres are rich, very rich, from the money they get on work of Indians." He moved his fingers together, to indicate that money passed between thumb and finger.

"But Padre Payeras and Padre Sarria both wear habits that are patched, and they have wine only once a day, because the rest is traded to feed Indians and keep the rancheria San Carlos de Borromeo from being sold for taxes."

"Phew! That is all a pose. They hide the money so you won't know. Sarria is going away from here anyway, patched habit or not. He is going to the Mission Soledad in the Valley of Howling Winds. Even the Mission there is falling apart, because the Padre took the money."

"No. Not our Padres taking money." Juan shook his head.

"They go away from here after a while, don't they? They go to Spain or Mexico. Well, they take it with them, fool!" He stooped lower. "They are keeping the governor and his soldiers from helping the Indians, Old One. What José Maria

Echineada wants to do is to give every Indian some land of his own, take him away from the hard work at the Missions, and let him work for himself. The governor wants to give you cattle, and seeds to plant, and implements to work with. Then you will be able to put your heads as high as Spaniards, and go to fiestas like they do. All your life will not be slaving with sore fingers from sewing to put money into the Padres' hands."

"Juan is an old man, too old now. There is food, good tortillas, and meat, and music, at the Mission *rancheria*. The Padres give us as much as they can—" he looked up at the soldier's eyes "—after taxes for the soldiers are paid."

With a quick impatient flip of his whip that seemed accidentally to hit Juan's shriveled legs, the soldier moved away, to talk to younger Indians piling fire under the soap vats. Juan noticed that the man was careful to pick places where there was no Padre to listen to his words.

"Indians are not doing this hard work today at other Mission *rancherias*. They have taken what they can get from the Mission and gone to land on the hills. They have revolted from such slavery." Juan heard the soldier tell this to the Indians as they wiped sweat from their faces. "You are fools to sweat like this, when the governor himself wants to help you to freedom."

After a bit he talked more quietly, because the men had drawn closer to listen, and Juan heard only a soft "And I will use my power with the governor to see you get good land from the Padres for yourselves. Horses, too, and cattle of your own. The Spaniards and Mexicans are getting it—why not you?"

Padre Payeras was coming up the hill from the orchard, where plowing was going on. The soldier moved away.

"Don't be locked up this night or ever again," he advised, in a low voice. "They have no right to lock the doors."

Juan wondered. After all, the soldier was right! Mission lands had belonged to Indians long before Padre Serra had come to sing beautiful chants under an oak. Indians had

99

hunted, fished. Everything was theirs then, with no taxes, no governors, and no flags to bother with. Now the Spaniards hunted the deer, which were getting scarce; and fishes were no longer so plentiful that an Indian had only to make them sleepy by throwing the leaves and roots of wild cucumber into a pool, and then dip them out with his hands.

Even gentile Indians like Te-mo were suffering because of the Padres and soldiers and Spaniards and white people who had come in. They had to hunt harder because so many people were here. Te-mo said his woman could not have any more babies; too many mouths to hunt for, and it took too much of an Indian's time. Juan wished he was not so old and shriveled in arms and behind. He would join the young ones, take off the pantaloons, and go to the hills.

In the hills you just burned down the tule huts when fleas were too thick. An hour's work and you had a new hut at a different place with new things to look at. Not like the thick adobe walls of the Padres, that earthquakes cracked, and then must be patched. Only a few fleas were walled up in the patched cracks.

Padre Payeras arrived in the compound, hot and dusty. He nodded to the soldier and took a drink of water from the gourd.

"The governor has ordered that the Reverend Father Sarria proceed to the Mission Soledad," the soldier said. "From what I hear, there is trouble with the neophyte Indians there. They are revolting, and refuse to work as they should at the *rancheria*." He held out a letter. "Here is the order in writing from Don José Maria Echineada."

Juan saw Padre Payeras grow white under the sweat and dust on his face. "I will give Father Sarria the order," he said, and walked toward the church.

The bell for midday rang out on the clear air. Padre Payeras paused before he entered the church. "You will stay and eat with us, Captain?" he asked. "There is fresh corn from the field."

The soldier nodded.

Padre Payeras went into the church, the Indian men came up the hill from work in the fields, and the women left their looms and soap-making.

The soldier sat under the tule shelter with the Padres. Juan looked toward Loreta who was with the rest of the sisters, apart from the others. Her knitting was beside her. There was no time to waste, for the cold rains would be on them before long, and socks must be ready.

Padre Sarria blessed the food, thanked God and San Carlos for making strong backs and willing hearts that produced it for all to enjoy. His eyes seemed sad as he looked over the faces of the Indians before he sat down to eat.

When the meal was over, and all were taking ease and siesta, Juan went up to Sarria.

"I heard the soldier tell that you are going to Soledad. Juan would like to play a chant, from Padre Amores that you never knew, to bring good omen on the journey."

Sarria smiled. "Play tomorrow, Juan, just before I go. Blessings will be needed, my son, and you have been faithful to the Padre who gave you the fiddle."

The soldier rode off on his chestnut horse. Indians and Padres went to work. The shoes didn't go so fast that afternoon, because Juan's mind was too busy. The young Indians resented it when he found hidden knots. They didn't want to take out stitches so that shoes would be smooth for señoritas to walk in.

He heard the Padres talking together as they cut raw-hide thongs in the shade. Padre Sarria shook his head sadly.

"I feel that trouble over the Mission land is very near to us, Padre Payeras. In Monterey the other day, I heard that Californians were promised that *they* were to be officials, and now Vallejo and Alvarado say they will fight because Mexicans have sent twenty-one Mexicans to be administrators of Missions. They claim they will break up Missions so there will be nothing for the Mexicans to administer. Vallejo and Alvarado may be behind this revolt of Indians at Soledad and then Mission Land would be easy to take if our combined strength is broken."

The Angelus bell rang. Indians washed and walked into the Mission for prayer. Juan looked a long time tonight at Loreta. Her face was lighted by the candles from the altar. She was very happy. After the Amen and his bow to the cross, Juan did not glance as usual toward the face of "Our Lady," so calm in her niche. Some Satan inside him would not let him lift his eyes.

The hot meat soup was ready and felt good to Juan's insides. He was used to the queer food of the Padres now. It had been a long time since Padre Serra and Padre Crespi had given him the first taste of Spanish food, from their own hands. So many Padres had come and gone. Some died, some sailed to Spain, some to Mexico, with perhaps the gold from selling the shoes that he made. Juan sighed, rested his bones for a bit, and watched the young Indians talking and laughing in groups.

The call came to be locked up. Instantly there was a babble of voices! A quick rushing in and out of the rooms where Indians slept! Even married Indians in their tule huts were running. Padre Payeras called again. No one obeyed his commands. There were no soldiers to help!

"Come! It is time for rest!" the Father Sarria called. "There is confusion. What is wrong, my children?"

Men dashed into the long adobe room and rushed out with their things.

"Come along, Old One," a young Indian called. "If you can't run quick enough, we'll drag you," and he caught Juan by the pantaloons.

"Wait!" Juan cried. "I must get the fiddle!"

"Aye, the fiddle. Let him get it. We will have music by the fire tonight."

Swift as a bat, Juan reached up to the nail for the worn bag, and ran fast as his legs would take him, in the crowd that had knocked Padre Payeras over as he tried to force them back and shut the door.

"To the hills!" The cry rang through the compound, and blotted out the voices of the two Padres. Married Indians and their women ran, too. Children were dragged.

"Loreta!" The word came as a cry from Juan's mouth.

He was caught up and dragged. "She will be happy. A sister. They will always take care of her. They must, for she has given her vows to God," a young Indian said.

After that Juan felt better. Loreta was safe, and happy. Her face had showed that only tonight at Angelus. He ran hard, following the crowd, and clutching the precious fiddle under his arm. Finally his heart was beating too fast. He could not get his breath. His heels lagged behind the rest.

"Come on, Old One!" Two strong youths caught him up. He was carried along by the armpits faster than ever he could have run on his own legs. "We need you, Old One, to make music for us. Your music will be fine now that you will have land and cattle of your own, and freedom to hunt! You will play for us instead of the Padres."

It was all very exciting! Juan had never lived through so much excitement before. A revolt was wonderful. Now they were free to lie in the sun, and fish and hunt as they pleased.

The soldier was up on the tall hill to meet them. "Bravo," he called. "You are free!"

They made a fire in no time, these young ones with strong arms and active legs, and then called Juan to play. They cried a cheer to the soldier who had come from the governor to free them.

The fiddle was charmed, now that all the strings were there! Juan found that he could play fiesta music he had heard that night so long ago at the street dance in Monterey when Miguel was alive. He played what he had heard over and over. Indians danced. There was even wine, taken from the Padre's stock.

CATHEDRAL IN THE SUN

It was almost as wonderful as a fiesta when a boat came in from far away!

Juan played until his fingers grew tired and his arms ached from holding the fiddle to his chin. Exhausted, he dropped the instrument to his lap.

"Fiddle on, Old One!" a young Indian cried. "Why do you think we brought you?"

Juan shook his head. "No more tunes will come. My arms are tired and fingers, too."

"Fiddle on, or we will crush chilicote seeds and give you a potion that medicine men use to put old ones out of their misery," a voice cried from the rim of the fire.

Up went the fiddle, on and on the dance tunes, until Juan's head whirled. His fingers grew numb from pressing the strings —and he knew no more.

Chapter XII

A SMELL OF SAINTS: 1829. 1830. 1831

THE soldier who led the Indians to freedom was ready to leave the next day after they had all feasted and toasted him in wine and food that had been taken from the Mission.

"I must ride quickly to Monterey to ask the governor for your land, and seeds, and horses and cattle," he said. "He will claim stock from the Mission and tell the Padres what they are to do."

Juan looked at the sun on the hillsides and thought how fine it was to eat and drink and not have to sit on his haunches all day sewing shoes. Indians had plenty of meal ground by the great stones, and several whole beeves. A real fiesta every day now! He could play the fiddle as much as he wanted. Whenever a bird song entered his head he could put his fingers on the strings and try his hand at bringing the call out of the shining box. The tunes he knew were demanded a dozen times. Only two or three days, now, until the soldiers would be back, with more horses and cattle. Why hadn't someone thought of this sooner?

A scout went to see what was going on at the Mission. He was to keep watch and sound alarm if the Padres were coming after the escaped Indians. Surely now it wouldn't be so bad as the old days, for now soldiers were helping Indians to get away instead of bringing them back. The Padres would not beat even if they did come to the encampment.

"Play for us, Old One, or you shall not have the soft tasty bits of meat that only the old can chew with their shriveled gums," a youth cried, as he stretched his gleaming muscles in the sun and smoked tobacco.

Juan played. It was nice to be needed. But the third day came and went, and no soldier with horses and cattle came over the hill. Juan was tired of continually playing the violin. The Indian who had been sent to watch said that Payeras and the Indians who had remained were tilling the fields as usual, and that the sisters were helping to harvest the corn—all sisters except Loreta, who was knitting and minding babies.

"Father Sarria left on a white horse, with an Indian and a pack," he said. "I suppose he is taking gold with him that we have earned."

A sudden hurt went through Juan. Padre Sarria had gone! Gone without the promised chant. Juan O-nes-e-mo had made that promise in his heart to Amores in heaven, and the promise had been broken! All the rush and excitement and happiness of this new freedom had made him forget Amores. Juan was an old man. He would perhaps never see Sarria again to tell him how it was about forgetting. And Amores, who had made the scratch possible through this very fiddle Juan now played on the hillside? What would he think when he looked down? Too many thoughts bothered the brain of an old man. It was better to go off by himself and play the chant with the hope that Amores would hear and understand.

He slipped away under the low, thick branches of a big oak, and sat down with his back to the gnarled gray trunk. He tuned again, to make sure the notes would be true before he played to Amores.

Very softly Juan played. The leaves sheltered him with their cool green; hornets buzzed accompaniment as they hunted for insects. He made the sweetest chant he knew, the one that had brought sea-otter skins from Te-mo. He hugged the violin for singing such beauty.

"Here, Old One, out of that. We want no Padre music!" Two Indians came under the boughs. "We want lively tunes to make us forget that the meat and tortillas are low, and our stomachs gnaw." They wrenched the fiddle from Juan's hands.

"No!" he cried. "You will break it and no more songs will come."

"Then see that we have fiesta music to cheer us to freedom. No church music. You work your fiddle to make happiness, because you are too old to hunt or fish. There is no food for mouths of lazy Indians." They tossed the fiddle back into his lap.

The corn and meat were lower the next day, and a council must decide what to do about it. There was no sign of a soldier on the road from Monterey. No Indian wanted to hunt. All wanted to listen to Juan playing, and be free. Why should anyone work? There was a fight. Finally two Indian women took riatas and brought a yearling from the hills above, a yearling belonging to Señor Joaquin. All hands ate to capacity that night and the women were to grind acorns for meal the next day.

Padre Payeras walked into the *rancheria* about dusk. He looked tired and his habit was covered with dust. He was alone. A murmur of dissatisfaction ran around the fire.

"Did you come to give us our land and the cattle that belong to us?" an Indian demanded.

"No, I came to see how you poor children were faring in the wilderness," he said, and sat down to pull the weeds from his habit. "Satan came to you, in the shape of that soldier who rode into the compound and told you to run away."

"We want land of our own. We do not want to slave for the Mission and Padres," a tall, handsome Indian cried.

"Have you land of your own now that you have run away?" the Padre asked. "Have you good food?"

There was a murmur.

"Will you answer me?" the Padre asked quietly, and seemed unafraid.

"The soldier has gone to tell the governor we are free. He will bring the cattle and give us land," someone said from the darkness.

107

"And so you wait—" Payeras nodded his head, understanding. "You had better come back with me to the Mission, and help harvest the corn for winter. If you want land and cattle of your own, I will see that you get them, but waiting on a hillside for a soldier to come with food will only make you weak from hunger."

"We will take from the Spaniards cattle range and corn fields," an Indian cried excitedly.

"God and the Spaniards will punish you for taking what is not yours," Payeras told them. "The Spaniards do not understand that you are but runaway children, and will hang you by the neck when they catch you."

A murmur of uneasiness ran around the fire. Juan wondered if the women who had taken Joaquin's yearling would be hanged. Spaniards had sharp eyes. This freedom wasn't such freedom for an old man. His fingers were as tired from playing music as they had been from making shoes. Was he free if he was not allowed to play chants, or rest in the sun like the others? Somehow, now when he had the chance to play all the time, the fiddle had lost charm. His fingers were not so tender on its neck. Juan's eyes met the Padre's in the gleam of firelight.

"Loreta is sad, Juan. She wonders if her father eats corn and warm soup that is good for an old man. Twice she has asked San Carlos to look out for you."

"But she is happy. The Padres will look out for her because she gave her vows to God." Juan repeated the argument of the Indian who had induced him to run away.

"Poor Juan," Payeras said, and looked around at the rest of them. "Poor children all. Do you realize that the missionaries alone cannot do all the work to grow the food? If we perish and lose the Mission lands and cattle, the sisters will perish with us. Many hands working will produce for many mouths. It is by the work of head and the work of hands that all live." He bowed his head in grace, and took from his bundle some jerky and a tortilla or two. Juan watched the Padre eat his supper

108

by the fire of hostile Indians and wished that Pablo was here. Pablo was in the thick of things. He knew every time a governor was changed or sent away, and he knew about soldiers, even to what women they liked.

The Padre ate in silence. The Indians watched him. Juan thought of this freedom on the hillside, away from sewing shoes, and from tortillas, and hot soup, and Loreta. Right now his head buzzed wearily from too much fiesta music. His arms were tired and his fingers sore from the fiddle and its strings.

When Payeras had finished eating, he lay down by the fire to sleep. He didn't seem to fear the disgruntled murmurs or the black looks that were sent his way.

In the morning at sunup, Juan heard beautiful music. He rubbed his eyes and looked. Far above, on the hillside, he saw the solitary figure of Payeras. The Padre knelt facing the sun, his hands clasped in prayer. Music came from his mouth.

Juan pulled his fiddle from under the blanket, looked at the sleeping Indians around him, then softly he played on Padre Amores' fiddle. Freedom might be all right, but the music it brought from the fiddle didn't make him as happy as that lonely song on the hillside.

Payeras came down to the encampment. He asked them if they would bow their heads to bless the food. Some Indians did, and others were defiant, for there was no sign of food. The acorn meal had to be ground and leached before they could boil it.

The Padre opened his bundle, took out five tortillas. Carefully he broke the precious cakes into tiny bits, and gave a bit to each Indian. When he had swallowed his own share of the tortillas, Payeras folded carefully the cloth that had held the food.

"Again I ask you to come home, poor ones. If you want land, I will see that you get it, with God and San Carlos to bless you. I can do no more." He picked up the pine stick and started back toward the Mission.

There was silence in the encampment. All eyes watched

109

the Padre's brown back as he walked around the hill and out of sight.

Juan put the fiddle in its bag, crossed himself, and turned his face toward the sea and San Carlos de Borromeo. Loreta would be waiting there. She had missed him even if she was only a girl instead of his son. Sewing shoes was not so bad.

"He does these things to get fools back to work for him!" an Indian cried angrily. Juan paid no attention, but trotted on.

Soon he heard the patter of many feet on the hard ground behind him, but he didn't turn. He wanted to catch up with the missionary.

A mile or so along, Juan came upon the Padre resting under an oak. He was reading the little book with yellowed pages that he always carried with him. He looked up and smiled. Juan dropped down on the leaves beside Payeras. Other feet stopped suddenly in the distance.

"A rest is good, for the earth seems hard today," Payeras said. "Perhaps it is because my feet are sore from treading in the fields."

Juan nodded, trying to get up courage to explain about breaking his promise to play a chant when Sarria was leaving. There was silence. Words would not come to Juan.

"The earthquake cracks in the church were made larger by a small temblor night before last. We will have to patch them, Juan," the Padre went on as he put his book away. "You know? The cracks near the niche where 'Our Lady' keeps watch?"

"Wide?" Juan managed.

"Quite. I'm afraid they look badly to San Carlos, and make the saint think we do not love him so much as we did, in good years."

The Padre got up, and together they walked along the trail. Footsteps again sounded behind, but neither the priest nor Juan turned to see who was coming.

"Juan, you told me how it was with Indians and the Fra Junípero Serra and the corn," Payeras said after a while. "How you had to be taught over and over again to plant it, and how

110

you dug it up a lot of times because you did not understand that if you left it in the ground it would grow more corn for you?"

Juan nodded and they both laughed.

"It is the same with Indians. They run away and come back, and run away and come back, until they learn that God and the Padres are their friends."

Three dozen neophytes who had revolted, filed into the church when the Padre rang the bell for prayers that evening at sunset. They ate their stew in silence after the blessing was said.

Juan thought tortillas had never tasted so good. There was a great mound of them, too. Enough for everybody to have his fill.

That night Padre Payeras didn't hold up a pine flare and count Indian men. He didn't even lock up the door where they slept.

Juan glanced contentedly at the fiddle on the wall above his head, and then rolled up on his tule mat. He felt very sorry for Indians out on the hill who had no belly full of tortillas and warm stew that was made in the Mission pot. There were so many empty places in the long, low adobe room. It was better for an old man to think how beautiful Loreta had looked among the sisters at the side of the altar. She had smiled at him when she walked past in the procession.

As he went to sleep, Juan wondered just what the word "freedom" meant. He had worked even harder at playing the fiddle on the hill. Sewing shoes was easier and he could rest now and then without being yelled at, and his food threatened. Only the good God knew the real meaning of this word "freedom" that made people excited, and ready to fight or run away because of it.

The next morning, Juan was up before the bell rang for Mass. He took down the fiddle and went into the church. It was cool and quiet and smelled of flowers and incense, a smell of saints. The little flame flickered near the altar just as it had

111

before he went away. He said a prayer and then put his fiddle under his chin and played the long-promised chant. On his way out, Juan looked up and smiled at "Our Lady" so calm and serene in her niche. The earthquake crack had come very near to her but she smiled on. He felt happier now, and ready to take up the day's toil. It was better to have someone to lean on, if not a son, at least a Padre, and a daughter to smile at you as she passed by.

Chapter XIII

SHOE COMPETITION: 1832. 1833

THE Spaniards were very cross when Juan arrived in Monterey with the load of fresh fruit and vegetables.

"Why have you lazy ones not brought the vegetables for days?" a señora demanded with such anger that her big stomach shook as she talked. "Corporal Vincente has the christening tomorrow at the governor's church, for his twin girls, and we need vegetables to make sauces and fancy things for fiesta afterwards."

Juan did not look up from the vegetables and fruits that he was laying out, but he said a prayer and thanked the Saints for letting an Indian keep the beautiful gold nugget a while longer. He promised never to run away from the Mission and Saints again.

"I am sorry your vegetables didn't come when you expected, but all has not been well at San Carlos on the Carmelo," Padre Payeras told the fat señora. "We are doing the best we can."

"You missionaries are too soft. The Indians are running you!" she snorted. "But now Señor José Hijar will alter all that. Indians will no longer be lazy. They won't lie around mission rancherias any longer, but be forced to make their own way on the land. The savages." Her eyes looked black and angry as she glared at Payeras.

"Today we have eggplants that will make tried tempers soften with contentment, Señora Maria. The tomatoes have just the right amount of ripeness, and they are going cheap." The Padre's voice was calm.

At the mention of a bargain, the old woman stooped as low as her great stomach would let her, and expertly fingered the tomatoes. The wind blew her voluminous black skirts against the squatting Juan, and he brushed them away with impatience. Was this fat one telling things she really knew, or just talking with her mouth to anger people?

As Señora Maria waddled away with her load, Don Marquena slipped off his bay mare, tied the reins to a lichen-covered redwood post, and came to greet the Padre. Juan, from his place on the ground, watched the glistening silver embroidery on the sides of the Spaniard's breeches.

"Have you heard that Hartnell's school is nearly ready?" Marquena asked the Padre. "A college for California, like they have in England where Don Hartnell came from. A big adobe affair it is, and took over a year to build." Don Marquena gave a spit into the dust, and Juan saw a hornet fly to see the moist spot.

"That is good news," the Padre said. "Always news of learning is good news."

"Maybe so, but I don't think many will go to his school." Marquena stooped and helped himself to a brown pear from the pile at Juan's side, and then dropped a square bit of money on the cloth. "He's going to teach the boys Latin, French, German, and writing of essays, mathematics and *philosophy!*" He bit into the pear; Juan saw the bump in his throat go up and down, and the bite of pear was gone. It would be nice if Indians at the Mission could have all the pears they wanted to eat fast like Don Marquena ate, instead of saving them to sell and pay taxes.

"Hartnell's going to give special attention to Christian doctrine and morals, and habits and manners, and charge two hundred dollars a year for it!" Marquena laughed. "What our boys need is to learn to fight for themselves, and to drive a good bargain, instead of so much German and French and essays."

"But any knowledge helps to sharpen the wits for business," the Padre said softly, and Juan saw him look toward Don Cooper's house. "The world has ever the need of idealists like

Don Hartnell. The mind must be supplied as well as the purse and the stomach, Don Marquena."

"Yes, but think of the softness! This is what is necessary for a boy to go to college next month at Don Hartnell's." Marquena pulled a bit of brown paper from his pocket, and read aloud to Padre Payeras.

" 'Each boy will be required to have his own horse, two complete suits of underwear, and necessary top clothes. He shall furnish his own books, a piece of carbon for writing, and two rolls of cartridge paper to write on. If he uses this paper in a wasteful way, parents must furnish more, as the school cannot undertake to supply extra paper to students.' "

Juan saw Marquena fold up the notice. "We'll have our young men as soft as green cheese if we pamper them the way Don Hartnell would have us do. It will be all essays on Philosophy and no one to do the work!"

"You are too practical, Don Marquena. You said our grinding stones wouldn't work. Remember, it is God's plan that there shall be some philosophers and poets, as well as merchants and money lenders."

"Ah, Padre, gold will ease hunger when philosophy won't!" Marquena called out with a smile, as he strode toward the shop where silver things were made.

As Juan sorted over tomatoes and ate the ones the last señora had pinched so much that they were soft, he wondered if this big new word philosophy was like the bump sickness that Spaniards had brought on the ships along with tortilla pans. It sounded like a sickness, but the Padre had not crossed himself; he had even been pleased about the word. Perhaps Indians didn't get this sickness. For comfort he felt once more at the little gold nugget that Señorita Guadalupe Boronda had given him.

The Padre said he was going to the governor's church and would be back before long. He warned Juan to keep the money safe when he sold the vegetables.

Pablo drifted up to Juan. His eyes were bright, and he

115

kicked the yellow dirt with his toes. "A long time since you came," he said casually. He always talked like this when he was rolling gossip under his tongue and nearly ready to spit it forth.

"The corn has to be harvested these days," Juan said.

"But you don't harvest, Old One," Pablo grinned. Then he softened. Leaning down he pretended to pick out vegetables as he talked in Room-se-en. "So much has happened since the last moon, Juan. More than in a man's life before—" Juan saw that Pablo's heart was beating furiously under the thin cotton shirt. "Soldiers tell Indians to run away from Missions, then promise things. They were put up to this by the governor. He wanted Mission lands for his friends." Pablo took a breath. "Then other soldiers headed by General Vallejo went up into the hills to fight Indians, and bring them back." He leaned nearer. "Soldiers killed some Indians because they caught them taking cattle."

A great hurt went through Juan. Were San Carlos Indians hanging from trees for buzzards to make fiesta?

"It is all terrible. Spaniards are fighting against each other. Any day now, Mexico sends us another governor in place of the bad Echineada. His name is Figueroa."

"Come, Pablo. Have you the vegetables?" Don Feliciano Soberanes asked, and gave Pablo's rump a good-natured poke with his whip as he passed. "The women will scold if we are late."

Juan and Pablo jammed vegetables into Pablo's basket, and in no time he was off after his master, who was by far the finest-dressed Don in Monterey. Don Soberanes had a vest that was bright with gold sewing, and the tight-fitting trousers were flared just right. Even his sombrero had the broadest filigree band on it.

What was an Indian to think, Juan wondered, if even the Spaniards and Mexican governors themselves did not think alike? So many governors, too. Pablo always told of a new one. He was glad to be back at the Mission, away from all this trouble and hanging and freedom. He would never tell Pablo that he, too, had been a fool and run away to the hills. Padre Payeras wouldn't tell and Fray Abella, the newest priest, didn't often come to Monterey.

There was a new Indian neophyte christened before San Carlos Day that year. He was tall, and very young and strong, and he came wandering into the mission compound by himself to give his heart and hands to God. He was from far down the coast, and could ride young horses and break them in for others to ride.

Fr. Ramon Abella was pleased, for the new one could speak Spanish. They named him Antonio Prealta. There was no need to point out the "blue law" to him. That was the writing that said that anyone not singing out as loud as he could at services would be in stocks four hours. Antonio sang beautifully, and he loved singing. Juan noticed that it was not long before the young Indian looked on the face of Loreta as he sang the chants.

There were few converts now, and Mission lands had been cut down, for many Indians demanded ranchos of their own, instead of living at the Mission. After cattle, seeds, horses and implements were given to each family, from the already meager supply at the Mission, there was a scrabble to keep things going on what was left.

Juan worked hard on his shoes, for he had no helpers now. The Indians who could do rougher work were needed. This new Antonio did not have to be watched at his toil. He had worked for Spaniards down the coast, and knew life away from the Mission. He told Fr. Abella that the gentile Indians were beaten by Mexicans if they didn't work well. There was no one to look after them.

"An Indian has to work for Mexicans if he wants to eat," he sighed. "Spaniards control the range and hunt the deer. They drive an Indian away from fishing streams." Antonio willingly did the work of three men for the comfort he gained from his religion.

117

One day when Antonio was breaking colts to be sold to rich Spaniards, and the Padres were busy at the soap vats, Loreta came and sat by her father. They both worked for a time in silence. Juan knew what she wanted to talk about, for he had seen which way her glances turned at eating time, and during the procession out of the church. She had a smile for another besides her father on the way to Mass. That was as it should be. Young to young.

"Antonio has fine muscles," he said, without looking up from the shoe sole.

"And a good heart," Loreta murmured.

Juan smiled to himself. Loreta's fingers shook at her needles as she spoke the words.

"His voice is strong with manhood. I like to hear him sing," Juan said. "The cracked song from an old man's throat is nothing to charm the saints and bring better days to the Mission."

Loreta's eyes were tender. She put her hand on his thin arm. "But you play the fiddle. No one can play the fiddle as you do."

Juan's heart sang with happiness. But now was no time to talk of fiddling. He looked into her eyes. "If you were ever to drop a son, Loreta, would you like the boy to be the son of Antonio Prealta, the strong one?"

Her smile was like the picture of the Madonna that Payeras owned. Juan hardly dared breathe for fear her beautiful face would change from its happiness. She nodded.

"He is a Christian, and studying the catechism. He came here because he wanted to—"

Juan smiled. "Men are not saints because they learn catechism and come to church." But he knew by Loreta's eyes that she didn't believe what he told her.

Padre Payeras and Abella both smiled when they saw Loreta talk with Antonio.

There was a hard struggle after San Carlos Day. The rain came and there were so few shoulders to carry the work now.

Old ones only sickened in the wet and had to be dosed with *yerba de veba* to draw the rheumatism from their bones. This took time. It was better to leave them by the fire. But Mission taxes went on, and Padre Payeras said Mexico had taken away the "Pious Fund"—money given to the Padres as a gift to help Indians understand about God.

Father Prefect came to San Carlos and they planned a fine Christmas Mass. Juan worked extra hard to make the candles. Perhaps this glorious Mass and lots of candles would attract attention of the Blessed Mother and her Son, and bring better days to San Carlos after the New Year.

Loreta went out into the wet fields to gather toyon berries and greens, and made up the lost time by knitting in the dark.

Juan's shoes were not selling so well. There was a fad among señoritas now, to wear different shoes that came around the horn on "Boston ships." The price for Mission-made shoes went lower and lower until Juan knew they did not even pay for the food he ate. Such was the fate of a man too old to do anything but sit on his behind and sew, and think, while others worked.

Loreta herself made the manger for Christmas, and Juan carved the shepherds and the sheep and a cow or two. As he carved he thought of that time long ago, when he had worked on the statue of "Our Lady," and pleased Father Crespi. The sheep looked more like dogs, but Abella and Payeras said God would understand and Jesus was kind of heart.

Antonio Prealta wanted to make and hang the star, because this was his first Christmas at the Mission. He had saved some silver thread that had raveled from the dress of a señorita when the silver crochet work on her full skirt had caught on the door at Señor Hartnell's store one day. Carefully he tied sticks crossways to make a star, then wound each stick with the thread. It glistened! It sparkled, and was like a real star.

Juan watched them when Antonio showed Loreta the star. She smiled. "It is beautiful enough to guide anyone to the manger, Antonio."

119

Then, when Antonio's back was turned, Juan saw her quickly pull a lopsided point into place, and tuck in the ends of thread so that the star would be prettier.

The church was filled for the midnight Mass on Christmas. Spaniards and Mexicans, and Americanos and Englishmen all came to hear the Indian neophytes sing about the birth of Jesus. Many of the Indians who had run away from the Mission, and now had ranchos of their own, came too.

Juan's heart felt sorry when he saw these old ones who had worked and prayed beside him. Their clothes were ragged, and their faces sad in the light of church candles. Pablo said some of them couldn't make enough to eat on the land, and had to work for Spaniards.

The candles burned so brightly that they dazzled Juan's eyes. There were so many of them to honor Jesus. The Padres and Indians sang, and Juan was pleased that he could play Padre Amores' fiddle for those Indians who had come back to pray. His cracked voice singing would have spoiled the songs, and everyone must make music for the birth of Christ Jesus.

Antonio Prealta sang alone, then, a beautiful Gloria that soared as if it had wings. Juan gasped for breath, it was so beautiful. Loreta did not look up from the floor while Antonio sang, but Juan saw that her face was very happy. To her, Prealta's voice must sound like an angel's voice.

The wet came on after Mass. Padre Payeras hurried toward Juan.

"Help us urge the Indians to stay the night, Juan. Tell them they will not be locked up as of old. They are free! Today they are invited to share with us the fiesta of Christ's birth. An Indian must tell them!" His face was sad and he sighed, "Their minds have been poisoned so they do not believe what Friars tell them."

Juan called Antonio to help. Antonio must bring the Indians to him, for Juan's old legs could never go fast enough. Antonio was pleased to be helping, and smiled on Juan, and

120

said he would tell every single one that Juan, "the fiddler of San Carlos de Borromeo," had an invitation.

When they drew around the church door, Juan told them: "You are invited to stay the night at San Carlos, out of rain and cold. Then you will be here early to join in the feasting. We feast for the birth of Jesus, and have food together, and happiness." He watched the faces. Some were eager at the word food, some sad, perhaps, because it was for only one night they could stay. "Padre Payeras said to tell you that we are never locked up now, and you will not be locked up this night. You are free."

"Look here, Reverend Father," Don Juan Bautista Cooper said to Padre Payeras from behind. "You haven't enough food to feed all these! You are having a hard time as it is!"

"God knows, perhaps it will be the last time we will be together, with the Pious Fund gone, and colonists coming from Mexico any day now," Payeras said. "The great Serra would have liked us to share with them. We will make out, Don Cooper."

"As you will," the kindly rancher murmured, and moved toward his horse.

That night every inch of the adobe room was filled. Some Indians even slept in the sheltered places in front of the church.

There was a great noise in the compound just before dawn. Were the grizzly bears now so bold that not even the San Carlos was safe?

Juan got up and went stiffly to the door and opened it. The others were only moving sleepily on their tule mats. Juan saw Antonio Prealta and another Indian run toward the gateway. Soon Padre Payeras came running past. Juan decided he would brave even the wet ground under his bony feet to see what was happening. He hobbled along.

In the dim, cold light, Padre Payeras stood aghast for a moment, and Antonio just looked. There was something on the

121

ground. A great, dark hump! Juan shivered with cold, but went on. As he reached the place, Padre Payeras put his hands together and looked up.

"Oh, God, bring many blessings on those of your children who did this kind deed," he said aloud.

From the other side of the adobe wall there came voices, English and *Americano* voices, as well as Spanish, singing a Christmas carol about God blessing everybody who had no fear! And then the song died out as horses galloped away.

At the feet of Payeras were two beeves and six sacks of corn already ground. There was another bundle, a smaller bundle that was very heavy. By now all the Indians and Padre Abella had joined the crowd. Padre Payeras picked up the bundle and carried it through the damp cold air toward an adobe building. Antonio held a candle while the Padre opened the package with fingers that were red with cold and shaking a little.

Glistening rock candy! A great pile of it gleamed under the feeble rays of the single candle. There was enough to put a stick of it in the hands of every little Indian child at the Mission.

"Don Hartnell did this!" Juan cried. "Only he has the beautiful sweet from far away. He has it in his store in Monterey!"

"Don Hartnell was not singing alone, behind the wall," Abella said. "Don Juan Bautista Cooper, too, was singing; for he always flats the notes."

"The good deed will sharpen all his flat notes as God hears them," Payeras said, and told the Indians to make ready for Matins.

Chapter XIV

WRECK: 1834

THERE was a week of rain that ended in a terrible wind for the New Year, and then the next day the sun was hot. It made wet earth steam in the Mission compound.

Padre Payeras came over to where Juan sat with his back in the sun. Old bones could soak up a lot of warmth after so much rain. Even the adobe sleeping quarters smelled musty and damp, now.

"Antonio Prealta wants to marry Loreta, Juan," the Padre said and swung the tassels of his habit. "She looks favorably on him, too. She tells me she will keep on knitting socks for the Padres." He sighed and looked toward the lush, green hills. "But there will not be so much need for socks soon. The Missions are to be turned into just pueblos, or towns, with a parish priest in charge, if Hijar under his new title of Commissioner of Colonization has his way. There is already talk that the governor will send all Indians who are married or have been baptized for fifteen years, away from the Mission *rancheria*, onto land of their own."

"You mean me?" Juan asked. "I am to take land and go from here?" He waved a hand toward the tower, the tower that his own hands had helped build so round and beautiful. He could see now the day he had climbed to place the cross on it! "I put stones in the church, Padre Payeras!"

"These new Mexican governors do not understand, my son. We have tried to tell them." Payeras sighed. "But Hijar is determined."

There was a squeeze in Juan's heart. He could not speak. He stretched his skinny legs in the sun and looked down his bony body.

123

"Juan is old and shrinking. Maybe die before Hijar comes to put Juan out?"

"We hope not, Juan, and that you live a long time. Perhaps the new governor will make some changes." Payeras turned to warm his own back in the sun. "Antonio says he and Loreta will look out for you if we have to leave here and go to Branciforte by Santa Cruz."

"Antonio is a good worker," was all Juan could manage.

The Padre was quiet a minute. "If Loreta marries Antonio, they shall have land and a start of cattle and seeds, and a horse or two. . . . Perhaps it would be better that they have a place established, just for safety's sake, Juan."

"The old who cannot work are a burden to the young," Juan said. "Some animals I have seen eat the old, to make room for the new."

"Hush!" The Padre's voice was harsh. "You must not go back to a savage!"

"Look!" came excitedly from Indians beside the soap vats. "A horseman is coming fast from Monterey! He rides well. He is an Indian!"

Soon Pablo came rushing into the courtyard. "The colonists' boat from Mexico," he roared. "They came last night, and the colonists were making fiesta, and Juan Gomez, the master of the *Natalie*, was making fiesta—"

"Lower your voice, Pablo, and you will have more breath, my son," Payeras said.

Pablo lowered himself from the horse, but there was too much excitement to lower his voice. "The crew of the *Natalie*, they wanted fiesta and kisses from the señoritas, so they came ashore." Pablo took a great breath, maintained a dramatic pause as he looked around him at the faces of the Indians and priest. "The *Natalie* dragged anchor in the great wind. There was no one to tend her. The *Natalie* is wrecked!"

"Pablo!" Payeras gasped. "The Mexican colonists' boat?"

Pablo nodded. "People are rushing to the beach and carting away good things that colonists had on the boat. Señor Abrego

124

is to have the boards for his house. All belongs to the people when a wreck comes, the Alcalde says so! San Carlos de Borromeo should have some! A voice inside told Pablo to come." He grinned. "The horse went slow up the hill, but I make him go like Satan down to the Mission." Pablo patted the animal and said an endearing word into the pricked-up ears. "Don Soberanes is very busy today with headache from too much fiesta. He will not miss Pablo."

"The Indians could use things. Shall we let them go?" Father Payeras asked. "Surely they have as much right as anyone to the wreckage."

"There will be a fight with Mexicans," Abella said.

"But there is always a fight, wreckage or none."

"Then we will send some young, strong men and three ox carts." Payeras paused a minute. "And I shall ride over after them on my horse, to see that no harm comes of it."

"Antonio!" Abella called. "Put the oxen to the carts. You go with Esteben and Ruez to Monterey to pick things from the beach! I'll attend your fires and watch the fat render."

In no time the oxen were ready. Pablo started back to Monterey ahead of them in case the headachy Don Soberanes should call for him and he would not be there!

Just as the carts were pulling out, Payeras put up his hand. "This will not do!" he cried. "There should be women to cook and mind what the men bring back on the beach. The men cannot do everything. There are some who would take from the Indians if their salvage is not guarded."

He turned in his saddle. "Maria, you are old and make fires well, and Teresa for the tortillas—" There was a slight pause, and Juan saw the Padre glance at Antonio who stood waiting by the oxen, thongs in his hands. "Loreta, put by your knitting. Your young legs can run to the water-line and bring back to the fires what the men fish out."

Soon the women had shawls on them and were ready.

"One to a cart to ride," called Payeras. "Loreta, take this first cart, and then you pull off, Antonio." There was a creak,

125

and the cart went lumbering noisily out of the compound, followed by those bearing fat Maria and Teresa the toothless.

"You are very good to look on, Loreta," Antonio said to the girl who sat knitting as she rode over the bumps. "I have a present for you." He reached into his cotton shirt and pulled out a tiny bundle of silver thread. "I took it carefully from the star so no threads would be broken—for you. Maybe it is an omen for us, that star." His hand felt warm and made happiness glow in Loreta as she touched it to take the thread.

"The silver thread will go on the christening robes of our son, Antonio. The son who will be strong like you," she told him, and watched his chest go out quite a lot, and his step quicken.

Father Payeras rode up on his horse. "What you two salvage today shall be your own. You will need it for starting a rancho."

"We do not go away to a rancho as long as you are at the Mission," Antonio told the priest. "There are few enough hands for working the land now."

"Bless you, Antonio," Payeras said. "You are both good workers and do not listen to the tales that are inspired by Satan. If you plant crops and tend land as you have been taught to do, you have nothing to fear. Then, when the work is done in your fields and your cattle on range, there is many a job for willing hands and stout backs. Spaniards and Mexicans pay Indians to do it; not much, but all helps."

· "And we will look after Juan as I told you," Antonio reminded Payeras. "He needs to sit by fires now."

The good Padre laughed. "He can sew shoes for all your children, Antonio, beautiful shoes, for Juan knows well how to make them, and he will put music into their souls by way of fiddle strings." He rode off to look at the view of the wrecked ship from a high hill.

When they got down into Monterey and reached the beach, the tireless Pablo was there. "Señora Cooper said that this was truly an ill-fated ship that the Mexicans bought from France.

126

This ship carried a man named Napoleon Bonaparte from the Island of Elba, far away. He was a sad man, and his sadness was not gone with the new name of the ship. There is an omen."

Payeras laughed. "Omen nothing! Just the lack of a crew, Pablo. No ship can sail itself. Not even the memory of Napoleon Bonaparte can help it. The same way Missions cannot run themselves."

Antonio and his comrades went to work. There were many boxes floating on the small surf waves, and three were landed in no time. Indians were quicker and surer of foot than Spaniards and Mexicans, who were just running around shouting, as far as Loreta could see.

"What's this?" a voice demanded. "Have we also Mission Indians joining in the rabble?" The tall Mexican kicked at the boxes. "This may have in it valuable things for the colonists!"

Father Payeras was instantly behind Loreta. "You speak truth, Señor, but even flies have the right to eat off a carcass," he told the Mexican in a low voice. "There have been enough buzzards taking from the Pious Fund in Mexico." The man turned away and spat in the sand with disgust.

Antonio came up with a board, smooth and lovely. "This will go over our door," he smiled. "Now when I go back, watch me, Loreta. I swim better than any out there, and do not tire."

Loreta watched, and murmured a prayer that he would not be caught in sea moss and be dragged to his death as her grandfather had been on Point Aulone one spring morning before the flowers were in bloom. Her father was frightened of sea moss and told her never to swim in the sea, for moss was like a devil waiting for Indian bodies that never returned.

She reached inside her voluminous Mother Hubbard and pulled out a cloth with tallow in it and rubbed a bit on her hair to make it look well and shine. Maria had taught her that. Maria said Indian men liked to see their women's hair shine.

127

She was not yet Antonio's woman, but he wanted her, and with so many smiling-eyed Spanish women about, well, it paid to keep tallow on the hair.

When eating time came it was nice to have Antonio so close that she could hear his jaws cracking on the meat. Some day she would be cooking over a fire for him, with no eyes to watch what she did. Loreta's heart was singing. After the food she ran harder than ever to the water's edge to take things from the men.

"It is time to go," Payeras called when he came back from talking to the priest of the governor's church. "We must make it over the hill before dark. There is work to do at San Carlos."

Antonio looked longingly at the wooden chest they were trying to pull ashore, but when the Padre called he started toward the beach. Suddenly out of nowhere a woman appeared. She was a Mexican. "Oh, Mother of God, there it is! My own grandmother's chest," and she put her head in her shawl and started to cry.

"Antonio, Esteben, Ruez!" called the Padre. "All together, work to bring the chest to shore."

Loreta was proud as she saw Antonio's muscles move under his bright skin. He was so strong, so fine to look at. She smoothed her hair. The three men worked a long time, and then brought the chest with them and set it down.

The woman ran across the sand to where they were and crouched next to it. "Mine!" she cried, her arms around it.

"But it is ours," Esteben said. "Anything afloat that we get is ours."

"No—no—" the woman wailed. "It is my own, my grandmother's chest I was bringing here to the land of milk and honey the governor promised!"

"It is ours," Esteben insisted without moving. "The Alcalde said so."

"You savage! You have murder in your eyes. You would steal the grease from a holy altar! Get from my sight!"

Padre Payeras came up. "No, Señora. He has no murder in

his eyes, only fear for his rights!" he said quietly. "Esteben makes candles for the altar at Mission San Carlos. He is a Christian and not a savage. Only his color is different. He has loves, and hopes, and, God forbid, hatreds, the same as those who persecute him." Payeras then turned to Esteben. "Take the chest, my son, to where this woman wishes it to be. It is your gift to her. Perhaps an Indian may yet bring light to darkened hearts."

Chapter XV

THE OUTSIDER: 1834. 1835

THE next time Juan went into Monterey with vegetables, he saw the great pile of lumber that Señor Abrego had salvaged from the ship. Juan was worried over this wood that was to go into the new house. After his carrots and onions and cabbage were set out in the shade, he ran to Señor Abrego's newly opened store.

The storekeeper looked up from his work and smiled.

"Pablo tells that Señora Cooper says that there is a curse on the *Natalie*, Señor Abrego. A man named Napoleon Bonaparte was sad, and the curse was not lifted when the Mexicans bought the ship and called it a different name."

Abrego just laughed.

Juan felt hurt inside. "Perhaps if you build this new house from the wood of the boat you will have bad times, and few children for your old age."

"Don't fear, Juan, Señora Cooper was just making a little flurry of excitement. She is beautiful, and her eyes shine when there is excitement as a beautifier for them." He gave Juan a little tobacco. "Go and soothe the fear away from you with this."

Pablo came for vegetables. "Figueroa is not handsome in eyes of señoras and señoritas, but he is sorry for Indians, Juan," he said and picked out a cabbage.

"Then he will not send Juan away from Padre Abella and Payeras at the Mission?"

Pablo shrugged and pulled a braid of onions toward him. "That Vallejo has changed his song, Old One. He has already told the governor how sad it is for Indians to be turned from

130

Missions too soon." He looked knowingly at Juan. "That is because the good Dons, José Castro and Feliciano Soberanes and Francisco Soria were so cross and talked to the Governor against turning away the Padres. The governor is very sorry for Indians, to see them so poor with bad Spaniards already stealing away some of their land."

"Don Feliciano Soberanes is good, Pablo," Juan said thoughtfully. "He gave rubbing liniment to Juan, for the old bones."

Pablo was not interested in old bones; he was too young for aches yet. "Vallejo will only watch for his chance. He and his nephew, Alvarado, and their friends, do not change coats so suddenly and become saints, O-nes-e-mo."

"I have news, too, Pablo. It is about Loreta and Antonio, instead of governors who don't know their own minds."

Pablo was instantly all ears. Juan knew he liked to take back some gossip to the kitchens of Don Feliciano Soberanes. To talk was important to Pablo, and a mouth must have something to work on!

"Antonio from down the coast?" Pablo asked.

Juan nodded.

"He is an outsider! He is not Room-se-en."

"But Antonio is good. They had marriage ceremony in the Mission by the Padre one day." Juan grinned. "Padre Payeras said they might as well, that Loreta was thinking only Antonio and dropped stitches so that Padre Abella lost all of the heel to his sock. We had extra food too."

Pablo sniffed. "At Señor Soberanes' is always good food and plenty."

Juan closed his ears to that temptation. "Loreta looks beautiful as a saint, now, and they have already built a tule hut on the land that Padre Payeras pointed out as theirs." Juan looked at the surprised Pablo. This was something that happened and Pablo didn't know. "The Padre and Indians helped build a big tule place for them."

"That Antonio is an outsider," Pablo insisted. "You see,

there will be a curse on them," he sniffed. "Loreta should have taken for a man at least from the Room-se-en on the Carmelo."

"Maybe you?" Juan asked with a laugh. "Pablo, you are too old to bring strong sons now. With so many people living on the land, Loreta needs strong sons. There is not food enough for weak ones who cannot work."

Pablo spat in the yellow dust, gave a black look to Juan, and picked up his basket of vegetables.

"Loreta and Antonio are to have a fiesta soon with plenty of beans and meat and then we go to sleep at the new rancho, but we will keep on working at the Mission. The Padres need all hands there to work." Out of the corner of his eye, Juan noticed that Pablo had paused to listen. This was too exciting to leave, this news. "You had better come to the fiesta for Loreta and Antonio."

Apparently Pablo's mind was not on the fiesta. "You will do well to let them go alone to the hut," he said. "Your presence there might affect Loreta's strong sons," and he trotted off in the direction of the house of Don Feliciano Soberanes.

Juan thought about the words of Pablo all the way home. The oxen were weary from extra work and did not hurry. They even paused frequently to switch the flies with their tails. Juan did not push them, for he had known what it was to be pushed at the hand of soldiers, and he knew the bite of flies on the back when he was too heavily burdened to put them off. It would be better for him to stay at the Mission as long as it was possible so that Antonio and Loreta could have full time to work their new land, after evening prayers, and no old man's bones to be rubbed with liniment. Maybe Pablo was right about the strong sons being affected by a weak old man! It would be hard enough to work at the Mission and till their own land, too. Loreta had told him she promised God and the San Carlos that she would serve the Mission always.

There was great feasting and games from noon until time for Angelus on the day that Loreta and Antonio and Juan were to leave their places in the sleeping rooms of the Mission and go to the tule hut on the Carmelo. Juan played the fiddle, a grand mixture of dances and chants and bird songs. Only the bell in the tower, calling all to service, stopped the music.

"Don't you think it would be a very good omen if I played tonight at prayers the chant Padre Amores played the night Loreta was born?" Juan asked the Padre as they walked toward the church. "It might help her in dropping a son, when God is thinking that way."

Payeras nodded. "The chant would be beautiful tonight, Juan. Which one did Amores play?"

Juan didn't know. It was the one that made quiet inside you.

When the services were over, Antonio went to the ox cart that was already loaded. "Come, Juan, there is a place for you to ride," he called. "And a strong young arm to help you, too."

Juan watched the last rays of the sun on Loreta's brown skin as she busied herself putting things into the cart. He wanted to look well at her today, so that he could often shut his eyes and see her just as she was now, happy and beautiful and quiet.

"Come, Juan," Antonio called. "We have not much time to miss the rough places in the road before dark."

Juan stood a moment with his fiddle under his arm, smiled at them both and turned to Padre Payeras. "Juan will stay, Padre," he said quietly. "Young to young. Juan will work harder on shoes and not ask once for people to rub his bones if he can only stay here. When Hijar's men come to shove Juan out, maybe they will come too late!"

Payeras put his hand on Juan's shoulder; it felt warm and comforting. He smiled a bit, which was good. "Juan, your hands worked to build the church. You shall stay here as long as there is protection for you." Instantly the Padre's voice changed. "Be off, Loreta and Antonio, before Satan catches you in the dark. It will be a short time enough until morning when you will be back again to work. No knitting tonight, Loreta, for we want no more raveled socks." He murmured the

133

blessing as Antonio bowed his head, nodded obedience, and used a touch of rawhide to the back of the oxen. Just as they were pulling out, the handsome Don Feliciano Soberanes rode along Camino Real on his fine-stepping chestnut horse. He stopped to watch Antonio and Loreta in the cart.

"New householders?" he asked the priest.

"Yes, a marriage, Don Soberanes. They are going to their rancho."

"Ah!" Juan saw Don Soberanes put his hand into the embroidered pocket of his coat, and bending low, he gave a gold nugget to Loreta. "I wish you well. Remember that Don José Manuel Boronda is schoolmaster up at Tularcitos, if you have need of his services, Señora." And laughingly, he turned and rode to where Padre Payeras and Abella were standing.

"We have news from Mexico," he said. "Heaven knows they don't bother much to hear from us. The government only sends communication about every two years!" He slipped from his horse, and Payeras motioned an Indian to take it. "Padre Real, a Mexican priest, is coming here to manage things, I'm told."

"Come in, Don Soberanes, and have a glass of wine with us," Payeras said. "We are dependent upon such visitors as yourself, who tell us the news."

They all went toward the tule shelter where Padres ate. Juan squatted down to sew some bits of color to shoes before dark. It was better to think of satins than to think how much he wanted to be with the sweet-faced Loreta who had so often rubbed the very pain from his bones with her soothing hands.

"Figueroa has been duped by Vallejo and the others," Soberanes sighed. "But then, the poor man is not well. He has already sent in his resignation to Mexico and only waits for another to relieve him. It may be our cold fogs bother him."

"Again it may be our hot politics!" Payeras answered. "So many hatreds. Figueroa is a good man and wants to do right."

"I am irked that I rang the Mission bells and said High Mass when some of the Mexican colonists arrived safe, Don Soberanes," Abella said. "It may be I was only sounding our death knell, ringing in the destruction of the Missions that Fra Junípero Serra labored so hard to found."

"Figueroa would need to be wise as a dozen serpents to escape being taken in with fine speeches. We have silver tongues in Monterey, now, as well as pretty faces," Soberanes murmured, and lifted his wine to sip and be comforted. "Already Alvarado and some others have plans for doing away with Missions. Alvarado has plans for being governor, too." He sighed. "In some Spaniards and Mexicans there is no good."

"Don't say that," Abella cried. "You mean our eyes can see no good in them."

"As you like it; but any man can have his thoughts, Padre."

"You have done your best for us," Payeras said.

That night Juan thought of the things he had overheard. He couldn't sleep for thinking of so many governors and soldiers, and Directors of Colonization, all trying to get the Missions and lands away from the Padres.

There were such a lot of people now. Other places in the world must have many more people than Carmelo, for they had come from everywhere. Spaniards by dozens, good ones and bad, and then whole boats of Mexicans, and English traders to get hides and tallow, and some to stay and take up lands. Now these new *Americanos* in "Boston ships," with shoes that señoritas liked better than Juan's shoes, so that he couldn't sell his work so easily. Don Soberanes had told the Padre there were nearly four hundred people in Monterey and Carmelo. If more settlers came, where would they stay? All land would be gone. His Loreta with O-nes-e-mo blood in her had land, now, unless the governor took it away. Suddenly Juan felt very lonely.

Only the fiddle would take away the frightening thoughts of what would happen to one old Indian, Juan O-nes-e-mo. He groped in the dark along the wall. It was comforting to his fingers when he felt the bag. The Padres looked sad most of the time now. There was seldom even a twinkle in their eyes.

CATHEDRAL IN THE SUN

No time to talk of the old days and hum a new chant for Juan to try and play on Padre Amores' fiddle when the shoes were finished. Padres' tongues were always busy about what they were going to do when they could no longer stay at the Mission. In the dark Juan played a little song to San Carlos.

Chapter XVI

PEAR BRANCHES OF SAN CARLOS: 1835

"IF we plant corn right away it will be ripe before the rains come again," Antonio said as he walked beside the ox cart. He smiled, and reached up to press Loreta's hand against his own. "I can till and you bring water from the Carmelo. With our hands working together, Loreta, we will prosper and show the Padre how well we treat the land he has given us."

"Onions, too, we'll plant, and tomatoes for sauce like Spaniards have," Loreta told him, her heart full of happiness for this warm hand against hers. "Abella is sorrowing, Antonio. He seems to feel that the Padres will leave San Carlos de Borromeo very soon."

"If we work harder at the Mission, maybe Alvarado and the others will think it pays to keep the Padres. Let them charge high taxes. San Carlos will pay them and keep the priests."

"So few hours of daylight to work, my Antonio." Loreta shook her head. "And even an Indian must rest."

In front of her own tule hut, Loreta paused to look up at the spring stars before she went to work at unloading the things from the cart. "They have come out tonight, Antonio, after so much fog. Perhaps they shine a happiness to us."

Antonio didn't speak; he just came close to her and looked up, too, and the warmth of his body so near was comforting.

The next morning, Loreta was on her knees for prayer beside Antonio, long before light came into the sky. Silently they ate the tortillas Fr. Abella had given them from the Mission, and then hurried out to the little plot of land where Antonio was to plant corn.

Loreta's back ached that first day when it was time by the

137

stick in the ground to leave for the Mission and her work of knitting. But after a few weeks she no longer noticed it. The ride rested her, bumpy as it was.

By the time the hills turned golden, things at the little rancho were coming along well. Rabbits ate only a few of the tomato plants and Antonio's corn was high and filled with tassels. Loreta was to drop a baby before it was time to put the Christmas star over the altar at San Carlos de Borromeo. They couldn't use the silver thread for making the star, this year. It would be on christening robes, as Loreta had promised.

Juan was delighted about Loreta's child. He would have a grandson, now! He would teach the grandson to fiddle, and when Juan finished with the Padre's fiddle, it would go on to Loreta's son! There would be an O-nes-e-mo to fiddle in memory of Padre Amores at the Mission.

Fr. Abella looked a little sad when Loreta said he was to christen the baby when it came. He even shook his head. "I won't be here, Loreta. Fr. José Real, the Mexican priest, will christen your baby. He will be coming over here to the Mission for Mass sometimes." He lowered his voice. "When we are gone to Branciforte on the other side of Monterey Bay."

Juan could hardly breathe. "You leave? All Padres leave?" he asked. But it was a silly question. In his heart he knew that Hijar had at last caught up with Juan O-nes-e-mo, Mission Builder.

"Yes, before another moon we leave."

The Padre looked out over the fertile fields and to the hills beyond. "The lands are to be divided, and stock and sheep and horses." He paused a moment and lowered his voice so that Juan could hardly hear. "Serra's dream is fading fast, and his poor children will get less than half of what they worked so hard to earn." He turned suddenly. "You will have the strong shoulders of Antonio to lean on, and tender, loving care from Loreta, so count your blessings, Juan, and play often on your fiddle to the good San Carlos. Let him know that at least Juan O-nes-e-mo has not forgotten the brave spirit that led him to

138

the Mission. And always help the other Indians who are less fortunate than you are."

"But with no Padres to tell us, Indians don't know what to do," Juan said.

"Oh, that is all to be managed beautifully," Padre Payeras cried angrily. "Pio Pico and Vallejo and Alvarado are all taking over Missions, and a friend of theirs, José Joaquin Gomez, is commissioner here! He is to manage the affairs for Indians at San Carlos from now on."

"Vallejo!" Juan cried. "He is the señor who would not give me money when he took pears to eat in Monterey."

The Padre only sighed, and looked a long time at the Indians working at the soap vats. "Vallejo will not be satisfied with mere fruit. He will most likely have his share of Mission stock now."

"Indians will watch," Juan said.

Payeras shook his head. "The Indians and Padres are losing the game, and the Picos and Vallejos and Alvarados have won. From poor settlers they will turn suddenly into rich men. These men will keep what belongs to Indians until others come and take it away from them."

Juan could not think. There was such confusion in the days that followed. The Mexicans came, and ate and drank, and counted sheep and cattle, and divided them. Some of the best horses that Antonio had broken were taken, along with many cattle and sheep, to the Rancho National in Salinas Valley to be used for loans to new settlers. Some cattle were to stay on Mission range, and the rest were divided among Indians, who drove them away to the little ranchos that Commissionado Gomez gave them.

Juan was very sad. If Don Soberanes and Castro and the other good Spaniards who had made a fight for Indians couldn't stop this, what could a hundred San Carlos Indians do?

"Here!" called a friend to Gomez through yellow dust that arose from many hoofs. "Don't give an Indian that fine steer.

I will take it and pay the Mission for it!" A riata was around the animal in no time, and it was taken away from Antonio.

"But it was given to me by the Padre Abella days ago," Antonio said. "That steer is mine, and Loreta's. She is a Mission sister!"

"Give him two skinny ones," Gomez shouted to a Californian, "and let's get on with this business. My throat's as dry as parchment."

Antonio took the two skinny heifers, and added them to the band that Loreta watched.

Padre Abella looked white and tired when he rang the bell for Angelus that day. Juan knew that it was the last Angelus for Payeras and Abella in San Carlos. They were to leave after Mass in the morning.

The Californians washed in the trough and came into church. They gave off the feeling of a finished job, done to suit them, as they swaggered past the kneeling Indians to their places closer to the altar.

Juan thought Fr. Abella's voice had never been so tender and loving as it was that last Angelus. The altar was shining with light. And when Juan turned to leave the church, even the statue of "Our Lady" was still smiling and serene in her niche. But then, she could not see that all the corn was gone from Mission bins, and that Mission cattle and sheep and horses had been driven away today. "Our Lady," being a saint and not interested in such things, would never know that there was nothing left in the compound but the great grinding stones too heavy to move, and two carts that were to carry away the Padres and their things before sunup.

The *Comisionádo* and his helpers were anxious to be away after Vespers. They shook hands with the Padres and wished them well and a pleasant journey, then gathered up the papers, and swung onto their horses.

"We will have to race a bit to be in Monterey in time to shine properly at the Cascarone Ball," the one they called Temerez cried. "Let's be off."

Juan could see that Padre Real, the Mexican priest, was upset. He was to stay on until this new pueblo of Carmelo was established, and then he, too, would go over the hill to Monterey and the Presidio chapel, for the two churches were to be united by order of the government.

Loreta and the other sisters had cooked a meal from their own share of Mission food. They even put a bunch of yellow Mariposa lilies to decorate the table. There had been little time to spare, but Loreta had used it to scour the dry hillside for the yellow beauties. They were Padre Abella's favorites of all. Each year he greeted the lilies as old friends, and the Mariposas had arrived barely in time to say their farewell to him this year.

Antonio and Loreta and some other Indians who loved the Padres slept that night in the long adobe room, with bars on the windows, the room that had sheltered Juan O-nes-e-mo for so many years; the home his hands had built.

The next morning after Mass, there was great bustle around the compound. Loreta made tortillas for the Fathers to carry on their trip, and a hot stew in the pot of hollowed-out stone, stew that would keep hot for hours. Antonio was going over the ox cart. There was nothing an old man could do.

Juan went into the sleeping room and brought out the two pairs of sandals he had made for the Padres, sandals cut from the strongest and best leather in the whole cowhide. He found Padre Abella writing last entries in his brown book. The priest was delighted with the parting gift.

"This is to make easier your feet on the lumps," Juan explained.

"Bless you, Juan. If I could only return the compliment for Indians! There will be so many hard lumps along the path for Indians."

Juan didn't understand what the Padre meant, but he was happy when he saw Abella sit down and try on the sandals. They looked so out of place, so new, peeping from under the patched and faded habit the Padre wore.

141

Finding Padre Payeras was hard. No one had seen him. No one knew where he was, not even Abella.

Juan called softly at the door of the little room back of the church. He searched the Indian burying ground, and around the adobe buildings that were so much in need of repairing, but no Payeras. Then at last Juan came upon him in the orchard. He was standing alone, looking hard at the gnarled old pear trees. His hand rubbed the bark lovingly. Juan stood quietly a moment. But the Padre was used to the silent feet of Indians, for he looked up and his face was very pale.

"Poor old trees. They have seen many Padres come and go, Juan. They have seen revolts and thievery and pirates, and dry years and wet, and still they go on, growing and giving forth their fruit." He smiled. "There is a great lesson in these twisted branches, Juan, a lesson for missionaries to take away with them."

Quick as a flash, Juan was cutting switches of pear. "You take them with you, Padre," he said. "Father Lasuen brought these trees in switches like Juan gives you. Borica was governor then, and Juan helped to plant them. Long, long ago, when Juan was a young man."

"Are the trees as old as that, Juan?" Payeras cried. He counted with his lips. "Why, that was forty years ago, in 1795!"

Juan didn't know years. "They were only just planted when the prisoners landed." He nodded toward the sea. "Ten men and a woman, from a ship. They came from a long way called Botany Bay, and Captain Dorr brought them. There was trouble." He caught himself up. "Old ones like Juan think about what is gone and forget now." He held out the new sandals to Payeras. "Put them on so that you will walk away from the Mission with Juan's good thoughts on your feet," he said, and smiled.

Padre Payeras laid down the bundle of pear switches and took off the old sandals and then slipped his toes into the new

142

ones. With a quick toss, he threw the old ones away, far down into the orchard.

"Off with the old, Juan, and on with the new!" Resolutely he picked up the branches and walked toward the Mission. Juan saw that Payeras' eyes were very bright.

"What have you?" Father Abella cried.

"Pear branches, to start new trees," was all Padre Payeras said as he carefully tucked them into the cart.

"All is ready," Abella said softly. "The sun will be up and we have a long way to travel."

"Juan will travel to the top of the hill with you," the old man cried, "and play chants all the way on Padre Amores' fiddle."

Payeras shook his head. "You are too old, Juan. It will only tire you."

"When Juan plays chants, San Carlos will not let him be tired," he insisted. "I will rub the feet with hot rocks, as my father did when he was old and had to walk a long way."

Loreta came up to them. "Let him go," she said quietly to the Padres. "It is the only way he knows to show his gratitude." She turned to Juan. "I will take you in the ox cart, so that all your strength will go into the fiddle music."

The three carts pulled out of the Mission compound.

Juan saw Padre Payeras, and Abella, too, give a blessing to the little group of Indians by the gate. The Padres didn't look back after that.

Juan played the bird calls he loved, and then the chants. He saved for the very top of the hill, that was high and nearest the saints, the sweet chant that was for Padre Amores in heaven.

And as he played Juan found that Padre Amores was telling him about the nugget. When the carts stopped on the hilltop to rest, Juan took from the belt of his pantaloons the bit of cloth that held the gold. Carefully he unwrapped the precious gift, then, with stiff joints complaining, he got out of the cart

143

and went over to where the Padre Payeras was soaping the wheels. He waited patiently until the Padre had finished, and then touched the brown sleeve.

"Padre Amores in heaven tells Juan to give you this nugget that Señorita Guadalupe Boronda gave Juan long ago." He dropped the bit of gold into the Padre's hand.

Payeras looked at the nugget, and then nodded his head. "Yes, Juan, Padre Amores asks me to bless it for the grandchild of Juan O-nes-e-mo, Mission Builder." The Padre's lips moved in prayer, and then he put the gold back into Juan's rough hand.

The sun shone suddenly from behind the mountains, and the Padres rode down toward Monterey.

Juan sat in the ox cart at the top of the hill and played as long as he could see them, and then he put the fiddle away in its faded bag.

Chapter XVII

JACK PREBLE ROUNDS THE HORN: 1835

JUAN sat in the sun making shoes. Every minute or two he paused to glance inside the hut and look at the naked baby on the cowhide. No doubt about it. José was a boy!

"You have many things like your grandfather, José!" Juan mumbled. "You have no teeth either, man. It goes hard for O-nes-e-mos without teeth." Then he laughed, and called in Spanish to Loreta who was tilling the vegetable garden.

"Better feed the boy. He will starve. O-nes-e-mo and Prealta men need good food to make them strong."

Loreta looked up, nodded, and a faint smile played across her face. Then she tilled on. "I'll finish this row, and then feed him," she said.

Juan went back to his shoes. Doña Allen, who was a Boronda in Monterey, had ordered three pairs of the best from him. Her tiny feet were not made for shoes that came on "Boston ships." He had picked the softest leather, and was sewing beautiful stitches on them. Doña Petra was as good as she was pretty to look at, and her husband, Don Jorje Allen, was very kind to Indians.

As Juan sewed, music drifted up from the fandango houses in Los Beracos, the frail village made of tule huts where most of the Indians were living now. A whole row of huts was there, with three saloons, and three fandango houses, and dancing girls. Violins and guitars played dance tunes night and day at Los Beracos. Some of the Mission Indians had already killed most of their cattle to get the hides for drink and girls. Juan sighed, and cut off the thread on the toe of Doña Petra's shoe. The Californians and others were always wanting Indians to kill their cattle and sell the hides.

145

Loreta came slowly up the hill and sat just inside the hut. Little José saw her and started crying. She filled his mouth with her nipple and he began drawing at her brown breast.

"Los Beracos music is not music to me," Loreta said. "It is sadness, and forgetting the Padres and good San Carlos so soon." She looked off toward the oak-dotted hillside across the river. "But my Antonio never comes down from Los Laureles Rancho that he does not go to the Mission—for a prayer."

"He is good," Juan said and took a thread to tickle young José's nose. He watched the baby stop sucking and rub his face with his fist.

"No," Loreta smiled and pulled away the thread. The baby went back to his sucking. "Let him eat in peace. He has soon enough to learn of irritations and sadness in the world."

Juan tickled the baby's head this time, but José sucked on. "But I am doing this because my grandson is soon to be christened, and must get used to tickling and water on him. An O-nes-e-mo should not cry and make bad noises in the church that his grandfather helped build."

Loreta looked down and stroked the little brown head. "José will not be christened in San Carlos de Borromeo. I went to the Mission today to see about it when you two were sleeping. He will have to be taken to Monterey. A notice on the door says the priest comes once a month for Mass, and for San Carlos Day. Don Cooper stopped on his bay horse and read it to me."

"No priest at the Mission?" Juan could hardly believe what Loreta said.

She shook her head. "People have already taken away tiles from some buildings to put on their own roofs. I saw Mission tiles on a settler's house as I walked home."

"I made those tiles, with Miguel and Pablo," Juan said, a squeeze in his heart. "I rolled them from flat cakes of mud, and pressed them over my leg to make them round. Father Pujol and Padre Antonio Jayme laughed when they came on their pilgrimage to San Carlos and saw the tiles drying in the

146

sun. Father Pujol said that a long time from now, people would know what bony knees Juan O-nes-e-mo had, because there is a knee hole in this tile." Then suddenly, as he rambled along about old days, a plan was born in Juan O-nes-e-mo's head. "You have garden things to sell in Monterey?" he asked in a firm voice. "The onions, and perhaps a few tomatoes?"

"Maybe a few, and cabbage, but Mexicans will buy them right around here," Loreta told him.

"To Monterey the vegetables go!" Juan cried.

"But Antonio has no time to take them. He is getting money for breaking horses now at Los Laureles Rancho," Loreta said gently. "And I must mind José, and garden, and grind corn, or we don't eat."

"To Monterey the vegetables go, and Juan takes them along with Doña Allen's pretty shoes, that will be finished tomorrow. The Padres gave Antonio and Juan oxen to drive, and Antonio made a cart. Juan has often gone to Monterey with fruit and vegetables to sell before now."

José lost the nipple and started to cry. Juan watched Loreta trying to poke it into his mouth. When she looked up, she said, "Very well, but be careful—"

"You talk to the wrong toothless one!" Juan said hotly. "Tell things like that to José who sucks and won't understand anyway." And he went at his sewing with new vigor.

"You are missing the gossip with Pablo," Loreta said, as she put down the sleeping baby and pushed a fly from his face. "Is that why you must go?"

"For a grandfather there are many more things to see to in Monterey besides gossip."

The next morning, before dawn, Juan and Loreta knelt at prayer. After tortillas, Loreta helped load the cart with vegetables. Juan wrapped the shoes in an old bit of cloth that had once been pantaloons, and tucked the bundle under the cabbages, so that the shoes would not be lost off the cart when

147

it hit a bumpy part of the road. He was well on his way before the sun came from behind Toro Hill.

Juan stopped at San Carlos de Borromeo, and tied his oxen to the gate. He prayed a few minutes in the church that was dark and empty, except for "Our Lady" in her niche beside the door. It seemed queer not to see the glow of the sacred lamp, but the saints would understand that the Padres had gone.

When Juan came out, the sun was blinding after the darkness. Then in a minute he saw! Mexicans were taking away boards from the doorways! Some had tiles and were carrying them to carts.

"No, not the Mission," he cried, but even to his own ears the voice sounded weak and cracked. "The good San Carlos looks down on what Indians and Padres made, and a curse will come on you."

They only laughed, and took a cabbage from his cart.

"The Mission is deserted," one said. "The lumber and tiles might as well be used."

Juan climbed into his cart and drove on. What could an old Indian do against the rush of newcomers here in Carmelo? Why, there must be five new families now, some of Hijar's people, no doubt, for a boatload of them had to be put somewhere when they landed in Monterey.

The sun was straight overhead when Juan finally pulled up the winding road to Doña Jorje Allen's house on the hill back of the governor's church. There was such a sweetness of pinks and roses of Castile in the little lady's garden. The tule roof had been replaced by tiles, made with Indians' hands, and bought from the Padres at the Mission Carmelo.

Two dogs ran out to bark at Juan. An Indian boy, Basillo, called them off.

"What is it, Basillo?" Doña Allen called, and came to the door with her sewing in her hand.

"Juan with the shoes, Doña Petra. Could Juan speak for a moment with Doña Petra?"

She came along her garden path to him. Gracefully she walked in her full, soft silk dress. Her little hands were still holding the fancy embroidery she had been working on.

"Of course. I am anxious to see the shoes, O-nes-e-mo."

Juan pulled the bundle from under the cabbages, and unwrapped it. Then he stood back from the cart, to let her see.

"They are beautiful!" Her eyes were shining. "We must have two more pairs." She took the shoes in her little hands, and felt their softness. The red satin patches looked well in the sunlight. Juan knew that no Americano shoes off a "Boston ship" could ever be so beautiful.

"So—vain one!" A soft voice came over her shoulder. "Shoes again!" Don Jorje Allen was smiling at the little lady. "How much are they, O-nes-e-mo?" He jangled money in his pocket. "And you must go back to the kitchen to have some food. We are about to eat."

"I want to speak," Juan said quietly. "Juan has a grandson, now. José—"

"Bravo," Don Allen cried.

"Hush, Jorje," Petra said. "O-nes-e-mo wants to tell." She put a hand over her husband's laughing mouth.

"There is no priest to christen at San Carlos now," Juan went on. "José must be baptized in the Presidio chapel, a notice says." He looked up at Don Jorje Allen, the tall Englishman. "Juan built San Carlos, working right with the Padres, so his grandson cannot be baptized there, because there is no priest."

"Oh, Jorje," Petra cried and her eyes begged. "It's so little to ask, when he has given his life to the Mission."

For a minute Jorje Allen didn't say anything, only looked all over Monterey, and out to the bay. The wind blew his light hair. Then he turned to Juan.

"Go and eat, O-nes-e-mo. Then attend to your vegetables and I will see what can be done."

Pablo was pleased to see Juan. He couldn't buy vegetables from him because he had already bought Don Soberanes'

149

vegetables earlier. He explained that he was in a great hurry to go to the wine shop, for company was expected at Casa Soberanes. Then he squatted on his haunches to impart the news.

"You should have been here before, Old One. We have had big doings in Monterey!"

"Not pirates?" Juan asked. "Don Allen didn't say anything."

"He maybe thought you knew the news. Everybody knows." Pablo sniffed. "Governor Figueroa died and his body was lying for a long time in the Royal Chapel so that all could see him. He had a beautiful uniform with even a sword and hat. Fr. Garcia Diego came here to Monterey and Fr. Bernadino Perez, too, and Fr. Real was very busy watching over the body. Yesterday there was a procession of soldiers, and cannons fired, and the dead governor sailed away. He is to be buried, so they say, in Mexico." Pablo stopped for breath.

"I have better news than a dead governor," Juan cried. "I have a grandson, Pablo. Loreta said you were to be godfather to little José when he is christened."

Juan watched Pablo swell up with pride. He was so pleased he didn't even notice when Don Soberanes' wine bottle went over.

"I will give the baby a holy medal," he said. "And when he is older, I will pay for him to go to school. I have no children, and work for money, and still own my stock—"

"Pablo, Loreta is sad. A notice says that the priest comes only to San Carlos de Borromeo once a month for Mass, and San Carlos Day. We will have to bring José into Monterey." He sighed. "Only this morning I tried to stop settlers from taking away the tiles we made—for San Carlos."

"But why can't José be christened on San Carlos Day?" Pablo cried. "The priest will come then, and what is better? Little José can honor the San Carlos. I will have a new suit by then with gold trimmings on it."

"I told Doña Petra Allen, and Don Allen said he would

see," Juan said. "Don Allen understands how it is with an old Indian."

Pablo smiled knowingly. "Juan is not so old but what he knows the most pious Señora in Monterey. Do not fear, Old One. José will be christened in the Mission if it is at all possible. The priest, Fr. Real, will do much for Petra Boronda. And don't forget that Petra made Jorje Allen be christened in church before she married him."

An Indian child came running up, her eyes wide with excitement. "Pablo, Pablo!" she called. "Quick, Don Soberanes is upset. He wants wine. They have waited long, and sent me to find you."

Pablo jumped to his feet, grabbed the wine bottles. "I will have my new suit for José's christening," he called over his shoulder to Juan. "A grand one with gold threads. I'll have a medal for the child, too." He ran down the yellow, winding street as fast as he could with such big wine jugs.

The real business of the day was finished now, and it irked Juan to sit by the vegetables. He put away some of the finest tomatoes for a present for Doña Allen, and made short work of what remained. He had only to call out the prices two or three times before old señoras wearing black dresses, and whiskers on their faces, came from all directions, like buzzards, to buy the fresh vegetables cheap. They even forgot to hold their black shawls tight over their heads, because they were so excited. Two long-toothed ones were soon fighting over a cabbage. They exchanged ugly looks and words flew so fast that neither heard the other.

"I will cut the cabbage," Juan cried, pulling at them. "Each shall have half at the same price."

They had no time for Juan. They were calling each other rabbits and oxen and goats, and Juan's weak voice did not come to their ears.

"Here, here! I shall take the cabbage if you must fight over it!" Don Allen was laughing. "Give it to me." He tossed a

151

coin to Juan, took the cabbage from the hands of astonished señoras, and ran to Abrego's store. Soon he came back and then smiled and presented half a cabbage to each.

"My regards, Señoras, and now cool your anger." Jorje Allen then turned on his heel to face Juan. "It will be possible for Juan O-nes-e-mo's grandchild to be christened in the San Carlos," he said, gaily. "I have seen Father Real."

Juan thought his heart would burst from happiness. He couldn't speak but instead caught up the cloth which had carried the shoes, and filled it with tomatoes. Silently he handed them to Don Allen. As their eyes met, something loosened Juan's tongue. "Tomatoes, from little José to Doña Petra and Don Jorje Allen."

"When do you want the christening, O-nes-e-mo?"

"San Carlos Day. It would be a good omen, then, and the priest would have only one trip to the Mission."

"San Carlos Day it shall be then! I will tell Father Real."

Juan put a hand on the fine cloth of Don Allen's sleeve. "Doña Allen is so beautiful. Would she be José's godmother?"

"I will ask her. If you do not hear, then know that she will come to San Carlos de Borromeo on San Carlos Day to be a godmother." He called an Indian to come and carry the tomatoes to Doña Allen, and then said good-bye.

Juan waited until Don Allen was around the corner of an adobe, and then ran after the Indian. "If you eat any tomatoes, I will kill you next time I come to Monterey, for I shall ask Doña Petra's Indian how many tomatoes were in the cloth." He did his best to look threatening.

Seeing that the young boy was properly terrified, Juan turned and went back to his cart. Swiftly he prepared for the trip to Carmelo.

The day before San Carlos Day, Juan and Loreta put tule brooms and José into the ox cart along with food for a few meals, and started for the Mission.

"Antonio will come on horseback as soon as he can," Loreta said. "He is going to fix the place that is cracked and mend the roof where it leaks to show San Carlos that we have not forgotten."

On the road they met several other neophyte Indians who were going to the feast of San Carlos. The other Indians also felt the need of a bit of work before the Saint should be worshipped at the abandoned Mission.

It seemed strange to Juan to ride between gates swaying crazily from broken hinges, into a compound where three cows lay chewing in the shade of the wall. Wood rats had been busy along the beams, and the empty church needed cleaning. Dust was yellow on the smiling statue of "Our Lady" in her niche and a wood rat had made his nest behind her.

There was little for Juan to do while Loreta and the other women worked in the church, and some of the men cleaned the cow manure from the compound where the fiesta was to be.

He minded José, and told stories to the children who gathered around of the old days and fiestas at San Carlos. While he talked, Juan made wreaths out of the flowers the children had gathered and dumped on the ground before him. One wreath for the statue of the Saint tomorrow when it was carried in the procession. One wreath for Padre Amores, who had been so kind. And a beautiful wreath to put at the feet of the patient statue of "Our Lady" who kept watch over San Carlos now that all the Indians and Padres were gone.

Toward dusk, Antonio rode into the compound on his chestnut horse, the horse that he had broken for Abella. Juan almost thought for a minute that it was the horse he had broken for Padre Amores, but that had been too long ago, and the governor had taken Amores' horse over the hill as taxes. Amores was dead. Old men were forgetful.

"I stopped in at the rancho on my way from Los Laureles and gave the animals feed," Antonio said as he turned his horse loose. "That made me late. I can't see to patch the roof now. I'll have to do it in the morning."

153

Juan was a little dazed—seemed to be mixed up. "But tomorrow is San Carlos Day. That is the one day of the year that Indians eat and feast and do no work." He told this to Antonio. "You must not mend the roof tomorrow. Padre Amores will not like it."

Antonio paused and Juan saw him stare into his eyes a moment and then make for the river. After a while he came with freshly brewed willow tea.

"Drink it, Juan, for you must have fever." He smiled as he handed the rough clay cup. "Don't you remember? José, your grandson, is to be christened tomorrow."

The hot tea made Juan's insides warmer. The mist cleared from his brain and his eyes. Of course. "José Carlos" was the boy's name. Juan would stand up near the font when the Padre said the words!

The church was swept and the altar piled with green pine boughs. All was ready for the coming of the Padre tomorrow. Loreta helped to cook the evening meal, and the youngsters ran happily around the compound.

"Like being back home," Loreta said. "Only there is such loneliness now at the Mission, without the Padres and the prayers and the silver altar ornaments." She sighed. "And so few Indians to worship."

Two dozen Indians slept that night on tule mats in the compound. Juan noticed that the old sleeping room was cold now, for there were many cracks and the door had been taken away. It would be warmer if the door was on and locked as in the old days.

In the morning, the priest arrived in time for early Mass. Right after that Loreta took little José to the river to scrub him. Doña Allen was coming to the services for San Carlos, and to be a godmother to little José. The priest had told so, as he busied himself putting the statue of San Carlos right for the procession.

José yelled when he was washed. He wouldn't stop yelling even when he had his beautiful white christening dress on him,

154

the one with the silver threads that were used only last year for the Christmas star.

He fell asleep at the breast after a while, and Loreta laid him down while she washed and dressed herself. Then they went back up the little trail to the compound.

Antonio had fixed the roof even before the priest had arrived to say Mass. He was weary now, Juan could see by the way Antonio's feet were dragging. The young father went with Juan to the river and helped him wash up.

"Who is to carry the Saint today in the procession?" Juan asked.

Antonio didn't answer, but stooped over the river and washed his face. Then he pulled out of a bundle their clean clothes.

"I asked who will carry the Saint this year?" Juan repeated.

Antonio smiled. "You will be one, Juan, and I hope that I will be another, if God wills. I have never carried the Saint."

"You have not been here as long as Juan, Antonio. When your grandson is christened, maybe you can carry the Saint." He smiled at the tall, handsome man before him, and Antonio laughed, too.

When the bells rang out, there were two *marineros* waiting to see the San Carlos service, and Don Allen had come with the dainty Petra. Pablo was there in a new suit with a leather jacket and stars on it! Pablo's fingers shook as he opened a little box and took out a tiny gold medal. He gave it to Loreta.

"For my godchild, that he may be blessed, and be as faithful and pious as his mother," he said, and there was a softness, Juan saw, in Pablo's eyes as he looked at Loreta.

"You are right, Pablo. Loreta is a good girl. Many a pair of feet would have been cold without her devotion and nimble fingers to knit socks," Don Allen said.

Juan thought he had never seen a Señora so beautiful in the face as Doña Petra when she stood at the yellowed font with his little brown grandchild in her arms. A Madonna she was, her eyes like stars as she repeated the vows that José Car-

155

CATHEDRAL IN THE SUN

los Prealta's spiritual needs would be attended to as long as she, Petra Boronda Allen, should live.

After the christening the Indians went to kneel at the altar. It was hard for Juan to get down. He thought of the time when Loreta was tiny and would not be still, and he had asked the kind San Carlos to remember she was only an Indian baby and forgive her. Now here she was, strong and fine and beautiful, kneeling beside him, the mother of his grandson, with Antonio, her husband, beside her.

This was the first time Juan did not play his fiddle on San Carlos Day, for he had to carry a corner of the statue under its blue satin canopy. Pablo made beautiful clear ringing on his triangle at the back of the church as the hymn started, and the bearers picked up the statue.

"We came to thee, Oh happy Saint,
To claim thy care and love;
To beg thy guidance through this life
To endless bliss above."

Padre Real sang, but Juan's heart ached as he walked. The church was nearly empty except for a few Spanish and the two marineros who had come over the hill from the boat in Monterey bay. And the voice was not Padre Amores', so clear and beautiful. And hardly any Indians except the ones who had come last night.

Juan could not sing. His heart wouldn't let his throat loose. Behind him in the procession he heard Loreta's sweet voice above the others.

"Oh, pray for us, San Carlos,
For dangers hover near;
Oh, pray that God will give us strength
To conquer every fear."

Out of the door they went, and Juan noticed that the tall Vincente, across from him, slowed down his pace so that Juan did not have to breathe so hard, and he was grateful.

156

"And when we've triumphed over sin
And death's dread hour is nigh
Oh, pray that God may angels send
To bear our souls on high."

That was the end. Juan was glad, for the statue had grown heavy and he needed rest now, and quiet.

The heads bowed while Father Real said a prayer. San Carlos had been honored. Juan wondered what the good Saint thought when he saw among the people honoring him, the very ones who had taken away tiles with the knee of O-nes-e-mo marked on the inside.

Doña Petra smiled at José, and gave Loreta a beautiful medal for him, before she got into the cart to go home. Don Allen shook Antonio by the hand, and then warned Juan not to let womenfolks fight over his cabbages again.

The barbecue was ready, but Father Real didn't stay. Loreta helped to pour wine and pass tortillas and meat to all. Antonio gave out beans from the stone pot.

Some Spaniards were there with guitars and violins, and sweet-voiced Mexicans sang. Juan sat on a mat in the shade to watch. The two marineros were making merry and danced a marinero dance. They seemed to be enjoying the fiesta of San Carlos. Loreta came with José to sit near Juan. After a while one of the marineros came seeking shade. He wiped sweat from his brow and said in good Spanish that it was too hot under California sun to dance English dances. He sat down beside Juan.

"I haven't had such a good meal in a year," he said. "They give us very poor food on the boat, and no good place to sleep. We're practically slaves to the master of the boat."

"Today was special. San Carlos Day and my grandson christened," Juan said.

The young marinero smiled and wished the baby well.

"A lot of English here. I've seen them on the street in Monterey," he told Juan.

157

"Don Jorje Allen and Don Juan Bautista Cooper, and the schoolmaster Hartnell, are all English," Juan told the *marinero*. "They are good to Indians. Honest, too."

Suddenly the boy turned to Juan. "I've a mind to desert the ship," he said. "I'm sick of poor food and no rest and a lot of hard work."

"You are young," Juan said and noted down on the upper lip of the fair young man.

"But I'm strong. I can work." There was a twinkle in his eye. "And I am honest, too."

"They will catch you, and then put you in irons," Juan warned. "Juan has seen this before now, when a *marinero* deserted a ship."

"I'll hide. I'm willing to risk it. I'll die if I do not get food and rest."

"You are young," Juan insisted.

"Eighteen."

"I do not know years. Indians grow like the grass without measuring."

"We will hide you," Antonio told the *marinero* after he had talked to Loreta. "Loreta says it is bad to have no rest and not enough food, and that Englishmen here can give you work."

"I'll do anything you ask, if only you'll help me. My mother is a widow in England. There is nothing there for me. I want new country. I'll work!" the youth cried excitedly. Juan saw that his hands were raw and rough from work and were shaking now.

"Hush! There are ears to hear you. *Marineros* often try to leave the ship at Monterey, because of señoritas and the gentle climate," Juan said. "If other ears are listening, we cannot help you hide."

"You're right. I'm sorry. But if you knew how I've suffered—"

"What about your *comero*, the other *marinero*?"

"He's homesick. He wants England, but he'll never tell."

158

It was arranged that Antonio, Juan, and Loreta were to start with their cart along the road, and the young *marinero* was to join in the races and games of the fiesta. Then after a while he was to follow along the winding road to the hills. In the willows near the village of Los Beracos, Antonio would meet him with an empty ox cart. He could hide in the cart.

"You are good. I'll repay you a thousandfold for this," the boy said. "Jack Preble never forgets those who befriend him."

"Perhaps it is the San Carlos who does this," Juan murmured. "I have been beaten by soldiers, too. I know the running-away feeling."

Antonio smiled and called good-bye to all. The cart creaked out of the compound, and nearly bumped into the cows that were coming home as usual to the ruins, their night quarters.

Chapter XVIII

ENGLISH MEDICINE FOR BONES: 1835

JUAN liked this *marinero*, Jack Preble. He had a smile and
a willing hand for work, even if he didn't know all the
words to talk in Spanish. He understood about Juan's old
bones aching, too.

"I know what will help you," he said early the next day.
"You draw the cold from the ground. You should have a bed,
up from the earth, to keep out the aches."

"No, only Spanish in Monterey have beds with lace covers.
Not Indians. Always Indians sleep on the ground."

The young *marinero* just stood and looked at Juan for a
minute, thinking. "You said Indians didn't have corn before
the Padres came. You ate acorns and roots, didn't you?" he
asked a bit crossly.

Juan nodded.

"Now you like corn better, don't you?"

Juan nodded.

"Then let me make you a bed to help your aches. If you
don't like it you can go back to the ground." With a set jaw,
young Jack took tree branches and made a framework which
he lashed together with rawhide thongs. Then he laced thongs
back and forth to make a platform. Juan watched, and was
afraid of this new thing. You could fall off a platform in your
sleep.

"Be still and see," Loreta said in Room-se-en language to
Juan, as Jack worked. "Remember José Manuel Boronda
thought the great grinding stones would work, and he was the
only one; they *did* work and made Indian women feel better
with no grinding to do."

160

"Now we'll put straw on this, and then your hides," the marinero told Juan as he straightened up and looked at his work. "You will like it. In England we all have beds, and sleep better, too."

"All Indians have tule mats in Carmelo and sleep good," Juan insisted in spite of Loreta's shaking her head at him.

"But this is progress," Jack cried excitedly. "Don't you want to improve? To live better without aches?"

Juan didn't know. He watched Loreta put her hand on the marinero's arm. "It is fine," she said and smiled. "If Juan will not sleep in it, I will. The old are always against things they do not understand." Then she went to till the garden.

After a while, Juan sat on the platform, but he couldn't trust it enough to take his feet from the floor. It was nice to sit on, and did not make old muscles pull on sore bones so much as squatting on the floor.

He sat very quiet, not daring to move for fear this new thing called a bed would fall to pieces under him. Because he didn't want to meet the eager eye of young Jack, Juan looked out across the land below, and wondered what Indians in the Mission compound would think of Juan O-nes-e-mo perching up in the air like a bird to sleep! He tried to figure ways for an old Indian to be sharp enough to get his own way against Loreta and this young marinero they had taken in.

Then he saw Loreta drop her tilling stick and come running toward them. "Quick, hide," she cried. "Marineros and a soldier coming! Over the hill on horseback. They may be looking for you!" She darted toward the ox cart. "In here! I'll cover you with grass."

Young Jack caught up his coat and sprinted for the cart. He was curled up in the bottom before Juan had time to pull himself from the bed. It took so long for stiff joints to move. After they were started, it was not so bad.

As Juan helped Loreta to pile straw over the marinero, he kept an eye out for the little posse that made a cloud of yellow dust down on the road. When no blue of Jack's clothes showed through the straw, Juan scuffed out the tracks made from *marinero* boots. Loreta went to her garden and returned with several heads of cabbage.

"Sometimes a wind comes," she said to the cart. "A cabbage or two will hold down the straw."

Juan was pleased that Loreta remembered the wind. An old man forgets, and Indians must always be awake and not let mistakes slip in and cause troubles.

Down at Los Beracos the music was going in the fandango houses, and now and then loud voices came up through the trees.

"They will go there first," Loreta nodded in the direction of the music. Then she went in to give the breast to little José who had started to howl.

Juan laughed. "Men all make noise about drinks," he said. "The little ones cry for want of them, and old ones because they have had too many." He took up the shoe he had been sewing before the *marinero* insisted that he try the bed.

Horses' hoofs clattered on the hard dry earth in front of the hut. Juan watched the men dismount and throw the reins over their saddles.

"Seen a *marinero*?" a tall, ugly-faced man in a sailor's suit asked. "One's deserted. A youngster."

Juan nodded his head. "Yes."

Out of the corner of his eye, he watched Loreta. Her face did not change, but as she looked down on José, Juan knew she was upset at his words. It was well to frighten her a little, to make her more careful next time, and to train her never to move a muscle of the face so it would tell a tale.

The man smiled and looked at another man. "You see, I was right. Preble wouldn't stick around Monterey."

"Where'd you see him? Where is he now?" the soldier demanded.

"He was at the Fiesta San Carlos yesterday, at the Mission," Juan said and held up the knitted cap that Jack Preble had forgotten. "This his cap?"

"Sure, that's it!" They were excited now. "Where'd you get it?"

Juan only smiled. "A different cap from Spanish. Maybe someday my grandson will wear this cap." Juan pointed to the little brown head against Loreta's breast.

"So you hooked Preble's cap in church, eh?" The man threw back his head and roared with laughter. "That's a good one. A savage in a sailor's cap." Then they all laughed and Juan joined them.

"Look under the bed," a man cried. "I don't trust these brownskins."

"A nice bed," Juan patted the new straw, and smiled as the man got down on his knees to look under. "You want the cap?" he added, and held the knitted black cap toward them.

There was a sniff. "Keep it. You've most likely all of you tried it on. It'll be full of lice by now." Then they laughed again. "Quite a hatful for young Jack Preble."

"He'll be past worrying over mere lice when he gets into irons," the tall man said. They looked around the cart, and into the shelter where the oxen stayed in wet weather.

Juan took up his sewing again. Then he had a thought. He reached into the old cloth that had once been pantaloons, and fetched out a pair of dainty satin-trimmed shoes.

"You like pretty shoes for your women?" he asked.

"Look at what the old man is showing!" the youngest of the posse cried. "Anna wouldn't look bad in those."

Juan smiled. "I make shoes for best families in Monterey."

"Better not trust your girl in those. She might do a dance with someone else while you are at sea," the man laughed. But after a while they each took a pair of Juan's shoes, and he had, in exchange, a big knife, a belt buckle of silver, and handkerchiefs from England.

"Did you look over in the fandango houses for the *marinero?*" Loreta asked in a low voice as she laid little José down on the bed.

"Not yet, we saved the best place for the last! Come on."

163

They mounted the horses and tied the newly purchased shoes to their saddles.

"If you would like food, I can give you fresh things," Loreta offered. "You are welcome."

They shook their heads, and put spurs to the bellies of the horses. "Good luck to Preble's cap and to you two," a man called as he turned his horse in the direction of Los Beracos.

For a minute after the men had gone, Loreta was silent, then in a low voice she said, "We forgot the cap. They might have caught him."

Juan sniffed. "The young are careless about small things. It still takes an old Indian to lead soldiers away from what they are after, without telling even one little lie. 'Our Lady' and Jesus will not be angry!"

"You must stay there, *Marinero*, until we see them go away from the fandango houses. They might come back," Loreta whispered into the cart as she made to pick up twigs for the fire. "Eyes at Los Beracos may have seen you here."

Toward sundown, Te-mo came riding up to the hut. He was very proud of the horse he rode, a horse bartered from a Mission Indian. Juan saw that even Te-mo's joints were stiff, for it took the Indian a long time to get off his horse. He came and sat down on the mat near Juan.

"The Mexicans came and burned down the *rancheria* two nights ago," he said. "They told me the land was theirs. They showed me papers. I had no papers to show them."

"Where are your woman and children now?" Juan asked.

"In the place of the big oak, up on the hill." Suddenly Te-mo saw the new thing the *marinero* called a bed.

"What is that?" he cried.

"Your bones hurt, Te-mo?" Juan asked, trying to keep eagerness out of his voice.

Te-mo nodded. "Nothing helps now for Te-mo's aching bones, not even *yerba la vebra*," he groaned. "Only under the ground for maggots, will take away Te-mo's aches. Sweat house only tires me."

164

Juan pointed to the bed. "You sleep on that. It takes away aches. A marinero told Juan, and fixed this cure for him."

Te-mo took another look at the bed.

"You sleep on it, Te-mo, and then tell Juan if the aches are better," Juan insisted. "It is very fine. Te-mo was good to Juan with sea-otter skins. Now Juan will let Te-mo sleep on the bed." He moved José from the bed and urged Te-mo to lie down, and then held his breath as the Indian took both feet from the floor to try the platform. "The marinero says that old Indians draw aches from the ground. You sleep here, aches go."

Juan waited. Nothing happened when Te-mo stretched himself out on the bed.

Finally the old Indian smiled. "The marinero was right. Takes away hardness. Te-mo will have one."

Juan drew himself up. "Only this one that the marinero said things over, cures aches." He came closer. "You can have this one. You let Juan have sea-otter skins that time."

"No, no," Loreta objected. "It is your bed, Juan. The marinero made it for you."

Te-mo turned on his side and thumped the bed. "Ten cowhides I will give for this."

Juan paid no attention to Loreta's black looks. "It is yours for ten cowhides, but first the hides, before Te-mo takes away the bed that brings peace to bad bones."

The old Indian sat near the fire and ate tortillas Loreta gave him. "My sons will bring the hides and take away the bed in the moonlight tonight. Te-mo wants no other night without the bed." He hobbled to his horse and took the animal to a rock so that he could climb more easily to the saddle.

The dance music was still going at the fandango house in Los Beracos. Juan heard the voices of English marineros there. He took tortillas out to marinero Jack Preble in the cart.

"It is better that you stay until they are gone. A drunken man shoots quickly and is often cruel."

Loreta blessed the food and they ate. Juan looked down into

the garden already tilled for rain. "It has been a good day, to-day," he murmured. "I sold shoes, and the bed. Much better day than selling vegetables in Monterey."

"That is because of the marinero," Loreta said. "Without him, the men would not have come here to buy shoes. And you would never have had a bed to sell if the marinero hadn't made it." Then she sighed. "I am sorry you let Te-mo have the bed. You would not part with Padre Amores' fiddle. The bed was a gift, too."

Juan thought back. "I was willing to let Te-mo have the fiddle once, to get scratch for you," he murmured. "But San Carlos saved the fiddle for Juan. Better Te-mo fall off the platform than Juan breaking his bones."

It was late, and still songs and laughter came from the fandango house. Te-mo's sons arrived with the hides, and took away the bed, the three of them lifting it on their heads so that they walked inside a cage. That made Juan laugh. He folded the stiff hides and put them under his tule mat, and then curled up to sleep.

"I will watch to help the marinero," Loreta said and sat looking at the light at Los Beracos.

Finally hoofs sounded on the road, and roistering voices called compliments to the ladies. Then the posse headed back over the hills to Monterey.

Loreta went to tell the marinero that it was safe now. When he climbed out of the cart and shook his cramped legs, she got up her courage.

"My father was afraid of the bed you made. He had Te-mo, a gentile Indian, try it first. Te-mo liked it so much that my father let him have the bed for ten cowhides. Te-mo's sons brought the hides and took the bed away." She lowered her voice. "I am sorry. It was beautiful and would have been comfortable for an old man."

There was only a good-natured laugh. "Juan is clever, a bargainer. Ten hides is a good price for a bed. I'll make him another to sell."

166

Chapter XIX

TREACHERY: 1835

THE English trader stayed in port for repairs to her keel. Jack Preble was restless. He wanted to be away from hiding and at work.

"Not until the sails are unfurled and she goes," Juan told him. "There are eyes and tongues that would do you harm. An old man knows the young find days very long, but time spent in irons is not worth much."

When Jack's raw hands healed a bit, Juan taught him how to make shoes, and found that in no time the young *marinero's* fingers were as nimble as his own. The boy soon figured ways to make work easier, short-cuts that Juan frowned on at first, and then later adopted.

Toward the end of the week Antonio rode in for a meal. He was on the way to Monterey with two fine horses that he had tamed for his master, José Manuel Boronda. They had been sold to officers at the fort.

"How is it going?" he asked the young *marinero.*

"Slow enough. I don't like to take advantage of good nature this way. The boat should be on its way by this time."

"Jack is good," Juan said, as he sipped hot stew made from rabbits and the vegetables that Loreta grew. "I taught him to make shoes, and now he is quicker and better at it than the master."

Loreta was pleased, and smiled at Juan. "He made a bed for Juan," she told Antonio, "but Te-mo liked it better and gave us ten cowhides for it. Jack will make the grandfather O-nes-e-mo another and the little José shall sleep on it, too."

A thought came to Juan. "Antonio, you have horses going to Monterey?"

167

Antonio nodded.

"Then take the hides Te-mo gave for the bed, and bring back as many soft, tanned hides as you can get for them," Juan said. "With the new shoemaker we are running out of leather, and I must teach him to make saddles if he is to be a ranchero."

"A pack will do the horses good," Antonio said later, as he strapped the hides to the shining brown backs. "Do you want me to sell the shoes, too, Grandfather O-nes-e-mo?"

Juan was pleased at being called grandfather. He smiled but shook his head.

"In trading, Antonio, you are too kind-hearted. Juan can get more if he bargains his own work."

Loreta left little José beside Juan, and climbed on the back of Antonio's horse to ride down the road a way. Juan took up his sewing, and Preble cut out soles. Heat waves quivered on the yellow hillside, and flies made little black patches on bits of food that had been dropped on the ground around the opening of the hut. The two men worked in silence for a time.

"I am a blacksmith by trade," Jack said.

Juan looked up. "What is that?"

"Heating iron to shoe horses. A forge to make the iron the shape you need. Cart wheels would be good with iron bands around them, O-nes-e-mo. They would not wear out so fast, or shake apart."

"When you are free, that would be good to do," Juan said. "Long ago, the Padre said iron bands might come on the ship from Spain or Mexico for the cart wheels, but Juan never saw any."

"I was only an apprentice boy to a smith, but I learned a lot before I ran away to sea." Jack looked off toward the hills. "My mother most likely misses me. She will be waiting for me to come back on the ship, waiting with a treat of ham and marmalade and a good cup of tea." The boy sighed, and Juan saw the lump move up and down in his throat.

Juan did not know ham and marmalade the boy spoke

168

about, but he knew the meaning of a sigh. He often sighed himself, since the Padres had gone from Carmelo. His own lump stuck halfway in his throat sometimes when he thought of the light from beautiful candles and the music and singing, and then he saw that the Mission was dark, and silent, and cold, with only swallows to make noise in the old bell tower.

Loreta came along the hot yellow road. Her bare feet made no sound. She sat a few minutes to rest, and brushed away flies from the face of her sleeping José. After a while she went to work in the garden.

Midday eating-time passed the next day, but Antonio did not share the stew and the beautiful berry *empanadas* that Loreta had made from dried berries, as a special treat. They all laughed when the *marinero* called them "tarts," and said he had tasted better ones in England!

When the sun was low and very hot against the eastern side of the hills, Juan looked up from waxing a thread and saw a horseman racing toward the hut.

Don Juan Bautista Cooper was off his horse before Jack Preble could hide himself in the cart, for Juan had not been able to call alarm to Loreta and old men are slow on their feet.

"Stop!" Don Cooper cried. "Who are you?"

The boy stood by the cart white and frightened. "Jack Preble, sir," he said.

Loreta ran up the hill. "He is our friend," she told Don Cooper. "He is English and good and would kill himself rather than go back to the boat to such poor food and no place to sleep."

Jack Preble stiffened himself. "She's right. I would kill myself. I never want to go back. I won't go back."

Loreta went close to Don Cooper. "He is English like you, Don Cooper. You would not let an Englishman be put in irons and punished because he needs food and sleep?" Juan saw Loreta smile up into the big Englishman's face.

"No, Loreta, I wouldn't," Cooper said. "That is not what

169

I came for." He turned to Juan. "Antonio is in great trouble, O-nes-e-mo. They caught him trying to trade ten of Señor Rodriquez' hides that were stolen."

"No!" Juan cried. "He did not steal them. They were my hides that I gave to him to trade."

"That's what he said, O-nes-e-mo, but the brand was on the hides, and Rodriquez knows that now you do not rope well enough or ride a horse swiftly enough to rope, and kill, and skin, ten cows. Rodriquez' range is very near to Los Laureles where Antonio Prealta works—" Don Cooper was looking right into Juan's eyes. "It is an Indian's word against a Spaniard's word." He paused. "In a Spaniard's country."

"No—" Loreta said. "Te-mo gave the hides for the bed that the *marinero* made for Juan O-nes-e-mo."

"Yes," Jack Preble put in. "I made the bed and the old man sold it for the hides."

"Antonio told that, too," Cooper shook his head. "But Rodriquez is sure that Antonio is a thief. The Alcalde has sent soldiers to bring Te-mo."

"I'm going to Monterey and tell them. I know! I made the bed. I'm no Indian. They'll believe *me*." The words were short-clipped and determined. Juan looked at the white face of the young *marinero*.

"No—" Loreta said. "They will catch you and put you in irons."

"I'll not let an innocent man be branded a thief when I can defend him!" The boy ran to the little pasture, and raced after a horse.

"Loreta, get the ox cart. Old bones cannot stand such speed as horses make." Juan sighed. "I will go. If Te-mo is there and Juan is there, that will be enough." He moved gently off the mat, for his joints were very stiff today.

Don Cooper just stood watching the excitement, and then his eyes met Juan's. "You'd better go, Juan, but there is Spanish anger abroad. That is why I came to tell you on my way home." He climbed his horse, and rode over to the pasture

170

where Jack Preble walked beside a horse. "Do you realize that
the jig is up for you if you go to Monterey now? You'll be
sent back to England in irons, boy."

Juan saw the *marinero's* face turn white.

"These people are my friends," he said. "They took me in.
It is my turn to help them. Surely that Spaniard will hear me
out and take my word." He walked on past Don Cooper.

As Juan helped Loreta put the yoke over the head of the
oxen, he saw that Loreta had heard the *marinero*. Her hands
were shaking.

"Maybe they won't take your word," Don Cooper called.

"Then I will have done my best." The boy was on his horse
now. He rode swiftly to where Juan and Loreta were working,
and leaned over to shake their hands. "Most likely I won't see
you again," he said. "I thank you for all you have done, and
I wish you well."

"No—" said Loreta in a low voice. "You will do no good
by going."

"But he will!" Don Cooper cried excitedly. "He has stuck
by his friends. He's a bloody Britisher to the bone!" He rode
up to the three, and put a hand on the boy's arm. "The boat
left this morning. There's work for you, lad, down the coast at
my rancho when you get through helping Antonio. I like a
man who is not afraid of irons when it comes to doing right."
Don Cooper spurred his horse, and they watched him gallop
toward the road.

Loreta insisted on taking José and riding with Juan in the
ox cart.

"He is my Antonio," was all she said, when Juan told her
to stay at home and mind José.

"You're right," the *marinero* said. "But it's no place for a
woman with a baby if the Spaniards and Mexicans are filled
with anger."

"He is my Antonio," Loreta repeated, and climbed into the
cart.

"I'll ride ahead and tell them my story, and that Juan O-nes-e-mo is coming." Jack Preble dug his heels into the horse and raced toward Monterey. A strange sight he was too—a sailor on horseback, with his cap awry on his blonde curls, and the wide bottoms of his blue mariner's trousers flapping in the wind.

It was quite dark when the ox cart creaked through the winding street of Monterey toward the house of the alcalde. Loreta had given little José the breast in order to have him asleep and quiet when they arrived.

There was a light in the front room, and horses were tied to trees at the side of the house. It took Juan quite a time to limber his joints enough to get out of the cart. Loreta helped him down, almost lifted him. It was bad for an old man to be so slow. His heart was pounding so much that it was hard to breathe.

"I am praying to the good San Carlos," Loreta said quietly at his side. "He has helped us often before now. Do not be afraid." Her arm tightened on his, and it gave Juan strange comfort. He stopped to murmur a prayer himself to "Our Lady" before he knocked at the door of the Alcalde's house.

The door opened, and a beam of light shone out into the night. Light from a sperm-oil lamp that was fixed to the ceiling. Juan couldn't keep his eyes from this new light!

"Here is O-nes-e-mo," a man called into the room.

Juan walked in, and Loreta followed with little José in her arms. The door closed behind them and Juan just stood there with Loreta by his side.

The low adobe room was full of Spaniards and Mexicans smoking pipes. Te-mo was between two soldiers. Jack Preble, very white in the face, was leaning against the wall, and over in a corner on the dirt floor was Antonio, his hands and feet bound by rawhide thongs.

"Well?" The alcalde, a thick-necked swarthy man, raised heavy black eyebrows and looked right into Juan's eyes. "You came. Now what have you to say?"

Something hurt inside Juan. There was so little to say when

172

a Spaniard looked at you that way. He had seen governors and soldiers have that look when they were around Indians, and he already knew what it meant.

"The hides were not Antonio's," Juan managed. "They were Juan's, traded by Te-mo for the bed that the marinero Señor Preble made."

"You see? I told you," Preble put in excitedly. "I made the bed."

"Hush, you," the alcalde said angrily. "What good is the word of a runaway marinero? A newcomer. A seagoing foreigner who takes our trade." The alcalde turned toward Te-mo.

"Te-mo is here. Let him speak about the hides."

One of the soldiers gave Te-mo a prod, and Juan saw an angry twitch to the Indian's mouth. The eyes were sullen.

"Te-mo has never seen the hides," he said quietly. "I do not even see Mission Indians. I am a gentile Indian."

Juan's heart pounded so much that breath would not come.

"Well?" demanded the alcalde, looking at him.

"Te-mo has the bed," Loreta said from behind. "The bed the marinero made—"

"This is no petticoat trial," the alcalde roared. "Out with the woman. This is a man's place to talk." He motioned to the soldiers to put Loreta out.

She went quietly. Juan saw her look a moment at Antonio, before the door closed behind her.

"You don't give them a chance," Jack Preble cried. "You're unfair. I was there. I made the bed and saw Antonio strap the hides on the horses."

"Your opinion is not asked, Runaway." Soldiers moved to the side of the boy. The alcalde stuck out his chest. "I'm not to be talked to that way. I am representing Governor Gutierrez in Monterey." Then he turned to Te-mo.

"Do you have a bed?"

The Indian nodded.

"Where did you get it?"

173

"My sons made it after I saw O-nes-e-mo's bed," Te-mo said. "They only copied the bed the *marinero* made."

There was a loud, long, laugh that seemed to fill the room. "What a trial!" Don Hartnell cried. "We really should take a few minutes off to drink to Te-mo who lies so well."

The alcalde turned good-naturedly to Don Hartnell. "What do you mean, Schoolmaster?"

Hartnell stood under the light, his pipe in his hand. After a hearty laugh, he said, "Why, Alcalde, Te-mo said that he was a gentile Indian and never even saw Mission Indians. He seemed proud of the fact. Then he turns around and says after he saw Juan O-nes-e-mo's bed, well, he just hopped home and copied it! How could he see the bed if he did not go to see Juan O-nes-e-mo? You swallow *that* against the word of O-nes-e-mo, Mission Builder, to whose grandson the Señora Petra is godmother?"

The room was in an uproar. Pipes came out of mouths that turned up in laughter.

"Well done, Schoolmaster," someone shouted. Even the oil lamps fluttered with excitement.

"Maybe there *is* something in this Latin learning after all," a voice called out from behind Juan. "The schoolmaster has sharp wits from writing essays, maybe?"

Don Hartnell cackled again, such a merry laugh that made everyone want to laugh with him.

"That's a jingle. How did Te-mo see the bed, if Te-mo didn't see the Indian who owned the bed?" Hartnell sang. "Let's make a song of it."

"Give the hides to Señor Rodriquez," the alcalde ordered soldiers. "Turn Antonio loose. Te-mo is the one to punish for this. He is not a Mission Indian, so doesn't know truth. Punish Te-mo so well that never again will we be gathered to hear of *his* sins!"

Juan saw the alcalde's eyes glisten with eagerness for an Indian's punishment—any Indian's punishment. They would probably *hang* Te-mo.

"Be careful about what you say of truth, Señor! Those are dangerous words. There might be others who are not Mission Indians in this crowd. Those who sometimes *stretch* the truth," Don Soberanes cried gaily. "Come to my place and we'll celebrate."

Juan was pushed back against the wall in the rush of feet toward the door. Black looks were gone now, and eyes sparkled with merriment. Jack Preble circled around and stood next to Juan, and they waited for a chance to get out.

Don Hartnell passed. He put his hand for a moment on the shoulder of young Jack.

"Careful, boy, do not be too indignant with these people. You are an outsider, an Englishman. Some day you may want to have land of your own and be a settler as we are. Officials do not forget those who step on their toes," he said in a low voice. "And remember, ridicule and laughter provide a way of fighting that saves gunpowder and lives." With a wink he passed on and out of the door.

Loreta moved into the light that came from the doorway and helped Juan through the dark, toward the ox cart. He was glad he didn't have to look again at Te-mo. A Satan surely had worked inside Te-mo to make him say he didn't know about the hides. Juan mumbled prayers as he walked. He asked the Good God and the Lady of Sorrows to forgive the soul of Te-mo who didn't understand and was not a Mission Indian.

Loreta helped Juan into the cart. The sons of Te-mo brushed near her as they walked to their horses. A low hiss came to her ears. "For *this* O-nes-e-mos will suffer until the sun is dark," the tall one told her in Room-se-en. He hit Loreta hard in the back with his elbow and then moved on.

"San Carlos watches over us always. Do not fear, Loreta," Juan managed, as soon as he could put some of the terrible fear from his own heart. "O-nes-e-mos are faithful to San Carlos." He hoped the saint was not too busy with Spaniards and Mexicans and Americanos to notice the prayers and troubles of Indians.

175

"I'll ride in the cart," Jack Preble told Antonio. "I know you would rather ride your own horse."

"I must ride Don Boronda's horse back; the one I rode to town on yesterday," Antonio said. "But it would be nice to ride in the cart with Loreta and little José. I see them such long times apart."

"Then let me ride the horse I came on, and lead the other, and you drive the cart!" Preble begged. "At least I can do that. I'll hurry ahead, and when you arrive there will be a fire and maybe some stew all hot."

"He is a good man," Antonio said as Preble went off with the two horses, and he climbed into the cart beside Loreta. Little José whimpered under his covering, and Loreta fed him as they creaked over the road toward Carmelo.

Juan crossed himself when they passed the Mission which already showed cracks of moonlight through the ruins. Sadly he looked up in the bell tower, but there was no bell. Someone had taken the sweet bell away from the Mission. What would call Indians to prayers now?

It was nearly dawn when they arrived at the rancho. Jack Preble had been as good as his word, and there was the warm glow of a fire to welcome them. A pot bubbled with stew.

Loreta did not speak until after Antonio had his food to eat. Juan was content to sit on a tule mat near the fire and warm his aching bones. There had been fog and wind, and the ride home was a bit cold for the old.

"You made a good friend today, Señor Jack," Loreta said as she sat down by the fire. "Don Juan Bautista Cooper is a good Englishman. Indians work for him and he feeds them well, treats them good. They like him."

"And Don Hartnell, too," Juan put in. "He talked to you and by the eyelid-drop Juan knows he likes you."

"Someday I won't be just a runaway," Jack said hotly. "Someday I'll be a settler, a landholder like they are now, and I'll get it back at those people who won't let an innocent man

176

speak, or give those who come to defend him, a chance! You see."

"Indians are used to that," Juan sighed, as he saw the boy's set jaw. "What can you do when even the Padres that came first have been turned out?"

The boy mumbled something Juan could not understand, about "laws." But Juan grew suddenly tired and it didn't matter. Jack was like all young gulls, high flights but short ones. It was better not to fly so high, but to keep flying. Juan settled down on his tule mat to try to sleep and forget for a time that this was a Mexican country now, and Indians must do as Mexicans thought.

Chapter XX

THE TREE OF THREE CROSSES: 1835

JACK PREBLE often dropped in to see Juan and Loreta on his way from Monterey where he went to do business for Don Cooper. Juan, too old now to go alone and sell his shoes, counted time by the visits of the young *marinero*, for he brought news.

"Just came to see if you sold the second bed I made for you," he would say, and grin.

Not long before Christmas, he arrived one day at the little rancho just after Juan, Loreta, and Antonio had returned from a pilgrimage to the Mission.

"The Mission is bad now," Juan sighed. "I am ashamed to have San Carlos hear Indians singing from such a cracked church."

Winter rains had melted adobe walls of mission buildings now that there were no tiles on the roof to shed water and protect them. Juan said that the cracks in the church had widened in the last earthquake until there was a hole in the roof above the niche of "Our Lady," and a beam of sunlight came across her face and faded the paint.

"Who has charge of the Mission?" Preble asked. "Surely they'll fix up the roof."

"Romero is the one," Juan sighed. "But he says there is no money for missions. The Padres' fund is used by Mexican settlers, and Mission stock put on settlers' ranchos, so there is not even a hide to sell."

"Why don't you ask the governor?"

Juan looked into Preble's blue eyes. "You are new here. Indians know better than to bother governors. That only makes them think about Indians. Alvarado, the secretary, already thinks too much about getting land and stock away from Indians."

Preble kicked the dust. He watched Loreta as she made tortillas for a while before he spoke. "Loreta, do you think we should repair the Mission?"

Juan saw that Loreta did not look up. She only nodded.

"The Padres were good to Indians. Juan helped to build the Mission, and arranged the altar there. . . . Juan is too old to fix the Mission now. So few Indians remember how good the Padres were."

Preble spat far out in the yellow soil. A bit of dust came up.

"I'm not much on churches myself, and I wouldn't know a saint if I met one on the road, but I've a strong back and a willing pair of hands," Jack said. "If we could find a few other people to work, we can perhaps keep the church from going to pieces."

"Yes," Juan nodded. "That's the way San Carlos thinks. Juan cannot work, but the fiddle will sing for you as you work, and call attention to the saints that we have not forgotten them."

"We will have a fiesta, Marinero Jack," Antonio said. "I will help. Don José Manuel Boronda will be happy to have Antonio work for the Saints after Mass on Sunday. His sister, Doña Petra, is José's godmother."

Loreta was pleased. "The food will come from here," she cried. "*Empanada*, tortillas with herbs, frijoles—"

"I will ask Don Cooper if it is all right to bring Indians to work." Preble was excited. "We will meet after the priest has gone away on Sunday."

Loreta looked kindly at him. "Perhaps the work will go easier on the back and hands, if Jack comes to hear Mass first, with Antonio, and Juan and Loreta."

Word went up the Carmelo for faithful Indians to come and work and make fiesta after Mass on Sunday. Jack Preble was to spread the news to Indian converts working on the great rancho of Don Juan Bautista Cooper.

The very next day Loreta started Juan to work about fiesta food.

"You, Grandfather O-nes-e-mo, and little José, must sit in the sun and pick out rocks from the dried beans, and get them ready for me to cook," she said, first thing after prayers and tortillas.

Juan wished he could move quickly as Loreta did, and no bones to hurt. In an eye-wink she had the beans in front of him, and José on a mat beside him.

José was no help at all. Soon the boy was busy trying to shove a dried bean into his belly-button. The bean slipped out of his little brown fingers and he carefully picked up another one, to have a new try. Juan stopped work to laugh at his grandson. Loreta didn't seem to mind. She looked up from her hoeing, shaded her eyes from the sun, and smiled at them. She knew that an old Indian and a young Indian had many things about them the same, and neither old nor young could be counted on for much.

But there was to be a different fiesta on the Carmelo after Mass on Sunday. A vaquero rode up to the tule hut one morning and leaned from his horse.

"Antonio lies dead and swelled up, in the gulch near the spring of Weeping Eyes," he said. "No one knows when he was shot." The vaquero looked sadly at Loreta who stood with José pulling at her skirts. "We covered him with oak branches to keep the buzzards away for a while. Te-mo's sons were seen around."

Loreta's face didn't change. She put her hands together, leaving the baby to keep his balance the best he could on wobbly legs. Then Juan saw her lips move in prayer. He bowed his head, and tried to remember all the words of the prayers for the dead that the Padres had taught him. But he was dizzy, and an old man forgets, and Padre Amores was calling for the fiddle, calling for sweet music to show Antonio the way to the new world where he was a foreigner, a stranger. Juan shoved himself along on his haunches until he could reach the fiddle bag.

"Anything I can do?" the vaquero asked. The words came from far away, through so many thoughts.

"Just tell the Father Real at the church in Monterey," Loreta said. "I will go with the ox cart and fetch Antonio. Only two days until Sunday Mass. Proper time so that Padre Real can say Mass for Antonio, and we will bury him under the oak of Three Crosses where Father Serra used to bless the Indian bodies."

"I'll tell him," the vaquero said, and turned his horse toward the road again.

Juan didn't look up. The fiddle strings were in need of tightening. Tuning was heavy business for stiff fingers.

Loreta sat down and pulled little José to her so that he sat on her lap, and was encircled when her hands were together in prayer.

Juan put the fiddle to his chin and played as sweetly and softly as he could with knobby fingers. He hoped that the holy music would push Los Beracos fandango music away, so that Loreta could say her prayers without hearing the jangling guitars. It was better for an old man to help this way than to offer half-forgotten prayers. Padre Amores had told him God understood things without words.

After a while Loreta got up and cooked tortillas. She fed Juan and José, and put a few of the cakes into a bit of cloth, then hitched the oxen to the cart.

"If the buzzards haven't eaten him, I will bring him back," she said. "Take care of José." Another thought struck her as she started toward the road, for she turned. "If I do not get back in time, you had better take José and walk to the Mission, so that the Father will know I am coming," she said quietly. "Sometimes vaqueros find wine or the smiles of señoritas make them forgetful." Without looking again at José, Loreta drove toward the hills.

181

José played with his grandfather, but did not seem to listen when his grandfather fiddled for him. Not even the most beautiful chants affected the baby. At last, when thoughts were as heavy on Juan's chest as the meat from old grizzly bears, which always made him feel heavy in the stomach, he tried the hymn to San Carlos and sang the words.

> "Thy purity has won for thee
> A crown of fadeless light.
> Oh, may its radiance shine on us
> And cheer the gloom of night."

The baby wasn't even listening. Instead he threw great handfuls of yellow dirt up and let the dust fall onto his head. But the hymn brought light and beauty back to Juan. It made him think of the young Antonio who had put up the star only last Christmas; Antonio who had been the father of his grandson, and yet never even carried a corner of the statue of San Carlos in the procession. Juan was an old man and had carried it many times, and was ready to die, yet he went on living.

Why not mend the roof and fix up the Mission in honor of Antonio Prealta who had walked into the Mission to become a neophyte such a little time ago? Not even two Christmas Days had he spent at the Mission, but he had done much good. Antonio would be looking down from heaven along with Padre Amores and the rest. He would be pleased if the Mission was repaired in his memory.

Loreta understood when she came back, and was glad that Juan had prepared great pots of beans, and ground as much corn as he could. She threw hides over the cart where Antonio lay on a bed of ferns, and hurried about the necessary work.

"The saints will be good to Antonio if we do his share of work on the Mission. He will watch us and smile," she said.

When they arrived on Sunday, young Preble rushed up. He helped Juan off his horse, tied the reins of the ox cart for Loreta, and helped her down. He even carried José on his arm.

Juan knew that the young *marinero* was eager to give out comfort, but no words came when he saw Loreta's calm face.

"I'm sorry, I didn't know. I brought Indians to work," he told Juan.

Loreta looked at him. "Afterwards we will do the work. That is what Antonio wanted most of all to do today," she said. "On the packhorse is food. I made plenty for everybody."

After Mass, and the service for Antonio at the tree of the Three Crosses, repair on the Mission began. Loreta worked as hard as any. Juan saw her carrying load after load of adobe for patching cracks. She pulled weeds from inside the room where Juan had spent so many years of his life, and she dusted the statue in the niche by the door, and piled green bay branches around "Our Lady" so that the sunlight would not fade the paint and the rain would not weather her.

There was too much roof to be mended, and too few hands to do the work, but when the bats began to fly from the bell tower and it was time to leave, the Mission looked better. Antonio slept under the hill at the north of the church where there would be no Padres, no Christmas Mass with a star this year, no sugar candy from Don Hartnell, and no beef from Don Cooper. Father Real said that Midnight Mass would be in Monterey.

Loreta went alone into the dark church. The only incense now was the pungent scent from pine boughs and the bay leaves around the solitary statue. Loreta prayed to San Carlos and "Our Lady," crossed herself, and came out. Near the door was Jack Preble. He moved toward her and put his hand on her arm.

"I'm not much. Only a runaway foreigner," he said softly, in halting Spanish. "But if praying to saints makes you so calm and beautiful and good—" he paused, "I'd like you to tell me the words, and show me how."

Juan had been waiting for Loreta, too, but now he hobbled away on his sore feet toward his horse. The good San Carlos had touched the heart of *marinero* Jack, and it was for Loreta

183

alone to help the saint. Little José was sleeping in the cart that had carried his father to the Mission for the last time. Juan leaned over and pulled the rabbit fur cover closer around the baby, and sat down to wait until Loreta came to help him up on the horse. Queer how much alike old men and babies were, he thought. Both had to wait for someone to care for them. The only difference was that the old already knew happiness, and trouble, and the struggle, and the young were just waiting to have all these things come to them.

Chapter XXI

ALVARADO CHANGES HIS STYLE: 1836

LORETA was bewildered. So many people came now to collect taxes on the rancho. First, Secretary Alvarado had sent a man for five hides. Then Governor Gutierrez' soldiers arrived with a paper saying that twenty hides must be ready by next light of moon. If Loreta did not have the hides ready, forty head of cattle would be driven away.

Antonio had taken good care of the small herd that Padres had given them, and Loreta had helped on the range in wet weather when the calves came, so that every animal could be saved and the herd would grow larger, but forty head of cattle was such a lot for the governor.

"We will not give him forty," Juan said weakly through his wheezes. "Juan can scrape fat from hides and help you peg them in the sun. We will have twenty by light of moon."

"But the rodeo—I can't hunt cows alone," she sighed. "Someone must help to get them in the gulch."

The next day when Loreta was grinding corn so that there would be enough to eat while she was in the hills after cattle, Juan slipped through the trees and made his way slowly down the trail to Los Beracos.

A winding road divided the rows of tule huts in the Indian village on the river. Music was loud, and there was this new wine in jugs that addled the head. Whiskey, they called it. Juan went into the fandango house. Women sat on the floor smiling at men drinking out of jugs. For a while they paid no attention to Juan in the opening, then a woman looked up.

"The grizzlies must have picked his bones without killing him," she laughed, and pointed to Juan. "What's he want here?"

185

The men roared with laughter. One tall man came over to Juan. "Well, Comero, a drink? Perhaps you have a cow to pay?"

Juan shook his head. In a corner he saw a half-Indian he knew, Cabez. He hobbled over, and was conscious of eyes watching. He touched the Indian on the arm.

"Antonio is dead. The governor wants hides for taxes. I will give you some if you will help Loreta cow hunt," he said in Room-se-en.

"Cabez busy now—" the Indian answered in Spanish and rolled his eyes dizzily. "Can't bother."

They all laughed again. Juan didn't know what to do, so he just went out of the tule hut.

A gentile Indian at Los Beracos finally agreed to come to the rancho and kill and skin the animals for the tallow and all the meat for grizzly bait.

"Not the tallow, too," Juan cried. "Only the meat, all the meat."

The Indian shrugged his shoulders, and dug in the dust with his toes. "Mission Indians want too much. Tallow, too, or I don't come."

"All right, tallow then," Juan agreed. "Will you help Loreta cow hunt?"

"If it does not take too long." His eyes looked into Juan's. "But three hides," he put up three fingers.

Juan nodded. "Three hides."

Juan was exhausted when he finally reached the rancho again. He was glad of marinero Jack's bed to rest on. His breath came hard and made loud wheezes. He couldn't work on shoes that day. Loreta was very tender to him, when he told her what he had done. She even held the bowl of soup for him while he drank.

The next day Loreta made a pot of rabbit stew and tortillas enough to last. Before she rode off with the Indian, she tied a twisted rawhide riata around José, who toddled about. The other end of the rope was fastened to the supporting sticks of the hut.

"José walks some now, Grandfather O-nes-e-mo," she said to Juan and smiled. "You can pull him in to feed him, or when the sun is too hot. You will not have to make your bones sore by moving them."

The day was long. Juan had trouble making a fire to heat the rabbit stew. A bee stung José on the bottom, and the boy roared a long time because Juan was slow mixing mud to take away the hurt. While Juan was plastering him, the baby ate up one of the red satin patches Juan had cut for a shoe. There was no more satin left. Babies were squaw business.

Juan was weary from tugging on the rawhide riata to keep the boy away from troubles. The extra work made his arms ache and the breath go out of him far too fast. As a last effort for peace and quiet, he reached into his pantaloons and pulled out a bit of cloth. The little boy's body was warm and comforting as he sat close to Juan and watched to see what was in the cloth.

The gold nugget, worn bright from hard horny fingers, gleamed in the sun for a bit, then, quick as a bird for a worm, José picked it from the cloth, put it into his mouth and swallowed it! He set up a loud roar when Juan ran a bony finger around his mouth to see if the gold was really gone.

The grandfather sighed. He was too weary now to care what happened to the gold. Perhaps the nugget blessed by a Padre would quiet the boy, and give some peace and silence to an old Indian. It would not be too high a price to pay for rest. the nugget was for José anyway, the Padre had said that when he blessed it! Now José had it inside him, and there was an end of it! Juan rolled up in the hides on the bed, covered his ears so he couldn't hear what the child was doing, and went to sleep.

Someone was shaking him, hurting the sore arm. "Juan O-nes-e-mo, are you alive?" a voice called.

187

Juan rolled over and opened his eyes. It was nearly dark now.

Marinero Jack stood looking down, a smile on his face.

"A nice grandfather, you," he cried. "Look at José." Jack held the baby up at arm's length. "He was eating honey out of the pot with both hands when I came," Jack said. "He's sure to have a belly ache. Where's Loreta?"

Juan waved up the hill. "After cattle, for hides to pay taxes to Governor Gutierrez."

"Alone?"

Juan shook his head. "An Indian man with her to help kill cows. Mo-he-to."

"Juan! You shouldn't have let her go alone like that!" There was hurt in the marinero's voice.

"But taxes. Hides must be ready before light of the moon. What can an old man with crippled legs do? Indian women always work all right."

Jack sighed and put the baby down. "Better get a fire going," was all he said as he set to work.

After a while the marinero held José's legs and arms while Juan tried to wash off some of the stickiness, then they all had stew together. José, with a full stomach, was soon asleep.

"She should be coming most any time now," Jack said as he filled Juan's pipe and lighted it.

"Long way to hills," Juan murmured. "But why are you here so late? Don Cooper will be angry."

"Governor Gutierrez and Secretary Alvarado had a fight today over the running of the Customs House in Monterey. Each thinks the other is a thief," Jack said. "Don Cooper kept me there with him."

"People killed?" Juan asked, eager for news that came so seldom now.

"None. Alvarado and his men started a revolution and sent a cannon ball through the Governor's house. That ended the revolution. Governor Gutierrez gave up and the people chose

188

Alvarado for Governor and Guadalupe Vallejo for Military Commander. Gutierrez sails for Mexico soon."

Juan shook his head. "So many governors. Another maybe by next moon." Then he had a thought. "Now Governor Gutierrez is going we won't need to give soldiers twenty hides?"

Jack laughed. "There's always taxes, no matter who's governor, Juan."

"Pablo told Juan this would happen, long ago," Juan said. "Pablo knows. He hears many things at Spanish houses in Monterey when he goes to carry things for Don Soberanes. Pablo said Alvarado and Vallejo would be changing their hides again soon, to show new clothes and make people forget."

"What do you mean?" Jack asked. "Alvarado is popular. They chose him for governor."

Juan sniffed.

"Why do you sniff? The people agree with Alvarado. Isaac Graham, the Americano whiskey distiller from the Pajaro valley, came over with others to help Alvarado. They think it is time that Californians have some say about the administration of things here. Mexico cares only for the money, not the people."

"Long ago, Vallejo, who is Alvarado's uncle, ordered Indians hanged with grapevines," Juan told this man who looked so very white and clean in the glow from the fires. "That was when you were sucking. But an old Indian doesn't forget."

Jack sighed. "But some Indians were bad too, Juan, and they had to be punished. Indians stole cattle and made trouble. Things couldn't go on with Indians working hard at the Missions, and learning only catechism and songs, and not how to look after themselves. That only made them steal when there was no one to feed them."

"An old Indian doesn't forget," Juan repeated.

"That's no way, Juan, to hang onto old hates, old fights. We must look to changes for the better and bury what is

189

past." The marinero's voice was young and eager. "He's a poor man who never changes his mind. See how pleased you are with the bed, and you would have none of it at first."

Juan nodded. "Yes, Juan's bed is better than old days on the ground. Perhaps that is what the good God sends young for—to look ahead when the old are tired and want only rest." He was quiet, thinking for a minute. "But you will be a clever young crow, Marinero Jack, if you change people from fighting over land."

"Loreta! I hear horses." Jack said suddenly.

Juan listened. He heard nothing but an owl screech far away in the trees below Los Beracos. "Englishmen have good ears, when they want to hear," he laughed. Jack laughed, too, but he listened harder than ever and soon went out into the dusk to listen.

Loreta rode in alone, leading three burdened horses by rawhide ropes. She slid wearily off the horse. Juan hunched up to the fire and poured her some stew, but before Loreta ate it she looked at the sleeping José.

"We killed, and the vaquero skinned in the hills so he would not have to carry grizzly bait so far," she said and smiled at Jack who sat quietly watching her. "He took four hides for himself."

"Only three he was to take," Juan said.

"He took extra because he had to work with a woman and the woman would not do things in the hills that he wanted to do," Loreta's voice was low. "I told him that if he touched me, San Carlos would put a curse on him and he would die."

"Such a country! Cutthroats and rapers—even down to the savages. I'll go after him. I'll kill him. Who is he?" Jack cried in disgust.

Loreta ate some stew, and then shook her head. "No need. He will not come back. It is better you think of the prayers I told you, than killings, Marinero Jack." Then she asked Juan how his wheezes were, and if José had been a good boy while she was away.

Juan thought it was better for an old Indian not to tell of the high price he had paid for a sleep, so he didn't mention the nugget in the bowels of José.

"He was a sweet boy when I came," Jack laughed. "We had to wash the honey off him."

Loreta didn't laugh. She put away her bowl and dropped quickly to a tule mat. In no time she was asleep.

Jack covered Loreta with a rough blanket that she had woven, and helped Juan to his bed.

"I must go now," he said. "Don Cooper needs me at the rancho in the morning. We, too, must have hides ready for taxes. I will attend to Loreta's horses and put the skins down."

Juan nodded, and soon heard hoofs die away in the night. Marinero Jack had no more news for an old man's ears after Loreta had come home and was asleep.

Chapter XXII

A NEW CHANT FOR JUAN: 1836

JUAN could no longer make the tedious trip to Monterey for Mass in the Presidio church. Besides, there had been complaints that his wheezing disturbed others at their prayers.

Loreta washed herself and José, and saddled the horse. Then she propped Juan up in his bed, and put water and food where he could get it when he wakened from his second nap. The sun was not yet up over the rim of Mt. Toro when she set out for Monterey with her little boy in front of her on the saddle.

The rains had been gentle this year, and no bad blowing of wind. Fresh juicy grass tinged the brown hills and made them look like the brown and green changeable silk dresses that señoritas wore.

When she reached the Mission San Carlos de Borromeo, Loreta paused and looked up for a moment at the beautiful, lichen-covered tower that her father had helped build. She could not pass without a prayer in the deserted church; a prayer for all those who had taught, and prayed, and built and then gone away.

As she turned to leave, Loreta smiled up at "Our Lady" in the niche, and the Saint smiled back through her covering of dust. Being a woman like Loreta, she would understand that women must go on working, and praying, and living, for the day that was and the day to come.

Loreta needed the blessing of our "Lady of Sorrows," when she saw José! She had left him sitting on the great grinding stone while she went into the church. When she came out, she found him covered with mud. He had discovered a hollow where water collected, and he lost no time filling it with dirt to make mud which he plastered on himself as his grandfather had done for the bee sting. He smiled at her through a caked face.

Loreta sighed, wiped him as well as she could, and put him on the horse. Perhaps by the time they reached Monterey the mud would be drier, and she could brush it off him.

Not many Indian converts came to Mass at the governor's church. They were dazzled by the Spanish and Mexicans and Californians who passed in to services swishing full-skirted black silk dresses. Each Doña had an Indian servant to carry her blanket, for there was nothing but tiled floor to sit on.

Pablo, gossiping with men, smiled at Loreta, and Doña Petra nodded pleasantly in the doorway as bells pealed.

Loreta held José close to her as she prayed for Antonio in heaven, and for Juan in the tule hut on the Carmelo. Would Jesus please help to make Juan's wheeze better and not so noisy, so that he could come to church?

The altar was bright with candles, as in the old days they had shone at Carmelo when Loreta had arranged the altar and helped make candles. The Mass was the same, but something hurt Loreta's heart. Perhaps it was because so few Indians remembered to come, or maybe because she thought of "Our Lady" keeping her watch without even one candle to cheer her.

Jack Preble came up as Loreta waited for the Spanish and Mexicans to go out of church first. He smiled, looked down at José, and picked a bit of dried mud from the child's brown hair.

"Is Juan too weak to come?" he asked when they were outside.

Loreta nodded.

"Will it be all right for me to ride home alongside your horse? I have some liniment for Juan's chest. I think it will help. My mother sent it to me in the box that came from England on the last boat."

"Juan is old, *Marinero Jack*," Loreta sighed. "Perhaps the

193

liniment will only be wasted on him. But he would like you to come and stay to eat with us—" she paused, "and Loreta would, too."

There under the oak tree beside the church door, the *marinero* smiled, and put a warm, comforting hand over Loreta's for a moment. "I'm glad you want me," he told her. "There may be some work I can do for you."

José cried when they were on the road. Loreta gave him a tortilla to eat from the white cloth she had brought, and then she stopped and took off her shoes and hung them on the saddle. "Shoes are for Doñas, not Indian women," she said as she got back on the horse.

The blue sky had clouds today, white fluffy clouds that made light and dark patches on the side of old Mt. Toro as they moved southward. Meadow larks sang from the top branches of chaparral. "Don Cooper has a fine rancho where I have charge of Indians," Jack Preble told Loreta. "There is a little river running through, called the Sur. Big sycamore trees grow there with light-colored bark that looks ghostly when you see it in the moonlight. Deer graze in herds like sheep when evening comes. They are not afraid."

"The mountains down the coast are very steep, Juan says, and they go right to the sea. Not much flat land to till." Loreta pulled the limp body of the sleeping José up closer to her on the saddle.

"There is a small place where vegetables grow, that is all. But canyons have trees, giant trees called redwood. Don Cooper is cutting them down to make posts. He will have enough to sell."

"Don Cooper will be a very rich man, then," Loreta said.

"I will be a rich man someday, too, Loreta," the *marinero* cried. "Anyone can be a rich man here in Alta California if he works and uses his head. Mexicans will give a man land if he is a decent citizen and lives here two years. The hills are full of wild horses to be had for the breaking."

"That was what Antonio did for José Manuel Boronda at Los Laureles," Loreta put in. "Antonio could tame horses fast."

The marinero didn't seem to be listening about Antonio, for he went right on talking.

"And there's thousands of acres for cattle to roam in. Hides and tallow always bring good trade. The Boston ships will take all we have around the horn."

"But so many of the cattle Antonio and Loreta had, have gone. A different brand is on them. More taxes and there will not be enough hides to pay them."

"The wild Indians are stealing cattle," Jack said. "They have been stealing Don Cooper's cattle, too. They kill them and eat them and sell the hides."

Loreta looked off at the oaks across the Carmelo and saw that they were tipped with bright new leaves. "This was Indian's country first," she said quietly. "Even flies must eat, Marinero Jack. Wild Indians do not change brands. They have no irons to heat."

"You saw someone changing brands, Loreta? Who did you see?"

Loreta shook her head. "Indians here have enough trouble without making the foreigners angry. Antonio was shot. Loreta doesn't forget that."

"But the law!" Jack cried. "It can make them stop stealing."

"The law cannot bring Antonio back to life again, Marinero Jack."

Juan was still propped up when they reached the rancho. He had eaten only one tortilla because his breath was hard.

Loreta watched Jack Preble rub Juan's bony chest with strong-smelling medicine, and cover it with rabbit skin, fur side toward the chest.

"That'll loosen her up," he said cheerfully. "Then a hot stew inside you and you'll be a new man."

But Juan was not a new man. The cold fog came in, and the

sun did not shine through for several days to help warm up old
bones. Loreta watched his dull eyes, and made him drink willow tea for the fever and to help warm him up.

Then one night about dusk, when the red-headed woodpeckers in the old stump by the door took to scolding and
bowing at each other before they settled down, Juan grew suddenly worse. His dull eyes turned so bright that the light in
them answered the candle when Loreta put it beside his bed.

"The fiddle," he whispered to her. "When you have finished
lighting the candles around 'Our Lady,' get Padre Amores'
fiddle. He is here at the Mission asking for it. The Padre wants
to play his fiddle for Juan and show him a new chant."

Loreta crossed herself and murmured some prayers for the
dying as she reached for the worn bag, and put it near Juan's
hands.

"No—no!" His voice had come back suddenly and sounded
very angry. "Do not give Padre Amores' fiddle to Juan. Give
it to the Padre. Amores wants to play."

Loreta took the bag away again.

"Why don't you give Amores the fiddle so he can play?"
Juan's eyes were still brighter now, and his heart was beating
so hard that Loreta could see the pulse in his neck. "Music,
quick, for Juan. Amores is asking."

Would the good God tell her what to do? Loreta tried to
think. If Juan kept using his strength this way in anger he
would not last, and the priest was so far away now. It would
take a long time to go over the hill to Monterey.

"Music!" Juan insisted. "Padre Amores wants his fiddle that
he left to Juan."

Loreta took the fiddle out of its bag, and without even tuning, put it under her chin and drew the bow across a string.

"Satan!" the old man cried excitedly. "Satan has the fiddle!
He is playing. Loreta, get the fiddle from Satan and give it to
Amores." He grew frantic, and picked at the coarse blanket
with knobbed, bony fingers.

A sudden thought came to Loreta. Quickly she pulled the

cover around Juan. "Loreta is going after Amores. Do you hear, Juan?" she said. "Keep very quiet and still, and Loreta will bring Amores' music for you."

He smiled then and was quiet.

Loreta caught up her shawl and ran through the dark toward Los Beracos. Someone there played the fiddle. Many times had she heard the fiddle in fandango houses.

Loud singing and the *hota* dance were going on. There were lots of candles in the little room. Loreta stood in the doorway gasping for breath enough to call. Guitars, and a jangle of bells to dance to, and Indian flutes made from hollow elderberry stems, but no violin.

The din stopped to give the dancers a rest. Now was the time. From the door Loreta called. "My father is dying! There is no priest for miles and my father is calling for fiddle music; for a chant. Please, will someone come to him and play for a minute? I heard fiddles here sometimes."

"Isn't she beautiful—for an Indian?" came to Loreta's ears from a man with bleary eyes.

"No one here plays the fiddle," a tall Mexican said. "That man has gone."

"Maybe a flute? A reed flute will do," Loreta begged. "Please come with music for my father. Music is sacred to him. It is all I can do."

A girl in a purple satin dress pulled away from the arms of a man and came toward Loreta. "I had fiddle lessons when I was a girl," she said, "but I haven't played since then, and don't know any chants."

Loreta clutched the satin arm. "But it will be fiddle playing. He won't mind, and the saints will forgive us."

"I know a Christmas song," the girl said. She pulled up the skirt of her dress and tucked it in at the waist, leaving a scarlet petticoat for all to see.

"We'll *all* go and sing a Christmas song," a drunken Mexican called, and tried to pull himself from the floor.

"You'll all stay where you are!" the girl's eyes were fiery with

197

anger. "Is there no decency to you?" She turned to Loreta. "Come on. I suppose I'll ruin my shoes but that can't be helped."

Loreta led the way along the trail through the fog. "You shall have the most beautiful pair of shoes you have ever worn for this," she told the girl. "My father made shoes for señoritas in Monterey, and did not take the last ones to sell. There will be a pair your size."

"The fiddle," Juan was crying. "Loreta! Where have you put Padre Amores' fiddle? He wants to play for Juan, and Juan can't see to find it."

"Hush," Loreta said tenderly, as the fandango girl picked up the violin and began to tune. "You hear, Juan? The tuning?"

"The tuning," the old man smiled and nodded. "The Padre has found his fiddle."

Softly, with uncertain fingers, the girl played an old Mexican Christmas carol.

"A new chant," the old man whispered. "Amores has a new chant now to teach Juan."

It was not necessary for the girl to stay away from the fandango house very long, for Juan O-nes-e-mo, the Mission Builder, had gone to learn the new chant before the Christmas song was finished.

Book Two

LORETA OF CARMELO

The Mission as it appeared in 1879 showing remains of original roof before any restoration work was started. Drawn by W. K. Fisher.

Chapter I

MEXICAN FIRE IN CALIFORNIA: 1836

THE long spell of foggy weather was broken at last, and hot California sun once more warmed the Valley of the Carmelo.

Loreta Prealta sat on the ground beside her tule hut. As her hands worked at pulling husks from yellow ears of corn, she lifted her eyes to the golden hillside, and wished that San Carlos, the Patron Saint of the Mission, could have made just one more sunny day for her father, before Juan O-nes-e-mo's bones were taken over the hill to Monterey, so far away from the Mission he had helped to build on the Carmelo. Her father longed for one last warming by the sun on his poor, old body, and he would have liked to be put away near the beautiful tower he had built; the tower where swallows flew in and out, showing green-tinted wings, and where the wind made sighing noises when there was a storm at sea. Loreta had begged them to let Juan's body stay near the work of his hands, but now that the Spanish Padres were gone and the Mission deserted, and only a Mexican priest in Monterey, there were no ears open to hear the words of an Indian woman.

She looked at her brown son as he made his way to her on unsteady legs. He was busy trying to pull a bit of duck down from a finger sticky with honey. When the feather stuck to the finger of his other hand, and was changed back and forth several times, José gave up trying. He sat his bare little behind on the ground and roared with anger.

Loreta went to the baby, pulled away the feather, and was pouring water on his hands to wash off the honey, when she heard the clatter of horses' hoofs on the other side of the hut.

Could this be another Mexican for taxes? She had already paid Alvarado's man twenty hides, and another man before him ten hides! Her father had helped her scrape the fat from hides for taxes just before he died!

She walked around the hut. Two Mexicans were sliding off their horses. One, a small fellow with a wrinkled face and crafty eyes, saw Loreta as she looked at him.

"Here you, Indian," he called in Spanish. "You're on my land, and I've come to tell you to move off of it."

Loreta drew herself up as became an Indian woman who was eighteen years old, and taught by the Padres at the Mission; then she walked slowly to where the men stood. Wind from the sea blew her brown cotton dress tight against her straight young body. Her bare feet made no sound on the hard-baked yellow ground.

"This land belongs to Loreta Prealta," she said quietly, when she was near to them. "When Padres left the Mission on Carmelo they gave this land to Loreta and Antonio, because we were Mission Indians." She took her stand by the oxcart that Antonio had made such a short time ago. "Taxes have been given already to the Mexican Government."

The man came closer to her. His face had a worried look to it now. "Who is Antonio," he asked, "and where is he?"

"Antonio was the father of my boy, and husband to me. We were married by the Padres," Loreta told these Mexicans, who were looking around anxiously. "He was killed by savage Indians at Los Laureles, the rancho of the Spaniard, Don José Manuel Boronda, so now his share too belongs to me."

"Well, you don't own the land," the man glared and pushed a paper toward her. "Governor Gutierrez signed this paper of mine. It says that the land belongs to me. You have no paper telling about your land. You don't belong here."

Her father, Juan O-nes-e-mo had often told Loreta that an Indian woman must never change a muscle of her face to give away the thoughts in her heart, for a face can tell to another, things that the mouth does not say. "Governor Gutierrez is no longer governor. How can a paper from him be good, when Alvarado is the governor now?"

"Can't you read?" he shouted. "This paper is dated 1836, before Governor Gutierrez left Alta California for Mexico. The land is mine. Alvarado and his crowd may think that they are rulers, but Chico and Gutierrez have sailed back to Mexico for five thousand soldiers and will bring them to fight Alvarado and the Californians who want to rule over Mexican country. This land is mine and is Mexican. Indians get off it."

Loreta sighed and looked over at the hills beyond the river. "So many governors have come here and taken land and taxes away, and never come back. Indians lived here in the Valley of Carmelo before Mexicans came, or even Spanish and Padres. Loreta Prealta is the one who *belongs* here. In the Padre's book, is written down the land given to Loreta and Antonio. That is all the paper Loreta had, but the priest in Monterey will know. Padre Real will tell you. It is written in a book covered with rawhide and tied together with thongs. They wrote it down the day stock and Mission implements were given out before Padre Abella and Payeras left. Loreta and Antonio saw them write it."

The man set his jaw. "This bottom land belongs to me. Get your animals off. I'm going to burn the tule huts and all the vermin along with them." He pointed to the hills at the north. "Up there is where your land is. You can't read." He tapped the paper again. "I'm not going to argue with a squaw. The huts are to be burned tonight."

"But I cannot grow corn for us to eat on poor hill land," Loreta told him. "There is no water except the spring of Weeping Eyes, and that is not enough for growing food."

"I'll give you work. You can wash for us and have food and a place to sleep. It will be better than hill land."

Loreta shook her head. "I will move the stock, and go to the hills—for a while," she told him. "It is time the huts were burned—time for new ones." She walked up close to this Mexican. "But the land is mine, and Father Real, the Mexican priest in Monterey, will give Loreta a paper, too."

"They still have faith in a sinking ship, don't they? Don't even have sense enough to know that Padres are less than nothing now," the man said, and turned to his comrade and laughed a laugh that did not bring happiness to Loreta's ears. "She'll be harmless enough—alone as she is," he added as they both mounted. "Handsome squaw too, with a straight back and a small bottom—and firm young breasts. Who knows? She may come in handy one day." He put a spur to the belly of his horse and was off.

Loreta watched the Mexicans ride toward Los Beracos, the little town of tule huts along the river, where some of the Indians had settled after Padres left the Mission.

"We'll go and hush their fandango music, and see if there's much fight in them." The words, shouted against the wind, came back to the ears of Loreta, as she turned to call José, who was pouring dirt on his head.

The boy didn't look up. Why was it, that José never came when he was called? He was a good boy in every other way. His attention was hard to get unless he was looking at you. She called again, then when he didn't turn, she ran down the narrow path after him. He was three years old now, and would have to help as much as he could with moving stock. He could at least sit at the openings and keep cows from coming out.

For a while José was set at pulling leaves from ears of corn, while Loreta worked as hard and fast as she could to harvest what was left. She was determined not to leave an ear of her labor for the Mexican to smack his lips over. If she had time, she would even come back for the corn stalks. They made good cattle feed. Loreta watched José a moment and smiled. His hands were so little and he had to pull so hard to get even one layer of leaves from the corn, but one layer was something when it went toward the whole work. She left him, and moved horses and a cart full of corn to the high place that the Mexican said was hers, and then came back to take from the hut the few necessary things for cooking.

For a long time Loreta looked at the bed that had belonged to her father; the bed made by the young English *marinero* they had hidden when he deserted his ship. Perhaps her man Antonio would still be alive if no bed had ever been made!

It seemed such a short time ago that she had gone to the Mission with Antonio and old Juan, and young José, to honor the good San Carlos on his day.

With other Indians, they had marched around the church that no longer had a Padre to guide the souls of Indian worshippers. They sang the beautiful chant that Padres had taught them, and then knelt before the abandoned altar to receive the blessing from San Carlos in Heaven. The saint would not forget faithful Indians whose fathers had built a church with a tower, to honor him, even though there was no Padre left to give the blessing words.

The day had been clear, with swallows wheeling around the yellowed tower of San Carlos. On the seashore, thin green waves turned over in the sun and then sent tongues of white foam up onto the beach.

There was not even the boom of heavy surf to spoil the sweet voice of her Antonio, as he stood, straight and tall, and sang the final verse of the hymn to San Carlos:

> "Oh, pray for us, San Carlos,
> For dangers hover near;
> Oh, pray that God will give us strength
> To conquer every fear."

When the fiesta started and meat was roasting, Antonio had seen the two English marineros standing in the shade, and he invited them to eat. The men seemed never to get enough, and it was then that the golden-haired Jack Preble told them about the bad food on the whaling ship—and that he had no place to sleep except in wet and filth.

That night Antonio and Loreta had hidden the young mariner in their cart, and kept him hidden until the whaler left Monterey bay for good.

And now here was the beautiful bed too big for one Indian woman to lift; besides, the cart must go through trees to get up the hill. Branches would catch on it. No, the bed must be left here, along with memories of her father sitting by the fire, and playing chants on the fiddle that Padre Amores had given him. The marinero Jack Preble would understand. She would tell him all about it next time she saw him, before he had a chance to miss the bed and ask.

Loreta made many trips up the hill. She took away all the corn, and as night closed in, she filled the cart to the brim with corn stalks, so that no shred of food or fodder was left. Wearily she lifted young José onto the corn stalks to hold down the load and ride to his new home; then she left the cart and walked through the gathering dusk to the hut.

Her hand touched the smooth, night-cooled rushes, and Loreta thought of the days when she and Antonio had worked with their hearts and their hands, to build this home; and the day when Padre Abella had come out from the Mission and asked God and the Saints to bless every Indian soul that came to live under its sturdy oak roofbeam. Perhaps tonight, the fire from the burning hut would shine out like a great, beautiful, candle, so that the Saints and Antonio and Juan, in heaven, would see that Loreta and little José were safe on the hill above.

José was trying to vomit when Loreta reached the cart. She put her finger into his mouth and pulled out a bit of cornstalk that he had tried to swallow; then she gave him a tortilla and prodded the oxen. The cart squeaked for the last time up the narrow trail, and the evening star came out. Loreta was glad it was the same star that had welcomed her to the hut. Now it was once more above her, glowing alone, as she climbed alone up the hill. Stars went on shining in spite of Mexican fires. An Indian woman would go on like the stars, long after Mexican fires had burned out!

Later, as she made things ready for the night, Loreta heard fiesta music and singing in the valley below. There was the crackle of flames, and she saw that Los Beracos was burning!

A prayer went from her lips for the kind-hearted fandango girl from the dance house there. She who had come in her high heels and purple satin dress and played the Christmas song on the Padre's fiddle so that Loreta's father could die in peace and happiness.

Loreta could not take her eyes away from the bright glow, as fire burned up the house she had helped Antonio to build. Her bones ached with weariness from the moving. She had paid out so many hides in taxes and yet here she was on the hillside, homeless and alone, with only her little son to comfort her. The story was always the same, fighting between governors and hides and tallow taken from Indians to pay for the fighting. In Monterey she heard how Gutierrez and Chico, the Mexicans, had sailed with a special boat to carry hides and tallow stolen from the Missions. With this they would buy soldiers to come back and fight the Californian Alvarado. Only sleep could take away the sadness.

José was very much excited over the trip to Monterey the next day. He seemed to like things that were different. Father Real was working among the flowers around the governor's church when they arrived. He was kind to the little boy and gave him a holy picture to look at while Loreta talked.

"No, my child," Father Real shook his head. "I have no book with entries in it. It was here for a time, but so many people were looking at it, governors, and secretaries, and alcaldes and others. One day I came from prayers and it was gone."

"Then there is nothing to show? Loreta has no land that the Padres gave her?" She could hardly believe that the loss of a book, a book made by Padre Payeras, could make so much difference to an Indian woman.

"I will go to the alcalde, to the other proper people and tell them about you," Padre Real said. "I will tell them I was there

207

when the land was given to you and swear to a paper. Everything will be all right." He patted her shoulder. "Now go into the church, child, and calm yourself with prayer. I will watch the boy while I garden here."

Loreta felt quieter and more at peace in the church with the little altar light glowing through the dimness. It was cool here and she was tired. Her prayers—she couldn't think of the words.

"Wake up, my child. You must be exhausted." Father Real's voice came to her. He was standing by her side, and looked tenderly at her. "Come and eat, and you will feel better."

After the food was blessed and eaten, José went to sleep, and then the priest told Loreta about the graveyard lot.

"You must bring some hides to pay for Juan O-nes-e-mo's grave in the cemetario," he said.

Loreta didn't understand. "My father must buy a little land to lie down in and rot?" she asked. "Indians never bought land to bury in at Carmelo. I did not buy land for Antonio who lies beside the Mission."

"That was different. Juan is over here in Monterey, in a graveyard with Spanish and others. It is like a pueblo for the dead, and lots must be bought for graves."

Loreta nodded, but she didn't really understand. "Juan would have liked to be where he could see the beautiful tower of Carmelo, with no Spanish and Mexicans. Juan did not want to rot in Monterey."

The Padre sighed. "But Carmelo is no longer a place to bury. We must all do as we are told, Loreta. Things have changed now."

"Things have changed now," she repeated. "What do I pay for this ground for Juan?"

"Two cow hides will do."

Loreta nodded.

Before she left Monterey that afternoon, Father Real went with Loreta to the alcalde and got a paper that was signed and had a seal on it. He gave it to her. "Keep this always. It is called a deed, a right to your land."

Such a lump went away from Loreta's heart. "Then I can go and tell the Mexican this is my land, and build again on the flat where Antonio and Loreto made their first house?"

The alcalde shook his head. "Gonzales is in possession now. We can't do anything about that. We can't take it away from him. This paper gives you the rest that Father Real heard Padre Payeras give you."

Loreta was bewildered. Mexicans could take away from her, and from dead Antonio, and Juan, who had lived there a long time, but they could not take away from the Mexican who had been there only one night. She wished hard that she could ask the Spanish Padre Payeras and Abella about all this business of different kinds of papers.

The next day Loreta was building a tule shelter for the oxen when she saw Jack Preble riding up the trail. He sat so straight and tall in the saddle that she was happy just looking at him. People thought well of the runaway English marinero now, and he was good to the Indians who worked under him at Don Cooper's rancho. There was no time to rub a bit of tallow on her hair to make it shine, but she smoothed it as well as she could before he came up to her.

Jack jumped off his horse and smiled into Loreta's eyes. "Take a good look at me, now, Loreta. See if you think I'm different."

She looked at his clothes—leather jacket, sombrero, trousers —everything was the same. He had no silver spurs.

"What is different, Marinero Jack?" she asked.

"Blind one," he laughed and brushed her eyes lightly with his fingers. "I'm baptized now, by Father Real. Behold Jack Thomas Preble." Loreta watched him stick out his chest. "You can see what a good influence you are on me."

"You couldn't expect Loreta to have the eyes of a Saint and

209

see the changes in your soul, could you?" Loreta asked. She was so happy. Now Jack would be safe and guided to right with the Virgin and Jesus to help him.

"You're as near a Saint as I'll ever see, Loreta," Jack said and took her hand. "I was baptized because I thought it would please you to have me in the church."

The warm hold Jack had on her hand took away all the weariness and hurt from Loreta's heart. She no longer felt a lone Indian woman, fighting a world of Mexicans and Spaniards and English and Americanos. This man had become a Catholic because he thought it would please her. But Loreta could think of no words to tell him how happy she was.

"Aren't you going to say you are pleased?" Jack asked her. Then, suddenly, before Loreta could even smile he was holding her very close to him, so close that she could hear the beat of his heart under the leather vest. "I love you, Loreta. I've loved you ever since that day when you told Antonio to help me, and you hid me."

Loreta was content to stay against Jack's strong body for a while, for it brought happiness. But he held her away, and looked into her eyes.

"Loreta, now is my time to help you. You can't get along alone as you have this last year since Antonio died. They've taken some of your land, and burned your hut. And now you haven't got even old Juan for company. I want to love you and make a home for you. I'm being naturalized as a Mexican citizen, and I'm a Catholic. I've already applied for a grant of land."

Loreta looked at him sadly.

"Marinero Jack, Mexicans burned my hut, even after taxes were paid."

Jack put back his head and laughed. "But I'm not going to be that kind of a Mexican. I'm with Alvarado," he cried. "We are now free from Gutierrez and that mad Mexican Chico. We will soon run ourselves, and not have all the riches of California go into pockets in Mexico City."

Loreta saw his eyes bright with excitement.

"Gutierrez and Chico had to be protected on the boat before they sailed, because they took so much hides and tallow from the Indians. As he left Chico shouted to Alvarado from the beach 'Bring up crows to peck your eyes out.' He swears he will be back to fight and we cannot have home rule, but we'll show him." Jack caught her hand. "But I don't want to talk of Alvarado and Gutierrez and Chico, now. I love you and I want to take care of you, Loreta."

"I would like you for my man, Marinero Jack. But you are very white, and Loreta is only an Indian woman. In Monterey some people look down on Indians."

She saw Jack's head come up defiantly. "The Indians have not only furnished land to some white people, they have furnished the man power to work it as well," he told her. "No, Loreta, you'll have to think up a better excuse for not being the wife of Jack Thomas Preble."

Loreta could think of no other excuse. Instead, she made special enchiladas and empanada, and they sat on the hillside with little José between them, and had a betrothal fiesta. The only other guests were two uninvited bluejays who stole bits of corn cake from the pot.

"I will stock your land with cattle, Loreta, and we will build a house here on this high hill where we can see up and down the valley of the Carmelo. No tule hut for Loreta Preble, but a beautiful adobe with a tiled roof, and a barn that will not blow down in every wind."

Loreta could not help smiling. "My father, Juan O-nes-e-mo, used to say that young gulls fly high, but come down quick, Jack. Perhaps it is better we do not fly so high, in adobe houses like Spanish Dons have."

Jack only laughed and put his arm around her. He crushed enchilada against her brown cotton dress, and it made a red stain.

"I'm not flying high," he cried. "I have been saving, and Don Cooper has good stock. With your land and my grant put together we will have a fine rancho, and I will add to it as I can."

Loreta thought of the hurt about the paper. "Be sure you get a paper with things written on it," she said. "Father Real couldn't remember how big Loreta's land was. Paper is better than just remembering."

Jack put his head close to hers, so that she could feel the rough bristles of hair on his face. "Poor Loreta," he murmured. "So many troubles in such a short life. But never will trouble come to you again if Jack Thomas Preble can keep it away from you." He put his mouth to her lips.

José fell into the enchilada pot and came up covered with sauce. He had to be taken to the spring for cleaning, so there was no more time for lovemaking at the Rancho of Weeping Eyes.

"That chap needs a father to touch him up a bit," Jack laughed. "He must learn to mind. He does not come when he is called. We will teach him to ride well, and cow hunt for his mother and father."

As Jack rode away, Loreta called after him. "Be sure and tell Father Real, so that our names are read in church for three Sundays." Then a great longing came through her veins. "Wait, Jack," she cried, and ran down the yellow trail. When she reached the horse, Loreta looked up into Jack's eyes. "Hold me to you again," she begged, "and I will be happy until next time I see you."

"Bless you," he said and was on the ground in a second. He held her so that the loneliness was going away again. In the distance came the loud squeal of José, who did not relish being left wet at the spring.

"Pray to good San Carlos that we will be many years together, Jack," Loreta said as he mounted his horse again. "So many things happen—"

Chapter II

MARRIAGE PROMISES: 1837

LORETA looked at the real gold wedding ring Jack had bought from the shop of Banales, the goldsmith in Monterey. No Spanish Doña in all California had a more beautiful ring, for it was fashioned out of a gold sovereign that Jack's mother gave him when he sailed away from England. On it were traced an anchor and a cross, in very fine lines.

"That's because I'm a runaway sailor man," Jack said when he showed the ring to Loreta in the back of the church while they waited for Father Real to marry them before Mass. "And the cross is for you, Loreta, because the first time I saw you, you were singing the hymn to San Carlos at the deserted Mission on the Carmelo." He smiled, caught hold of her hand, gave it a quick squeeze and dropped it. "Perhaps the only reason I'm marrying you is because the Padres at the Mission taught you how to knit such fine socks. Englishmen are fond of having warm, comfortable feet."

Loreta was pleased for the praise of her work, but she didn't let Marinero Jack see. "What about the stomach of a marinero?" she asked. "Perhaps it was the stomach told you to marry Loreta—just for tender rabbit stew, after such poor food on the whaling ship?"

"You've been so good to me, Loreta," Jack whispered in her ear. "I'll take good care of you—always." He turned then, to greet Don Jorje Allen and his wife, the beautiful Doña Petra, who was godmother to José.

Loreta noticed that Doña Allen had on a fine new black watered silk that was stiff. On her feet were beautiful shoes fashioned by the fingers of Juan O-nes-e-mo. Seeing shoes made by her father brought an ache into Loreta's heart. Juan

213

would be pleased today, if he could know that Marinero Jack was promising to take care of Loreta for always. She wished that an Indian woman could have a fine watered silk dress to wear when she made promises to the marinero and God, instead of just another loose brown cotton one that would wear a long time.

"I'll keep José," Doña Petra said. "I'll give him my prayer book and some holy pictures to look at, so he will be quiet and you can keep your mind on your holy vows."

José would have no prayer book or holy pictures. He stiffened his back and legs, and puckered his face all ready to roar, when Loreta gave him into the keeping of Doña Petra. But the golden-haired Englishman, Don Allen, was too quick for José! Before even one roar came out of the baby's face, Don Allen took from his pocket a small compass, and put it into the little brown hands. José soon forgot who was holding him.

Loreta's heart was lonely as she walked to the altar to say her marriage vows. The governor's church in Monterey was filled with strangers, except for Doña Petra and her husband, and Juan's old friend Pablo, who lived now in Monterey and worked for Don Feliciano Soberanes. To these Spaniards and Mexicans and Americanos, Loreta Prealta was only another Indian woman whose marriage made them stay longer in church that Sunday morning. The priest did not smile or say the words slowly as Padre Abella had done at the Mission on the Carmelo when Loreta and Antonio Prealta were married. This priest was a Mexican priest, in a hurry to be at Mass.

Such a little while it took to make the marriage promises, Loreta thought. Not even long enough to need a silk dress. This time would not be like the marriage of Loreta O-nes-e-mo to Antonio Prealta. After that service in the Mission on the Carmelo, Padre Abella rang the bell in the tower many times, so that it startled the swallows from their nests. There had been extra food that day for every Indian. Food set out in the shade of Mission walls. No one worked, until it was time for evening prayers, and then Juan had played extra chants on the fiddle that had once belonged to Padre Amores.

Now, when they came out of the governor's church in Monterey, people who had been to Mass were still talking in the shade of adobe buildings, and no one mentioned the wedding!

Don Jorje Allen wished Marinero Jack well, and then Loreta saw his eyes brighten.

"Did you hear of the excitement at our house a day or two ago?" he asked Jack. "Alvarado came to my place to talk Isaac Graham, the Americano, into joining with our revolutionary cause. He was just telling Graham that we could use Californians instead of Mexicans in high places at high salaries, when he glanced out of the window and saw Captain Munoz, one of Gutierrez' men, riding up.

"No," Jack cried, "what happened?"

"Alvarado ran out of the house and escaped on Isaac Graham's fastest and best horse. The one the distiller thought most of. You should have heard the bullets whistling around his head."

Then they both laughed and little Doña Petra pulled Loreta to one side in the shade.

"José has a holy picture in his stomach; it would be well to give him physic," she told Loreta, and then dropped her voice very low. "Your man is a good man, Loreta, but remember that Englishmen are very different from Spanish or Indians. They do not always see things the way a woman sees them. But there are ways to manage an Englishman, and you will learn." She pressed a holy medal into Loreta's hand. "May God and the saints always smile on the daughter of Juan O-nes-e-mo the Mission builder."

"Come, Petra, we must be getting along. Your baby will soon be wondering if she has a mother," Don Allen called. Petra hurried over to him and they went on their way toward the adobe on the hill behind the governor's church.

215

CATHEDRAL IN THE SUN

While Marinero Jack was speaking to Padre Real, Pablo sidled up to Loreta.

"You would have done much better to marry me—an Indian, when I asked you after Antonio died," he told her. "Twice now you have married outside the Room-se-ens of Carmelo. A white marinero might want to go once more to sea, and will leave Loreta to live alone."

"But, Pablo, you are too old, you were the friend of my father," Loreta said.

"I am the godfather to your José. Your father was old too, when he took his fourth woman. Polonia, your mother, was young like you, when the Padres joined her to Juan O-nes-e-mo." Pablo sniffed.

"And she died, Pablo. I never knew her," Loreta said thoughtfully. "It was hard for my father—raising a baby when he was already old."

Pablo sighed impatiently. "Young always want young—but sometimes they would find better shelter under an old oak than they find under new green wood that has not been through the toughening storms." Then he turned and shuffled off through the yellow dust toward the house of Don Soberanes.

Marinero Jack was very quiet in the ox cart as they rode back to the Valley of the Carmelo.

"Alta California, belonging to Mexicans, is a very long way from my mother in England, Loreta," he said after a while. "If I was home now, and just coming in from being married, my mother would meet us at the door of a thatched cottage, and we would sit down to a cold joint, and bread and butter and jam with plenty of good strong tea to drink." He looked off to the hills at the fresh green shoots on the oak trees. Loreta saw the lump in his throat go up and down, and she heard her Jack sigh.

"We will have special enchiladas, Marinero Jack. I made empanadas too, from berries," Loreta told him, trying to take away sighs that meant sadness in the heart.

216

"But that is only Indian food," he grumbled. "I don't want Indian food on my wedding day."

They rode along in silence for a while; Loreta prayed to the Virgin who understood the heartaches of a woman, and asked the Mother of Sorrows to send comfort to the English marinero.

The Saints heard, and answered Loreta's prayer, for the next time Jack spoke, there was strength to his voice.

"But if I'd stayed in England as my mother wanted me to, I'd still be apprenticed to the village blacksmith!" he cried. "I'd be selling sixpence worth of nails in a paper poke, or shoeing a horse while the owner makes a sot of himself in the public house across the road. That's no future for a lad!" He turned to Loreta, his eyes bright with excitement. "I'll show them! With your land and my Mexican grant I'll control more land than English gentry owns! Fancy young Jack Preble at nineteen being a landed gentleman! Won't my old woman preen herself and wag her tongue at the town pump when she goes for water? Every villager will know how rich her son is. The letter should reach her by Christmas."

"Maybe your mother could come to us, Marinero Jack. Then you would not be lonely for her," Loreta said, but soon found that this was not what her man wanted.

Jack shook his head. "No, she's better where she is—not knowing anything except what *I* want her to know."

As the months went on, Loreta decided that her man was very much like her young son José. He soon threw off homesickness in his eagerness to build a home and raise cattle of his own. José was the same; if he got into mischief, you had only to take his mind away from it by giving him something else to do.

Loreta worked as hard as she could to help Marinero Jack, and make him happy on the land, for always in her mind were the words mumbled from the toothless mouth of Pablo, that the English marinero would long once more for the sea, that he would go away and leave Loreta alone.

217

Chapter III

HOUSEWARMING: 1838

SUCH excitement! Loreta could hardly believe what she saw. Jack Preble and the vaqueros had just driven so many cattle from Don Cooper's rancho, that the hills behind the new adobe were thick with red dots. There was plenty of feed, too; winter rains had done well by the hills.

The adobe house was built quickly, for Jack paid Indians well, and gave them good food. Loreta wished that Te-mo's sons hadn't been among the builders. Te-mo's sons looked at her with anger in their eyes; Loreta knew the murder of Antonio Prealta was on their hands, and would never be washed off. But they had labored well on the house; she hoped that the work of their hands would not bring a curse to the house of Loreta and Jack Preble.

Jack rode up the path on his chestnut horse. Spring wind blew his golden-colored hair so that it swayed like a field of ripened barley. His face was happy. His eyes shone as he dropped off the horse and landed by her side.

"Well, old lady Preble," he called, "is the fire burned to coals? Today is fiesta day! Housewarming for the Preble adobe, with barbecue, and fine food, and plenty of wine for everybody to drink happiness to us."

Loreta nodded. "All is ready," she said. "The beef is roasting."

Jack walked with her to the pit under the great oak tree. Loreta was proud when she looked at the meat cooking on iron rods.

"Even the Borondas and the Marquenas will have big eyes when they see Jack Preble's new way to cook meat," she said.

218

Jack stuck out his chest. "You did well to have a blacksmith for a man, Loreta. We'll show 'em a lot of things along Carmelo before we're through." He gave the beef a prod. "I'll charge rancheros plenty to make metal plowshares for them and iron bands for wheels, but they'll find it's worth the price."

He turned to look at the low adobe. "We have as good a house as anyone," he said. "Maybe not so big as some, but it will stand wind and rain, and even José."

"It is beautiful, like a dream," Loreta told him. "I wish Juan could see." She glanced over the hills. "But the months while the adobe was building were good, too, Jack. The Indian tule hut Loreta made has brought us happiness. 'Our Lady' is blessing us. I will drop a child for you before the winter rains come again."

Jack hugged Loreta. "My child will never have to live in a tule hut. He will be born in a real house, with red tiles instead of a tule roof. Loreta Preble will not have to be as others and lie against the wall praying every time the wind blows, to keep the roof on."

Such a fiesta! The Marquenas and Rodriquez, and young Borondas, came, and Don Carlos Espinosa rode in on his beautiful white horse. Señor Vasquez was a little tipsy from whiskey when he arrived from Monterey. Señora María Berreto, the wife of Fabian Berreto, explained that Vasquez was not accountable, for he had a new son to be named Tiburcio, and the baby and the whiskey had gone to his head. A jug of whiskey and a son on the same day were too much for any man. There were toasts, and singing for the new house and the new son Tiburcio Vasquez. Mexican soldiers from Monterey played guitars.

Loreta was busy cooking and serving, and Jack made them laugh as he cut the meat with a great new knife. Señora Berreto was very kind and helped Loreta, who knew few Spanish women outside of Doña Petra Allen, who was a Boronda.

After the food came races that Jack started by the crack of his pistol. There was a heifer each for the winners. It was a grand fiesta like the ones Juan had told about in Monterey.

Loreta was proud that the women could stand in the shade of her adobe house to watch the races. Not many women came, and Loreta was disappointed, but Pablo, an old Indian friend of her father, smiled and nodded knowingly as he hugged little José to him.

"This has been a big year for babies in Monterey. The mothers are staying home to feed them."

Vaqueros rode their horses, and made them do tricks. There was a rope-throwing contest. As the wine and whiskey lowered in the bottles, the music grew louder and faster.

José's eyes were shining, and he ran around like a mad thing. Twice he was nearly under the feet of a horse. Jack yelled at the child but he did not even turn around. Loreta saw that Jack was angered as he strode out and picked José up by his pantaloons.

"I'll teach him to mind," he cried as he passed her. "I'll switch his little bottom until it's red, and he'll learn to come when I call."

Into the new adobe he went, with José under his strong bare arm. Loreta stood with the other women, and heard the switch strike, and José cry out with pain. Again and again went the switch. The screams of the boy reached Loreta in spite of the guitar music. Why did José have to be switched on this fiesta day? Her hands doubled up and tightened with the pain from the cries; she asked San Carlos to make José mind so that he would not be whipped.

Soon Jack came back and poured more wine for all.

Loreta rushed up the hillside and pulled some sage, and then went in to José. She wiped the little face, and put the crushed sage on the reddened bottom. The child whimpered. "You must come when your stepfather calls," she told him, as she held the face between her hands and looked into José's eyes. "If you don't come he will switch you, even though he loves you. He is an Englishman."

"José will come when father calls," the child nodded.

Loreta went to say good-bye to the ones who were leaving, for shadows grew long on the hills, and there were chores to be done on ranchos before dark.

When Fabian Berreto and his wife were ready to go, the Spanish woman put out her hand. "I wish you well, and would like you for a friend," she told Loreta.

"They're good people to know, the Berretos," Jack said when everybody was gone and they sat alone by the fire. "It was a fine party, we gave, with the right friends. I want you to take your place in the valley of the Carmelo, Loreta. Someday you will be the wife of a very rich ranchero. You must make friends with the Spanish people, and the English, and the Americanos. No longer are you just a Carmel Indian. You are the wife of Jack Preble with a fine adobe house and cattle—"

"And José," Loreta said quietly as she looked into the fire.

"José will be a better boy soon, and show proper respect for his elders, as he should," Jack told her. "I'm going to train him. Later, he will go to Tularcitos school to be taught by Don José Manuel Boronda."

"José doesn't mean to be bad," Loreta said. "The red places on him were deep. I put crushed sage on them."

Jack Preble poked the fire, then went into the house. Loreta was tired, for she had worked hard. She gathered up some things to carry. In the doorway she stopped. Through the dusk of the room, she saw Jack undressing sleepy little José. Carefully he put more sage on the red marks, and then tucked the baby into the small bed beside their own.

Loreta laid the things on the heavy table made of axe hewn boards. Jack came up and put his two hands on her shoulders. "I'm sorry I made welts on him, Loreta. It's hard for a sailor man to learn new tricks, and my temper got away with me," he said quietly. "But the boy must mind."

Loreta just nodded.

The new Preble adobe became quite a meeting place. Jack set up a building with the front out, and sent for a forge and anvil. Before long he was doing a good business making plow-shares and iron bands for the wheels of ox carts. He could fashion the irons for branding cattle, and was good at mending metal pots.

Loreta wondered if half Jack's business wasn't due to the fact that he invited customers to stay and eat. Always there was extra to cook. A lot of corn to grind, and only one pair of Indian hands to do it. Then, after the food, the men talked together about Alvarado, and how he was growing too bold, and blaming everything on English and Americanos, when it was really the Mexicans who stole cattle and took the land. There had to be a limit.

Jack did more talking than the others who listened. Loreta was afraid.

"There may be eyes and ears that will do you harm," she told him one night.

"No one can harm me, Loreta. I'm honest, and I do my share and take an interest in the country I have adopted. If more honest men did that we would not have so many rascals thinking they owned everything in sight. Evil ones are always at work."

Loreta only sighed. She had learned that Englishmen do not change their minds, and only hills listen to the talk of an Indian woman.

María was born two days before San Carlos Day. A little thing she was, and not so dark as José. Jack was kind, and rubbed the little María with tallow and put her in a blanket beside Loreta. Then he went to the blacksmith shop and came back with a bundle that was sewed in cloth. His face was alight, and he looked tenderly at Loreta as he drew out his knife to cut the sewing.

"It is a surprise for you," he cried. "I saved it. My mother sent it all the way from England!" He pulled out a great piece of meat that was covered with mouldy spots. "A ham, Loreta, an English ham to celebrate the birth of María."

Loreta looked at the meat, and wondered how English could

222

be so excited over such mouldy stuff when there was plenty of good fresh meat for the killing.

Jack was busy for a long time scraping off the mould, and boiling this chunk of meat in the iron pot. It smelled different from beef. Loreta lay on the bed and wondered if she would be able to eat the stuff, just to please Jack, who was so kind to her and glad about little María. But the ham was good—salty, pink and tender. It was not like anything Loreta had ever eaten before. Jack sliced some thin with his great knife, and put it between tortillas for her.

"It's pig. Cured with smoke in a closed hole," he explained, "and it keeps for a long time."

Jack came with still another surprise.

"Marmalade." He curled up his eyes with happiness and smacked his lips, and showed Loreta yellow stuff in a white pot.

The marmalade was made from oranges like the ones that came on boats to Monterey from Mexico.

"Now aren't you glad you turned English?" he asked as she ate the sweet, bitterish syrup. "I'll show you a lot of things, and you'll be able to lord it over some other people here. When the next boat comes in there will be an iron pot oven. We'll bake bread in it and not have to eat just these flabby tortillas. English people know how to live!"

Loreta didn't know bread and she liked tortillas, but now was no time to say so. Perhaps the boat with the iron oven pot on it would go down as a lot of boats did, and there would be no need to make bread.

But the boat didn't go down. Just a year later the pot arrived and with it from England and Jack's mother, came a little bottle of some stuff called yeast which must be kept alive to make more bread.

Jack experimented, and then taught Loreta how to bake loaves in the pot. He was very cross when it didn't taste right.

"Rot," he cried, and threw away the first bread she made alone. "You'll have to do better than that on bread before you're an English cook, and we can invite Don Hartnell and Don Spence to have some old country bread so they will remember their young days in England."

Loreta tried her best. When the bread finally suited him, Jack smiled, and picked out two loaves to take to Monterey, when he went with a load of hides. "This will make their eyes big. Bread is like heaven to an Englishman in a Mexican country," he said. "I will give Hartnell one loaf, and either David Spence or Cooper the other. If Cooper is in Monterey he will have it. I am proud of you, Loreta."

Jack was late coming home that night, for he stayed to see the fight between a grizzly bear and a bull, in the enclosure in front of Cooper's house.

"Such color," he told Loreta excitedly as soon as he had taken off his spurs and sat down with his pipe. "The señoritas had on their best dresses, and never were the Dons so fine in red sashes. Guitars played, and there was barbecue. All watched the bull charge toward the great bear, a four-hundred-pounder! It was no end exciting when the bear stood up on his hind legs to meet the bull. The crowd cheered as the bull tore up the dust. Then the bear gave one great swipe of his black arm and broke the neck of the charging bull. The crowd cheered some more. Guitars played for a contradance and hota. I didn't stay long after that."

Loreta saw Jack's eyes sparkle in the firelight, and his voice was full of excitement. She was glad he told her of the bull and bear baiting. It seemed like old days when Pablo used to come and tell Juan all about the doings in Monterey.

Jack kicked off his boots, and stretched his feet toward the fire. Loreta was proud of the socks that covered his feet. They were made from wool off a lamb that she had saved during wet weather.

"I gave Cooper the bread. He was pleased, Loreta, and so was Hartnell. They sent their compliments to you." Jack smiled at her, and Loreta saw him reach into the pocket of his vest and bring out something that was wrapped in a bit of

224

cartridge paper. "I saw this at Banales', the jeweler, and I thought you'd like it to remember the first fine bread you made for Englishmen." He handed her the paper.

Inside the rough brown package was a beautiful locket, gold, with a little glass window in it. Loreta rubbed the glorious disk with her rough hands.

"It shines, like something the saints would have," she managed from her full heart. "You are very good to me, Jack."

He smiled. "You put hair from your children, or from me, behind the glass in it," he told her. "It is as fine a locket as I could buy. Wear it to Mass on Sunday so that people will see that I treat you well. Some call me a Squaw man in Monterey, but what is that? At least I don't have to be afraid to go away from the rancho because you have eyes for other men."

"Jack," Loreta cried, "do not talk that way. God will hear and punish you. Say extra prayers tonight, so you will be forgiven, and the Virgin will look kindly—"

"Just the same it's true," he insisted. "The Mexicans are getting jealous of the Englishmen and these clever Americanos who come into the bay. I heard two talk at the trader's today. They said the Yankees and English are marrying all the prettiest señoritas and living like Dons on the fat of the land."

"Listening ears hear no good of themselves," Loreta murmured. "That is what the Padres at the Mission told Loreta long ago."

"I've known listening ears to save a man's skin before this, Loreta. Different times, different uses for ears," Jack said.

Loreta watched the locket pick up the bright flicker from the fire, and she smoothed it tenderly. She wished her father could have seen it. He had loved bright things so much.

"I think my hair would look well in it, Loreta," Jack said. "It is yellow enough to match the gold. Do you think the new baby will have gold hair?" He kissed her.

"I will ask the Virgin to remember about the gold hair," she murmured. "Then when you look at the baby you will think of this night when you gave the gold locket to Loreta."

225

Chapter IV

ROSE PETALS FOR LOVE: 1840

FOR Loreta, the days stretched out in one long struggle of trying to please Jack by cooking, baking, and serving him and his friends. José grew like a weed and was still whipped because he did not always mind. The child never tried to make excuses, only promised to come when he was called.

Loreta was sure Jack loved José. He had taught the boy to ride a horse so that now José rode alone to the Tularcitos school and had lessons and deportment from Don José Manuel Boronda, the brother of Doña Petra. Don Boronda complained some and said that José didn't pay attention and so did not do well with his lessons.

"Sometimes José even looks out of the door when I am talking to him, which is bad," Don Boronda told Loreta the day he came to order fire irons for the Los Laureles rancho.

Loreta glanced toward the smithy, and was glad to see that Jack was pounding the anvil and didn't hear. "I will tell José always to look at you, Don Boronda," she said quietly. "He is a good boy every other way and very kind to little María when I'm busy grinding corn and cooking." She smiled at the schoolmaster. "It is better that you tell only me when you have trouble with the boy."

But Loreta loved Jack Preble. He was good to her. He looked out for the cattle, and saved her rancho and the ranchos of many other Indians when the proclamations were nailed to trees along the road. Those proclamations said that Indians owning land must go and live on it or the Mexican government would take it away from them.

Jack saw the notice one morning and dropped all his work

226

at the smithy. "Ramierez will wait for his plowshare," he cried, and saddled the fastest horse he owned.

"Where are you going?" Loreta asked.

"Indians don't know the Mexican government is taking their land unless they are found living on it! Indians can't read. They are clever people who started this scheme for thieving land, but Jack Preble will ride trails and spread the news." He dug his spurs into the horse and was off.

Loreta was afraid she would drop her baby while he was gone. One night when the baby inside made her belly hurt, and she could no longer sit quietly by the fire with José, because of thinking that evil had come to her man, Loreta went into the bedroom and took the fiddle bag from its nail. Then she drew her little son close.

"In here is a shining fiddle that your grandfather Juan O-nes-e-mo played for the saints at the Mission to hear," she told him, and watched his brown eyes grow big with interest. "Once, long before even your mother was dropped, a kind Padre came all the way from Spain to teach Indians on the Carmelo about God and the Saints, and how to grow corn and grind it, and how to build adobe houses. The Padre carried this fiddle with him, and from it he brought bird calls, and music that angels know about. Your grandfather was a good Indian, and worked hard, so the Padre showed *him* how to make bird calls and chants. And then the bump sickness came to Indians, and Spaniards. The Padres crossed themselves whenever the curse of smallpox was even whispered. One day God told the good Padre of the fiddle to come to Paradise. Before he left, the Padre gave the fiddle to your grandfather, so that as long as an O-nes-e-mo lived, there would be bird calls and chants in the Carmelo—played on the Padre's fiddle."

José stood very still by Loreta's knee as she untied the strings of the bag and drew out the shining brown fiddle. He stared at it a long time, watching the light from the fire play on the curved wood, then he picked at the only string that was left.

"Maybe someday, your grandfather's fiddle will be yours

227

to make bird calls, José." Loreta said and hoped that the good San Carlos had put music into the soul of her son, so that an Indian would once more play chants to honor the patron Saint of the Mission, where Padres were no more.

José picked again at the string, then looked at Loreta and shook his head. "Birds are nicer to watch when they sing. Woodpeckers move their heads up and down when they call. José likes that better than fiddle calls—"

He pulled the worn velvet bag over the fiddle and patted it with his little brown hands, and then turned once more to watch the fire.

Loreta sighed, put the fiddle in its bag, and hung it up on the bedroom wall. Maybe the new baby would be a boy and play the fiddle?

Jack arrived home just in time to catch little Benito in the warm blanket Loreta had made for him, and now Loreta had a surprise for Jack.

"Look in the cupboard behind the door, Niño!" she called, and waited to see his face.

Jack was very happy when he came to the bed bringing the home-smoked ham on a platter that had come around the Horn on the last "Boston ship." "Did you do this?" he asked.

Loreta nodded. Jack's happiness was worth all the hard work and trouble she had up in the hills smoking the leg of pig with green willow wood.

"When Benito was almost here, and no ham from England, Loreta was afraid Jack would be sad," she told him. "José helped me and we smoked it in a hole on the hill, to make the California pig taste like the one your mother sent for the birth of María."

Jack was proud. Loreta could tell that, for the worry lines in his forehead were rubbed away.

"I'll have to pay attention to my new son," he said and smiled into Loreta's eyes. "I'll have to forget for a bit that Alvarado and Vallejo are fighting between themselves now and Vallejo has accused my good friend José Abrego of not dividing Monterey tax money equally between civil and military employees." He started to pace the floor, and Loreta knew already he had forgotten the little new baby.

"Vallejo wants the lion's share for his soldiers. Alvarado calls Vallejo 'Autocrat of Sonoma' and no longer visits him. They don't drink wine together now." Jack stood and looked down at Loreta for a minute. "Some say that Vallejo is massing his troops at Sonoma to operate against Alvarado. It's time the foreigners did away with Mexican Californians' rule and asked for their rights. Isaac Graham thinks we could overthrow Alvarado and Vallejo and their crowd if we stick together."

Loreta sighed, and shook her head. "You are thinking more about land and fights than you think about your son, Niño Jack."

He turned away from her with anger in his eyes. "You're only an Indian. You can't see that it is for the good of all that I think so much about politics," he said with impatience. "All you want is fiesta. Well, I'll give you a fiesta. We'll ask people to come and see the baby and taste the first ham smoked on the Carmelo." After that he didn't mention Isaac Graham or the troubles of Alvarado and Vallejo; instead he invited people for fiesta, and Loreta was glad. But she knew something was brewing in his mind.

Many people came to drink to the health of mother and baby. Even Fabian Berreto and his wife María came all the way from Pescadero Rancho to see little Benito. Maria consented to be the baby's godmother when he was christened.

After the Spanish and Mexicans had gone, Loreta noticed that Don Cooper and Hartnell, the schoolmaster at Monterey, and Don Jorje Allen and some other English and Americanos gathered close to the fire to talk low. Loreta was afraid of low talk. At the Mission long ago it meant trouble! Something was wrong.

"This makes a good place to talk," Loreta heard a tall thin man say. "The Mexicans will not suspect we are planning against them at a fiesta for the birth of a baby."

229

"We must be very careful, for Alvarado suspects us, and I hear he has made friends again with General Vallejo, who is right now in Monterey carrying out Alvarado's orders to arrest every foreigner except those married to native women or in the professions. Vallejo has lots of soldiers guarding the jail," Hartnell said. "Alvarado is afraid of so many foreigners coming in to settle land and carry on trade, and Isaac Graham, the distiller in Pajaro, has talked too much. He comes from Kentucky, and brags a lot, which makes it hard for us all. They are afraid we'll take the country."

"The women are behind everything," a man said from the dark. "José Castro, Alvarado's right hand man, says that a California cavaliero cannot woo a señorita if he is opposed in his suit by an Americano sailor, and these heretics must be cleaned from the land."

Everybody laughed then, and some of the fear in Loreta went away.

"Not women, but the fear of being brought to justice is what tugs at the liver of Alvarado," Abel Stearns said. "I told him foreigners would take away their money and trade, and Alvarado said we couldn't do it. He won't let us take our money and trade away."

"Foolish Mexicans," Spence cried. "Why, Americanos pay nearly eighty per cent of the customs in Monterey. We could not exist without foreigners."

"Not foolish Mexicans," Jack laughed. "You forget that Alvarado was born in Monterey. He's a Californian."

"He's a fool," Don Cooper snorted.

Hartnell laughed. "But you are exempt, Don Cooper. Alvarado himself said you would not be touched, and neither would Abel Stearns or Nathan Spear. Each of you three must have been born with a caul."

"I'm not an Americano," Loreta heard Jack say. "They won't be taking me. I'm being naturalized as a Mexican."

"But we all are naturalized. I suppose you think they forget that you're damned busy doing your duty as a citizen and

230

watching and talking a lot," someone said from beyond the fire.

"Castro is in on it, too. He's busy as a skunk stealing honey," someone else said. "A fine bunch of flowers they all are, when they're together."

"And now if you're all through talking of flowers and animals, you will stand up and have a riata put around you, and go quietly and lawfully to jail in Monterey," a clear, loud voice called from the dark. "We have you surrounded by soldiers, under orders from General Vallejo. The first man who makes trouble will be shot. Don William Hartnell and Don Juan Bautista Cooper and Don Jorje Allen will mount their horses and be off about their business."

Loreta heard loud cries and scuffling in the dust. She was weak from just dropping little Benito, and slow getting to the fire, where they were gathered, but she arrived in time to see a riata thrown over Jack's shoulders. It tightened around his middle, and pinned his arms to his sides. There seemed to be soldiers everywhere.

"Loreta! Loreta!" Jack cried. "Here! Look this way!" In the dim, red glow Loreta saw a soldier's rawhide switch cut across Jack's mouth. But the Marinero went on. "If anything happens, go to Don Cooper. He will help you. Remember, do *nothing*, until Don Cooper tells you it is all right."

Loreta saw soldiers with pine flares to light, gathering up the hides that were pegged out to dry, and she saw them take all the best irons from the smithy.

"Got any fire arms?" a soldier demanded, and pushed past her into the house. He took the gun from the rack by the door.

Loreta clung to it. "The gun belongs to me, to Loreta," she cried. "I need it." But the man wrenched away from her hold, and went out.

Like a bundle, Jack was tied and tossed on a horse and taken away in the dark.

A new baby; pride over the ham; and now, Jack taken away on a horse like a sack of meal! Where would they take him?

231

What had happened? Loreta dropped to her knees by the bed where María wailed, and while her hands were busy patting and comforting a baby body, Loreta prayed to the Virgin, who watches over orphans and all mothers of children, and asked her to intercede for an Indian woman with three little children, and bring Jack back to the beautiful adobe he had built.

Two days later, Don Cooper rode up under the great oak tree and tied his horse.

"They have taken Jack along with thirty-nine others as military prisoners in chains. They sailed at dawn today on the bark *Joven Guipuzcoana* for San Blas in Mexico," he told Loreta. "I tried to get the boy off, but I couldn't. José Castro went with them, and Castro never liked Jack." He smiled sadly at Loreta and took from his pocket a paper. "Listen carefully, Loreta, this is Alvarado's proclamation, and it is important." He unrolled it and read that Alvarado was informing his fellow citizens how "a sordid and venal faction, gotten up by some ungrateful foreigners whom you have welcomed to your hospitable soil, attempted to strip us of our most precious treasure, country and life, desiring to sacrifice to their unmeasured ambition the first authorities of the country. I congratulate you all on your escape from these people."

"Will they bring Jack back—" Loreta managed after a while. "Or will they kill him?"

"I don't think they'll kill him. That would be too dangerous. But they may keep him in Mexico."

"What good would my Jack Preble do in Mexico?" she asked.

"Oh, Loreta, if I could answer that, perhaps I'd know the answers to everything," Don Cooper sighed. "Jealousy and hatred and greed, make men do a lot of things, things that sometimes involve countries, and sometimes even the whole world. All we can do is wait, and hope for good news."

Loreta looked at little Benito. "Jack won't see Benito christened, then. Perhaps he won't ever see any of us again. It will be just like Antonio."

"Cheer up. Oliver Larkin, in Monterey, is a smart man. He knows people high up in the Americano capital at Washington, and he has written to tell what has happened to Americanos who were taken along with Jack. Maybe Larkin will cause trouble and get them back."

After that, Don Cooper told Loreta his plan. "You cannot take care of your children, and look after Jack's stock," he said. "I will manage the rancho for you, and send my best man, Manuel Boleno, as a foreman. He is good at selling, and can keep vaqueros at their work and away from too much whiskey." He smiled into Loreta's eyes. "If you have any trouble send for me, and I will come. We will keep strict accounting of everything, so that when Jack returns, he will see how well we have managed."

Don Cooper mounted his horse. "Manuel will be along tomorrow." He looked in at the open front of the smithy. "Better use grease on the iron and tools," he said. "Things rust very quickly, and Jack will be cross." Then he waved at Loreta and José and María, and rode away.

Don Cooper was kind, and his plan took some of the worry from Loreta's heart, for there were so many cattle, and so much riding to do. Jack had taught his two vaqueros what was necessary about watering and feed, but they were used to orders, and in just two days they were already staying around until mid-morning before they rode to the range.

Manuel Boleno came and brought his wife and children. They built a tule hut in the willows near the water, and the vaqueros went back to riding the range, just as they had worked for Jack.

The days were peaceful, with plenty to eat, and good friends dropping in, sometimes to stay a week at a time. Señor Fabian Berreto was not feeling so well, so he and María came and stayed with Loreta to get away from the heavy fog at Rancho Pescadero on the seacoast.

María was worried about Fabian's chest. Twice Fabian had seen Manuel de Alva, who knew about herbs, but it did no

233

good. Loreta and José made an Indian sweat house, and they put Fabian in it to sweat away the cough.

It was nice to have a Spanish woman living in the adobe. She showed Loreta a lot of ways to cook meat, and how to make sweet cakes, and then one day María ground petals of Castile roses in a stone mortar until they were a pink dough. Into this sweet-smelling dough, she carefully worked fresh clean tallow.

"When Jack comes home, Loreta, you put some of this pomade on your hair and on the neck where men like to kiss, and he will never go away from you again. That is how I keep Fabian so near me, when other, younger, eyes smile at him," she told Loreta. "Men like to close their eyes and kiss, and smell sweet rose petals all at the same time."

But María was soon to fail in her efforts with rose petals, for Fabian's cough grew steadily worse. Before next full moon the cheerful little man closed his eyes, and was no longer interested in sweet smells from ground-up roses.

Loreta was lonely for a time after María Berreto went home to Rancho Pescadero. The Duartes came in on their way to town, and Don José Manuel Boronda often stopped to talk. The Romeros brought fruit and cakes. Each time the neighbors came, Loreta would ask if there was any news from the prisoners in San Blas. No one knew. Their minds were now on grizzly bears that were taking cattle from the ranchos on the Carmelo.

José Manuel Boronda rode in from his Los Laureles rancho one morning and told Loreta that a bear had come right into the corral.

"He put his great arms around a calf and squeezed the life out of it before a single vaquero could stop him with a bullet," the Spaniard cried. "We must all band together and do something! Bears go up on the range and wait until cows open their mouths to bellow and then, quick, they grab the tongue of that cow and jerk it out. In no time the animal is dead and ready for grizzly fiesta." He said he was going into Monterey after Feliciano Soberanes, the famous grizzly hunter, and would bring him up the Carmelo to help rancheros rid themselves of the dreadful creatures.

But Loreta could not put her mind on grizzlies when her heart was aching to know news about her Marinero Jack in Mexico. What did grizzlies matter if her Jack, her golden-haired Englishman, was lying to rot somewhere among the cruel Mexicans?

When one full moon followed another, and coyotes up on the hillside yelped in the moonlight, and went away again more times than she had fingers, Loreta could stand the hurt no longer. She made extra food for vaqueros, left José to attend the little ones, and then took the white pony over the yellow road toward Monterey. Tied to the saddle in a cloth, were candles to light at the feet of "Our Lady" in the deserted Mission of San Carlos. Surely the statue would have pity on the sorrows of an Indian woman, and would send comfort and hope back to Loreta in the beams from the lighted candles.

When she arrived at the Mission San Carlos, Loreta saw that the last earthquake had made a wider crack in the side wall. Mexicans had taken away all but a few of the redwood poles that had once formed the Mission compound for cattle. She tied her pony to one of the lichen-covered poles, and took her cloth with the candles in it. Gray lizards sunned themselves on pieces of broken roof tiles, and clods of adobe that had fallen from ruined walls. A bluejay scolded at her and hopped around on the roofless room where Indians had slept after their hard work of rendering tallow or tilling the fields. Loreta tried to keep her mind on prayers when she saw that even the altar was tipped crazily, and the wood had rotted away. As a Mission sister she had placed the flowers on that altar, and washed the beautiful lace-trimmed covers, and polished the candlesticks until they reflected lights in their golden curves. Loreta and Antonio had put a star over that altar on the very first Christmas Antonio came to San Carlos!

235

"Our Lady" was very dusty in her niche at the back of the church. Perhaps God had sent the spiders to make a thick, soft web across her eyes, so that the statue would not see what was happening in the church. She would only be sad if she knew not even one Padre walked to the altar with the cross swinging against his patched brown habit.

Loreta lighted her candles and put them at the feet of the statue. She could not see the face of "Our Lady," for the spiders had been busy a long time weaving her gray veil. The mouth alone peeped out under the soft web; half of it was smiling, half of it sad, where Juan's knife had slipped so long ago as he was carving her.

"Don't feel sorry about her mouth," Juan had told Loreta. "The Padre Lasuen, when he came and saw my statue, said that the Good God understood, and that even Padres must be reminded that sadness goes with joy the world over."

As she knelt alone to pray, Loreta asked God to please send Marinero Jack back from Mexico, and bring once more the happiness to go with the sadness in the heart of an Indian sister of Mission San Carlos.

Lighting the candles and saying prayers made Loreta feel better. She came out into the sun once more, and smiled when a bluejay scolded at her. Now she would go to Monterey and hunt for Pablo.

Pablo was the best one for news. He got things straight from the Indians at the washing hole, and they heard it direct from servants who waited in the big rooms of Americanos and Mexicans and listened to the talk.

"Thomas Larkin, the Americano, is turning trouble loose," Pablo told Loreta as he met her coming out of Dr. Manuel de Alva's house where she had been buying medicine for little Benito's cough. "The Americanos at Washington have sent to tell the Mexicans to let out the Americano prisoners or there will be a big fight." He leaned over close. "María Temaco was there. She was cleaning the floor, and heard it said that the Mexicans will turn the men loose and arrest José

236

Castro and keep him there. They laughed and said Americanos would be home soon because the Mexicans would not want to fight the Americano government."

"Then they are alive!" Loreta cried. "Are you sure of that, Pablo?"

"Women are like pigs," Pablo mumbled. "They squeal if you make them happy. Keep your voice low or you shall never have news from Pablo again."

"But it might be some other prisoners they talked about, not Jack."

At that moment the earth rocked violently and Loreta heard bottles clink and smash in Abrego's store. People ran out into the street from the doorways of adobe houses.

"See," Pablo cried. "See what the squeal of a woman can do! It even makes the earth's bowels rumble with disgust in an earthquake. I must go and help Don Soberanes save what wine can be saved," and he ran down the street.

Chapter V

STRIKE, CALIFORNIA STYLE: 1841

WHEN six months went by and Jack did not come back, Loreta was sure that Pablo had heard about the wrong prisoners, but she had little time for brooding. Benito coughed a great deal at night and in the early morning. A racking cough just like Fabian Berreto had suffered. Nothing stopped the cough, and the baby grew thinner day by day. Then there was trouble with the grizzlies on the rancho. Many cattle had been taken in the hills, and now the bold bears came right into the pen where the calves were.

Augustine Escobar, and Don Feliciano Soberanes, the fine grizzly hunters, were busy all the time now, but some of the bears were so big that they were dangerous to hunt. Wounded, they would go wild and kill the hunters.

Manuel Boleno had trouble to keep the vaqueros at work. They were all the time wanting to go grizzly hunting, and then when they did go, they were afraid and just climbed trees and sat looking at the bear.

"We'll build a stockade on the hill to catch the grizzly that's eating so many cattle," Manuel Boleno told Loreta. "I found another skin today. Men are not safe riding alone in the hills and I'm afraid for little José. He does not seem to pay attention when we warn him. Young are fools."

"José is a good vaquero," Loreta said. "And only seven years old, too. He understands what cattle are thinking, for he keeps them from stampeding when he drives them. Better than some grown vaqueros is José."

"He'll most likely be trying to understand what señoritas are thinking about in a few years, like the rest. Understanding

238

cows' minds may help him then," Manuel sniffed as he turned away. "Perhaps he will be seeing how high a whiskey jug has to be tipped without spilling whiskey into the nose."

Such excitement building the stockade! Loreta wrapped Benito in a wool blanket and carried him up on the hill in the sunshine to watch the men at work. José was wild with happiness, and little María ran after him with shining eyes. She fell down and picked herself up a dozen times without a murmur. Trees were cut, tall pines from the ridge nearest the sea where they grew well. Then they were hauled by oxen to the knoll above the adobe. A heavy timbered gate was put together with wooden pegs, and raised over the opening to the big stockade. Then Manuel dragged fresh meat in the dirt around the enclosure and put it inside.

Loreta watched Manuel examine the great V-shaped piece of wood which would release the heavy timbered gate when the bear took hold of the meat.

"Now try it out," he called. Then he caught sight of José. "Come, Vaquerito, you be the bear," he called. "Pull on the meat, and see if the door comes down."

José did not heed. He just went on watching one of the men test a post to be sure it was strong.

Loreta called to José, but he did not look up.

"Pull on the meat, Basillo," Manuel said to an Indian. "The boy is thinking of what is in a cow's mind."

Loreta wished there was more play in José. He seemed so quiet, always watching the faces of older people and not talking much himself; only when he was spoken to. His smiles were for little María who pulled his hair. He often gave her rides on the back of a calf, and told her she was a vaquero, and they both laughed. Queer that he did not want to be the bear and watch the great gate slam down, for now he jumped with excitement as Basillo pulled on the meat. But there was no more time to think of José, for Benito was coughing and the sun was low on the hill. It would be better to go into the house with the little boy.

239

Just at dawn the gate went down with a bang, and wakened everybody at the rancho. Loreta slipped into her dress, pulled sandals onto her feet and ran out. Manuel and the vaqueros were already there, climbing up in the branches of the big oak to look over the stockade and see the bear.

"The biggest one of all," Basillo called. "He is the grandfather of all bears, and we will need Escobar to sit in the tree and shoot him."

"No! No!" there was a chorus. "A bear baiting in Monterey for this one! A fiesta! Everybody will work better if we have a fiesta. Don Cooper has a bull waiting for this bear."

"Don't be fools," Manuel said. "There is the range to ride, and see if any other cows have been killed. One would think that now vaqueros were Dons in scarlet shirts and sashes instead of Indians who cow hunt."

"Fiesta," called Vincente, a tall dark Indian with a scar across his face. "We do not work unless there is a fiesta to celebrate the bear."

"Then you will not need to work here," Manuel cried out through the dim light. "There are others to take your place and be glad to eat well and have whiskey now and then without fiesta."

"Fiesta—" roared Alesandro, from another branch in the tree.

"Fiesta—fiesta—" The word echoed all over the rancho. "We do not work, unless fiesta."

Vincente, who was a San Antone Indian, kept at Manuel. "Rodeo time, and branding, too," he threatened. "But Indians don't work unless they have fiesta."

Loreta saw that Manuel Boleno was angry. "Let them have a fiesta," she said. "They have been good and worked well. Jack always liked fiesta and bear baiting in Monterey."

"You are easy," Manuel growled. "They will think they can have anything they want if they howl like a pack of coyotes."

"No, not easy," Loreta shook her head. "But Indians know the longing for freedom, for something different. I have never

240

seen a bear and bull fight with music and fiesta. It would be nice to go. I will take little Benito to the doctor when I am in Monterey."

Loreta thought Manuel looked at her with eyes that were not as usual, but he ordered riatas out, and soon the bear was tied by his legs and in an ox cart headed for Monterey. Manuel Boleno went ahead on a fine horse to spread the news of the big bear, and let all know about the bear baiting.

José insisted on riding his own horse to Monterey. He would not be like a girl and ride with the women and children.

María came running with her pink embroidered dress that Doña Petra Allen had sent her. She slipped on a bit of fat, fell with the dress on the dirt floor, and started to cry. Then Benito had a fit of coughing.

Loreto was cross because José just stood in the doorway swaggering like a man. He did not even try to help his little pet María stop wailing about her crushed dress.

"Help your sister," she cried angrily. "Find her another dress and help her get washed and combed for the fiesta. Don't you see that I must look after little Benito?"

"Dressing babies is woman's work," José said. "I am a man now. I am all ready to go to Monterey on my horse."

"Perhaps it would be better to leave such a big man at home on the rancho to look after things," Loreta told him. "All the vaqueros are gone to make fiesta. You can be the man and stay home." She wiped Benito's face with a cloth, and put fresh clothes on him.

José changed instantly, and fell to work on María's tear-wet, dirty face. He scrubbed her until she yelled. In no time he had her hair combed and a clean dress over her head.

"María can ride in front of me on the horse," he said quietly. "Then you can ride with Benito and we won't have to take the slow old ox cart."

"That is better, Niño José," Loreta smiled. "Your step-father would not hear such words from you without switching. Maybe he will never come back to us, and you will have to be

241

the man of our family. But remember, kind men help Indian women with little babies, and sick boys."

Loreta took warm blankets to shield Benito from the night air on the trip home, and they started for Monterey.

Manuel Boleno had done his work well. All was excitement in Monterey when they arrived. The bear baiting was to be after the midday meal, and some said that the stores would be closed. The soldiers at the fort would play the band, and Don Cooper invited all to eat roasted meat afterwards.

Loreta left José and María sitting beside the road near Don Cooper's house, while she went to see Manuel de Alva with Benito. The doctor shook his head.

"He is growing too thin. Rub him all over with tallow every night and keep him warm. That is all I know." He was a little man, and came up close to Loreta. "And don't you dare put him in a sweat house either, or you'll kill him."

"But the cough? You don't give me any news of the cough?" Loreta said. "That is what makes him thin."

"I don't know anything more to do for the cough. He'll outgrow it," Manuel de Alva said, and pulled down the vest under his long-tailed coat. "And now I must go to dinner. Today we have a bear baiting right after siesta."

Such a fiesta! A band from the fort played, and a señorita danced around a hat. People wore their best clothes. The old bear had a run for his money in the bull that Don Cooper had been saving for so long. Then came the meat roasted over the coals.

José and María ate too much and got sleepy, so sleepy that José couldn't ride his horse home, and that left María stranded. Basillo lifted José on the horse in front of him, and Manuel Bolena took María, and they led the boy's horse.

Little Benito had been excited and flushed as he watched the bright colors in señoritas' dresses and heard the band music. He had only one spell of coughing. Now he lay peacefully sleeping in Loreta's arms, well protected by blankets. Perhaps the treat had done Benito good. He had not been so quiet for

242

many days now. He was even snoring because he slept so soundly.

When they arrived home, Loreta laid the baby on the bed carefully, lest she waken him, and then took sleepy María out of her red dress. José's legs were long, now, and she couldn't manage, so she washed his face with cold water.

"Here, man of the house!" she cried in his ear. "Out of your pantaloons! Such a sleepy vaquero, a woman must undress him like a baby!"

The words lashed at pride and brought better results than the cold water. José slid out of his clothes and into bed naked.

When she went back to Benito, a queer feeling ran through Loreta's heart. The baby was not snoring, and he wasn't awake. Little Benito had outgrown his cough.

Benito's cross in the cemetario in Monterey had been weathering for six months when Jack Preble rode into the rancho and called merrily for his son.

Loreta sat by the door of the adobe patching the seat of José's pantaloons. The boy had been too ardent in teaching María how to climb the oak tree. He had slipped and hung himself up by the seat of his pantaloons; and stayed there until vaqueros rode in for midday meal to lift him from the snag that caught him. Loreta didn't look up at the sound of hoofs, for Manuel Bolena always rode in early.

"Well, a fine homecoming for a husband!" came from the horse. "Where's my wife Loreta? Where's my son Benito, and Niña María?"

Loreta could hardly believe her ears! Jack was off the horse and running toward her. Then he held her close, so close she could hardly breathe in the folds of his ragged leather jacket.

"I've waited eighteen months for this," he murmured in her ear. "It was a living hell at Tepic. I prayed to the Virgin for your safekeeping, Loreta."

"I burned candles for you in the church at Monterey," Loreta told him. "Their light brought you back to us."

243

Jack laughed. "No, Loreta, not lights, but a horse borrowed from a kind friend in Monterey, brought me home! A good stepper he was, too; even so, it seemed an age riding over the hill to you." His arms were still around her, and he held her close. His eyes searched the dooryard.

"Where's my son?" he asked. "He must be a big chap by now. I wonder if he will remember his father?"

Loreta sent out a prayer for words to tell her man the news that would hurt him so much.

"Why are you so quiet, Loreta? Have you lost your tongue?" Jack demanded sharply and looked into her eyes.

"Benito sleeps beside Juan, in the cementario in Monterey, Jack. He has been there a long time now." Loreta put her head against Jack's great shoulder so that she would not see his face. She could feel the muscles in his arm twitch when he heard the news.

For a minute there was silence, then Jack sighed a great sigh that was more a groan. "And little María?" he asked, as if he was afraid.

"She is on the hill with José, churning butter, by strapping a barrel of cream to a wild calf. It makes the butter in no time and Américanos and English in Monterey will buy all we make."

"Let's go and find them. I have brought María some little earrings," Jack said. "They are in my bundle along with a prayer book from Mexico City, for you."

Loreta clung to Jack. "The days were so long with you away—" she managed. "To see you, and feel you with my hands seems only like a dream that will fade."

"Poor Loreta, all alone, and losing little Benito—" Jack held her close again and kissed the back of her.neck, which made Loreta think of the rose petals that were mixed in tallow and waiting in the house for this moment. The sweet smell that would keep a man close to his woman.

They walked to the horse and Jack took off a small pack. Loreta watched him, and felt sad for his thin boniness, and the

244

clothes that were almost in rags. He would need tortillas, and the home-smoked ham that she had been saving. Good meat stews and plenty of this new butter that English liked so much would fill him out again. He had been so young, and strong, and stout when he was thrown on that horse and taken away. Now he looked weary.

"Has José been minding better?" Jack asked as he handed Loreta the prayer book bound in white leather. "If he does not mind, I will not give him the beautiful spurs from Mexico."

"He has been a good boy, Jack. He has done as much work as some of the vaqueros, and he is only a bit over seven. Why, he can keep cattle from stampeding when he drives them. Even Manuel Boleno admits José is clever at driving cattle."

"Boleno?" Jack raised his eyebrows. They walked along toward the hill. "What is Boleno doing here? He belongs with Cooper."

"Don Cooper said he was a good man and sent him to manage for us while you were away. Don Cooper comes to check up. Boleno keeps the vaqueros at work."

"Well, now I'm home we'll not need Manuel Boleno," Jack said. "I'm sure Don Cooper must miss him."

"They do not even have Mass at San Carlos de Borromeo now," Loreta told Jack as they climbed up the bank. "The walls are cracked, and sheep take shelter in the ruins. Juan would be sad if he could see. Only on San Carlos Day does the priest come over."

Jack sniffed. "Yes, they said everything would be fine if we had home rule instead of Mexican rule, with Alvarado as governor! As far as I can see, things are worse now. Everyone seems to be taking what he can get from California."

"What did they do to you in Mexico?" Loreta asked. "You are so thin and worn."

"It was not so bad after we got to Tepec; the Mexicans treated us well enough, Loreta, but it was the cruel misery going down. We were put in irons, and if we talked or moved too much we were hit over the head with a sword."

245

"Poor Niño," Loreta patted his arm.

Jack drew himself up as straight as he could. "But that was nothing; one man, Chard, was held down by two men while a third man cut the tendons of his legs with a butcher knife, and then left him to die. I heard Castro suggest 'scuttle the bark and drown the prisoners,' but he failed to agree with the master on the price of the boat."

"Niño, Niño," Loreta shook her head sadly, "it is a lot to pay for going against Mexicans for the good of all people."

But Jack was not listening; his eyes were looking far away. "They drove us under lash to Tepec sixty miles in two days with the sun burning down on us! Prison was fine after that."

Loreta leaned close to her man, and the great hurt in her heart grew so big she could not swallow for a time. "I will be very good to you now you are back, Marinero Jack," she said quietly, and he squeezed her hand in answer.

"The Mexicans gave us each $250 and apologized for the 'mistake' that Castro and Alvarado made," Jack sniffed. "It will take that much money to put fat back on my bones."

María didn't know her father, but she was pleased with the earrings. She put her arms around him and kissed him. When Loreta prodded the child, María admitted it was nice he was home.

José proudly showed the butter they had been making, and shook hands with his stepfather. "Now that you're home we can have some ham," he said. "We have worked hard smoking hams for you to eat at fiesta."

Jack put his arms around the boy and Loreta was pleased to see their heads together as they fastened the spurs to José's little shoes. José looked up at her. For the first time in his life, the child seemed really happy. "Don Preble knows I'm a man, you see that?" he said. "He has brought me spurs."

"You had better mind when you are called, or you will lose them," Jack told him, and gave José a playful cuff on the side of the head. A terrible look of pain went over the child's face,

246

and he held his ear for a moment, and then went off alone.

"A queer chap, that," Jack said. "Come on, María and Loreta, let's go make fiesta. Your brother doesn't know playing when he has it. We'll have to toughen him up a bit."

Jack declared fiesta for everybody the next day, and word went to the neighbors to come. All were to celebrate the return of the prisoner.

While the music played and food and wine went the rounds, Loreta was busy cooking. Boleno came to where she worked.

"Jack Preble has told me he doesn't need me," Boleno said. "I am leaving on the first of the month, but I am not going back to Don Cooper's as Preble thinks. I am going to a rancho of my own near Jolon."

"That is fine," Loreta told him. "Your wife and children will like having their own rancho."

"When I leave I am taking forty head of cattle from here—" Boleno spat in the dust, and his eyes met Loreta's. "You must say that was the agreement, and you gave the cattle to me—"

"But I didn't say that! You have had your wages, Boleno!"

"You gave fiesta to the men because they worked well. I have made them work and looked after your stock." He came up close and lowered his voice. "Jack Preble grieves about the death of his son. If you do not see that I get those cattle, I will tell Jack that you brought Fabian Berreto here with a cough that he gave the boy, and that you were so crazy for bear baiting fiesta that you took little Benito out into the night air and killed him."

"No—no—" Loreta brushed her hand across her eyes. She wanted to wipe the words away from her brain. "Loreta, his own mother, would not kill Benito."

"If Berreto had not come, there would have been no cough. Benito might be running around today, if he had not gone to Monterey to the bear baiting," Boleno insisted. "Jack Preble shall know this, unless—"

247

"You are touched by Satan, Manuel Boleno," Loreta cried. "You would torture a father about his dead son, just to get some cows!"

"Did you hear any news, when you landed in Monterey?" Loreta asked cautiously the next day as Jack sat with her under the oak.

"Only that the military rulers and the civil rulers are fighting among themselves. Each wants to be top dog. The Mexicans are sick of Alvarado and Vallejo making trouble. Everybody is fighting everybody else to get what they can of land and cattle."

Loreta went on mending Jack's tattered coat. "A sad thing has happened since you went away. Fabian Berreto took a cough—"

"Poor old Fabian, always getting something." Jack looked off over golden hills.

"María brought Fabian up here, for the change, thinking it would help his cough, but he died. He died here at our rancho."

"Fabian dead!" Jack sat up and rubbed his back against the tree to scratch it. "Where's María?"

"At the rancho Pescadero." Loreta hesitated. "Jack—"

"Yes?"

"When Fabian was sick, I told María to bring him here, because of the cold fog at the seacoast."

Jack patted her knee and smiled. "Bless you, always trying to live up to your prayer book, Loreta. You were beautiful that day I saw you first, singing in the Mission."

"Our little Benito caught the cough from Fabian Berreto and died, too." The words were hard to say, but Loreta had thought about this all night.

"Poor baby—" Jack did not look up; he poked in the dirt with a twig. "I didn't see him but a couple of days. I was so proud of having a son, Loreta."

"I did everything I could for Benito, and on the day the great grizzly bear was caught on our rancho in the stockade, I took Benito in to Dr. de Alva. We stayed to hear the music, and see the colors. Little Benito laughed and clapped his hands and forgot to cough. I wrapped him well in blankets coming home—"

"Why all this tale?" Jack interrupted. "We can't bring the boy back by talking about it."

Loreta took a big breath. "The tale must come out, Jack, because Benito died that night after we got home, and Manuel Boleno told me yesterday, that if I did not say to you that he was to have forty head of cattle for his new rancho, he would tell you I had killed Benito, by having Fabian here, and taking the baby to Monterey."

For a moment all was quiet. Loreta saw the lump in Jack's throat go up and down. Then he turned to her, with eyes full of tenderness. "I'm glad you told me, Loreta. It took courage to tell me—and forty head of cattle are not so many to lose." His jaw set. "Manuel Boleno is a skunk." He got up from the base of the tree. "I'm glad you did not let him force you into such an underhanded business. The forty head would only be a beginning of what he would get out of you." Jack knelt in front of Loreta, and took her face between his two poor chapped hands. "Always remember that I trust you, and will trust you until someone proves that you are not to be trusted, Loreta, because I love you." He got up and walked swiftly toward the tule hut near the river.

Loreta never saw Boleno and his family again. They were gone before sunset, and Jack set fire to their hut.

Chapter VI

AMERICAN FALSE ALARM: 1842

IN no time the smithy was going at top speed, for Jack had as
much work as he could possibly do. In his absence there
had been difficulty in getting iron plowshares made, and many
Spanish and Mexican rancheros had to go back to a sharpened
stick for plowing.

There was no resentment now in Loreta's heart over the
number of people she had to feed, and the amount of work for
one pair of hands. Sometimes she looked at the big barn Jack
had built, and the beautiful horses, and wished she had someone to help her cook, but that soon passed. She was pleased to
have her man back at home, where she could see him in the
smithy as she took skins from peppers, or peeled onions.

Jack was so full of talk about what Alvarado and Vallejo
were doing. He would even stop pounding the hot iron to tell
some passer-by what he thought; and that there was bound to
be trouble. Alvarado hadn't kept his promises to the foreigners,
for the help they gave him to become governor. Loreta saw
looks exchanged, and knew that some of the very people who
ate Jack's food and listened to him, were thinking opposite to
the way he talked. This made Loreta afraid.

Once she mentioned it. He only laughed. "Don't be afraid,
Loreta. Never mind the looks they exchange. I give them food
and help when they need it. They will never bite me. Jack
Preble lets them have horses and money. If you do good,
things work out, even if the mountain lions have taken six
calves this week."

Miguel Torres came oftenest to the rancho on his way home
from Monterey. He was usually drunk with whiskey, and car-

250

ried several jugs along with him in the ox cart. Miguel would stay a couple of days to sober up because he was afraid of his wife.

"She'll kick my breeches off me; she'll never even feed me if she sees me this way! María is a good woman, but she makes me wipe my feet too much, before I go into the house, and once she gets started talking, there's no way of stopping her. She turns her grievances against me over and over, like the sad sea waves." Then he would sidle up to Jack. "Preble, you are a good man. Come home with me and view my fine crops, and pay a well-phrased English compliment to María, will you? Then she'll be happy and forget to call her poor Miguel a worm."

Jack usually went and Loreta grew vexed about it.

"Now, Loreta," Jack told her. "You wanted me to join the church and be a good man, didn't you?"

She nodded.

"Well, I am doing my good works when I go home with Miguel Torres. You know his wife is a long-toothed, horse-faced woman, a scold. If I can cheer her up, I stop a fight between them. Surely that is doing good for people and making the saints smile. I know the saints feel sorry for Miguel." Jack patted Loreta affectionately. "María is not so sweet and patient as you are. We must not be too hard on poor Miguel." Then he rode away on his horse ahead of the worried Miguel.

Loreta knew Jack enjoyed smoothing the fur of the annoyed María Torres. He was pleased about this power he had over people. She went back to making bread in the iron pot. At least while Jack was away, José would be saved punishment for not coming when he was called.

A week later, Loreta was peeling onions under the great oak tree by the door, when a Mexican vaquero rode up and slid off his horse. Jack passed the time of day, as the man tied the mare to the post.

"What can a smith do for a vaquero now that the fog has lifted?" he asked.

251

"Nothing for me," the man grumbled. "Don Soberanes sends me to tell your squaw that an old Indian who works for him is dying and wants to see her."

"Pablo," Loreta murmured, and put the pot of onions away from her onto the ground so that she could cross herself. She looked up to see Jack lay down his hammer and stride over to the vaquero. With a quick dart, Jack lunged toward the man and smashed his great hand into the vaquero's nose. "You'll call her no squaw, trash that you are," he cried. "You'll call her Señora Preble, or I'll fix your jaw so that you'll never call anyone else by any name at all."

He wiped the blood from his hand on his breeches, and then picked the Mexican from the yellow ground by the collar. "Now, give your message to Señora Preble properly. Address her as Señora Preble." He shook the man, who was smaller and afraid.

"Señora Preble, Don Soberanes sent me to tell you that Pablo, the old Indian, is dying and wants you to come," the man said as well as he could through the blood that was running from his nose.

Loreta nodded, and said a prayer for the soul of her Jack who loved to fight, and another prayer for the soul of the dying Pablo; then she turned toward the house, to make ready for the trip to Monterey.

With Pablo gone there would be few Mission Indians of the Carmelo except Loreta Preble, she thought, as she brushed her hair with the wooden brush Jack's mother had sent on the last boat that came around the Horn to Monterey.

Jack soon followed her into the house. Anger was still black on his face, as he paused in the bedroom doorway and watched Loreta pull a clean dress over her shoulders.

"You are not going to Monterey to see Pablo," he said. "There is no need of it."

Loreta faced him. "Pablo was the friend of my father. As a little boy he helped to make the tiles for the roof of San Carlos Mission, from squares of clay that he bent over his legs and then put to dry."

"What the devil difference does *that* make? The tiles are mostly broken now. You're *not* going," Jack cried angrily.

"Loreta O-nes-e-mo is still a sister of Carmel Mission, and Pablo has sent for her now when he is dying." She gently pushed little Mariá out of the way, and reached into the corner for her shoes.

"I'm master at the Preble rancho, and *I* say you are not to go," Jack roared. "Didn't I just smash that vaquero's nose for calling you a squaw? I'm trying to turn you into something more civilized, someone who can mix with Spaniards and Englishmen, and then you go running every time an old Indian calls, and spoil all my hard work. If you keep on, why they'll be naming me a squaw-man to the end of our days." He came up to Loreta and shook her by the shoulders. "You stay here away from Pablo—and other Indians. There is plenty of work to do."

Loreta looked into the angry eyes of her Jack. "Pablo dies but once, Marinero Jack, and he is the godfather to little José. There will be work to do on the rancho when Loreta's bones rot in the cemetario." She turned from him, and reached up to the nail on the wall for her shawl, and then threw it over her shoulders.

"If you go to Pablo you need never come back here to me and your children," Jack said. "I'm sick of trying to tame a squaw."

Loreta drew herself up, walked to the door. "May God and the Virgin forgive you, and be kind to you," she said, and then ran out to José and told him to catch the white pony.

She drew him close to her.

"Your Godfather Pablo is going to leave us and go to Paradise," she told him. "He wants to see me before he goes. You must take care of María—be good to her, for I will be gone a long, long time,—many moons." She stooped and kissed him

253

and gave little María a great hug—and then mounted the pony.

All the way to Monterey Loreta prayed for the soul of Pablo. The words of Marinero Jack hurt; prayers for another would ease the hurt.

Doña Soberanes was very kind, and ordered an Indian to feed and care for Loreta's pony, and Don Feliciano himself took Loreta to the little house in back where Pablo was lying on a bed. He did not go in, but patted her shoulder.

"When you have talked to Pablo, come to the kitchen for some food," he said gently, and left Loreta by the low doorway.

Pablo looked very thin, and his eyes burned like the nuptial candles on an altar.

"Loreta," he said feebly, and put out his hand. "The priest has been, and I have made confession. Pablo wanted to see you and give you the paper for José, his godson." He reached a bony hand under the skins on his bed, and brought out a paper. "This is the paper telling of land that the Padres gave to Pablo when they left, and another paper telling that Don Soberanes has money belonging to Pablo. All goes to José, the son of Loreta O-nes-e-mo."

Loreta wiped sweat from the sunken eyes, and an Indian woman who sat by the bed, gave willow water to Pablo, to freshen his lips. Then he smiled at Loreta.

"Pablo saved his money and his land," he told her. "No whiskey drinking. No smoking Mexican tobacco; only gossip was Pablo's badness, and that has been confessed." He caught her hand again. "You would have done better to take Pablo for your man instead of that yellow headed Englishman. I hear he beats José when the boy doesn't mind. Pablo would not do that."

Then a pain went through poor old Pablo; his body shook, and his eyes closed. The Indian woman gave him medicine, but it was hard for him to swallow.

Loreta put her hand on his forehead, and sent prayers to the

254

good God and San Carlos to help Pablo, the Mission builder. After a time he was quiet again, and seemed to sleep. Loreta went out into the fresh air. The warm sun felt good on her back. Doña Soberanes sent a servant to tell her that food was waiting.

The sun had moved the shadows only the width of two fingers while Loreta was away, but when she went back, Pablo's soul had gone from the little house.

Doña Soberanes had Loreta stay the night, so that she could go to the Rosary for Pablo, and see him buried the next day.

"But my black dress—it is in the Carmelo!" Loreta said. "The Saints will think that an Indian woman gives them poor worship in just a colored dress for the funeral."

Don Soberanes smiled on Loreta then. "It is better to have worship in the heart that is covered by a cotton dress, than to cover sins with silk," he told her. "Your face shines with goodness, Loreta, and God understands about the cotton dress."

The next day when they came out of the cemetario after Pablo was laid away, Loreta saw Jack, with María on the horse in front of him; and José on a pony by his side. They were waiting under some big oaks by the roadside. María's face was dirty and smeared from crying, and her dress was on wrong side out. She called loudly to Loreta who walked behind the priest and two others.

"We came to ride home with you," was all Marinero Jack said to her, by way of greeting. "María has cried and wanted you."

"She cried because father gave her too much meat, and she's cranky because it is time for a physic," José said. "She wouldn't take physic for me or father—only you."

"I had to give her meat. A man should have some peace in his own house," Jack told Loreta. "Come, where is your pony? There is work to do at home."

No more was said about Pablo, then, but Marinero Jack held Loreta close and begged her forgiveness that night after

255

the candles were out. "It was well you went to see old Pablo, Loreta," he said as he caressed her. "If you hadn't gone he might not have left his money and his land to José. Someday if I look after his affairs, the boy will be a very rich man."

One day in October, while the hills were still yellow and waiting for the first rain, Miguel Torres rode into the rancho. He was greatly excited. "You should come to Monterey, Comero Jack. Big doings. Alvarado has his hands full now. He will give up. What you said has come to pass."

Loreta saw Jack's eyes brighten. His chest came up with pride.

"What did I say, Torres?"

"Why, that the Americanos would take Monterey!" Miguel shouted. "Their boats are in the bay right now. They have sent messages. I was in the saloon waiting for courage to ride home to María when the boats arrived, and I thought of my good Comero, Jack Preble. Come to Monterey and see! Americanos threaten to land one hundred and fifty soldiers and take the fort."

"Wait while I catch a horse," Jack cried, and dropped everything. He raced to the pasture and clapped his hands for his favorite horse.

Loreta ran to Jack. "No, Marinero," she begged. "Don't go and leave Loreta. Something will happen."

Jack only glared. He pulled away from her hold on his arm, and flung the saddle onto the horse. "Do you want me to stay pounding iron in Carmelo, when there is something important going on in Monterey? How does an Indian woman get such power to judge what a man is to do?" Without looking back, he rode away with Torres, and soon was blotted out in the cloud of yellow dust.

Loreta stood a moment, watching that cloud, then she turned, and ran up the hill where José and María were fastening barrels of cream on the backs of calves. She waved her hand to attract José's attention and beckoned him.

256

"I must ride over the hill," she told the boy. "Food is in the cupboard. Get it out when the sun is high, and tell the vaqueros I will be back any minute. Do not feed too much meat to María and be a good boy." She patted him and felt around his neck to see if the holy medals were there, that Pablo and Doña Petra had given for his christening. Then she kissed María. "Do as your brother tells you," Loreta said. "He is man of the rancho today."

José's face shone with happiness. "A man does not undress babies and put them to bed," he told her. "You must come home by the time María says her prayers."

Loreta gave his bottom a spank. "Saucy Niño, you soon take on manhood, don't you?" She ran toward the corral and caught a white pony.

Loreta took the old Indian short-cut over the mountains to Monterey. It would never do for Jack to see her on the road. Her heart was aching as the horse plunged through chaparral and scarlet poison oak. Why did Jack have to be in on every fight? Did the saints have no control over him? Were the English as bloodthirsty as gentile Indians who didn't know the good God and the mercy of the Virgin, that they must go to fights? The hoof beats made a chant to her prayers as she rode along, and the sun grew hotter on her bare head.

But there was no fighting in Monterey! As Loreta went down the hill, she saw the boats anchored, and foreign soldiers at the fort. The street down near the shore was filled with people. Not even an Indian woman was to be seen at the washing hole. Bands were playing.

Loreta tied her horse in the willows just outside town near El Estero, and made her way along the winding, dusty street. She had forgotten her shoes and wore only a blue cotton mother hubbard, but none of these things bothered her. Where was Jack? What had happened to make a fight turn into bands playing? Maybe these Americanos were a queer tribe that played music after they killed people. She walked close to the wall of Don Cooper's house and tried to be inconspicuous in the crowd that was hurrying toward the bay.

"Alvarado told me he gave up to the Americanos from kindness of heart so that no Mexicans and Spanish would be killed," Loreta heard a little wizened man tell another, tall man.

"Such talk! He hadn't enough men to fight, that's all, and no powder. Soldiers without gunpowder are no good. They can't keep the enemy at a distance by making faces."

Loreta stepped noiselessly in bare feet on the hard, worn ground. She kept pace with the men to listen.

"They didn't even make a face," the old one said. "I was there myself, when the Americanos landed a hundred and fifty men and took possession of the fort. The Americano soldiers gave tobacco to our soldiers."

The sun was hot and directly overhead when Loreta wedged her way into the crowd near the Customs House.

Governor Alvarado was there, and the alcalde of Monterey. Mexican soldiers from the fort wore their best uniforms, and a lot of Americano soldiers were there in uniforms. A fine-looking man stood by the flagpole, and Alvarado bowed low to him.

"That's Commodore Jones of the Americanos," a señorita said in a whisper to Loreta. "He and his soldiers took the fort awhile ago."

"What will happen to us?" Loreta asked. "Will they kill us?"

The señorita laughed. "No. They are about to put up another flag for us to look at and we will have a fiesta with a ball tonight. The Americano soldiers are merry-looking men. I have a new yellow satin dress to wear." The señorita giggled to a friend near. "The Indian woman doesn't even know we are taken over by the Americanos."

A trumpet sounded; a band played. Loreta saw the Mexican flag come down, and a pretty red, white, and blue flag go up while they played a beautiful chant that Juan would have liked. The great Commodore Jones made a speech and wanted everybody to be happy. He told them that he had not come to kill, but to take Monterey because the United States was at war with Mexico.

Alvarado bowed again to the Commodore as a salute came from the Americano boats in the bay. "If you will please be so kind as to lend us powder, Commodore, we will be glad to salute you and the United States. We have a gun that works, but no powder for it at present," Alvarado told the Commodore.

"Your request is granted, Governor Alvarado." Commodore Jones waved a hand and ordered sailors to give gunpowder to the Military of Monterey.

Soon there was loud booming that hurt Loreta's ears. She turned her face to press it against the wall of the Customs House, and covered her ears.

"Fiesta, fiesta. Strike up the music," came from all sides, as a parade of soldiers led by Alvarado and this new Americano Commodore Jones walked along the street toward the plaza.

Loreta saw Jack swaggering along with the soldiers, talking English instead of Spanish, and laughing. She sighed gratefully that he was still alive. Everyone said there would be no more fighting now the new flag was flying. It was better that an Indian woman go over the hills to her children before Jack Preble saw her in a blue mother hubbard and no shoes. Loreta needed no fiesta today, now that she knew her Jack was safe.

José had been very busy. He boiled the very largest ham he could find to make a fiesta for himself and María. "A fiesta to celebrate that I am the man of the rancho now," he told Loreta. "A man must have a fiesta sometime. María only squealed when I made her eat. That is how girls celebrate fiesta."

Loreta sighed when she looked into the pot at the charred remains of the big ham she had been saving for San Carlos Day.

259

Jack did not come home that night, but he was back in time for midday meal the next day, and he brought Miguel Torres with him. This was the first time Loreta had ever seen Miguel sober on the return trip from Monterey. They were both in fine spirits, and Jack was full of talk.

"The Americanos took Monterey with salutes!" he told Loreta. "There was a dance in the streets after the American flag was raised. Then, when everybody had a fine time celebrating, the old Americano Commodore found out that the United States and Mexico hadn't declared war at all! It was *his* mistake. The old boy only *thought* Mexico and the United States were at war and grabbed off Monterey."

"Then the flag is not up? The red, white, and blue one?" Loreta asked excitedly.

"How did you know the colors?" Jack looked at her with narrowed eyes.

"You told Loreta yourself that the Americanos long ago stole the colors from the beautiful flag of England," Loreta said, and nodded toward the tiny British flag that was draped over the picture of Jack's mother.

He smiled then, and seemed pleased.

"What flag is up over the Customs House now?" Loreta asked again.

"Commodore Jones of the Americano navy hoisted up the Mexican flag again. He made a lot of apologies and gave a salute to Mexico!" Jack's eyes danced with joy, and Torres joined him in laughing. "So we're just where we were day before yesterday, Mexicans again, with Alvarado frightened to death, and preparing to fight against the new Governor Micheltorena, who has already landed in San Diego with his army of pardoned criminals."

"José and María made fiesta yesterday, too," María said, as she crawled into her father's lap to be petted. "We boiled a ham because José was man of the rancho."

"Where is the ham? Bring it out, Loreta, for Miguel to have a bit. We'll celebrate being Mexicans again."

"It was burned, Jack. José didn't put enough water and the ham boiled dry."

"That boy needs a hiding!" Jack's face was black. "Such a waste of good food that takes time to prepare."

"He's little yet, too little to understand about ham," Loreta said. "I'll give you some of the new cheese we made, and bread baked this morning."

After Miguel had eaten bread and cheese washed down with some good wine, he became very quarrelsome.

"I've made a mistake laughing with you because the Americanos put up their flag," he cried excitedly. "*I* am a Mexican." He pounded his chest. "Those Americanos are *terrible* creatures. They have insulted the Mexicans and the Mexican flag. I'm going right home to María and tell her the news. María will give them a tongue lashing. I'll tell you she will, when Miguel lets her know what happened in Monterey yesterday."

Jack chuckled and helped him onto the horse. "Off with you then, and let María do her worst. Maybe she'll forgive you for staying away so long," he cried, and slapped Miguel's horse on the flank.

When Miguel had gone, Jack turned to his own horse and pulled a beautiful black embroidered shawl from straps behind the saddle.

"For you, Loreta. I'm sorry for what I said to you yesterday when I rode away, and you were begging me to stay," he said in a low voice. "I prayed at the church this morning and asked forgiveness for hurting the soul of an Indian woman. You don't understand. A man goes crazy when there is talk of fighting. Of war! He forgets to be kind to the woman who asks him to stay at home with her. It must be the excitement." He draped the shawl around Loreta's shoulders and then stooped to kiss her. "You are very patient with a sailor man, Loreta."

"I am glad you did not fight," she said. "I would like to give you another son and make you happy, Jack. That is all I can give—myself and some children to you. Perhaps the saints

261

don't send a son to us because you always want to be in fights?"

Jack laughed, and went to work building up the fire in the smithy. "Wear the shawl to mass on Sunday. It is prettier than the one Señora Rosalies wears."

Chapter VII

PIANO: 1843

"THERE'S to be a Cascarone Ball in Monterey on Tuesday night," Jack told Loreta one day as he slid off his horse. "Don José Abrego ordered Captain John Smith to bring him a piano around the Horn. Smith has just arrived with it! Don Abrego says nothing short of a Cascarone Ball will do as welcome for the piano." He picked up little María and tossed her into the air. She squealed with joy. "Smith brought three pianos. Abrego claims his is the most beautiful of them all. When I left they were feeling the shining legs and looking at the carving. Vallejo gets his piano up at Yerba Buena where Richardson sits almost alone as collector of the port."

"I have never been to a ball," Loreta said. "I do not know the dances."

"That doesn't matter. You have eyes, haven't you? You can watch. The señoritas are dressed in their best and throw kisses as well as cascarones. It is very gay. I want you to go and show your pretty silk dress and the shawl I brought you. We must make cascarones, too, and do our share."

"The Spanish do not like Indians to dance among them, Marinero Jack. Long ago Pablo and Juan said Spanish make Indians dance by themselves in another square."

"You are my wife. You'll go," Jack told her. Loreta saw that her man's jaw was set. "Today I bought another piece of land. We now have eight thousand acres, Loreta O-nes-e-mo Preble. We are landed Dons without the name." He stuck out his chest and Loreta thought her Jack looked a little like the new cock he had brought home not so long ago. "We'll have the name, too, some day, just as Don David Spence has it. If a

263

Scotchman can be a Don, so can an Englishman when he acquires enough land and cattle to be important."

"You said we must make cascarones for the ball," Loreta said. "Are they sweet cakes?"

Jack threw back his head and laughed. His eyes danced. "Sweet cakes, but not to eat," he cried. "It is high time you stopped being just a Carmel Indian on the land and took to Spanish customs, if you are to be civilized. Cascarones are egg shells filled with bits of fine cut paper. When a man sees a señorita he wants to dance with, he crushes the egg over her head. If it breaks, he can dance without an introduction. She's bound to dance with him. That's why cascarone balls are such fun. Señoritas use cascarones on men, too."

Loreta was horrified when Jack blew the insides out of every egg in the house, and then set José and María to cutting paper and filling the shells through the hole in the end. "The eggs —Jack," she said. "We cannot eat them all. They will spoil."

"Forget it! This is our chance to shine among 'em in Monterey. We'll show Spaniards and Mexicans that there's nothing small about the Prebles. We'll take the *biggest* basket of cascarones." He smiled and patted her. "Who knows? Wasting a few eggs may help to turn an Indian woman into a Doña."

Loreta shook her head over the wasted food. It was bad to throw away good eggs and fill the shells with paper. They didn't have enough paper to cut up. Jack grabbed the cherished pile of letters that were written crisscross in his mother's fine hand. They went into the shells.

"She'll write me more letters," he told Loreta.

When Jack had gone up on the ridge to see to the cattle, Loreta busied herself. Before long she bundled José onto a horse, with a great pot of eggs cooked in chili and tomato. "Take them to the Mission Indians who huddle in misery over at the rancheria," she told the boy. "They may have sold their land and cattle for whiskey, but they must eat. You get back as fast as ever you can, and say nothing, or your stepfather will whip you."

264

José was delighted over the adventure. He smiled knowingly and galloped off. Little María stood by Loreta as she watched him away. Loreta prayed that the Virgin would look out for the boy. After all, José was young, and absent-minded sometimes, and somehow different from most people. She had promised to serve the Mission always. Surely the saints would protect her child when he was carrying food to Mission Indians who had little but what they stole.

Jack came riding into the rancho before little José returned. Loreta set out bread and cheese and some of the cooked eggs.

"Where's José? Can't he even have sense enough to come when it is time to eat?" Jack asked as he took off his spurs, and then held his hands before the fire to warm them.

"He went to feed Indians," María piped up, as she leaned against her father's leg. "A big pot of eggs."

Jack's eyes were black with anger. He looked into Loreta's very soul. "Is that right?" he asked.

Loreta nodded. "I cooked the eggs we couldn't use and sent them. The Indians at the rancheria are Mission Indians and they need food. You are so generous and good to me, with silk dresses and a lot to eat. Loreta was a Mission sister, Jack." Even to her own ears, Loreta's voice sounded weak and frightened. "Padre Payeras and Abella told Juan and Loreta to help Indians after they were gone to Branciforte—"

"Some of those very Indians are stealing my cattle, Loreta, you know that. They have long ago forgotten the Padres."

"Perhaps if the rich people like Jack Preble would be kind to them, Indians would remember more prayers because of gratitude. Spanish and Mexicans cheated them out of land for a few bottles of whiskey. Indians didn't understand, Jack."

"Come here, Loreta," Jack said. "Are you proud to be the wife of a rich man?"

Loreta nodded, and walked over to him. She wondered what this Englishman wanted of her.

"You're beautiful when you're frightened of me," Jack told her. "I like to frighten you sometimes, to bring out the starch

265

in you." He pulled her down beside the fire. "I want you to do good, Loreta, but I don't like this back door giving when you think I am away. Give openly for all to see. I'll send a beef over to the rancheria tomorrow before we go to the ball. That ought to make the Indians happy." He kissed Loreta and put his arm around her.

Soon José came, bringing the empty pot. Loreta saw that the boy was frightened. "Come in," she said, as he looked at her with questioning eyes. "Your stepfather knows and is glad you were such a brave boy to ride over to the rancheria with food."

There was a look of great relief on José's little face.

Jack had been very critical when he looked Loreta over before they started to the hall. Her dress of stiff black silk hung right. He saw to that. And he pulled the big gold locket from the folds of white lace at her throat where it was hidden.

"Most of the women will have dresses without necks," he said.

Loreta saw that his eyes were disappointed in her, and there was a hurt in her heart.

"But you are an Indian and older, and your breasts are flabby from suckling babies, so perhaps it is better you have sleeves and a neck to your dress. After all at twenty-four a woman should not try to look like a señorita."

Now, as she stood in the bright flickering light from the pine flares and listened to the music and watched the dance, Loreta understood why Jack had been upset over her clothes! Her dress was a dress to wear to church, and here everybody, even the men, wore bright-colored satins. Señoritas in rustling silks had no sleeves at all! They showed their necks down to the very nipples on their breasts, and pulled a soft scarf over them when a man looked too long.

Dons whirled around in this dance Jack said was a waltz, and the tails of their yellow or red, or blue, or green satin coats flew out so that the silver buttons twinkled in the light. Their

266

breeches were only to the knee and trimmed with gold braid and silver thread. They were like a garden of flowers, swaying in the wind, to Loreta who stood next to the wall watching, with Jack by her side.

And then a señorita laughed with her eyes and crushed a cascarone over Jack's head so that bits of paper sprinkled on him. "Come dance," she called. And away he went to form part of a group that whirled around holding hands.

Loreta stood in the shadow and watched Jack dance. She thought of San Carlos Day long ago when she had seen him first, dancing a *marinero* dance in the Mission compound while everybody clapped and laughed.

A contra dance started. Guitars and fiddles played fast; there was a mad whirl. Bits of paper made the air white, and men laughed. Now Jack danced with another señorita in a blue satin dress. She looked up into his eyes as they whirled away together.

"Why aren't you dancing?" came from behind Loreta in halting Spanish. "I'd like to try it with you, if you can keep your feet out of the way so I don't step on them."

Loreta turned. The man was rosy, with blue eyes that twinkled. He was not a Spaniard or a Mexican, for he was quite light-skinned, and he wore the blue clothes of a *marinero*. He took Loreta's hand and pulled her into the light. "Come on. We can hop around in circles like the rest. I'm not much of a ladies' man, and I'm a bit of a runt in the bargain, but I will keep you from being knocked down," he said, and smiled into Loreta's eyes.

"I don't know how to dance," she told him.

"You'll never learn younger!"

The *marinero* could dance well. In no time he showed Loreta how to sway with the beat of the music. She watched others and did what they did, and felt light and happy inside.

Once when she was a bit slow and got in the way of another couple, the *marinero* was comforting. "Don't let them bother you," he said, "I've heard tell that the best dancers are usually the poorest cooks."

After a while a drum pounded. The music stopped. Don José Abrego stood at the very top of the street at the plaza end. He pulled away a great white sheet and there stood the beautiful shining piano that had traveled in a boat for two years.

Doña Josefa Abrego played a Spanish song and everybody sang. Then Don Abrego clapped his hands. "There is food and wine for all," he called. "Drink a toast to the new piano!"

"And a toast to the beautiful lady who plays it," a voice cried. Far down the street someone started singing a gay song.

"Stay here out of the crush. I'll get your wine," the marinero said.

Loreta stood against the wall watching the crowd as it moved toward the long, candle-lighted refreshment table. Jack was talking now to a señorita in a green dress, and she laughed. He waved to Loreta.

"I'll be there in a minute," he called.

Jack and the marinero arrived at the same time.

"Who are you?" Jack demanded crossly, as he looked at the wine and cake.

"Jack Swan, if it is any of your business," the man said, with a savage glance at Jack. Then he smiled and handed Loreta her wine and cake.

"That's my wife," Jack told him.

"Well, if I was a high-combed rooster like you and had a pretty wife, I'd see that she had a good time instead of leaving her to stand alone in the shadows." The marinero bowed low to Loreta and turned away.

Jack was glum on the way home. "I'll bet the sailor is a bloody Englishman. They're always ready to fight," he said after a long time.

"Just like you," Loreta nodded. "The marinero, Jack Swan, dances well."

268

"But not so well as I do," Jack said. "*All* the señoritas tell me I dance well."

"I don't know—" Loreta murmured. "Maybe they are right. Maybe they just want you to feel good by telling you that. The señoritas know Jack Preble is proud."

"Next time there is a ball you shall dance with me, and find out for yourself that I am lighter on my feet than the little marinero."

Chapter VIII

TALLOW, WISHES, AND FIDDLE STRINGS:
1844. 1845

JACK PREBLE butchered every two weeks. Most of the meat was sent to Indians at the rancheria across the river, or given to any other ranchero who cared to come for it. The hides were what Jack wanted. He still made saddles the way Juan O-nes-e-mo had taught him, and there was a ready sale in Monterey for Preble saddles.

It seemed to Loreta that she would never catch up with the tallow in her candle-making. Every time the bottom of the vat began to show, Jack butchered again. José was a help now, with fingers clever at putting in wicks. The little boy seemed delighted when a box of candles was ready for market, and twice asked Jack if he could go along to see whose house they would light.

Jack had just finished butchering early one morning, when an earthquake came. The rumbling underground frightened María, and she screamed. There was a look of terror on her face. José watched the frightened baby for a second, then turned to Loreta.

"What's the matter with María?" he cried. "Is something biting her?" He ran to the baby and commenced to rip off her clothes.

"José, don't you hear it? The terrible rumbling noise in the earth?" Loreta asked as she picked María up. "Any child would be frightened."

José shook his head, then listened. "There is no noise."

As Loreta held María to her and tried to soothe the frightened child, a sadness came over her. It was all very clear now why José didn't mind well and why Don José Manuel Boronda, the schoolmaster, had long ago complained about José's

270

lack of attention and given up trying to teach the boy. José couldn't hear well. He heard when he was watching your face or when you were close, but not a noise from a distance. She pulled the boy near and brushed her hand tenderly over his little ears. Loreta wondered if it would be well to tell Jack.

But there was no time to think further of José. Another temblor came. The barn was shaking crazily. María screamed louder. Loreta prayed as she watched a great crack widen near the door of the adobe.

Jack came running from the pen where he had been butchering. "Get away from the house," he shouted. "The tiles may shake off and kill you!"

The terrible rumble kept up. José just stood. He was near the house, not facing the way his father called. The tiles were slipping! Another shake came. Loreta started toward José.

Like lightning, Jack dashed past her to the child, and pulled him away just as a great block of tiles crashed to the ground.

Loreta saw her man's face grow red with anger. Without a word, he loosened little José's pantaloons.

"I'll teach you to be mulish and not mind!" he cried and raised his hand to strike.

Loreta pushed the screaming María from her. With all her might she clung to Jack's arm before he struck the second blow.

"No," she cried. "He's deaf! He couldn't even hear the rumbling a minute ago. He asked me why María screamed."

The din was frightful, for José was bellowing at the top of his lungs and Maria screamed with fright. Jack just looked at Loreta for a minute.

"Are you trying to protect him, because he is a boy, and Antonio's son?"

"No, Jack, I just found out. Trust me. You said you would!" she begged.

Jack's eyes met hers again, and his hand dropped to his side. "Why didn't you tell me before?"

"I didn't know—until he asked me why Maria screamed."

271

Loreta saw José pull himself right side up. "Why did you whip me on account of the tiles?" he sobbed. "It wasn't my fault they fell down."

All was suddenly quiet except for the whimpering of María who buried her head in Loreta's blue cotton dress.

Jack's eyes were tender. Loreta saw that his hand shook when he pulled the boy to him. "José, I'm sorry I whipped you this time, and all the other times. I didn't know you couldn't hear when I called." He brushed back the black hair. "What would you like most of anything in the whole world, José? If Jack Preble can give it to you, then you shall have it."

"To go to Monterey with you and see who burns the beautiful candles José makes from the tallow," the child said with eager eyes. "And maybe look at a ship."

Jack held the boy to him for a moment in silence, then loosed him suddenly. "Quick, everybody into his best clothes. We go to Monterey with candles. A fiesta for José Prealta, with ships, and barley sugar from Milton Little's shop. We'll see what damage the earthquake has done in Monterey, too. Maybe even houses two stories tall have fallen."

Loreta shook her head. "There is so much work to be done. The tallow and the meat and the vaqueros to feed. It is better that only the men go, with no women at their heels."

"A fine mother you are," Jack called. "When José wants to make fiesta, who works? We'll take the candles to Doña Petra Allen, and José shall see where they burn. We'll go to the church and light a candle for José's grandfather, and another for his father, Antonio, and another for his kind gossipy godfather, Pablo, who left him a rancho when he is twenty-one."

Less than an hour later they were on their way, leaving old Vincente, the Indian, to fix the roof and feed the vaqueros when they came in.

José's eyes were shining. He rode his own horse, and galloped ahead, and then came back to the ox cart where Loreta and María rode beside Jack. He called to them to hurry up a bit.

"José hasn't been to Monterey for a treat since the bear baiting when you were away," Loreta said. "The day that little Benito died."

"We'll take him to see Stokes, the druggest and pillroller, and find out if there is anything to do for the deafness," Jack said.

"Perhaps Don Jorje Allen would be better," Loreta told him. "He is a dentist and a surgeon, too, and we go to his home anyway. Doña Petra is always kind to Indians."

She saw Jack wince at her words. "I'm no Indian. I don't need anybody's kindness," he said. "I can pay for what I get."

They stopped at the deserted Mission. Loreta wanted to make a prayer to the good San Carlos and to renew her promises.

"I'll wait out here," Jack said. "Someone passing might steal our candles and saddles from the cart."

Loreta looked up at Juan's beautiful tower. It was still lifting its cross into the sky in spite of the ruined church that supported it.

The Mission smelled damp and mouldy, and there were great cracks in the south wall, so that soon a big chunk of adobe would fall in. Weeds grew waist high between the floor tiles. Some startled bats flew from the dark corner near the door.

When she knelt to ask San Carlos to bless her, peace came over Loreta; a feeling that the saints understood and were giving their blessing to a lone Indian woman who prayed in the deserted church that her father had labored to build. Maybe Juan saw Loreta, and knew she hadn't forgotten the good Padres.

The green bay branches Loreta had piled around "Our Lady" last San Carlos Day were still there, brown now, and moulded. She reached up to take them away and discovered that someone had been shooting at the Saint. Her nose and eyes were nicked with bullet marks!

Loreta ran out to the cart and snatched a candle from the

273

box belonging to Doña Petra Allen. Then she took a few flowers from the bouquets she had picked to put on the graves of little Benito and his grandfather.

"Give me your flint," she demanded of Jack.

He dug into the pocket of his vest and handed her the stone. "What are you up to?" he asked crossly. "Be quick. This is José's fiesta day. The boy deserves as much time as he wants."

"Go on, go on," she cried. "I will catch up. The oxen walk slowly." As she ran through the weeds toward the church Loreta murmured a prayer, lighted the candle, and placed it in the niche beside the Saint. Then she scattered the flowers around it. Surely this would help "Our Lady" to understand that the bullets did not come from the hands of Indians whose fathers or grandfathers had so patiently carved her face and robes, and even built the niche to shelter her.

As Loreta hurried out of the church, clutching a single Castilian rose, she stumbled on a tile that had fallen from the roof. It turned over and rocked. On the inside was the imprint of the boney knee belonging to her own father, Juan O-nes-e-mo! Gently Loreta picked up the tile and leaned it against the church wall, not far from the door, and then ran on through the trembling heat waves. She paused only a moment to drop her rose for Antonio who slept alone on the hillside.

Before the ox cart had reached the top of the hill, Loreta caught up with it. She was glad to ride now, and gradually to breathe more comfortably. Besides, she had to put on her shoes, so that she would look proper as the wife of Jack Preble, the ranchero of Carmelo.

Loreta thought Doña Petra Allen was never so lovely as to-day. She was very kind to José and gave him sweets, but he was too excited to eat them. She let him sit on a little stool with a gorgeous green-feathered bird embroidered in wool on the seat of it, while Jack talked to Don Jorje Allen.

Presently Doña Petra held José in her lap and explained

274

about the beautiful picture of the virgin that was on the wall. This virgin held a white dove to her breast and wore a wreath of flowers on her head. Then Don Allen looked into the boy's ears, and put some warm oil in them.

"What is wrong with them, Don Allen?" Loreta asked.

"One eardrum is gone. An abscess when he was a baby must have caused the trouble. He will never hear better, Loreta," Don Allen said. "That is why sometimes he hears and sometimes not. It depends on which ear is turned toward the speaker."

"I will remember the Niño in my prayers," Doña Petra told Loreta in a gentle voice, "and I will burn candles for him."

"Candles! That's one reason we brought him here, Doña Allen," Jack cried. "We were nearly forgetting. José makes the candles we sell to you. His one wish was to come to Monterey and see whose house they light."

Loreta forgot how tight her shoes felt, as she watched Doña Allen clap her hands. "Basillo," the little lady called. "Bring chocolate and cakes, then all the candlesticks and we will put in new candles made by José, and light each one with a wish, for my little godson. This will be a fiesta of the candles."

Little Guadalupe and Tula Allen wanted to make wishes, too. Soon all the children were quiet, wishing and watching, until there was but one more candle to light.

"This is my wish," Doña Petra said and took the paper spill from Basillo. She bowed her head as she lighted the taper. "To José, maker of light. May he hear voices of Saints with the ear that is deaf to the troubles of the world." Then she held him close, cake and all, and gave him a holy picture of Joseph.

The earthquake cracked a few walls, but nothing serious had happened. Jack drove the ox cart down to the wharf, for there was a boat to see.

On the way back, he pointed out a small, low, adobe building that was very new. "Your friend, the little *marinero* who dances so well, owns that," he told Loreta. "He's just finished building it. He made pies to earn money for it. Pies the way I taught you to make them, Loreta. He's going to have a saloon and a boarding house for sailors."

"Then you know him well now?" Loreta asked, relieved, for she had felt sorry about the black looks at the Cascarone Ball.

"Everybody knows him, and Britishers have to stick together in wild parts like these," Jack told her.

Just then Swan appeared in the opening that was not yet a doorway. He waved and called them to stop.

"What do you think of my place?" he asked. "Even the earth groaned and quaked when the last daub of adobe was put on this morning." He shook hands with Jack and smiled at Loreta, and then miraculously brought a tiny whittled boat from his pocket and handed it to José. "Sorry I don't have girl stuff, too, for the little one."

Jack nodded toward the house. "You can't do much now until the walls dry. Come home with us. I'll get Gomez and Torres and we'll have a grizzly hunt. You need a holiday before you tie yourself down to keeping a saloon and boarding house."

"Don't mind if I do," Swan said. "I'm only a water dog; maybe I won't be much good at a grizzly hunt, but I know I can run damned fast when anything's after me." He clapped a hand over his mouth. "I won't do it again," he told Loreta.

That night Jack Swan told yarns by the fire. His fingers were busy whittling. María screamed and stiffened herself so that Loreta had to spank her at bedtime. The little girl liked to sit on the lap of the marinero. He was cutting out a doll for her with his knife, and María didn't know a doll. She wanted to stay up to see what this round-topped thing would be.

"You go to sleep. The dolly will be waiting for you in the morning when you open your eyes," Swan told María in halting Spanish.

After a while Jack Preble got up and went to the cupboard. Loreta saw that he brought more wine and then he tossed rolled-up fiddle strings onto the table.

"Swan brags that he is a fiddler. I bought strings in town today at Milton Little's store. Go fetch Juan's old fiddle, Loreta, and we'll see if he can turn out a tune for us."

Loreta went to the bedroom and took the velvet bag from the wall. It was dusty now. The fiddle had not been out since she had let José look at it so long ago.

Jack Swan's face was happy as he drew the fiddle from the bag. "It's an old one. A beauty," he cried. Then he removed the broken strings tenderly, and replaced them with new ones.

Loreta was pleased that the marinero was so kind to Juan's fiddle. "It was my father's. Padre Amores gave it to him, for playing chants in church," she said.

In no time the violin was tuned, and Swan played gay dances that pleased Jack so much that Loreta saw tears of joy in his eyes.

"English tunes! The ones my mother played on her piano!"

Then there were sailor jigs, and finally a beautiful chant that Jack called "God Save the King."

"We'll take the fiddle along on the bear hunt," Jack said when it was time to turn in for the night. "It'll be good to listen to English music around a campfire while we wait in the dark for the grizzly."

Loreta put her hand on the fiddle. "Juan's fiddle stays here."

"Yes, Preble, your wife is right," Swan said.

Jack's eyes burned with anger when he looked at her. "Our hospitality, Loreta! You are forgetting yourself. A ranchero is bound to make his guests happy, and Swan likes to play the fiddle. He won't hurt it."

"Juan's fiddle stays here."

"Then I don't count for anything? You don't care about my wishes and happiness?" he asked. "What I say goes at the Preble rancho, and I want to take the fiddle."

"Juan's fiddle stays here," Loreta spoke quietly, but her heart was pounding so that she could hardly breathe. "You have Carmelo land that the Indian Loreta brought you. You have the work of Loreta's hands, and her love." She put her hand on Jack's arm, but he shook it off. "The fiddle must be saved for your son Loreta expects to drop about the time corn is ripe."

The next morning when they were nearly ready to leave, Marinero Swan came up to where Loreta stood by the door. "You did right to keep the fiddle at home," he murmured. "May the young 'expected' be a fine fiddler. Such a fine fiddler that he'll sail to England to play at a command performance for the King himself!"

Jack came around the corner of the house, and the little bowlegged marinero rolled off toward the horses.

Loreta turned from the fog, and went back to her work in the house. She looked at the picture of Jack's mother, with the British flag over it, and wondered what the stern-faced woman in the white cap would think about a fiddler from Carmelo.

Two days later the men came back. They brought with them good spirits and smiles, but no bear. Swan's eyes drooped with weariness.

"What do you think happened?" Jack asked. He laughed and gave José a kindly pat. "A heavy mist came on and the trees were dripping. We built a fire at dusk, near the place where the grizzly had been seen, and put the umbrella over our stuff to keep it dry. We tied it with thongs so that it wouldn't blow away, and then went after the horses. It is dangerous to let horses wander away when grizzly hunting!" He looked slyly at Swan and they both laughed.

"Torres got drunk, that is what happened," Loreta said. "You didn't hunt the bear."

"Drunk nothing!" Jack cried. "Wait till I tell you! We came back to the fire and saw a great, dark grizzly sticking his paws into the fire and throwing it all around. We were frightened, because a grizzly like that is not to be angered. Torres and I

278

sprinted for the first tree and climbed it, but Swan here was too short to catch on the branches. He clung to the trunk so frightened that he couldn't move. Finally we pulled him up by the coat. We all held tight to the tree limbs, watching the black bear dancing back and forth. We shot at him until we had no more powder, but still the bear didn't stop dancing and throwing the fire around."

"Oh, Jack," Loreta cried. "Why must you go hunting for troubles this way?"

"We grew so tired of holding on that our arms and legs ached," Jack told her. "Then this morning, tired, frightened, and stiff, we saw when light came that the bear was only the umbrella blowing through the fire."

"No more grizzly hunts for me," Swan groaned. "My joints will never be the same again. I'm too little as it is now, without being frightened into smaller room."

Romero dropped in just as they were eating the supper of boiled ham that Loreta cooked as a treat. He had just come from Monterey and was very much excited.

"Castro is fighting the Americano Colonel Fremont over by the Salinas," he told them.

"Not Fremont that bought horses from wild Indians for butcher knives and beads?" Jack cried, excited.

Romero nodded. "He said he was only getting supplies then, but he was really preparing to attack. He's up on the Gabilan mountain-top right now, and Castro will get him! Castro told him to leave but he wouldn't. The Americanos are talking too much. Americano settlers complain about Castro's rough-shod ways. That is because Castro has control of tax money."

"We should go," Jack shouted. "Larkin, the Americano Consul, has been good to us, and has done everything he could to keep peace. Alvarado and Castor and the politicians sent the kind-hearted Micheltorena back to Mexico because his soldiers stole a few chickens. Micheltorena couldn't help it if Mexico gave him jail-birds for soldiers. But this time we

279

should fight with the Americanos against Castro and Alvarado! Pío Pico is still after Mission land and stock up north!"

Romero looked black and went away without eating. Loreta called him from the door to share the ham, but there was no answer. When she came back she saw the marinero standing near Jack. He had his hand on Jack's arm.

"I'm older than you," he said. "And I've found out it is well for a hot-headed Britisher to keep out of other folks' dog-fights. You'll be happier and live longer, if you stick to your rancho and take care of the woman you picked. She'll be needing your help soon, in bringing up this son she's getting ready for you."

Jack looked into the fire. "I suppose you're right," he said. "But I love a fight."

"You were a prisoner in Mexico once, because you like to fight," Loreta said as she ate some English bread baked that day in the iron pot.

"It really doesn't matter," Swan said. "The Americanos are clever, and the people of Monterey are luke warm on Mexico. Why, I'll bet they don't even know there's not a Mexican flag or any flag at all flying over the Customs House now! But I've noticed it," his eyes sparkled, "because I saw a fat little Mexican take it down one morning not so long ago. He was alone, and his black eyes looked defiance at me when he saw I watched. He knows that the Americanos will eventually take over California, and isn't giving them the chance to haul down the Mexican flag."

"But I should help the Americanos," Jack insisted. "They have been good—"

"Just let things work out without getting a shot in your own breeches, Johnny Bull—that's my advice," Swan told him. "The Americanos managed their fights before you came over here."

It seemed to Loreta that as her body grew heavier with the new baby, she heard nothing but fighting. Jack was always on

280

the road to or from Monterey, eager for news of Fremont or somebody else. Each morning she gave thanks for Swan, the marinero, with his sound advice. He was the only one who could talk sense into the hot head of Jack Preble of the Carmelo. When the Americano Colonel Fremont finally gave up and went further inland with his soldiers, Loreta gave thanks to the Virgin. At least the temptation for her Jack to join Fremont was removed for the time.

Chapter IX

REAL AMERICAN STUFF: 1846

MARIA BERRETO came to vist Loreta for a few days. Her eyes sparkled, and she couldn't hold her news even until she laid off her things.

"I've sold the Rancho Pescadero," she told Loreta. "It was very lonely out there in the middle of four thousand three hundred and ninety-eight acres, with only an old Indian or two and the vaqueros. You know it extends for miles along the coast and no houses to see, only the woods."

"What did you get for the land?" Jack asked and bent to fasten leather on a saddle long overdue.

"Five hundred dollars! Think, just a bit less than twelve cents an acre! I'll build myself a house in Monterey where I'll see people and be able to visit around, and know what's going on."

"That will be nice for you," Loreta said as she husked corn for dinner and watched the little, dark woman settle herself in the doorway where she could see both Loreta and Jack as she talked. María reminded Loreta of a hen settling herself on the nest to lay an egg; she preened a bit at the white fichu and wiggled into a comfortable position.

"I'm told that Swan is doing well at his saloon and boarding house," María said as an opening. "The first drink is on the house. He tells the sailors that, when he goes down to meet the boats, and promises that their clothes will be washed and mended too, and pies for dinner made by his own hands."

"He is a hard worker," Jack told María. "He deserves to do well."

"They say he sometimes takes in sixty dollars a night, on the drinks."

Loreta looked up from her corn. "I wish he didn't sell the marineros whiskey," she said more to herself than María and Jack. "Whiskey is making thieves out of Indians who used to go to Mass at the Mission and be good."

"He'll be doing a bigger business once they let the sailors off the Americano warships that are anchored in the bay these last five days!"

Jack dropped the saddle to the ground. "What are you talking about?"

"Oh, didn't you know?" María raised her eyebrows in surprise. "The Americano Commodore Sloat and his boats are in Monterey. Anita Gomez says that every night the Americano Consul Larkin goes out with papers to the ship and then he comes back home again. Anita thinks they are waiting for Governor Pío Pico to come so they can take California away from Mexico. There is no ranking officer in command at the Presidio right now and that makes it bad. Larkin must do everything."

"It's come!" Jack cried excitedly. "The Americanos are ready to take Monterey. I'm going!"

"I wish you hadn't told him, María," Loreta sighed. "For nearly a week now I've kept him away from Monterey. I hoped he would get some saddles finished."

"But why is he excited?" María seemed surprised.

"Yes, why is he?" Jack came up to the wash tin, and plunged his head in and out again. "I'm excited because now when the Americanos take over we'll have better administration of our taxes. Better laws!" He blew water from his nose. "If there is any fighting to be done, Jack Preble wants to be in on it!"

"I'll go back with you," María said. "You can take me in the ox cart. I'll not let the Americanos have my new land in Monterey where the house is to be." She was out of her chair and putting on her feathered bonnet in a second.

Loreta's eyes met Jack's and he looked cross.

"I'm not going in the ox cart, María Berreto! Do you think

283

I'll spend the time riding with an old lady when I can gallop fast and be there quicker for the gunplay?" Jack called out as he wiped his face and then rushed into the house for his coat. "I'm going to Monterey on my fastest horse."

María just stood for a minute. "Then I'll ride one of your horses in my best silk dress and leave my ox cart here." She said this with so much determination that Loreta saw the feathers on her bonnet shake. "No one will look at the bony shanks of an old woman if there is a fight on."

"But I thought you were going to stay with me a few days," Loreta begged. She had looked forward to María's visit, and was very much disappointed.

"I will come another time. Tell the vaquero to saddle me a horse, Loreta."

Indian vaqueros have good ears, and the word spread fast. Before long everybody on the rancho except Loreta, José, and little María had gone down the dusty, yellow road toward Monterey. No one, not even Jack himself, looked back to wave at Loreta as she watched them out of sight. They were in too much of a hurry to get to the fight!

Loreta put her arm around the shoulder of her tall young son. "I pray the good Virgin every night, José, that you will never know war and guns, and be tempted by a fight as your stepfather is now. Only Satan himself makes people fight."

"But I want to go, too!" José said. "I'm big enough, and I want to see the boats!"

Loreta smiled at him. "But you are a man now, José, and sometimes it takes a bigger man to stay at home and mind the rancho."

"We will play vaquero, José," María said. "I can rope better than you can."

But José sulked. "I don't play vaquero with a *girl* in skirts," he grumbled, and threw two rocks at a ground-squirrel that had come out of a hole to sun his back.

Loreta was worried. It pained her heart that Jack was so eager to fight, so anxious to get off. Perhaps he would be killed, but he didn't think of that! What was happening over the hill in Monterey? The very thought tortured her.

"I will run away to Monterey unless we make fiesta," José told her. "If I am man of the rancho, and stay at home to look after women, we must have a fiesta!"

Loreta had enough. She grabbed José and spanked him. "We have no fiesta for such a boy. It is your place to do as you are told!" she cried. "And your mother always thinking you are such a good boy. Why do you have to say such things today?"

José yelled.

Suddenly a pain, sharp and meaningful, went racing through her body. Loreta pushed the boy away. "Get a horse, take María on in front of you and ride as fast as you can to Don José Manuel Boronda's at Los Laureles Rancho," she cried. "Tell Doña Boronda that a baby is coming to me, and ask her if she will send someone."

The boy stopped crying instantly and seemed to understand. He ran to get a horse.

When the children had gone, Loreta built up the fire and put the ham to boil. The pain came again, sharper than the one when she had spanked José. In that moment, Loreta knew that no matter how fast José rode to Los Laureles, he would not be in time. She murmured prayers, and with difficulty, forced her pain-racked body to the cupboard to get the blankets she had woven for the new son.

When at last her clothes were off and she sank gratefully onto the bed Jack had made for her, Loreta was very weak. Another pain came. She thought of the Blessed Mother who had brought Jesus in a manger, and remembered her blessings. Loreta Preble had an adobe house, and a bed, and a ham boiling. The fiddle in its bag hung on the wall beside her.

Maybe this baby would be the son who would once more play chants in the Mission? Then Juan O-nes-e-mo and the Saints would hear them, and know that an Indian sister was still following the teachings of Mission Padres long gone.

285

A pain came. She said a prayer and remembered how much better off Loreta was than Polonia, her own mother who had dropped a baby on a hillside after she had walked all day to escape pirates at the Mission. A pain came. . . .

The baby cried. It was little and red-headed, but not a son! Loreta reached for the blanket. Last time, Jack Preble himself cut the cord that joined little Benito to his mother. Now she did it herself and wondered if this new baby still had a father alive and breathing. After a while she would clean up everything, and the Spanish and Mexicans and Americanos would find that a Mission Indian could still manage alone. Long after midday eating time José returned with María, cross and hungry.

"There was no one at Los Laureles," he cried running into the house.

"It doesn't matter, we don't need anyone now," Loreta said in a voice so low she wondered if he would be able to hear her. "You have a sister. She came while you were away."

The children both looked at the baby in the blanket beside Loreta. María forgot to cry for food. "It is like my dolly," she said. "Did Jack Swan, the marinero, bring it for you?"

"No," Loreta told her. "I got it to surprise your father when he comes home."

José sniffed the air. "We are to have a fiesta with ham after all," he sneered. "I suppose it is because of this silly girl?"

"Because you were good to ride to Laureles," Loreta told him, and hoped the saints would forgive her for deceiving a deaf boy to make him happier. "Now you go see that there is water on the ham. We don't want it to burn again, or your father will be cross. Then feed bread and cheese to María and yourself. You must be the man and help now. When the ham cooks we will have fiesta. Now go, and let the new sister and your mother sleep."

It was quite dark when Loreta opened her eyes. The children were quiet, and there was the smell of boiling ham. She tried several times to get up and walk, but her legs refused to hold up her body. Finally she called.

José came running through the dark. "Is it fiesta time?" he asked. "I kept María quiet for so long, but she's very hungry now. I said the prayers you taught me, and showed María the holy picture Doña Petra gave me, to keep her still."

"First go and get a candle, and light it in the fire," Loreta told him. "Then I will have to lean on you and María because you are both so big and strong. We will lift the ham out and make fiesta."

Loreta could hardly eat. It was so dark. Why didn't Jack come home? Perhaps he was lying dead somewhere by an adobe wall in Monterey.

José and María ate ham and bread and boiled corn, and grew sleepy. After a while they went to bed. Still Jack Preble didn't come home.

It was gray with light when Loreta heard horses and drunken singing. Jack clattered through the kitchen and made his way to the bedroom.

"Be careful, Niño," Loreta said quietly. "There is a new baby here beside me on the bed."

"Loreta!" His voice sounded eager, but she couldn't see his face because he stood in the shadow by the door. "My son! He came wrapped up in the American flag!"

"No, a little girl," Loreta said, but Jack did not hear. He was racing through the kitchen. She heard his voice shrill and happy.

"Come! Come everyone," he called. "Come, drink to my new son that came wrapped up in the American flag. We have good days upon us in Carmelo now."

Loreta sighed, but she was happy Jack could yell and run. Anything was better than thinking of him lying dead by the roadside in Monterey.

Candles were lighted in the kitchen. Feet clattered on the hard-packed dirt floor.

287

"Go after Romero and Torres," Jack called. "They must come, too, and drink to the baby. A fiesta! They are only a mile up the road by now, my good friends, Torres and Romero."

There was loud talk and bragging among the vaqueros, and soon Jack came into the bedroom. "Let's have a look at him," he said. "I've got to produce him or they can't drink to him."

Loreta was too tired to argue, and besides, she had learned long ago to let Jack Preble, the Englishman, find out things for himself. It was the quickest way to make him believe what was true.

"Be careful," Loreta warned. "Don't bump into the doorway."

Soon there was a great roar of laughter in the kitchen!

"The Americano flag makes you see wrong," someone cried. "For a girl we get two drinks!"

Jack brought the baby back after a bit. "Why didn't you tell me?" he demanded crossly, "instead of letting me make a fool of myself like that?" But he didn't wait long enough for Loreta to answer.

The laughter and noise kept up. Loreta covered her head with the blankets, and held her little red-headed daughter close to her heart.

It turned out that there was no fight at all in Monterey. Just music, speeches, and a lot of soldiers in blue uniforms. Then an Americano "Stars and Stripes" was hauled up on the pole near the Customs House.

"The salute was fired," Jack told her, "and all hands stood at attention while the band played a tune. Everywhere men cheered. Then the band marched up the street and serenaded Consul Larkin."

"What did the Mexicans do?" Loreta asked. "Was anybody killed?"

"Killed? Of course not!" Jack cried. "A few long-nosed, bewhiskered Señoras put up shutters and sulked, but the señoritas decked the balconies with roses, and made eyes at the

288

handsome Americano officers and soldiers. The Americanos are fine people. California needs them now, and Mexico could not hold California longer. Changes must come."

"Did they sack the church?" Loreta wanted to know. "The Padres always warned Indians that soldiers and pirates first sacked the churches on account of the golden altar ornaments."

"If you had been there yesterday, Loreta, you wouldn't resent the Americanos. Commodore Sloat read a proclamation from the balcony of the Customs House, saying that citizens who didn't want to live peaceably under the United States government would be allowed time to dispose of their property and move out of the country, or else they must remain observing strict neutrality. He's leaving Mexican judges and alcaldes in their offices until things are arranged. The churches will stay in possession of the Fathers."

Loreta ceased to listen for a minute, and murmured a prayer of thanksgiving. Juan and Padre Amores would be pleased with the Americanos if they knew.

"And Americano soldiers told me that Commodore Sloat ordered his soldiers not to fire a gun, and warned them not to annoy the women, or steal from the people of Monterey, but treat them so courteously that the Americanos would never have to be ashamed of taking California away from Mexico. Sloat is governor until someone else takes over, and now Monterey is Capital of California!"

Jack's words came to Loreta through her meditation. She kept her eyes closed, and was thankful for this Americano Sloat. He must know and understand the sorrowful heart of an Indian woman, who feared for her husband, Jack Preble, the fighter. No guns. Peace! A sister of Carmelo could sleep at last with no fights to disturb her dreams.

Chapter X

BRICKS AND BOARDS: 1847

LORETA sat sewing one morning in the smithy while Jack worked on saddles. Just before noon, Don Cooper rode in to tell them Jack must take his land papers to Monterey and have them recorded now for Americano land taxes.

"Too bad José Abrego feels he can't serve as an officer now that Monterey is in American hands," Don Cooper said. "Abrego is honest and intelligent, and he's had a hard time with the management of mission funds. It makes things bad for him, being married to a half sister of Alvarado, when they have differences of opinion in their official capacities."

"Don Abrego is good," Loreta said. "He tried to save the last remaining San Carlos land from being auctioned to Pío Pico's brother."

"How about a bit of ham and some of Loreta's good bread and preserves, to cheer you up, Cooper?" Jack asked. "The sun is high. I'll wager you smelled the ham cooking."

"Well, seeing you ask me, I'd enjoy some ham." Don Cooper smiled and slid off the saddle. He patted little María on the head, and pulled barley sugar from his pocket. "For a reverend gentleman, and a chaplain off a boat, Walter Colton, the American alcalde of Monterey, is making out well," Cooper said as he settled himself in the shade.

Loreta folded her sewing and hurried to the house, but she could hear the talk from where she worked by the kitchen door.

"What's Colton up to now?" Jack asked. "I've had to stay around the rancho and get a few saddles made. People are out of patience waiting for them. I may as well be in London for all the news that comes from Monterey."

290

"Last night I saw Colton and a file of soldiers going toward the Washington Hotel so I just trailed along to find out what was causing the excitement. They surrounded the place and arrested about fifty gamblers busy at a bang-up Monte game."

"Was there a fight?" Jack cried. "I wish I'd been there!" Loreta saw him stop work. His eyes were eager.

"No fight at all. Colton just took them into the bar room and put his hat down on the floor. 'We're building a school-house here and need more money. Each of you is to pass along in front of me and drop a twenty-dollar fine into the hat,' he told them."

"You don't mean it!" Jack was very much excited. "Any of the gamblers bolt?"

Don Cooper laughed. "No, sir, they paid right up. One chap called out to the rest when he saw Colton's stern face: 'Come, my good fellows, pay up and no fuss. This money goes· to build a school where I hope the children will be taught better morals than they could gather from the gamblers who help pay for it.' They all laughed when the hotel keeper paid a hundred dollars into the hat as his fine."

"Colton is a smart Yankee," Jack said, "but high handed and liable to have a fight on his hands one of these days. He's broken up two gambling houses already."

"I can tell you another bit of news, too. You see, I want to treat you well on account of the ham." Don Cooper waved his hand at Loreta, who waited patiently by the door for them to come and eat.

"Washington Bartlett, the first American alcalde at Yerba Buena, has given orders that the little village is now to be called San Francisco. Such a fuss over a place where so few boats put in." Cooper snorted.

"The name's bigger than the town," Jack said as they walked toward the house and their dinner of ham.

Loreta had to go to Monterey with Jack to sign papers. She was startled by the changes in the town. Streets were full of

291

people. Building was going on everywhere. Across from the Washington Hotel near the plaza, a man named Botchson was building a wooden house. Not a single bit of adobe in it! Folks stood watching men put the boards together. Jack joined the crowd. Loreta went to Milton Little's shop for thread and calico.

"Business is good," Little told Loreta, "but now there are twelve stores in Monterey. Heaven knows how we'll all make a living."

"So many houses," Loreta said. "I haven't been to town since before Margaret, my red-haired baby, was born, and she is over a year old now."

"Have you heard? George Dickerson's got a brick kiln. He's going to make baked brick and build a mansion for himself. Monterey is to have the first brick house and the first wooden house in California." Little measured off the turkey-red calico for a new dress that María fancied. "There'll be quite a race, what with brick and wood. Botchson had to sink a boat to make a wharf so he could land his Australian sawed lumber, the other day. He claims he has enough lumber to put up six houses, and he'll have them ready for living in by the week's out."

Loreta smiled. "The Australian builds houses fast like Indians make tule huts, but tule and wood burn. Will a wooden house stand earthquakes?"

"Maybe we won't have any more earthquakes." Little took spools of thread from a big box behind the counter.

"Indians used to say that long ago," Loreta told him. "But God sends earthquakes once in a while to let us know he still has power enough to shake the earth, in spite of so many people."

Jack was very much excited about the wooden house, almost as much excited as he was about fights. "The wood came in sections from Australia ready to be put up," he told Loreta as they went down the busy street toward Jack Swan's boarding house. "Mr. Botchson's wife is an invalid. She was afraid they wouldn't find a house in wild California, so she planned the house and had it made with each section numbered. Even an English sailor can put it together, which is saying a lot. That shows what Britishers can do when they want to!"

Loreta smiled at him. Her Jack's chest stuck out as proudly as if he had done the business himself.

"But the woman thought it out," Loreta told him. Jack didn't let on he heard her.

The marinero Swan had built onto his boarding house! A long building was now attached to the first low saloon, and a great wooden inside shutter hooked up to the ceiling and then dropped to make a wall.

"It's my theater curtain," Swan cried when he took them in to see the place. "Jack Swan, the pie maker, has built the first theater in California for his mariners. The soldiers at the fort come, and we shove back the beds, let down the wooden curtain and give dramatic sketches. Acting is better than brothels for spending the time of evenings, and far easier on their purses."

"What kind of sketches?" Jack asked. "London music hall songs and dances?"

"Have a drink and think better of me," Swan motioned to an Indian boy in the other room behind the bar. "Our first theatrical performance was *Putnam, or the Lion Son of '76*. We played to a crowded house. Monterey is full of people now. The Americanos have started the serenading habit." His eyes twinkled.

The young Indian came to where they sat. "A glass of the finest wine and some of that cake I baked, for Señora Preble, and whiskey for us." When the boy had gone, Swan told them there was so much business now that two helpers were necessary to keep up the good service. "Better come to our next play. We're doing *Damon and Pythias*."

Swan, busy as he was, walked with Jack and Loreta to their ox cart. Suddenly Loreta saw something she couldn't believe with her own eyes! A tall Indian appeared in a blue uniform

293

with gold epaulets and a pointed hat. His black hair hung down to his waist. Around his neck was a silver chain with a large silver locket on it. He walked past them with an air of importance, and glanced out of the corner of his eye to see if they were looking at him. Swan saluted.

"What in thunder do you call that?" Jack asked. "Is he a general in the American Army or has your whiskey gone to my fizz?"

Swan threw back his head and roared. "We even put on street shows now. That's why there's a boom in Monterey lots!"

"That was one of Te-mo's sons," Loreta told Jack.

"You mean a son of the wild Indian who took Juan's bed, and made trouble about the hides?" Jack cried.

Loreta nodded. "Maybe Antonio's blood has been on his hands."

"How'd he get the masquerade costume?" Jack asked.

"Not long ago a bunch of wild Indians raided a farm and stole a hundred or so horses," Swan told them. "Colton sent soldiers after them and brought them into town. This chap was the leader. He entered court and was civil but defiant. They couldn't pin evidence on him and his outfit, so the next thing to do was to scare them. They took him out and stood him next to the wall and said they were going to shoot him, but he didn't even wiggle an ear. Then Captain Mervine told the Indians they were acquitted."

"Who fixed the old cove up in a blue suit and a locket?" Jack asked.

"You don't give a man a chance to finish." Swan was cross. "Colton is a Yankee and clever. He told the Indians about all the ships, and guns, and soldiers, that would be after them if they ever stole anything or raised a rumpus. Then he rigged out the whole party with fresh blankets and red handkerchiefs, and put a uniform on the chief, with navy buttons and the silver chain and locket. The band played 'Hail Columbia' and the Indians became part of the American Navy, vowing

eternal allegiance to the Americanos! This chappie thinks he's
a general in charge of Indians around here, and he's Johnny
on the spot to stop trouble, before it ever happens!"

The men just laughed, but Loreta was thankful that Americanos were not Englishmen who liked fights. The Alcalde
Colton knew how to keep gentile Indians from taking ven-
geance and perhaps killing innocent people later, when the
trouble was forgotten.

Don Jorje Allen hailed them. "You'd better stop at the
house," he told Loreta. "Doña Allen has been waiting many a
month to see you. She has something for José, her godson,
and she's worked her fingers off making it."

On the way home they stopped to leave the candles for
Doña Petra Allen. The little lady was happy and excited over
the new wooden floors in the adobe.

"No more dust," she told Loreta, her eyes shining. "A dirt
floor is bad. Don Jorje bought wood as a surprise for me. It
came all the way around the Horn."

After a few minutes, Doña Allen went out and came back
with a beautifully embroidered red velvet coat. It had medal-
lions in silver and gold thread, with tiny hearts as flower cen-
ters.

"For my godson, José Carlos, the vaquero," she said proudly.
"It is a long time since I have seen him. A few prayers for
him are stitched in with golden threads."

Loreta was filled with love for the little lady. Her mouth
and throat would not give words.

"José thinks he is a man. He will be pleased with the vaquero
coat," Jack said. "He is proud to stay home and look out for
things. When he comes of age he will be able to manage the
rancho Pablo left him."

"The coat is beautiful," Loreta said after a while. She ran
her work-roughened fingers over the velvet and looked into
Doña Petra's tender brown eyes. "I will tell José how your
face was shining when you told me about sewing prayers into
his coat with your golden threads."

295

Doña Allen smiled and her eyes filled with moisture. She picked some St. Joseph lilies, and a pink rose from her garden as they were leaving. "Put them near 'Our Lady' for me, Loreta, as you pass by San Carlos de Borromeo on the Carmelo. The Saint must be lonely. My father often told me how hard Juan worked to carve the face of the Saint, and the pleasure Padre Crespi took in helping him to paint the robes. Petra Boronda Allen doesn't forget Juan O-nes-e-mo and Loreta and other faithful Indians who worked so hard, even though the church they built crumbles in the winter rains."

Jack was silent a long time as they drove home. Finally he spoke. "When the next boat with lumber comes, you shall have a floor in your adobe."

But Loreta didn't get her wooden floor when the next boat came in. Gold had been discovered! Great yellow chunks were being washed out along the American Fork, so a traveler said.

Jack only laughed and blamed the cheap whiskey in Post's saloon. He called Dickerson crazy when he left the kiln and the first small wing of his brick mansion to join a dozen others and go in search of gold.

But a week later when Colton, the alcalde, sent a messenger to the American Fork to find out if the gold stories were true, Loreta noticed that Jack was as excited and eager as anyone, and very impatient for the messenger's return.

María was sick with a sore throat the following week. She seemed to be choking. Loreta tried vinegar and apple to break the film of phlegm that bothered, but it would not work. The little girl only grew hotter and choked oftener.

"I'll ride over to Monterey for old Dr. Calahan," Jack told her. "He'll know what to do for my pet. Doc Canfield is more of a scholar with his museum filled with snakes and dried things, but he's too shaky in the hands. Calahan puts what he knows into practice better."

Loreta looked into her man's eyes. "You won't forget to bring Calahan right away? Even if the messenger is back tell-

296

ing stories about gold? Loreta is an Indian. She remembers it is almost time for the man's return."

Jack's eyes twinkled in spite of his worry over little María. "You're a smart one, Loreta. Jack Preble can't fool you!" He kissed her. "Calahan will be here as soon as I can get him." And he left her to go saddle his horse.

Loreta went into the adobe and up to the bed. María's face was very dark-colored now, and she was having trouble in breathing.

The day seemed long to Loreta. José was good to help. He minded little Margaret well. Every hour or two he would come and stand in the doorway and ask if María was any better. His face was so sad that it hurt Loreta, when she shook her head to tell him the bad news.

María's color was suddenly blacker! Loreta grew frightened. She ran to the door and tugged at José's arm. "Ride into Monterey for the priest," she told him. "María is dying. If you meet Dr. Calahan on the way, tell him to hurry faster. Tie Margaret with a rawhide to the oak tree. It is better that she should be away from the poor María, in case she should catch the bad throat."

For a minute, José didn't move. His great brown eyes filled with tears. "María can't die!" he screamed suddenly, and raced to the barn for his horse. "José will tell the doctor! José will say prayers! María shall *not* die!" He disposed of little Margaret by the tree with lightning speed, and was off down the road in no time.

Dr. Calahan arrived not long after. "I met the boy, going for the priest, Loreta. I hurried as fast as I could. You can't push a horse beyond his strength."

Loreta led him into the room where María lay. The doctor took one look at the child's black face, and dropped his bag on the floor. He opened María's mouth and rammed his finger down her throat in an effort to break the film that strangled her.

297

"Diphtheria," he murmured. "There's not much chance. I've never been able to save them. We don't know what to do to kill this film." He stood up now, and held the thin little wrist between his long fingers, and watched María's face.

"She's gone," he told Loreta after a few minutes. "I couldn't have saved her anyway."

Something went numb inside Loreta. She looked down into María's little face. The struggle for breath was over, and there was a strange look of relief where before there had been terror.

"Don't kiss her or get near her, and burn all the bedclothes. Sprinkle the place with lime chloride, or you'll all get the bad throat," Dr. Calahan said, and gently pushed Loreta away. "Better boil all the clothes you have on before you go near that one." He nodded toward Margaret who sat playing in the dirt with two pearl-lined abalone shells.

Father Ramirez came, and Jack rode in behind him.

The Father sprinkled holy water and said prayers, and Jack knelt on the earth floor between Loreta and young José, who sobbed during his prayers. Calahan stayed too. Afterward, while Loreta fixed the men something to eat, she heard Calahan talking to the priest.

"It would be better, Father, if we could bury the little one up on the hillside under a tree, while you're here. Diphtheria is dangerous, and I'm afraid for the others, afraid of spreading it at a funeral."

Loreta's heart hurt. Poor María, not even the flowers and procession that other children had when they were put away! But little Margaret must be thought of, and José, and Jack, and herself.

Jack sat in the doorway and held his head in his hands. Father Ramirez tapped him on the shoulder.

"We think it best to bury her right away, Señor Preble," he said gently.

"Yes, yes," Jack got up. "But there is no coffin! I have no boards for a coffin for my little pet."

Loreta left the cooking and went over to Jack.

"Little María is the child of an Indian woman. Loreta will make a beautiful bag from the white calf-hide on the bed, and sew it with thongs, as Indians made bags for burying in when the Padres first came. We will turn the white hair inside, and it will look beautiful next to María's little face."

Jack looked up. He put out his hand and caught Loreta's, giving it a quick, understanding, squeeze, then dropped it again and went on with his thinking.

Loreta told José to feed Margaret, who howled, and strained at the rawhide rope. Then, while the priest and Dr. Calahan ate the food she set out, she went out into the barn alone to sew the little hide coffin for María. As she bored holes for the thongs that would hold it together, Loreta remembered Doña Petra sewing prayers into José's coat with golden threads. With each pull on the rawhide thong, Loreta murmured a prayer for tiny María in heaven.

Late that afternoon, after the priest and the doctor had gone, Jack went into the smithy. Loreta saw him at work in the slanting golden sunlight. He heated iron and cooled it. He pounded hard. She was sorry that her man thought no more of a burying that he went right back to work. After a while Jack came and showed her a pretty iron cross fashioned with María's name written like lacework across its bar. There was a tiny rosebud carefully fashioned, at the end of the name.

"That's because my little girl hadn't finished living. There was so much more world to unfold for her," he said and took Loreta's hand. "Let's go up the hill together and put it on María's grave."

Chapter XI

GOLD AND WICKEDNESS: 1848. 1849

LORETA had come to Monterey to have a Mass said for her father Juan O-nes-e-mo. She was standing in the plaza beside Jack when the messenger arrived from the gold fields. He dismounted in a sea of upturned faces, and pulled from his pockets lumps of yellow gold which he passed around through the crowd.

"It is gold!" he cried. "Look at it. Bite it. I picked it up along the American Fork!"

"God help us," an old Mexican roared. "Just another way the Yankees have of making us reconcile ourselves to their flag. It's a Yankee invention to fool us, I tell you."

"I'm willing to be fooled," Banales cried. "This is pure gold."

Instantly there was a furor in the plaza. Banales, the jeweler, knew gold! People hurried away. Colton stood beside Jack. He looked sad. "They'll all be going now," he said. "Half the town has already left without even waiting to find out if the gold stories were true."

Jack Swan came up, and told Loreta he was sorry about María.

"The dolly you carved went with her," Loreta told him. "I put it in her arms."

The marinero's Adam's apple worked up and down. "Bless her, maybe she's better off," was all he said, and turned to Jack. "I'm going to the mines, Preble. I can't afford to stay here with a bloody boarding house for sailors. I'll make my pile and come back and fix up the theater."

Before Jack and Loreta were ready to ride over the hill to Carmelo, people who were loaded and waiting for the report tightened thongs on pack horses. Bakers, merchants, bartenders were on their way. An Americano woman, who had just set up a boarding house, pulled up stakes and left on a donkey she bought at a high price.

Within a month every Indian servant in Monterey had gone, and Colton, the alcalde, and General Mason were cooking their own meals.

"It was funny," Jack told Loreta. "I went hunting Colton to ask him about the lots I bought, and found him in his own kitchen peeling onions. They had everything to do with, but not even an Indian. A General of the United States Army was toasting a herring for the two of them!"

Jack sat a long time beside the fire. He didn't talk, just looked at the flames. Loreta wondered if he was grieving for little María. She felt sorry that he seemed to resent red-headed baby Margaret because she turned into a girl when he wanted a son.

Finally Jack stretched himself. "I'm going to the gold mines," he told Loreta. "Not to mine, but to do blacksmithing! I can make as high as sixty dollars a day there."

"But the rancho?" Loreta asked. "Who will take care of the cattle? Three of the vaqueros have gone. José cannot do everything."

"Vincente, the Indian, says he is too old for hunting gold and will stay. He can cook and mind Margaret, while you help José. You'll manage all right. Soon the rains will come. They say a hundred pounds of flour costs twenty dollars at Stockton and at the mines two hundred dollars. I can make a fortune in no time. They'll need new tools made and old ones sharpened, and there's mighty few blacksmiths. I can charge them whatever I like and they'll be glad to pay when the tools are used to dig for gold."

Loreta saw that Jack had planned everything. There was no use even telling him that she wanted him to stay because in seven months more she would be dropping another baby. He had made up his mind.

301

"Well, why don't you tell me you're glad that I was apprenticed to a smith and know how to heat and pound iron, Loreta?" he cried excitedly. "We'll be very rich some day on account of it!"

Loreta managed a smile. "Not even gold can make me glad to have you away, Niño Jack."

He came over and pulled her down beside him. "I'll make my pile as quick as I can and be back to you before long," he told her. "Perhaps in less than a year."

"Indians don't count time by years," Loreta said. "Some years have been long on the Carmelo with many troubles. We lived through them together, Niño. The time you were a prisoner in Mexico was very long."

"But I'll be coming home every little while to bring the gold for you to keep! That won't be like the time in Mexico when you heard nothing."

Loreta only sighed and packed his boxes. Not even the sudden death of Don Jorje Allen, and the funeral, kept Marinero Jack from going to the mines.

As the months passed Loreta, heavy with the baby inside her, worked as hard as any ranch hand; she wondered what was happening to her Marinero Jack at the mines. So many tales came from those who returned, about the terrible fevers that came to people who slept on the ground and got cold, and about the ones who died from bowel trouble. And yet those same people only stayed in Monterey long enough to get strong and well again and then they went back.

Jack came home in six months to leave gold with Loreta. He carried it in a tubular bead belt, with rings on the end to hold the gold in the hollow.

"No one knows where I carry it," he told Loreta. "An Indian woman made it for me. When you want cash, go to Monterey and get money for a little of the gold."

He was surprised that Colton had managed to get his new

Capitol building finished with laborers at thirteen dollars a day.

"A fine building," Jack said, "but Monterey is dead, asleep, with everyone at the mines. San Francisco is much busier, because the miners go there to the port to spend their money. There's gorgeous gambling houses now, and fandango houses with French girls in them. Some of the best gambling places are just big tents and the boys put gold dust right on the tables. You'd never know San Francisco—it used to be little Yerba Buena with only a dozen shacks."

"Monterey is not dead," Loreta said with sadness. "A ball or a cascarone festival nearly every week, and meriendas out on Cypress Point. The Americanos have learned to serenade."

"But there's no money around!" Jack cried. "You should see the spending up near where Comstock is taking out the gold!"

Before long he was gathering up a load of merchandise and whiskey to haul back to the mines. "Might as well," he told Loreta, "the horses have to go anyway and they can just as well pull a load. I'll sell things for six times more than I pay for them."

"Riding range is hard," Loreta told Jack. "I'm almost ready with the baby and José cannot do everything. Won't you stay until I drop the baby? I'm bound to give you a son this time, Jack."

"I can't hang around another month," Jack cried. "Why, all the gold and miners might be gone by that time. I've got to make hay while the sun shines." And then he told her a long story about how hard things were to get, and how gold prospectors carried light packs on their backs, and used their frying pans to cook with, and then used them to wash out gold in the creeks, until they could get better pans for washing.

"But you can live here on the Carmelo and work at the forge, and we can all be happy, and no worries about sickness," Loreta told him.

303

"I don't mind, I don't stay where fevers will get me," Jack said, with excitement in his voice. "I'm taking pattern after the young easterner Charles Crocker from Troy. He worked at a forge for $11 a month and his board, and now he is making money fast in his dry goods store in Sacramento, and goes around in fancy clothes. Don't worry about me, I'll sleep in a bed of nights. Buck up and be a good one like your Indian forefathers. They weren't pampered. I'll be back home again in no time."

Chapter XII

SIX YEAR WAIT: 1850

BUT young Jack arrived and grew to be a good-sized boy without a father's smile. Fever didn't take Jack, but he was bed-ridden from an accident, and sent word that he had scurvy, because there were no fresh vegetables. Onions were auctioned off, and knocked down to the highest bidder.

Loreta hoped the baby would be a fiddler like his grandfather, the Mission builder. Music in the soul was better than thoughts of gold or fighting.

Each Spring when the fresh new shoots of growing things came up through the moist brown earth, Loreta followed the traditions of the Padres, and went to gather yerba buena and sage, and horehound, and the yellow-green buds from willow trees. These herbs she would carefully dry for tea in winter, to cure coughs and aches, and bring hunger to tired stomachs.

As she walked alone through the sweet-smelling woods, with the leaf mold as a cool carpet under her bare feet, Loreta would wonder how many more Springs must come and go before her marinero Jack had enough gold from the mines.

Sometimes a spotted fawn and its mother and father would run ahead of her, or nest-building wrens would stick up their little tails and scold her as she passed by hollow oak logs. All these things made Loreta lonely for her man—her companion. Wood creatures were satisfied to live together on what they could find in the Carmelo. Indians had lived like wood creatures before gold, and English, and Americanos came.

But the years went on. Each lush Spring gave way to grass-brown Summer. The fawns lost their spots, and the poison oak on hillsides turned red in the Fall—and then came the long gray rainy days of winter, but still Marinero Jack could not leave the gold fields and come to his family on the Carmelo.

Jack would write a letter each fall before the snow came in the mountains, and Loreta took it to Doña Petra Allen to read to her.

Always the news was the same, about how much money was to be made. He mentioned twice about a man called Collis Huntington who had opened up a hardware store in Sacramento, and had taken in as a partner Mr. Mark Hopkins. Mark Hopkins had started small, in Placerville, using oxen to haul goods from Sacramento, and was now growing rich in this new partnership. "Only a few years now, and I'll be like them, top hat and all."

Once, after six years, Swan, the marinero, came back to see how his saloon was going, and he rode over to visit Loreta.

"I'll tell Preble all about your son," Swan told Loreta, and pointed to the boy. "About how he smiles, and the number of toes. What I can't remember, I'll make up so that the yarn will be a good one. Trust a sailor for a good yarn."

They both laughed a bit, but Loreta wished Jack would come home and said so.

"No use wishing," Swan said. "Preble's boiling with the gold fever. When he goes after supplies, he hits for San Francisco so it won't take too long. He's making money selling things and pounding out tools, and I expect he's going to stay as long as there's anything doing and then come back to Monterey and knock folks cold with his riches."

José came in and sank wearily on the floor near the fire. Little Margaret went and sat in the crook of José's arm. She was seven years old now and had to do her share of work tending little Jack and watching the sheep up on the hill. Meat brought high prices now, because it was shipped by boat to San Francisco and then taken to the mines.

"There was a fine newfangled boat in Monterey bay today," Swan said while they ate. "A boat run by steam. The

306

Indians saw it first and told of a boat on fire that didn't burn up. I was talking to one of the sailors, and he says it's the coming business for getting goods and passengers around in a hurry. Beats even the new stage coach."

"I'd like to have a look at that boat," José murmured. "I don't see anything but the hind ends of cattle on the hills, and springs that water them. I never have a chance to go for a merienda at Cypress Point like the Borondas and Romeros do."

"But you are the man of the rancho, now, José, and the Romeros and the Borondas have their fathers. Your stepfather is at the gold mines," Loreta told him.

"Boronda girls have dollies, and play. I have to watch sheep," little Margaret whined. "All I play is vaquero with sheep on the hillside."

Little Jack was the only one who didn't whine. He sat by the fire, and fished pieces of charcoal from the ashes at the edge, then shoved them into his mouth. When he looked up there was a wide, moist black ring on his face, but he smiled.

"Let José go to a merienda and to see the boat," Swan told Loreta. "He'll never be young again." Then he pointed a finger at little Margaret. "Next time I go to San Francisco, I'll send, by Wells Fargo, a doll to Margaret Preble of Carmelo. Be sure to inquire at the office each time you are in Monterey."

Loreta looked up and her eyes met the eyes of the marinero. Perhaps he, too, thought now, with an ache in his heart, of the dolly he had carved for another little girl.

"But that will cost a lot to send," Loreta said. "You are too generous. Perhaps you will—" she paused to gather courage for the words, "you will cut out a doll with your knife for Margaret as you did for little María."

Swan shook his head. "No. Times have changed. There are more beautiful dollies to buy." He looked off at the hills, "We can't go back to the little Marías and their wooden dollies again."

There was a long silence.

307

"Speaking of Marías," Swan said, after a while. "Have you heard what María Berreto has done?"

"I don't often go to Monterey," Loreta said. "María lives in a very nice house there. Last year I visited her."

"Well, she's sold Pescadero rancho again, when she doesn't even own it. A man named Gore paid her four thousand dollars for it this time, and only took her word on a bit of paper! The first buyer didn't change his deed to the Americano records. Someday, somebody's going to wake up and there'll be fireworks."

"But how could that happen?" Loreta asked.

"Gore saw the property and heard Berreto owned it. María didn't disabuse his mind when he asked her if she would sell it to him, and she took the cash. He went back to where he came from, thinking he owns the Pescadero. He lives somewhere in the north."

"That is wicked. The saints will surely punish María, who is a Catholic and knows better," Loreta said. "But then, there is much wickedness now. Saloons and fandango houses with women and gambling, right on the road near to San Carlos that my father helped build! They even play gambling games inside the very walls of the ruined Mission, and make picnics there, with lovemaking on moonlight nights. Vincente, the Indian, stopped to make a prayer one day, and saw a drunken soldier. 'If you are a Saint, then dodge this,' he roared at 'Our Lady,' and he shot at her eyes." Loreta sighed. "That is why the pious pray and put crosses on the road to Monterey. There is an avenue of crosses there now."

"And I thought those were grave markers," Swan said.

"Grave markers for evil!" Loreta spread jam on another piece of bread for little Jack.

"Things have changed a lot around here," Swan scratched his head without taking off his broad-brimmed hat, and the hat bobbed around so that little Margaret laughed. "When I was in the Bola de Oro yesterday having my whiskers trimmed, José Soto had to leave me, to tend the bar. He poured out a

308

drink and then came back to his scissors work on me. The
customer tossed off his drink, and told Soto that there'd been
so much thieving and devilment around, that some of the
men had formed a vigilance committee to hunt the criminals
and hang them! They think the law is too slow in dealing with
thieves and rapers."

Loreta crossed herself. She had hoped for peace. "What
does the Americano Alcalde Colton think of the hanging?"
she asked, and remembered other days when Indians were
strung on wild grapevines.

Marinero Swan just looked at her for a minute. "Why,
Loreta, don't you know that California is now a state in the
United States, and has been for two years?" he cried. "They're
taking the capital from Monterey to a town called San José,
and they've already done away with the alcalde, and elected
an American, Philip Roach, as Mayor of the Town of Monterey."

"An Indian woman up the Carmelo cannot ride after cattle
all day and wash for her children, and cook, and keep up with
the news," Loreta said wearily. "But the threats of hangings
are worse than being a state or a town instead of a pueblo."

"They've already hanged William Otis Hall from the rafters
at Colton Hall. It's no threat," Jack said.

Loreta looked at the marinero for a time. "And maybe
these people hunting and hanging are themselves thieves. It
is a good way to cover tracks, joining the hunt. Indians know
that trick, too."

"That's what I told Soto!" Swan cried. "Takes a thief to
catch a thief. Loreta, you may be here alone with only children
to help you on a ranch in the wilderness of Carmelo, but
you've a lot of sense. Jack Preble can be thankful for you."

As he left, Swan promised to tell Jack Preble many messages, and urge him to come home to his family. The sailor
leaned close to Loreta after he had mounted.

"Gold is where you find it, Loreta. I've lost more money up
there in the hills than I've made, and I'm getting out before

309

it gets me out. I had to put a plaster on my theater the other day to carry on and take another chance at the glitter." The mariner smiled at Loreta and then nodded toward the two little children and José. "To my mind, Jack Preble's got a lot more gold on the Carmelo than he'll ever find at the mines."

He turned his pony and rode off. Loreta had a feeling of terrible loneliness. José looked at her a minute.

"When can I take in a merienda?" he asked. "There's to be one on Monday and the Borondas are going. The marinero Swan told you I would never be young again."

"You shall go to the merienda," Loreta said. "You have earned a treat and I can manage alone."

Chapter XIII

ARRIVAL AND DEPARTURE: 1854

ONE November night when the chores were finished, Loreta built up a roaring fire and hung a pot of water on the crane; then she shouted for her great gangling son José to bring the wooden tub that Jack had bought in Monterey so long ago.

"Everybody's to be scrubbed tonight," she told them. "San Carlos Day tomorrow, and your mother was once a sister of Mission San Carlos de Borromeo. We have services at the Mission and make fiesta for the Saint."

Little Jack didn't want to be scrubbed and set up a howl when he was stripped and plunged into the tub.

"Hush," Loreta cried. "The good San Carlos will hear you and think you do not love him enough to be clean on his day."

She motioned to José to put more wood on the fire and have towels ready to wrap the boy. One woman with children to wash and fiesta to make, as well as a bath for herself, had no time for monkeyshines.

As she lathered Jack with home-made soap she had learned to make at the Mission, and the rosy glow from the firelight played on his wet little body, Loreta wondered what the boy's father would say when he saw him. There had been a letter nearly two months ago, read to her by Doña Petra Allen. It said that Jack Preble would come back soon to his rancho in the Carmelo, and would be glad for some of Loreta's cooking. He hadn't mentioned Jack, the baby he had never seen. Little Jack was nearly six years old! Loreta sighed. Often now she saw the effect of gold on men and women! Marinero Swan must have been as good as his promise and told Jack Preble to come home.

José took the dripping boy onto his lap when Loreta finished the scrubbing. The big brother was tender, and rubbed carefully the wet blond pate. Jack stopped roaring.

"Now you, Margaret," Loreta straightened up for a moment to rest her back. "Why do you sit playing when you should be undressed?" she cried, as she saw the little girl cuddling the beautiful, golden-haired wax doll that had come on a boat all the way from San Francisco. "I have no time to waste. José must take his bath, too, and the water cools."

Margaret put the dolly down with great care. Her eyes watched the precious baby while her mother undressed her.

"Just a face wash, and my ears," she smiled disarmingly at Loreta. "The Saint cannot see under my clothes because it wouldn't be nice of him to look."

"Saints see everything without looking!" Loreta said and plopped her into the tub.

"How can they see without looking?" Margaret asked.

Loreta just lathered the child's face with soap instead of answering, and Margaret was soon busy sneezing. The question was forgotten.

San Carlos Day was clear, with a sky deep-colored as the back of a bluebird. The rain had come early, and cattle on the hillsides never looked up from their feeding. Loreta drove the ox cart with Jack and Margaret and the food. José rode his horse. In front of him, tied to the saddle, was the fiddle of Juan O-nes-e-mo, in a new turkey-red bag, made specially for the Saint's day. No one was able to play the fiddle but it could be carried in the procession.

Loreta and her family were the first ones to arrive at the Mission. For a minute, she stood without moving. She thought she would never again catch her breath because of the great ache in her heart. The roof of the Mission San Carlos de Borromeo had fallen in! Broken tiles lay on the floor, and the heavy rains had melted away part of the south wall.

Loreta O-nes-e-mo had given her promises to the Saint, as

312

a sister before the altar of San Carlos. Now she must worship instead of sorrow, and let the Saint know she was faithful. She lifted her head high and burst into the hymn of her fathers.

> "Oh, pray for us, O happy Saint,
> While on the sea of life
> We struggle with the wind and waves,
> Oh, aid us in the strife."

The terrible pain in Loreta's heart was eased a bit with the hymn. She smiled and turned to the children beside her. Little Margaret had tears in her eyes.

"The song was beautiful," the child said.

Jack was busy feeling a rock he had picked up.

"You and Jack drive the cows out of the church, while I clean off the altar," Loreta told her daughter, and patted the little head. "Then go and get the flowers we picked to decorate 'Our Lady.' The statue of San Carlos is in Monterey, so we can't have a procession, but the Saint will understand."

Loreta was all action. She motioned José to wipe the bird droppings and cobwebs from "Our Lady."

"Quick," she said into his ear. "I sent the little ones to the cart for flowers. We must not let them see how badly the Saint has been treated while she watches alone at San Carlos Mission. Your Grandfather carved the statue."

José nodded and there was understanding in his eyes. He wiped very hard and very fast with the new red bandana Loreta had given him to celebrate the Saint's day. When the children came with the flowers and bunches of red berries, there was no dust on "Our Lady" and José's finger-nails had scraped off all the bird droppings.

José lifted each child up to place flowers at the feet of the statue, and Loreta saw little Margaret's face shine with happiness as she crowned the Virgin with a wreath she had made all by herself from the first red toyon berries.

Only Romero came to the fiesta of San Carlos. The Mission Indians at the rancheria had been turned off the land and

313

pushed farther up into the hills by a newly arrived Americano who claimed that he now owned the land. Indians hadn't taken their papers to record at the time the Americanos took over. Everything was changed, now. But Mission Indians should never neglect the Saint on his day, no matter what happened! Loreta felt a hurt.

Romero brought his candle and lighted it from one of the two Loreta had placed on the altar to honor the Saint and the Mission builders. Afterwards he marched with them around the church singing the hymn to San Carlos, and they all knelt among the broken tiles to pray and ask the Saint to bless them. Loreta thought of Juan and his tile-making.

No one knew there had been a service for San Carlos, and no one seemed to care, except some crows that cawed from the old pear trees in the Padres' orchard far below the Mission. The crows were disturbed.

José made a fire. Loreta shared the fiesta food with Romero, and then they talked while the children played hide and seek in the ruins of the Indian buildings.

"The evil ones are beginning to suffer," the old Indian said. "Two brothers who shot at the Saints went mad and killed each other not far from here. Now they are no more." He crossed himself and sighed. "It is quite a walk here from Monterey for an old man. I am working now for Soberanes. Did you know that Don Soberanes had a grandson, little Benito? They had a big christening at San Carlos Church in Monterey."

"I don't hear much news," Loreta told him. "When I go to Monterey I have to come right back, for there is a lot of work to do and only my young José to help. I miss Don Jorje Allen's pleasant smile. Doña Petra mourns him. Her eyes were sad when I went to have her read Jack's letter to me."

"She is a good woman. The Saints will ease the pain in her heart," Romero said, then stiffly and slowly pulled himself from the ground. "I must start back. An old man does not walk as fast as a young one." He took his stick made from a pine branch, thanked Loreta for the fiesta, and then waved at the children.

Loreta gathered up the remains of the food, and called her brood. San Carlos Day was over, now, and there were chores waiting at the rancho.

As the cart turned up the Carmelo, Loreta took a last look at the cross that bravely held its arms to the sky. Its base was the Mission tower her father helped to build. She said a prayer for Juan O-nes-e-mo, then glanced at the turkey-red bag on the front of José's saddle. Padre Amores' fiddle had been silent today, for there was no one to play it, but if Juan and Amores looked down they would know it was still safe and well cared for.

The last of that week Jack Preble arrived home! He was thin and had a limp, and there were gray hairs on his temples, but Loreta saw that he was still stately and proud, and his eyes were bright. He was very much pleased with small Jack, and held him constantly. Loreta was glad that Margaret didn't notice the extra attention her father was giving the boy. The little girl seemed relieved that someone else was taking care of Jack. She listened to her father's talk and cuddled the beautiful wax doll.

"The mines will do something yet for California, you'll see," Jack said as he jogged the little boy up and down. "There's a young eastern fellow called Leland Stanford, a lawyer practicing in Placer County; he and Huntington and Crocker and young Mark Hopkins are putting their heads together to have a railroad with trains to come out here to California from New York at the other side of the country! They are carriages run on rails." He patted the face of little Jack. "Maybe this boy will have a ride on them, and remember that his father knew all about a railroad a long time before it was even built."

Loreta shook her head. "Too many new things, Marinero Jack. It is better not to tell a young crow too much. New things are very dangerous."

315

Jack only sniffed and said trains had been tried already along a place called the Hudson River in another part of the country. "You're an Indian, a squaw. You don't know what is good for the young who will follow us," he told her.

And then he mentioned that boots cost a lot of money up in the mines. "I thought often of Juan. He could have made money with his shoes. Loreta, I'm through with the mines." He tapped his hip. "I got a crack on the hip bone when a wheel flew off while I was working near a donkey-engine. It's stiffened my leg a bit, but I'm as good as ever." He looked up at José. "The boy is taller than I am, and almost ready to be off on his own rancho."

"He has worked well while you were away, Jack," Loreta said. "He's stayed home instead of going to fiestas, and minded cattle and taken good care of his mother and brother and sister."

"I'll make it up to him," Jack called. "He shall have cattle and implements, and a house built on his land when the time comes."

Loreta repeated the stepfather's news in a loud voice to José and he was very much pleased.

"His hearing is worse, now," she told Jack, "but he does pretty well by watching the mouth."

"I'll toughen him up a bit," Jack shouted and smiled at the boy. "He should know men and men's doings. Hanging around women's skirts too long is not good for a nineteen-year-old boy. Why, he's a man without being a man! We'll begin celebrating tomorrow, and see if we can stir the dead old town where only escaped geese wander in the streets! Swan came on the boat with me from San Francisco. Things have gone hard with him. He made money but lost it. I hung onto mine, and just worked at the forge and sold things and salted the big profits away." Jack beat his chest with his doubled-up fist. His body swelled with pride.

"Is Marinero Swan poor after all his work?" Loreta asked.

316

"Sunk his money in mine stock that was no good. He's still got the saloon and boarding house."

The next day, right after dinner, Loreta took Margaret and the little boy in the ox cart. She was to visit with Doña Petra Allen while José and his stepfather went to see Jack Swan and attend other men-folk's affairs in Monterey. José was eager to race ahead but Jack rode along beside Loreta.

"I want you and the children to see the darkey at Post's saloon on the road to Monterey. He's a freed slave, and sings without opening his mouth. Post pays him good money as an attraction. I saw him when I stopped there to get a drink," Jack said as they rode along.

"What's a darkey?" Margaret asked. "A bird that sings without opening its mouth?"

"You'll find out when we arrive there," Jack laughed and patted her shoulder.

Margaret found out when they got to the saloon, and she saw the great black man. She was frightened to death and ran out of the place and climbed a nearby tree where she sat on a limb and screamed until the black man was sent away and José climbed up to fetch her.

"That nigger's a remarkable chap," Jack told Loreta when they were on the road once more. "He's freed by his master. Now he's earning money to buy his brother from slavery by singing at Post's."

"Where do people buy and sell these black folks?" Loreta asked.

"At the other end of the United States, that we belong to now. They are having troubles and revolts about these negroes that must work for nothing—they are called slaves. The nigger came here to California because we don't believe in slaves."

"Before the Americanos came, there were people who branded Indians in Monterey and made them work hard. Is that slavery?"

327

"They don't do that any more, Loreta. Don't think about such awful things when we are on the way to celebrate."

Soon the men were off ahead on their horses, for there was nothing to keep them back with the ox cart now.

Doña Petra was pleased to see Loreta and the children. The women sat in the shade of the adobe and talked about sewing. Doña Petra showed Loreta some fancy work she had been doing. A fine altar cloth, with new stitches in embroidery. The garden smelled sweet with roses and honeysuckle. Doña Petra's little boy Alonzo was nine years old, and played well with Margaret and little Jack, until Margaret refused to be a soldier any longer. Then he bashed her over the head with a tomato he took from the pile where the Indian women were making sauce at the back of the house.

Margaret screamed as the red juice ran down her face.

"When I say you are my captain, you are my captain. My grandfather Boronda was a big soldier and he lived in this house. He made his men do what he wanted them to do."

"I won't be a soldier," Margaret screamed.

Doña Petra ran up and grabbed Alonzo. "For shame," she said. "You go and stand with your face to the wall by the fireplace while we all have chocolate and cakes." She grabbed him by the arm and pushed him through the door.

Loreta took Margaret around to the back of the house and washed the tomato off her face, but just as she finished, little Jack, who had been silently taking note of the affair, let fly another red cannon ball which hit his mother's skirt. He was promptly and thoroughly spanked, and started to wail. Loreta heard a snicker behind her. Alonzo was looking through the open window from his place by the chimney!

Doña Petra cut out some paper dress patterns for Loreta, and after a while they had supper of Spanish meat balls with rice. Loreta was expecting her men to ride up any minute. The children were growing tired, and she didn't want to wear out her welcome with Doña Petra.

318

Finally there was the sound of hoofs, a knock at the door, and Jack called. José was with him.

Jack's eyes were bright with excitement. "There's been a stabbing at the dance hall," he cried.

"We saw it happen," José said. He was wide-eyed and very much excited.

"Tiburcio Vasquez wanted to dance with a señorita who already danced with another man. Vasquez tried to pull her away and they started a fight—"

"Someone ran for the constable," Jack put in, "but before he got there everybody was fighting. I saw Tiburcio raise his hand with a knife as the constable came near—"

"They shot the lights out!" José roared. "When they were lighted again the constable was on the floor stabbed to death, and Garcia and Vasquez were gone!" The boy was bound to tell the climax before his father could possibly interrupt.

Doña Petra crossed herself. Loreta made a quick prayer for the souls.

"Men are getting horses now, and guns, to search for the murderers," Jack told Loreta. "I'm going to join the hunt. You'd better take the children and go home. I'll be along as soon as we've dealt with Garcia and Vasquez."

"I'm going, too," José cried. "I'm a man now. You said I'd been tied too much to women."

"All right, come along," Jack told him in a loud voice.

Loreta caught hold of Jack's coat. "I wish the boy didn't have to go man hunting," she said quietly. "I have a feeling—"

"Let him go," Jack said and pulled away. "He's got to be weaned from your apron strings sometime. It'll toughen him to make his own way later. My little Jack shall feel his spurs as soon as he's able."

Loreta sighed and turned back into the house as they rode off. Doña Petra helped her bundle the children up for the long ride home.

"These are terrible times, since gold and whiskey came into

319

California," the little lady said. "Hardly a night goes by when someone is not killed in a saloon or gambling place. Alcalde Colton tried to stop it, but now no one troubles."

Light was in the sky before Loreta heard the horses come in. Soon Jack stumbled into the adobe.

"Loreta, Loreta!" he cried in an agonized voice. "Loreta!"

She was out of bed in a second, and saw Jack's face dark and drawn in the dim light. He leaned against the door.

"Loreta, José's been killed! He didn't hear the order when the vigilantes called to stop, and he rode on as we were surrounding the place in the woods where we'd tracked Garcia and Vasquez. They couldn't see, only heard him, and thought he was one of the murderers. They shot him through the heart, Loreta." Jack covered his face and started to sob. He slid down and sat on the doorstep. "I hadn't been home long enough to remember that he was so much deafer than he was when I went away!" he managed, after a while.

Loreta watched the sky turn pink with the morning sun. She just stood, and thought about José, who had been so kind and good to her and the children. José, who was always longing for fiestas, but had so little time for play. José who was to have implements and stock and even a house built for him on the rancho his godfather had left him. José who was killed because of Tiburcio Vasquez, the baby whose birth was toasted at the housewarming of this very adobe!

Jack looked up at her. His face was wet with tears. "You aren't saying anything," he cried. "Don't you understand? He's dead! Our José's dead! And it didn't do any good. Garcia and Vasquez got away."

"I understand," Loreta said slowly. "José was killed—because he craved excitement and the affairs of men." She took a great breath. "Where is the son of Antonio now?"

"Doña Petra is watching over him. I went to her first, because she is his godmother, Loreta. I didn't know what else to do. Things happened so fast!" Jack got up and came to Lo-

320

reta. He put his arms around her and held her very close to his heart. "My beautiful Loreta. You have so many sorrows."

Loreta felt comforted with Jack holding her, but there were many things to be done.

"It will be better for us to go alone to Monterey and bury Juan's grandson next to him in the cemetario," she said. "Let the children remember José as they saw him around here."

After a minute or two Jack led her into the bedroom. "Try and rest. I will cook us some food, and make coffee, and then tell the vaqueros. Old Vincente will look after the children." He went out to the kitchen, and Loreta fell upon her knees and prayed for the soul of young José who had worked so hard and deserved great peace in heaven.

Chapter XIV

SPEED: 1856

MONTEREY was very dead for Jack Preble after the excitement of the gold mines. Americanos were scarce on streets that had once been so crowded with them, and the town was lazy and quiet and Spanish once more. Tinkling guitars and the honk of geese were the only noises now, except for the clink of money and glasses in the gambling houses and saloons. Once in a while even the geese were startled, and guitars stopped when a shot rang out, or raucous laughter came from a saloon.

"We'll make the Preble rancho a gathering place," Jack told Loreta. "There's no use going to Monterey now to see people. Dickerson is still at the mines and his brick mansion waits. Botchson, he's under the sod and his sickly wife is doing for boarders in the wooden house he built. She's ready now to marry again soon! Why, there's nobody around, except a few fellows that work on the whaling ships."

Loreta was pleased to be relieved of the cares of the rancho, and thankful that Jack was at last willing to settle down and stay on the Carmelo. She missed José, and tried to forget by devoting herself to cooking and housework. There was plenty to do, for Jack was shipping cheeses, butter, and potatoes regularly on the schooners that went to San Francisco. From the northern port the produce was hauled up to the mines and sold at a good price to men Jack had known.

The smithy was going again and folks stopped by often for meals and to talk, as well as to have their tools sharpened or iron hinges made.

One day Loreta took down the turkey-red bag and tried to

322

interest little Jack in his grandfather's fiddle, but the child turned away after a few minutes, and went back to throwing rocks at some crows that sat on the dead top branches of an oak. She sighed and was putting the fiddle away when José Marquena rode in.

"What do you think?" Marquena called to Jack in the smithy. "That fool George Romie has started to San José in a special speed wagon. He figures on making the round trip in six days. How can anybody go a hundred and fifty miles in a wagon in six days!"

"Romie is always anxious for new things," Jack said, and Loreta saw him lay down his hammer and poke the fire. "Why don't he ride a horse? What kind of a wagon is the thing?"

"Built all of wood and wheels two feet thick," Marquena said. "I looked at it. Why, the damned thing'll fall to pieces as quick as he starts tearing along the bumpy road with horses on it. Most likely he'll kill himself."

"There's always folks that take chances, getting places in a hurry," Jack said. "What's he going to do with the time when he gets there?"

"I told him he'd better arrange for someone else to look after his family in case he's killed," Marquena laughed.

"I'm going to have a cow hunt and branding next week," Jack said. "Better come over to the barbecue. Ought to be good fun, for the cows haven't been branded for some years and will be wild."

"Just as well to get your mark on 'em what with Vasquez running around loose with his thieves. They took some of Gomez' cattle, and the vigilantes found Vasquez and his crowd had eaten some and given the rest to Indians down near Jolon. He told the Indians to fill their bellies until the skin was tight, and make fiesta in honor of Tiburcio Vasquez, and he stayed there and saw to it that the cattle were killed before he rode off. The Indians were scared, but they liked the feed."

"I think Garcia led Tiburcio into thieving," Loreta heard Jack tell Marquena. "He was all right until he started running

323

around with Garcia, and he comes from a good honest family."

"Excitement, I guess," Marquena said. "These young ones are always after excitement. You heard about Garcia, I suppose?"

"No. What about Garcia?"

Loreta sighed and pounded the iron triangle to call them to dinner. Only the children came to eat.

"Why, we traced him down to his house near the Salinas river day before yesterday, and called to Garcia to come out. He wouldn't do it, so we fired on the house, aiming the shots to go through the wood. Garcia shot back."

"What happened?" Jack asked.

Loreta tried to keep little Jack busy with food, for she saw that he was straining his young ears to hear the blood-thirsty story. But it was no use. The voices were too loud and excited.

"Why, we got up on the roof and whittled to start a fire and burn Garcia alive in his own house, but he was too clever for us. He put his wife in front of him and they made a dash for the brush. We were afraid of shooting her, a woman, and aimed past her. We shot her arm and grazed it! The bullet went into Garcia's arm all right and he hid in the brush."

Little Jack's eyes widened. "They shot Garcia in the arm," he told Loreta, "and almost shot his wife! Did you hear? I'm going to be a bandit when I grow up! Bandits have fun."

Loreta put her hand over the mouth of her very young son, and prayed that the Virgin would help to weed the evil from his mind.

"We fired the brush, but it was too green," Marquena said. "Joaquin Torres was killed, and Layton, the Americano."

"Then he got away again?" Jack shook his head. "Anastacio Garcia must have been born with a caul. But we'll get him yet!" He clapped Marquena on the shoulder. "Let's go eat. The missus called us long ago."

Marquena smiled at Loreta and was very polite when he sat down to eat. "Father Sorrentine has made a pilgrimage to

324

Carmelo Mission," he told her, "and has located the caved-in graves of the Padres. He wants to try and restore and clean up the Mission."

"A Spanish priest will never get anywhere around Monterey now," Jack said. "Some of the evil Mexicans hate the church and the priests because they work so hard against the gambling houses and try to make the Mexicans come to church. When I went to Monterey the other day to sign papers, some gamblers were burning a priest in effigy."

"Father Sorrentine is a good man," Loreta said. "I will help him all I can."

"I saw you'd changed all the land into your name," Marquena said. "That was quite a chunk the young José owned."

"We have four thousand five hundred and ninety-one more acres on record now! The Preble rancho is the finest land in the valley of the Carmelo," Jack cried and held his wine glass high. He looked into Loreta's eyes and smiled.

"To Loreta who brought land, and the work of her hands to a marinero. May her eyes always shine bright as the candles on the altar during feast days." He lowered his glass and drank, and then added in a low voice, "And may she always have the patience of a saint with a stubborn Englishman."

Suddenly a terrifying, heartbroken wail went up from little Margaret, who had recently left the dinner table. Loreta ran out to her.

The little girl stood howling, the wax doll in her hand. The poor creature's face had melted in the sun and the nose was flat. The eyes had a queer, far-away expression and were running further away in the melting wax!

"I left her in the sun," Margaret sobbed. "She's melted. My darling Anita. She's dying! She's dying! Her nose is gone." Great tears rolled down the child's face.

Quick as a flash, Jack grabbed the dolly. "We'll fix her," he cried. "She'll be right as rain in a minute or two!" He ran to the smithy and plunged the blonde head of the doll into a wooden pail, then pulled it out dripping with water. With expert fingers he nipped at the hardening wax. Loreta saw a nose form and then the face was pushed back into shape.

"Now," Jack said, "let the wax harden and we'll smooth it with a knife. I have some paint, and we'll have new eyes painted on her before the sun sets." He held the child close as he gave her the dolly, and kissed her tenderly. In that minute, Loreta knew that Jack Preble loved his small daughter in his own strange way, even if he did set her to tending sheep until she cried from the weariness in her little legs.

When Marquena left the rancho, Jack called after him. "Don't forget the cow hunt. I asked Captain Davenport of the whaling vessel, but he said he didn't fancy going after our cows. Called them brush jumpers and said he'd rather hunt whales."

"Whalers are queer folk," Marquena said as he threw his leg over his horse's back. "I'd think they'd die from the stink of the whales when they're boiling out the grease. Maybe it softens their brains a little and makes them queer."

He waved goodbye, dug his heels into the horse, and was off.

Jack Preble's bad hip kept him at the rancho for long stretches at a time. The joint stiffened during foggy spells or when it rained, so that riding a horse was painful business.

Loreta would hear him holding forth by the hour in the smithy, to neighbors and those who dropped in for business, as well as the ones who arrived regularly around meal times. He would get red in the face and excited over riots and sacking and slaves in a place called Kansas, and he was irritated because at a convention of people, the Americano John C. Fremont was trying to be elected President of the whole country of America.

Little Jack was like a shadow in the smithy; a constant companion to his father.

The child was never asked to work as little Margaret must, tending sheep all day on the hills, even though he was large

326

for his age and had sturdier legs than his sister. Loreta was sorry that the father should show such a preference for the boy, and shelter him at the expense of Margaret, but there was nothing for an Indian woman to say.

On Sundays after Mass, father and son would stay in town for the afternoon bear and bull baiting behind the Pacific House. Loreta and little Margaret would travel back to the Carmelo in time to do the chores and feed the vaqueros an evening meal.

Only once did Margaret beg to stay. She wanted to hear the music and see the Spanish señoritas in their pretty dresses.

"No," Jack told her. "It's no place for a child like you."

"But I'm older than Jackie, and he's seen the bears a lot of times," Margaret begged. "I'd not be a *bit* of bother."

Loreta saw a black angry look go over Jack's face. "Mind what you are told and do not talk back to me," he said. "You've too much Indian in you! English children don't beg. They know better when their fathers decide what is best!"

He whirled on his heel, took little Jack by the hand, and walked toward the Pacific House without looking back at them.

Loreta put her arm on Margaret's shoulder, for there were tears in the child's eyes. Tears of hurt and disappointment.

"I know something better than old bear-baiting!" she told her daughter. "We'll stop at Doña Petra's and ask her for some of her moss-roses, and then we'll take them home and make sweet smelling grease from them, to scent little Margaret's hair and make it shine."

"But we won't hear music and see the pretty señoritas."

"Niña, it is better to wait as your father tells us. Then later when you are older, and very beautiful, you will go for the first time in a lovely rustling silk dress and lace mantilla, and all eyes will follow you."

"And will a lover come right to me, and want to marry me?" Margaret had forgotten the present in anticipation of the future.

327

"A lover will come, if you are good and say your prayers, and be kind to the Mission Indians and poor people," Loreta told her.

All the way home, Margaret picked the petals from the moss-roses Doña Petra had given them, so that at night before the fire, when the work was done, they would be ready for grinding into salve to make the hair smell sweet and shine.

As the months went by, Jack was more content with the company of his little son, and Loreta had her share of happiness in seeing them together. At least her fighting Englishman was at home, and safe, satisfied to raise produce and meat and make cheese to sell. There was no urge to go to the gold mines, and not much chance to fight.

Late one afternoon when little Jack had gone for a ride on his pony, Loreta took her sewing out to the smithy. This was the first time in months that Jack had been there without someone for company.

"Well," he said, and looked up from the hinge he was making for the Escobar's house door. "It's been a long time since you sat out here with me. I like it."

"There are always others visiting you in the smithy," Loreta told him, "and they must be fed, Niño Jack." She smiled into his eyes. "I came to tell you news. I am dropping another baby in the Spring." She watched him, thinking how pleased he would be, but an Indian woman could never tell about an Englishman. When she expected him to be happy, black ugly looks came into his eyes and his jaws set in anger.

"I don't want any more children," he roared. "We have enough already. They only die and make heartaches. Jack suits me, and you have Margaret to take care of you in your old age."

"Maybe the baby will be another fine tall son for you," Loreta said in a quiet voice. "A man cannot have too many sons."

"I tell you I don't want any more. That's enough!" Jack's eyes were bright and excited. "You must do away with this baby. Go to the Indian medicine man. Lord knows there's enough of them making trouble among the wild Indians. An Indian medicine man will do away with this baby. There must be herbs—"

Loreta hurried to put her hand over her man's mouth. "Do not say such things, Jack!" she cried. "Remember your vows to the church. What would Padre Real say, or Padre Ramirez—" she lowered her voice. "Don't let my fine, proud Marinero Jack say evil things that later he will be ashamed to have the Saints hear."

"I don't want any more children. I'll turn it out of the house if you bring it into the world. I'll not have a squalling baby around. I'm too old!" Jack was working himself up into a temper.

Loreta folded her sewing, and prayed that the Saints would be deaf to the noises made by a marinero who had been tempted by Satan to say things that were not really in his heart. There was nothing she could answer to a man who was in the hands of Satan, unless Saints put words into her mouth. Jack had the land of Loreta O-nes-e-mo and José in his name now. She looked at him. He was pounding violently with his hammer on the hinge. He pounded too hard and made a hole where he didn't want it.

"Damn!" he said without looking up.

Loreta walked over to her man. "Jack, the little boy you love so much now was once a squalling baby." She passed him and went into the house.

Half an hour later, Loreta took the path through the oaks toward the Mission. She carried a cloth tied by the corners. In it were some of the tortillas she still baked for herself in spite of Jack's English bread. Thrust through the knot of her bundle was one of the candles that Margaret had helped to make at last butchering.

It was quite dark when Loreta reached the Mission, but dark is nothing to a woman of sorrow who is seeking comfort from the Mother of Sorrows.

Broken tiles clinked under Loreta's feet, and a bat fanned her face as she picked her way to the ruined altar where she had promised her life to San Carlos. She lighted her candle and dripped a little grease on the altar to make the base of the candle fast, and then she knelt to pray. It was hard to pray to empty niches where Saints had been. Someone had taken the figures away. But San Carlos and Jesus would know, and "Our Lady" was watching from her place near the door.

Peace came. Marinero Jack was a good man. Satan had tempted him. An Indian woman carrying a baby inside must be patient—.

Voices of lovers came, soft and low, from the outside steps of the tower. Loreta prayed on. Once, the cross on her rosary hit against a tile, and she wondered if that tile carried an impression of Juan's knee. She prayed on— In the distance a horse clattered on the dry hard earth of the road, and then stopped. Perhaps more lovers.

"Loreta—Loreta," Jack's voice was tender. Tiles clinked under his feet as he came near to her. He knelt beside her, and Loreta saw in the light from one dim candle on the ruined altar, that Satan had left her marinero.

"Loreta O-nes-e-mo, forgive me," he said. "I knew you would be here, because you are so near to being saintly. Will you come home, Loreta?"

She nodded, and smiled, and handed him her rosary.

Chapter XV

FLOOD AND A HUMAN TASSEL: 1857. 1861

MARGARET was delighted with her new brother Ruez. "He's my baby," she told Loreta. "His face won't melt. I'm eleven, and too big now for the wax dolly anyway." As soon as Ruez was old enough, she took him along with her when she went into the hills to tend sheep.

Loreta was pleased with the arrangement, for then the child's cries would not bother Jack, who resented the slightest attention Loreta gave the baby. He seemed jealous of bright, dark-eyed little Ruez.

Loreta did not worry. The saints had sent a devoted little daughter to an Indian woman. She knew that up on the hillside, Ruez received his share of play, and love, and care from Margaret, for the baby's eyes followed his sister when she moved around the room.

There were few changes on the rancho, from day to day, except for the tasks to be done. Butter to churn, cheeses to be made, and butchering always, so that produce would be ready for the schooner when she put into Monterey every third week.

Loreta's smoked hams and bacon brought good prices in Sacramento and up in the mines. She often thought of José helping her to dig out that first smokehouse on the hills, and how many experiments they made before the pig was smoked to taste like the English ham Jack's mother had sent. Now she had a great log smokehouse, and an Indian to cut the green willows for her. Sometimes she smoked as many as twenty hams at a time.

Jack was always eager to ride to Monterey with the hams so

he could get the latest news of this war about slaves that was going on somewhere. He was interested too in things that were doing at the Capital of California in Sacramento. He came home one day in great glee. "What did I tell you? Charles Crocker, who was selling dry goods in Sacramento, is going to be a representative in the State legislature. He'll be pulling for that new railroad I told you about, and he'll try to get state help. You'll see—New York and United States will find out that California is on the maps."

But Loreta had no time for this Charles Crocker and his railroad, or what he was going to do in the Capital at Sacramento. She had too many hams to smoke. Jack would be angry if hams were not ready to send when the boat came in.

One morning Loreta started the smoke and sealed the door with mud. She was coming back to the house when their neighbor José Gonzales rode into the rancho.

"Where's Jack?" he called. "I don't see him in the smithy."

Loreta pointed up on the hill to where father was teaching son how to aim at a target on an oak tree. She shook her head. "Only nine years old and he's learning to shoot!"

"Good enough," Gonzales cried. "He may need the knowledge sometime with this war on."

Jack left the boy and limped down the hill. "What brings you?" he asked Gonzales. "Have some tobacco. It's the finest I've ever raised." He held out a deer-skin pouch to the Spaniard and they both sat down.

"They hanged Anastacio Garcia to the rafters in Monterey yesterday morning," Gonzales said. "A good job done, too!"

"How'd they catch him?" Jack was too excited to light his pipe.

"A woman, of course."

"Well, don't be so slow at unwinding!" Jack cried. "That's what you came here for, wasn't it?"

"It's a long story," Gonzales said casually. He pulled on his pipe, and then looked at Loreta with a twinkle in his eye. "Long stories take a while to tell."

"I could hit you with a hammer!" Jack laughed. "It's cruel to make a man wait. You shall pay high for your next plowshares for this. Go on, will you?"

"Garcia's wife got on the boat to ride to Los Angeles, last time it stopped in Monterey. A clever Americano was also a passenger. Garcia's wife is a pretty woman with not too many brains. The Americano flattered her, and she admitted that she was on her way to Los Angeles to meet Garcia and they were going to Mexico." Gonzales shrugged his shoulders and paused. "You know Garcia always said it wasn't safe to leave a pretty woman alone."

"Go on, go on, will you?" Jack roared. "I don't give a hang about pretty women. Get on with the tale."

"When the boat put in to Santa Barbara for freight, the Americano sent a messenger by land to the sheriff in Los Angeles, telling him where to catch Garcia. The captain didn't even tell Mrs. Garcia when they reached Los Angeles. While she was asleep one night they sneaked Garcia on as a prisoner and made the return trip without her ever knowing that the boat had put in to Los Angeles."

"The devil they did!" Jack laughed. "Pretty clever these Americans."

"When the boat docked in Monterey yesterday they sent Señora Garcia home and took Garcia out of the hold to Colton Hall and he was hanged. This morning people told her that if she wanted to see her husband he was at Colton Hall. I was there when she came. She saw him all right." Gonzales laughed. Jack laughed, too, for a minute. Loreta crossed herself and went slowly into the house. Poor Señora Garcia. She had been the means of her own husband's destruction. How could men laugh this way?

"It was a bit of a shame to make her suffer by looking at him like a tassel on the end of a rope," Loreta heard Jack say. "After all, *she's* never killed anybody."

"She talked too much, and she hid him!" Gonzales cried. "You're not going soft, are you?"

333

Loreta was glad Jack spoke that way. Even the eagerness of a fight had not made him forget the sorrow of a woman. Loreta saw Jack look off at the hills. He was not pulling on his pipe.

"I'm not going soft, Gonzales," he said very slowly, "but I'm not blaming her for hiding Garcia. He was her husband and she loved him."

"But not enough to control her tongue!" Gonzales cried. "It takes more than love to shut off a woman's tongue."

"Perhaps she talked because she was so happy about the chance of seeing him again. They shouldn't have tortured her."

Loreta went into her cool, quiet bedroom and gave thanks to the Virgin that her Jack understood a woman's heart so well. Someday he would be tender toward his son, if the mother of little Ruez was patient and kind. Maybe the good God was testing the faith of an Indian woman, by sending her a baby that the father didn't want.

Chapter XVI

THE SONG OF THE TURTLE: 1862. 1863

RUEZ was six years old and a merry, black-eyed little boy, when the great flood rushed down the Carmelo, sweeping everything in its way.

Loreta stood high up on the hillside with the children in the ox cart and watched an adobe house near the river gradually wash away.

"The Americano Captain Bralee helped pull up the flag of America the day I was born," Margaret told little Ruez. "It is too bad that his house washed away."

But Ruez wasn't interested in the man who helped raise the flag in Monterey. He squealed with excitement as chickens, and cattle, and wooden houses swirled down the great muddy river! Then suddenly his eyes widened, and he tilted his head to listen.

"The river sings a song to Ruez," he cried. "A song that says it is sorry to wash away houses and cattle and take the turtles from the places they like to live. But the water is glad to be rushing out into the sea." He sang a little song that sounded strangely like the rushing of water and the cracking of branches, and finally the banging of surf on the beach.

Loreta was afraid to breathe. For a minute the great rushing river that destroyed carefully planted fields was pushed from her mind. Ruez heard songs. He was an O-nes-e-mo!

The child came up and put his hand on hers. "Now listen, Mama mía," he said. "This is the turtle down where we play in the river bottom, telling the river not to wash her away." He made a queer, low blobbing sound that made Loreta laugh. She caught Ruez to her and hugged him.

"I hope you will always hear songs as your grandfather did, Ruez," she told the little boy. "It will make you happy as it did your grandfather."

"I can shoot ground squirrels and kill them the first time," Jackie said with a swagger. "That's more good than songs. Father says I shall have a better gun for Christmas."

Loreta looked at her oldest son, and then pulled him to her. "See that you always use the gun properly, Jackie. Garcia, the bandit, died by a rope because he used the gun to kill and rob other people, and Vasquez is in prison at San Quentin, with only bars and a small room, because he was led astray by Garcia."

"I know all that," the fourteen-year-old sniffed. He took aim at a crow and missed. Having lost face, he walked away from the group to meet his father who was coming up the hill.

Jack got off his horse stiffly. This had been a wet winter and the hip joint bothered him a lot. "We can be thankful that I had sense enough to build our adobe high on the hill," he told Loreta as he filled a pipe. "I tried to warn Bralee about being so near the river when I sold him that piece of land. You can't tell a sea-dog anything about land streams, and now he's cleaned out. The wooden rafters are floating away like matches."

As they sat watching, Escobar rode along the hill.

"I've lost a lot of cattle," he said sadly. "Good yearlings. I couldn't get them out of the gulch in time."

Jack stuck out his chest. "I could tell by the sky something was going to happen," he told Escobar. "My young Jack and the vaqueros drove the stock to the high hills. They're safe." He smiled and patted Jack's arm. "When my game leg acts up, I've a good substitute pair in this chap."

Loreta saw little Ruez turn his eyes from the river. He started over to his father. "I know a new song. I heard it from the river."

"What song's that?" Jack asked without much interest.

336

The sweet little voice piped up, but Loreta saw that Jack was not paying any attention. He was looking at the sad waste of hard work as parts of barns, made of wood that was hard to come by and took days of hauling, floated past them in the chocolate colored water.

"Quick!" Jack cried and pushed the singing child out of his way. "We can get ropes and pull out some of the cattle. See, they stop a little in the eddies and are trying to swim!" He hurried as fast as he could with the bad hip. Escobar and young Jack followed him.

Ruez just stood looking after his father. "Father didn't like my song! And I was singing it the best I know how."

Ruez sounded so hurt and disappointed that Loreta wanted to cry out. Before she could think of a word of comfort, Margaret whirled from the ox cart and caught the child in her strong young arms. "The song is so beautiful that it makes me quiver inside with happiness," she said, and Loreta saw her daughter look earnestly into the brown eyes of Ruez. "Always come to me when you want to sing. I wait to hear what the turtle says, and the song about the dry weeds blowing in the grass that sounds like bubbles."

"Has Ruez other songs?" Loreta asked.

The two children nodded. Then Margaret spoke. "Up on the hill Ruez has a pipe to play that we made from the hollow stem of elderberry wood. He calls the woodpeckers to him. They know him."

"Why didn't you tell me this before?" Loreta was filled with happiness.

"Because once father heard us and broke the pipe. He said that boys must grow up to be good vaqueros and able to look out for the great rancho that someday would be theirs," Margaret told Loreta. "We only play now on the way home and hide the new pipe in the crotch of an oak tree."

In the afternoon Jack decided that not even his bad hip could keep him in the Carmelo. He wanted to see what was

337

damaged in Monterey by the sudden downpour after a wet winter had softened the earth.

"We'll all go!" he told Loreta. "There is very little work we can do in the wet, and the children need a change. I can ride in the ox cart with you and my leg will be eased."

Margaret, in her best wine-colored wool dress that was made from a pattern of Doña Petra Allen's, jogged along in the ox cart behind her father and mother. Little Ruez and Jackie rode their horses. Jackie challenged Ruez to a race and Loreta took the chance to talk of something that persisted in her mind.

"Ruez is like Juan. He hears songs in the woods and water. I think that at last there will be a grandson to play the Padre Amores' fiddle," she told Jack as casually as she could, and watched out of the corner of her eye to see how he would take the news. "It will be nice to hear the fiddle play again, won't it?"

Jack spat far out into the road. "I'm not much on music playing for men," he told her.

"But you liked to hear Juan play."

"Oh, he was an Indian, but times have changed. Men nowadays must work hard and run ranchos, and put their minds to it, if they amount to anything. There's competition. More people coming. The easy old days of guitar playing and fiddling are gone, Loreta, and you might as well face it."

"Ruez shall do his share of the work," Loreta said with determination, "but his ears hear music, and at night after the work is done, it will be nice to have him play the fiddle for us."

"If he's got sense enough to play a jig or two it might be all right," Jack admitted.

"Today while we're in Monterey, I'll ask the priest about a few lessons on Juan's violin."

Jack didn't object and Loreta's heart raced at the very prospect. Now she would pray to San Carlos in the church in Monterey, and think hard that Padre Amores would know; then it would be easier for little Ruez to play the songs he

338

carried in his heart. She would even promise, for Ruez, that the boy would play chants in the church.

"I'm thinking to send Jackie to school where Francisco Soberanes is sending young Benito," Jack said. "He must get off the Carmelo and learn things if he is to carry on. Marcus Arais has a good school, and teaches them books as well as learning about crops. Young Jack will learn to speak English there, and be an English landed gentleman some day."

"That will be good," Loreta said, feeling happy that Ruez, too, would be having his chance at music.

"It will mean that Ruez will have to help me in the smithy as Jackie does now."

"But Jackie doesn't help," Margaret said behind them. "He only watches. Ruez is more help watching sheep."

Loreta was afraid, but Jack only pulled his mouth in a twitch, and clucked at the oxen for a bit more speed.

Loreta shook her head at Margaret behind Jack's back.

There was great excitement in Monterey. El Estero, always swampy with springs, had risen so that even the houses on high ground were flooded. All the low part of town was under water! Jack tied the oxen. Jackie and Rucz hopped off their horses, and the family walked to the low ground. Men were trying to save things from wet houses by loading boats from windows. Don Francisco Soberanes had no time to talk with Jack Preble about the school because his adobe house was melting right before everybody's eyes!

"Poor, poor souls, they're losing everything they own in that damnable water," Marinero Jack cried, and Loreta was proud to see how fast he was out of his coat and wading into the water to help salvage things from the houses. His eyes grew very angry when he saw young Jack standing on the bank watching.

"Who are you, to fancy yourself so much that you can't get wet to help unfortunates?" he roared at the boy. "Off with your coat and lend a hand before I stick your head in this muddy water."

339

Loreta took little Ruez and Margaret over to the church. Before they entered, Loreta brushed back the hair from her son's forehead. "Pray hard to the Virgin, my son, that she may intercede and help you toward making music. Your way is a hard one." As she looked up, her eyes met Margaret's. No word was said, but Loreta knew that the tall girl of sixteen understood.

After they had prayed in the peaceful church, Loreta went in search of the priest to ask him about music for Ruez. The Father was busy giving relief to the flooded and needy, and wanted help from the women. He didn't know of anyone who could teach fiddle playing. No one at present in the parish played. Surely Loreta hadn't heard a fiddle in church for a long time. Only the gambling places had fiddlers now. Mexican gamblers who hung fish heads around the necks of saints in effigy, and shot at them!

Ruez, instead of finding music, was set to the task of preparing vegetables for the stew that would go into the empty stomachs of the flooded ones. Loreta and Margaret helped to make tortillas. When they had finished work, the three went back to where they had left Jack.

"Why did you stay so long?" he asked crossly. "We've done all we could and were half a mind to go to Jack Swan's and leave you. We're tired and hungry and wet."

When he heard what they had been doing, Jack looked ashamed. "I'm sorry, Loreta," he said. "I might have known you weren't gassing with somebody. I'm an impatient customer," he squeezed her arm affectionately. "I'll buy you a present to make up."

Jack Swan was smiling and ushered the little family into the empty portion of his boarding house so that Loreta and Margaret wouldn't have to go through the bar. "It's a real theater, now," he said sadly, as he looked around the room empty of beds. "Not enough sailors stop over to keep it running. I'm living on what I make off the bar and the bit of tobacco I sell."

"What about the whalers? Don't they need boarding houses?" Jack asked.

"They build their own shacks, and spend little money. Most of 'em are Yankees staying out here until they make their pile. They pinch the pennies so's they can go home quicker. One whale the other day fetched seventeen hundred barrels of top notch grease, but few around Monterey will benefit!"

Swan set out a meal for them, and brought a bottle of wine from the bar. "I'm glad to have a snack with a Britisher for a change," he said as he poured their glasses. Then he lifted his own glass. "Give a drink to the future and be damned!" he roared. "It's all we got ahead of us. The feller that held the plaster on me foreclosed! Jack Swan's theater, built on a foundation of pics, is crumbling." He downed the wine at one gulp, and the smile never came off his face.

"You mean you've lost your place?" Jack cried.

Swan nodded. "Usurer's prices. I couldn't make it."

"Why didn't you tell me, Swan?" Loreta saw Jack's eyes sadden. "I could have helped you."

"The old bloke didn't give me a chance. Just clapped down. You see, I'd let the money go a day or two over to see what I could do. A day or two never made much difference before." Swan shrugged his small shoulders. "He clapped down one morning before even my eyes was open."

"Then how can you stay here?"

"The forked-tail devil gives me a chance to pay rent. That's how I stay here. Once my rent's not paid I'm on the streets." He was still smiling. "But the same divil as clapped down on me is in for trouble, don't you fear," Swan said.

"What kind of trouble?" Jack's eyes were excited now, as they always were excited at the mention of trouble. Loreta was used to that look.

"Why, our old friend, María Berreto, just figured Gore, who paid her four thousand dollars for Pescadero rancho, wasn't living in these parts, so she sold the damned rancho again to an agent of my forked-tailed devil! He took possession of the place and paid the taxes and fenced it. Now Gore is suing him, and María's gone. There's merry hell going on and lawyer's fees aplenty."

Loreta watched her daughter get up from the table and go around to where marinero Swan sat. "I'm sorry that you've lost your beautiful theater. I'll light a candle for you, and say prayers, because I love you. Once you made me very happy with a beautiful dolly."

"Bless you, honey, it'll take more'n one candle for the saints to see their way to helping an old sinner like me. But sailors don't sink easy." Swan pulled her down and kissed the crown of her shining black hair.

"Um—" he sniffed. "Don't you smell sweet of roses? Nice girl scent an old tar isn't used to. Makes me wish I'd weakened and got married."

Loreta saw Margaret's eyes shine with pleasure.

Jack ate his food in silence for a time; then he wiped his mouth and looked Swan square in the eye. "Promise me that you'll come up the Carmelo and live with us if you have any more trouble," he said. "There's plenty of room for you always. We'll build you a little house."

"What would a sailor do up the Carmelo?" Swan asked. He shook his head. "No, I'll make pies and sell whiskey to those not wise enough to let it alone. The soldiers pay me well to let them give shows for money in this room. I'll make out."

"Ruez hears songs in the woods," Loreta said without looking at Jack. "I thought perhaps the priest could tell us of someone to teach him a bit on my father's fiddle that you liked so well, but there is no one in the church now." She looked earnestly at marinero Swan, who had once been so kind and understanding at a cascarone ball.

"What ho! A young fiddler. And no pious feller to teach him!" Swan's eyes smiled at Loreta for a second and then he looked at Ruez. "Want to try a crack at it now in a saloon?" he asked the child.

342

"Yes!" Ruez shouted. "Please!"

Swan went out into the bar room to fetch his fiddle. Loreta looked for the first time at Jack. "It'll be a way to help the marinero by paying for the lessons," she said, and hoped the saints would forgive her for thinking more about her son's lessons than helping the sailor.

"Good idea," Jack smiled. "Loreta, you are a good woman. I wonder you stick by me, I'm so rough and thoughtless." He paused. "But I'm not always thoughtless, am I? And I love you."

Ruez was eager to know, and his little fingers soon learned the tricks of turning the pegs and tuning, even though a lot of people watched the lesson.

"Little duffer's got onto the tuning now. He's a good ear for doing it too," Swan cried, and tossed the tuning pipe to Loreta. "Take that along home with you so he can get the pitch right."

As they were leaving, Swan clapped Jack on the back. "He's got music in him, Preble, no doubt of it. He'll suck all I know about the fiddle out of me in no time."

Loreta saw Jack's chest swell with pride. For the first time, the father smiled with real love on brown-eyed Ruez.

"Now let's go and look at guns," Jackie begged. "You promised me one before Christmas."

"It's a long time until Christmas, and you'll wait. If this war and trouble over slaving lasts, you'll be carrying a gun with the business end of it damned busy. Then maybe you'll fill your own belly full of lead, and see how it goes, about guns," was the unexpected answer. "I promised your mother a present. We're going to pick it out." Jack smiled at Loreta when she looked sad. "Which shall it be, a shawl or a new dress?"

Loreta shook her head. "You've given me my present; one that makes me happier than any dress or shawl, Niño Jack," she said. "The promise you gave Jack Swan that Ruez is to have a fiddle lesson every Sunday after Mass."

343

"Pshaw," he said, pleased. "I was only helping the sailor a bit."

"Then, if you want to make me another present talk no more about war to Jackie and take Margaret to the bear and bull baiting next Sunday when you go," Loreta told him. "That would make me happier than a shawl. The child is grown up now, and wants to hear music and see the pretty dresses and merriment."

"She shall go," Jack promised. "She's beautiful as you were that day in church when I saw you first. I'll be proud of her in that wine wool dress." He seemed to be feeling pleased over everything.

"Now we can go look at guns?" Jackie asked. "Mother doesn't want you to buy her anything."

"I'll give you a gun in the behind if you don't stop pestering," Jack Preble told his favorite, and there was silence for a time, but eventually they stopped at the shop where guns were sold.

The next morning Margaret smiled at Loreta with shining eyes. "Do lovers just come right up to you and show their love at the bull-baiting?" she asked her mother. "Should I look the other way once or twice before I let him hold my hand if he does come?"

Loreta stopped kneading the bread, and watched her daughter for a minute. The girl's face was sweet and gentle, and her young body curved beautifully with budding womanhood. Loreta sighed for Margaret's dreams.

"The lover may not be at the bull-baiting, Margaret," she told her gently. "Your father saw me singing in church. The good God has as many ways to bring lovers together as there are people. You will know what to do when the time comes. Every woman knows."

Loreta could say no more to this shining-eyed creature. She bent over the bread tin and went to kneading the white dough.

344

Chapter XVII

DEAD MARCH FOR AMERICANO EARS: 1864. 1865

LORETA wondered if all Englishmen were as queer in their thinking as her Jack Preble. He was pleased with little Ruez and smiled when marinero Swan said the boy was clever with the fiddle, yet he never let the child have time to practice, even if he had to manufacture jobs to be done.

Young Jack, with his blankets, extra underwear, and paper, had gone to stay in Monterey where Marcus Arais was to teach him the classics and English.

"He shall have as good an education as the son of a Spanish Don, and he'll be a real English squire some day," Jack told Loreta proudly. "When I write home to England it'll make some of those stiff-necked ones squirm over class, with Jack Preble II, the son of a poor blacksmith and an Indian woman, belonging to the landed gentry."

"It is too bad that Don Hartnell died," Loreta said. "He was a fine school teacher, and good to Indians. Juan would have liked Jackie to learn from Hartnell."

"We can't go back to Spanish and Indian times. Things have to go on."

Monterey was quiet now, so far as politics were concerned, for the town consisted mostly of Mexicans, who preferred an easy life with gambling, and music, and hunting parties, to the bustle of San Francisco, or hardships at the gold mines. Money was not too plentiful, for tallow didn't bring such high prices, but there was enough to clink in bars and gambling places. The whaling industry in Monterey had made whale oil lamps the fad. Candles were used only in churches and at the mines, or by poor folks who couldn't afford a fancy lamp for burning the whale oil. The capitol had long ago been moved to Sacramento, which was nearer the gold mines and not too far away from the busy port of San Francisco. Monterey town trustees met only once a year. Trading boats called rarely, but there were still fiestas punctuated by a hanging now and then.

The Preble rancho was prosperous. Jack's saddles and hides brought a good price, and the smithy was handy for ranchers. "But I'll not be caught napping," he told Loreta one day. "I'm going to Monterey and make a deal for skinning the tan bark off some oaks down the coast. Tan bark is bringing high prices from the tanneries up north, and I can ship the bark from here by schooner."

Before he left, Jack laid out tasks for Ruez to do while he was away. There was a wicked twinkle in his eye when he saw his son sigh over so much work.

"You'll have to learn to work hard. Some day a third of all this rancho will be yours. If you can't work it you'll lose the land," he told the boy.

The dust stirred by Jack's horse had scarcely settled in the road before Loreta saw Margaret hurry out to the smithy.

"Quick," the girl cried, "go get your fiddle. There is a whole day ahead for practice. I'll cut and pile the wood for the fire." She grabbed the axe from Ruez. "I can work hard if you'll play me some of the songs you told me about. The one you hummed for the statue of 'Our Lady' that grandfather O-nes-e-mo carved, and the songs that came to you when I told you how pretty the señoritas looked at the bear-baiting."

Loreta had never seen Ruez so bright-eyed, so happy and eager, as he looked when he smiled at his sister.

"I've another one too!" he told her. "I heard it while I was heating the iron for father yesterday."

"What song is that, Niño?" Margaret asked.

Loreta's heart was squeezed with happiness when she saw her daughter's arm go around Ruez. The boy pulled away from Margaret, his thin bony body rigid.

346

"It's about the bear who felt sad because you didn't have a lover come up to kiss your hand, so he gutted the bull and then turned himself into a handsome lover for Margaret Preble!" he cried. "You see I heard you telling Mother that you missed your lover—"

"Play the fiddle then," Margaret said quickly and her face turned suddenly sad.

Ruez ran into the house and climbed on the bed. Loreta smiled when she saw how carefully he lifted the fiddle bag from its nail. She called to him.

As the boy came through the door into the kitchen, he pulled at the strings of the turkey-red bag.

Loreta put her hands on the young shoulders. Those shoulder blades reminded her of a picked chicken. "Ruez, it would be better if you didn't talk and think too much about lovers for your sister. You are not old enough to understand, and you hurt Margaret," she told him in a low voice. "She is sad now because she dreamed that the bear-baiting would be very different from the way it turned out."

Ruez pulled away. "But how can I help songs?" he asked, excited. "If a bear runs away and turns into a lover that sings a song for Margaret Preble, I must play it, because the song is here inside me." His bright eyes watched Loreta, and he pounded his bare brown chest.

The little boy's mind was on songs and not lovers, and talking would never change him. Ruez was a stubborn child. Loreta sighed, gave his thin cotton drawers a kindly spank, and sent him out to his sister. "Tell Margaret I will do her tasks in the house while the bread bakes and the beans boil for dinner."

Ruez drew soft sweet notes from the fiddle and Loreta thought of Juan O-nes-e-mo playing at the Mission when the work was done, and the gulls were winging their way toward the rocks where they spent the night. Even now, in her mind, she could see the white breasts of the birds turn pink in the rosy light of the sinking sun. The bells in the tower would

347

ring for evening prayers, and the Padres would start singing a beautiful chant—

Ruez stopped playing suddenly. Loreta came out of her day dream, looked out in the smithy, and saw a tall handsome boy about twenty leaning against the wall. He was gasping for breath and stared at Margaret with great frightened brown eyes. His heart was beating so hard that it bounced under the bare brown skin.

Loreta went out through the heat waves to the smithy. "What has happened, Comero?" she asked kindly. "You are afraid. Do not be afraid of us."

"He is after me—the Americano who tried to take away my grandmother's land," the boy said, and flattened himself against the adobe wall. "I heard you were kind and said prayers so I came here."

"Why does the Americano want you?" Loreta asked. She was aware of Margaret coming close up behind her, to be nearer the handsome Spanish boy.

"He tried to buy the Spanish land of my grandmother but I wouldn't sell. They would give only two hundred dollars for five thousand acres—and it is our home—our ground," the boy said, and looked anxiously around as if he was afraid of being trapped. "My grandmother is old, and kind, and simple in the mind because she has had much trouble—" He took a big breath; his heart was pounding hard. "The Americano came when he knew I was selling potatoes in Monterey. He talked kind to Grandmother about the children she had buried and her old home at Aragon in Spain. He piled gold pieces in front of her, and told her if she would make her cross on the paper she could have the gold!"

"No—no—" Loreta cried. "She didn't."

The boy nodded sadly. "She did, and was so happy to show me the gold when I came home— A bit more than a hundred dollars!"

"But why does he hunt you?" Loreta asked.

"Because of what I did to him."

"What did you do?" Loreta was almost afraid to ask. At least the boy hadn't killed the Americano.

"When my grandmother found out what she had done, and that our home and land was gone, she slashed her wrists. She bled to death alone in the straw of our barn. I found her the next morning." The boy could hardly finish the sentence.

With a sudden rush Margaret came past Loreta and put her arm around the shoulder of the boy. There were tears in her eyes.

"Poor one," she said tenderly. "We will look out for you—" and she kissed him on the cheek.

The boy was startled, and then broke down. "I am bad," he sobbed. "When the Americano came to turn me off my ground I waited in the chaparral and caught him with my riata and—"

"And *what?*" shrieked Ruez, who had been standing wide eyed.

"And cut off both his ears! They are only holes in his head now, so that even if he hunts me down and kills me, everyone shall know he is the Americano who stole land away from Magdalena Gonzales—and caused her death."

Loreta crossed herself, and asked the saints to think well of this boy in spite of his sins. He was so young; just about the age of José when he died—or even Antonio who had been the father of José . . . After all a man could *live* without ears.

A horse sounded on the road. The boy turned ashen, and began to shake.

"Behind here," Margaret said, and shoved him into the corner back of her wood pile. The rider was only Captain Bralee who had come for his stable latch from the smithy. When Bralee had gone, Loreta called to the boy.

"Come and eat, and then hide away in the largest of our three barns. There is a lot of hay. I will talk to my man, and we will see."

As the boy ate he looked into Loreta's eyes, and then away at Margaret. Ruez sat on the doorstep with his grandfather's fiddle, playing a gay little air that only he could understand.

"What is your name?" Loreta asked, and saw Margaret waiting anxiously to hear.

"If I tell—and your man should go to Monterey—" the boy began.

"Don't be afraid," Margaret said softly. "My father is a very good man."

"I'm Pedro Gonzales—and I'll probably hang for that pair of ears," the boy cried. "But I had to do it. You don't understand! I had to cut them off. The Americano killed my grandmother with his little pile of gold pieces and his lies!"

"No—no—you won't hang," Margaret told him. "My father will help you."

"But Gringos stick together against Spanish and Indians and Mexicans—the Gringos are never wrong!" Pedro insisted.

"Go into the hay and stop thinking of the Americano," Loreta said. "You will only be sick to the stomach. Throwing up makes people weak." But she knew how he felt. Alone with all the world to fight. She had felt the same way herself once long ago.

Margaret went to show Pedro the best place in the barn to hide. When she came back her eyes were very bright, and she hurried to finish the work before her father would be coming along the dusty yellow road. After things were set to rights and the wood piled high in the smithy, the little daughter came to Loreta.

"Pedro Gonzales told me I was very beautiful," Margaret said and watched Loreta sew. "Mama mía, do the words of a lover cut off the breath of a girl so that she is smothering, and her heart beats too fast?"

"Only the woman herself knows who is her lover," Loreta said. "The heart tells the mind. Things go wrong when you try to make the mind tell the heart!"

"He is good to look at. I'm sorry for his great trouble—"

"Here is his trouble," Ruez called from the doorstep. "Now listen to the music as I fiddle." He played a stern bit like a chant, and then the rhythm grew faster and faster—with two loud short notes at the end. "That's the Americano's ears dropping on the ground," he cried. "You hear it all in music."

"I'll thank you for hopping out of the way to let your father in," Jack Preble called. "What are you doing with that fiddle? Is there no work to be done on this rancho?"

The music had held them so that no one noticed Jack Preble riding in!

"But the wood is cut and piled," Loreta told her man. "The boy must play a bit to have his lesson for Marinero Swan on Sunday after Mass, or Swan will think he is not bright at music."

"All right, all right," Jack sank into a chair. "Let's have a glass of wine and a bit of bread to put me on until supper."

Then, as Ruez took the fiddle into the bedroom and began playing, and Margaret went up on the hill for a final look at the sheep, Jack told Loreta that the Monterey town trustees had met and passed some ordinances.

"They're going to fine any person fifty dollars who allows hogs to run in the streets of Monterey," he laughed. "But the worst hogs aren't the ones that grunt, more's the pity—for then a person would be warned by the grunt."

"What do you mean?" Loreta asked. Englishmen had queer ways of talking sometimes.

Jack drank the last of his wine and wiped his mouth. Loreta wondered if she had better tell him about the boy in the hay, but she decided that it would be better to wait until Jack had told *his* news. Men coming from town liked to talk.

"There's a legal fight on now, over the town lands that Ashley and a Scotchman bought at auction back in 1859," Jack told Loreta. "Ashley, president of the town board, was also the lawyer for the Scotchman. The town sold the land to raise money to pay Ashley's bill for defending Monterey pueblo lands before the U.S. land commission back in 1856. In 1859 when the land was sold, Ashley and the Scotchman were the only bidders, and bought the whole thing for $1002.50. Mr.

351

Ashley's bill of $991.50 was paid out of that. After expenses of the auction were taken out, Monterey had four dollars left!"

"And good pueblo land gone?" Loreta asked.

Jack nodded. "Now, years after, the town council has stopped making fiesta and music long enough to wake up and fight for what it has lost." He grew excited and limped across the floor to stand in the doorway. "But they'll lose, Loreta. They'll lose, because the Scotchman has already put up a bill to the legislature to legalize the sale."

Loreta understood. "Long ago, the Mission Padres said that Spanish and Mexicans were taking away Mission lands from Indians, and they would only have it until someone took it away from *them*," she told Jack. "Padre Payeras said that land fights would still be going on long after Padre's bones were rotted away."

"That's right," Jack nodded, and looked out to the hills. "Some take land by force the way Romans did in Britain, and some take land away from others by law, as Scotchmen do in California."

There was silence for a minute, and Loreta was about to ask if he knew Pedro Gonzales, when her man turned from the door and came up to her.

"We have our titles right. We will always be rich, and no one can ever say Jack Preble ever got his riches through dishonesty or legal shim-sham. Remember that, Loreta."

Loreta smiled into his clear honest eyes. "We can hold our heads without shame, Marinero Jack," she said, "and go down on our knees in church knowing that we have been honest and kind to Indians, as Loreta O-nes-e-mo promised the Padres she would be."

Jack sat down near her, and watched her peel the cooked peppers for a minute, and then he reached over and tipped Loreta's face toward him. "You'll always be able to say that," he told her. "God knows I like land and gold, but not enough to sear my conscience with the knowledge that what I've got belongs to another."

352

"Mother, did Pedro Gonzales bury the ears he cut off the Americano?" came the reedy voice of little Ruez from behind. "Because then I could play a dead march, like they had for the little Soto girl when she was carried around the streets of Monterey in a lace draped coffin."

"What's the boy talking about?" Jack asked Loreta. "Does he speak of Pedro Gonzales from Dry Canyon?"

Loreta nodded. "I hid the boy out in the hay. Americanos are after him." Quickly she told Jack about the troubles of young Pedro, and saw her man's eyes soften.

"Fetch the boy in from the hay," Jack roared. "The American skunk shall suffer for this, if Gonzales himself is not lying! I know the proper people to go to. Jack Preble is a power around here now! He has land and many thousand head of cattle—"

"Pedro doesn't lie," Margaret cried, from where she stood setting the table. "He grieves for his grandmother and the land—" she dropped the forks and ran toward the barn.

Jack turned toward Loreta. "Do you remember once, long ago, Jack Preble tried to defend an innocent person and was shoved away? I told you then that some day I'd have land and cattle and be something beside a runaway sailor."

Loreta nodded. How could she forget the night Antonio Prealta stood helpless and accused, and Jack had tried in vain to help him? Antonio had been shot not long after that.

"Be careful, Niño, Jack," she said quietly. "Americanos have different ways. Perhaps they will hurt you—"

"They don't dare hurt me," Jack said proudly.

Jack heard Pedro's story, ate his supper, and ordered a vaquero to saddle two fresh horses.

The boy was frightened. He seemed ready to bolt out of the door at the first opportunity.

"You can't run away from trouble," Jack said, and put his hand on Pedro's shoulder. "You have nothing to fear. I will protect you. I wouldn't blame you if you'd killed the Americano. Folks have been stabbed for less than that in these parts."

353

"No, Jack, no," Loreta cried out. "Don't talk about killing! God and the saints will never forgive you!"

Jack turned. "Maybe not—but folks around here are far from the saints. Those in heaven won't miss 'em. Times have changed, Loreta. We have to stick together and fight."

Loreta saw Margaret look a long time at Pedro. "You see, I told you my father was a good man," she said to the boy.

"Come here and kiss your father, Margaret. May you be as splendid a woman as your mother." Jack leaned from his saddle to kiss the girl, and a twinge went across his face as he moved the stiff leg in the stirrup. "It's a long ride back through the night—but morning may be too late for the little job we have on hand," he said.

Then he turned to the boy beside him.

"Have you the gold that Americano left with your grandmother?"

Pedro nodded.

"Come on then."

Jack kicked his horse and rode out into the darkness. Pedro sent a quick smile to Margaret and then followed.

Loreta stood beside Margaret and Ruez, and listened to the fading hoofbeats.

"I hope Englishman Jack is not in for a fight," she said as she shut the door. "This is just a job he loves."

"But it is a good fight," Margaret cried. "Two honest men fighting together for what is right can't come to harm!"

"Once, I thought that way too," Loreta told her.

"Now I can play a dead march for those Americano ears," Ruez called out.

Chapter XVIII

AN ENGLISHMAN SPEAKS: 1865

THE next day around noon, Jack rode in alone. He swung off the saddle and gave the horse to Ruez. Loreta could tell that things had gone to suit him, for he swaggered like a marinero.

"Well, Pedro is back on his land by now," he told Loreta and the wide-eyed Margaret. "A few of us took the Americano down to the Salinas River and tarred and feathered him. Pedro gave him back the gold pieces and we made the skunk sign over the land and confess what he'd done on paper. Then we put him on a horse and threatened to kill him if he ever came back into Monterey county."

"Was anybody killed?" Loreta asked timidly. She had worried all night about fighting and killing.

"Nobody killed," Jack laughed. "It was really quite a social affair for everybody but the earless American." He smiled slyly at Margaret. "Pedro sent his regards to you. By now he's most likely loading a cart of potatoes to deliver in Monterey tomorrow."

"You are a good man," Loreta murmured. "The saints will remember."

"I'm not so sure of the saints as I used to be, Loreta." Jack turned suddenly sad. "I used to think that if a man did good, things would be right for him—but a fine man has been shot and killed—a man who always did what he thought was right."

"Not Don Cooper—or any of the Borondas?" A great hurt went through Loreta, as she looked at the face of her man.

Jack's eyes went toward the hills and he shook his head.

355

"No, Loreta, you didn't know him. He was Abraham Lincoln, the President. The war is over, but we've lost a good friend who tried to do what he thought was right."

Loreta crossed herself, and said a prayer for the soul of this good man Lincoln. She asked Padre Amores to guide his footsteps to paradise, and bring rest to him.

"We'll soon be having our Jackie home for good," Jack broke into her prayers.

"Why?" Loreta asked, afraid for the boy. "Doesn't he learn well?"

"There's few lessons where the boy is," Jack laughed. "I met Francisco Soberanes on the street. His young Benito is home sick with a bowel complaint. They found out what was causing the trouble. Old man Arais sets the boys to stripping the leaves off of tobacco, then, as a special treat if they work well and say nothing, the schoolmaster gives them a few tablespoonsful of black-strap molasses that comes on the 'Boston Ships' and they think that it's fine. 'Americano sweets'—"

"But the sickness—?" Loreta felt anxious for her son.

"The bowel sickness came to little Benito because he was ambitious and stripped so much tobacco that the molasses treats were too close together, and physicked him until they thought he was going to die." Jack roared with laughter. "Soberanes would never have found out—if the boy hadn't taken sick."

"But our Jack—" Loreta began.

"Don't worry about our Jack. He's not liable to work hard enough to physic himself. He's too fond of breaking away to take a pot-shot at a few birds with that gun I gave him! It's a great bit of wit, the fathers paying for their sons to go and work for someone else. Here's one father that's learned his lesson."

"Then Jackie will be with us for Christmas celebration and see me as the Angel Gabriel!" Ruez called out. "Last Sunday the Father showed me purple wings and the white shirt I'm to wear when I call everybody to the manger in front of the church, where Margaret is the Virgin Mother bending over a baby!"

"Well, Gabriel, hop your white shirt over into the sheep pasture and do some herding," Jack told his son. "And don't toot your horn until you get to the church."

Loreta saw Margaret edge out of the door past her father. Her arm was held stiffly at her side, and two turkey-red strings hung down below her skirt. Juan's fiddle was walking out of the door right under Jack Preble's very nose! Women must do things quietly so that no trouble would come. Margaret had learned this without anyone to teach her. Loreta sighed, and wondered what the saints thought, when Padre Amores' fiddle must be sneaked out, and the lovely music from a boy's soul played secretly in a cleft of the rocks so far away from the house. She was sad that her Englishman, who was really good, could understand so little the heart of a child he had brought into the world.

Young Jack only scoffed at the Angel Gabriel. He sighed loudly with boredom beside his mother in the church, when Margaret, beautiful in her blue robes, bent tenderly over the babe while shepherds clustered around her and sang sweet chants. But he did chuckle a bit when Gabriel turned on the Evil One, in scarlet with hoofs, and played fast music that made the Tempter run away from the shepherds.

Loreta saw another pair of eyes watching Margaret with devotion and wonder. When the final hosannas came and everybody sang praises for the Christ Child, Pedro Gonzales sang his song for Margaret's ears alone, but an Indian woman understood. Once she had helped such a boy as Pedro to wind silver threads on wooden sticks to make a star for the Mission on Christmas.

When church was out, Loreta took her man's arm and hurried him over to talk to Doña Petra Allen. "The children must change their things," she told him.

357

Loreta heard Jackie brag to Benito Soberanes and the Soto boy, that he could smoke black cigars without being sick. She turned ever so little, and saw Pedro Gonzales standing close to Margaret in the shadows near the door of the adobe church. They weren't talking, but Pedro held Margaret's hand for a second, and smiled before they walked together toward the gate. Those two didn't need words!

"The Father tells me that your Ruez made up in his head the music he played," Doña Petra was saying. "You should be very proud."

Loreta nodded and smiled.

Jack stuck out his chest. "I'm not much for music, but it sounded all right, didn't it?"

"Some of the music reminded me of Juan O-nes-e-mo. I miss Juan. He made fine soft shoes—and played such beautiful chants at the Mission. It is well that his music has been passed along to his grandson." Doña Petra nodded and turned away as Margaret and Pedro came up. Ruez was just behind with his fiddle.

Pedro put out his hand to Jack. "This is a beautiful Christmas for me," he said. "You have made it beautiful and I am thankful to you."

"I hope you'll have a good crop of potatoes," Jack laughed, and turned to the cart.

Loreta took longer than usual to arrange the heavy hand-woven blankets, and fuss over the cart for the journey home, so that the young lovers would have a bit more time to look at each other.

"Come on, you're getting like an old hen. First one foot and then the other," Jack said crossly. "Let's be off."

Pedro still stood watching them in the light of the pine flare at the church gates, when the ox cart made the turn at the corner of an adobe wall.

It was wet underfoot and very dark when they reached the Mission San Carlos de Borromeo del Carmelo, on the way home, but Loreta found her candle, and took from the cart her bunch of berries. "I won't be long," she told Jack. " 'Our Lady' must be lonely over here in the dark and wet—away from candles, and music, and glitter, for the birth of Jesus."

Margaret caught up the toyon wreath she had made, and stood by her mother in the road.

"We'll go on slowly in the cart," Jack said. "You can catch up. My leg is aching and I want to get home, Christmas or no Christmas."

Loreta lighted the candle, and Margaret took hold of her arm. Together they picked their way toward the ruined Mission. The Indian buildings were now only low melted lumps of adobe.

"I saw men using some of this adobe to fix holes in the road when I came from taking butter to Martin's," Margaret said.

"Our Lady" was there, smiling in the dark. Someone else had remembered her, for a little bunch of pink roses was tucked in the niche beside her feet, and there was a stub of candle.

Loreta wiped the water away and fixed the candle; then Margaret crowned the damp head with her wreath of toyons.

There was something tender and beautiful about Margaret tonight. Her body was so slender and graceful as she reached up with the crown.

" 'Our Lady' looks kindly on lovers," Loreta murmured in Margaret's ear. "She smiled on your father and an Indian woman—and before that on Antonio Prealta—"

Margaret looked at Loreta a moment in understanding, and they both knelt to say a prayer for the lonely saint, on the birthday of her son.

Then through the darkness came the sweet notes of a chant! The chant Amores had taught an Indian long ago.

Loreta could scarcely breathe until the music was finished. The saints were hearing this too! The San Carlos heard! She finished her prayer and scrambled among the loose tiles at her feet. In a moment Margaret was by her side. They looked at the saint's face in the candle-light and went out.

359

"Did you hear it?" Ruez called eagerly from near the door. "Margaret hummed the chant over and over again—up in the hills—until I could play it! We wanted to surprise you, and make you think of when you were young on Christmas night."

Loreta caught her little son to her in the dark, and held him close. "Bless you—" she murmured. "The good God has been kind to an Indian woman." Then she gathered Margaret to her, for a moment. "You are good to remember the chant I sang to you—and help to pass the beauty of it into a violin again."

"But how did you manage to play the chant? Didn't your father scold you about staying?" Loreta asked, as they walked along the road.

"Oh, he doesn't know I'm not in the back of the cart!" the little fellow said cheerfully. "I slid out easy and didn't make a sound. Father is talking to Jackie. He wants to ride the range with the vaqueros now instead of working in the smithy. Father says he's to go and help strip the tan bark from oaks. We're all going to strip tan bark."

They didn't catch up with the ox cart, for going was slow in the muddy road, but Loreta was glad to be walking with her children in the dark on Christmas. A light shone in the house that was built on the land that Captain Bralee sold after the flood. Another Englishman lived there now, a tall, fine-looking man Jack liked. He was well educated and had worked in a great bank in London. It was comforting to see the light of this Edward Berwick, shining out into the night like a Christmas star. Good neighbors were better than gold in the valley of the Carmelo, Loreta thought, as she climbed the hill to the adobe, beside her children.

After the new year, Loreta looked far up on the hillside where Margaret knitted and watched sheep, and saw that Pedro Gonzales was with her daughter. It was well that both Jacks and Ruez were down the coast stripping tan bark. The good God knew when to bring lovers together, so that even the

360

fiddle of Ruez would not spoil things for them. Loreta smiled and soaked dried blackberries to make a special empanada for supper.

Margaret had not done much to the sock she was knitting, when the sun was low and the men rode into the rancho. Pedro jumped up from the doorstep and held Jack's horse for him.

"What? You here?" he asked. "Surely you haven't chopped off another pair of ears, Pedro Gonzales!"

Pedro flushed red and laughed along with young Jackie and his father. Ruez jumped up and down with glee. Loreta saw Margaret wince, and turn to set the table.

"Come in," Jack told Pedro. "Eat with us. I smell fruit empanadas that English call pies."

The men sat around the fire, while Loreta cooked, and Margaret moved quietly about the table. From the bedroom came soft notes from the violin.

"We stopped at Grag's saloon for a drink to warm us on our way home," Jack said. "A chap there said that Swan has just given up his little store. Couldn't make it go, poor chap." He spat into the fire. "And to think that one time the old sailor was worth forty-five thousand dollars! I wonder what he'll do now? He's getting so deaf you have to shout your lungs out at him."

"Swan passed me on the road yesterday and I gave him a lift," Pedro said. "He was going up into the hills with a pan and grub. He thinks he knows where there is gold."

"Then the glitter hasn't wormed out of his silly mind yet," Jack snorted. "I should think he'd never want to even look at a pan for washing gold."

"Poor Marinero, couldn't we put him up here?" Loreta asked.

"Too damned proud." Jack pulled up chairs for supper. "Shut the fiddle off, will you?" he shouted toward the bedroom. "I'd like to eat in peace."

Ruez came, and slid noiselessly into his chair. His poor

361

hands were skinned from working in the rough bark. Loreta wondered how he could finger the fiddle at all.

Pedro moved closer to Jack while Loreta and Margaret were washing the dishes, and young Jack was out attending to the horses.

"I came over to ask you if I could marry Margaret," Pedro said in a rush of words. "I love her and she loves me—and now I have my ranch I can take care of her."

Margaret stopped wiping the plate in her hands. She watched her father's face.

"Oh, you did, did you? Well, I say you can't marry Margaret. We need Margaret here. She's all the help her mother's got!"

Loreta pulled her hands out of the dishwater and came to the fire. "No, Jack, she has a right to her life. Don't say that—if Margaret loves—him."

"And what do you say about it?" Jack asked crossly. "Is the boy asking me or you about Margaret?"

"But she's my child too. Surely an Indian woman has a right to speak up for her child, Marinero Jack!"

Jack drew himself up. "Perhaps an Indian woman hasn't such fine judgment about what is good for her daughter. You weren't doing so well, Loreta O-nes-e-mo, when I took you on to look after. The girl is better right here on the Carmelo with her mother."

Loreta looked at the sad eyes of Pedro, and turned back to her dishwashing. She knew only too well that it was no use arguing with this Englishman when his mind was made up.

Pedro soon left. Margaret sat watching the fire. Jack emptied his pipe after his final smoke.

"You think you're being treated badly now, but some day you'll see that Jack Preble is a man of the world and no fool. Pedro Gonzales is only after this fine land I've worked so hard to get. There's many a prettier Señorita in Monterey than you he could have for the asking, but they have no land like you will have."

"He has a rancho now," Margaret told her father. "I could be so happy with him—and help him."

"We won't talk more about it," Jack said, and limped off to bed.

Loreta blew out the lamp and then drew her daughter to her. Together they watched the red coals in the fireplace crumble and make a smaller glow.

"No señorita in Monterey is more beautiful than you are, Margaret. I have learned that men sometimes say things they are ashamed of afterwards. Some day perhaps land will not mean so much to your father as it does now." Loreta kissed her daughter and went to bed. It was well to leave Margaret alone by the fire to dream for a while.

Chapter XIX

BAD MEDICINE: 1866

AS the months passed, Jack Preble had much more on his mind beside land and his daughter's love affair. The long trips down the coast to the tan bark camp proved too much for his lame hip in wet weather. He decided to put young Jack in charge of things, and let him haul the bark to Monterey. The boy was nineteen now, and a husky. He would have no more of school, and might just as well be doing something useful.

But the job went to young Jack's head. He felt important driving the fine eight-horse team into Monterey, and looked down on his mother and brother and Margaret. He began coming home later and later of nights. Twice he was the worse for liquor when he arrived at the Preble adobe.

Jack could see no flaws in his favorite son, and made excuses. "It's cold driving the team. Most likely he only had a drink to warm him and it went to his head because his stomach was empty. You women always think the worst."

Loreta only sighed and thought of the day nearly a year ago now, when Ruez had come racing to the rancho on a borrowed horse to tell his mother that young Jack was stupid with drink at Post's saloon, and the horses waited in the rain. Women might think the worst, but it had been young Margaret who rode over and drove the team with her brother lying drunk on the seat beside her. They put Jack to bed before his father returned from helping Escobar hunt a grizzly bear that was killing calves.

A row between young Jack and his father came on the day they went to Monterey for the christening of little Emma Butler, the daughter of bright-eyed Refugio Allen Butler, and

364

the granddaughter of Petra Allen. The little lady, whose eyes were sad now, because she was lonely for Don Allen, had invited the whole Preble family to the christening and fiesta.

"Think of that gay laughing-eyed Refugio Allen, who thought of little except good times and her guitar playing, having a daughter to be christened!" Jack laughed. "We must all be there on time."

But the christening, with Don Juan Bautista Cooper, and Dona Luisa Estrada as godparents to the baby was long over— and still young Jack, who was to drive in a load of tan bark, didn't come. Loreta watched the face of her man twitch with anger and his body grow restless, during the time that the fiesta was at its highest. He was surly while Refugio played her guitar and sang.

Finally he could stand the strain no longer. "I'll ride ahead. Something must have happened to Jack. A wheel may have come off the wagon. You come home when you're ready."

"Vasquez is at large again, Preble, but I don't think you need to worry about him tackling a load of tan bark with that husky son of yours driving the team," Don Cooper called to Jack as he was going out.

When Loreta left in the early twilight with Margaret and Ruez, the boy begged her to stop and take one peek at the medicine show going on in the grass-covered lot behind the Pacific House.

"Alonzo Allen says the man throws balls and gets two back for every one he throws, and I heard music from an organ grinder when we passed on our way to the church," he told Loreta. "Please let us go."

Ruez asked so little—and Jack never let Margaret and Ruez come into Monterey except for church and occasional shopping. "We will have to hurry then," was all she said.

"It is good to hear music and see lights here," Ruez cried excitedly as they walked along. "The field must miss the fiesta music and be sorry that señoritas don't come any more for bear-baitings."

365

Loreta and Margaret stood at the edge of the crowd. Ruez soon left them to elbow his way down near the organ grinder. A tall man in a gray top-hat and tailed coat stood on a platform and told stories in English. It was hard for Loreta to understand. The man talked fast and she was used to Spanish. Americanos laughed all around her. Soon another man came and tossed brightly colored balls into the air and sang a song as he caught them behind his head and under his knees. He pulled a red handkerchief out of his nose and poked it into his mouth. When he pulled it out again the handkerchief was green!

Loreta was so interested in what was going on that she didn't miss Margaret. When she turned, the girl was on the edge of the crowd looking into the eyes of Pedro Gonzales.

Loreta grew tired of standing. Twice the man had gone through his stories and the ball-throwing and handkerchief pulling. Twice a boy came through the crowd selling pink medicine in bottles for a dollar. People went and others came, but Loreta watched on. It was a small thing to let lovers look into each others' eyes by staying at a medicine show. An Indian woman knew that her daughter had hoped many months for such a meeting with Pedro. Ruez, down by the organ grinder, was unconscious of time.

The show was over. Ruez came to her with his eyes shining. "I can play all the tunes now on my violin when I get home," he bragged. "I listened hard."

"It is better that you play your own sweet music, Niño. Your notes are sweeter than any you've heard tonight."

"I know that, but I have to play tunes to please father—and now I have a lot in here." He tapped his head. "But the tunes in my head don't mix with the tunes that come from my insides, Mother. Those tunes are mine."

They walked over to Pedro and Margaret. Loreta smiled at the boy. "Ruez and I would like to talk of his music, and it disturbs the dreams of Margaret. Maybe you will take her behind you on the horse to the top of the hill, Pedro. Then we will be finished talking over the tunes and you can go quickly back down the hill."

"You ride in the saddle, and I'll get on behind; then I can put my arm around you," Pedro told Margaret when Loreta started away in the cart. He kissed her and then helped her up on the horse.

Margaret was bursting with happiness. Pedro's nearness made her feel that she would die when they must part again. His arms, warm and caressing, turned the dark road into black velvet beauty created specially to shield lovers from prying eyes. She leaned back against Pedro's chest. He kissed her mouth and her eyes and her brow. The beat of the horse's hoofs seemed like the ticking away of precious minutes they had together. Margaret wanted to stop time, and the beat of hoofs.

"I can't give you up," Pedro whispered. "The good God knows that we belong together, Margaret—even if an Englishman says no. I've tried for a year to forget you."

"I know—I know too, Pedro. You are my man. The lover I've dreamed of." Margaret sighed. "What shall we do?"

"Defy the Englishman. He is not God!"

"He is my father—I'm afraid."

Pedro's arms held her closer—and somehow, when he kissed her now, Margaret was not so much afraid of her father—.

"Run away. Your mother understands or she would not have given us this chance to be together! Margaret—I want to take care of you always. I have the rancho. We could be so happy."

"But the church banns. My father would stop the marriage!"

"I will meet you at the Mission, and take you to Monterey. You can go by the stagecoach to San Juan Bautista and wait for me. The banns will be read there—far away from the Carmelo and your father."

Clop, clop, the hoofs were carrying them closer to the parting. Pedro brushed his fingers tenderly over her eyes, and wiped away the tears. "You are so beautiful, Margaret, and so

367

good, that being away from you is killing your Pedro. Meet me at the Mission tomorrow night, after your father is asleep. We have the right to our love—and our life together."

They came suddenly upon the cart with Loreta and Ruez waiting. Pedro lifted Margaret from the saddle, and held her close a moment. Darkness was kind to lovers. "Tomorrow night at the Mission," he whispered. "I will be waiting."

"Tomorrow night at the Mission," Margaret repeated in his ear. There was a quick kiss and they walked over to the cart.

When they got home Jack was in a rage. "I met that lummox you brought into the world, drunk, and driving my finest horses so that they were white with lather! He was trying to make up the time he wasted in Grag's saloon," he roared at Loreta. "I'll not put up with it. A man can take a drink now and then to warm him—but I'll have no sot around the Preble adobe. He's cheated his own father by selling tan bark to buy whiskey!"

"Where is Jack now?" Loreta asked as she took off her best woolen shawl and folded it.

"I'm damned if I know! I told him never to come back here. I shoved him off the seat of the wagon onto his behind in the road and left him there. Then I tied my horse to the wagon and drove the team home. I've just finished wiping the poor horses down and given them a hot mash for their patience."

Loreta sat down by the fire and thought of young Jack. She wondered if his father had made the road to saloons easier by turning him from the home that was warm and comfortable. She wondered if the Room-se-en women in rancherias long ago had known the sorrows that an Indian woman knew now, or had all these things come with Spanish, Mexicans and Americanos who lived on the land? So many changes in the life of an Indian sister of San Carlos de Borromeo. Even young Ruez noticed the changes and was sorry that there were no more bear and bull fiestas with Spanish señoritas, and Margaret was not like Indian women—free to take herself the man she wanted.

"Make us some tea, will you?" Jack asked. "A fight makes me shake now. I must be getting old."

"Not old," Loreta said as she put the kettle on the fire that Jack had built to make the hot mash. "You have lived for a long time, with no fights, and the Saints are making you suffer for temper and anger, Marinero Jack. You must ask forgiveness—to stop the shaking."

"I'll be damned if I do. You should have seen those horses in a lather. No decent man could help anger. The cheat!"

"Let me play a jig for you, while the kettle boils," Ruez cried, eager-eyed. "It will cheer you, Father."

"Yes, lad, a jig—maybe one of my sons is worth something besides drinking. But mind, none of your fancy trills and twiddles."

Ruez sat by the fire and played the songs he had heard so recently, at the medicine show. Loreta sent a prayer to the Virgin and San Carlos for her other boy out in the cold. When next she looked at her fighting Englishman she saw that anger was wiped from his face and he no longer twitched. The toe of his boot tapped time to the music. The fiddle, played by his unwanted son, was bringing peace and quiet to Jack Preble.

Chapter XX

A BUSY WEEK: 1867

THE next morning before dawn broke, Loreta heard her man roaring at the vaqueros. She cooked the breakfast and wondered where young Jack had spent the night.

By sun-up, two Indians were already on their way to the tan bark camp on the coast. Jack came in and washed himself at the tin basin. Then he sat down, and, for the first time since their marriage, ate food without waiting for grace.

Loreta bowed her head over her plate and asked the saints to forgive her man.

"Send Margaret to tend sheep today. I need Ruez to help me in the smithy. There's lots of work, and I must get caught up so that I can go and see to the tan bark." Jack stirred his big cup of strong black tea. "There's six wheels waiting for iron bands, and Mr. Berwick wants a new kind of hoe made. He's going to plant pear trees, and figures on making a sunken dish of earth around them to catch water." He tipped back his chair and sucked on his moustache to clean the tea from it.

"I still have to work, I'm not as quick at making money as Rocker and Huntington and Stanford. They put their money in the railroad and two of them are Senators who have their way among law makers. They are to go to Utah and have a joining of the railroad that they dreamed about in the back of a store in Sacramento. Many's the time I've seen them come out of the shop of Huntington and Hopkins, together."

Loreta saw her Jack's eyes take on a far-away look for a minute, and then he got up from his chair suddenly, and laughed. "But that's all past. I'll wager neither Stanford nor Hopkins can hit that golden spike on the head at the first crack. It's better for Jack Preble to get at Berwick's hoe."

"Mr. Berwick is clever with his land—" Loreta said, and tried not to think about young Jack's breakfast this morning.

"It would have been well if our skunk of a Jack had seen fit to go to school down the road. God knows Berwick is paid little enough for teaching the youngsters in wet weather when they can't work, but the school was his own idea."

"Don't call Jack a skunk—" Loreta begged. "He is our son— and still young enough to make mistakes."

"Jack's a man; stubborn and a sot. He is a skunk!" Jack roared. "Long before I was his age I was making my own way!" He got up from the table and limped out to the smithy.

"In the night a song came to me about your hair, Mother," Ruez said as he mopped egg yellow from his plate with a bit of bread. "It is about the silver all shining, and mixed with the black. I want to play it for you—"

"No, no," Loreta told him quickly. "Not now. It is better for you not to make music. It might anger your father more, and he wants you to help him in the smithy."

"Don't you care at all about the beautiful silver notes?" There was sadness in the boy's eyes as he looked at Loreta.

"I want to hear the song!" Margaret cried. "Hurry into the bedroom, Ruez. You will have a minute to play while father is making ready!"

They ran away together and soon there was a tinkle of notes. Loreta kept watch. All would have been well, if Jack hadn't come around the adobe a different way from the usual one. He passed the bedroom first.

"Get out here, Ruez," he shouted. "There's no time for twiddling music. A few more shiftless sons and the Preble adobe will fall down on their lazy shoulders!"

The smithy fire was hot with red coals, and tools were laid out.

"You blow the bellows," Jack ordered, "and have tongs to grab the iron and plunge it into water when I tell you it is ready." The voice was harsh and full of impatience, and Lo-

371

reta heard Jack pound hard on the iron bands he was shaping for wheels.

"Quick! Drop it in water, stupid!" came tearing through the air and a second later a blood-curdling scream went up.

Loreta ran to the smithy. The flesh was seared on both little hands and arms, and Ruez' face was scarlet from steam burns. He jumped up and down screaming—then began to run . . .

Margaret ran too, but before she reached him, the boy dropped senseless in the yellow earth by the door of the adobe.

Loreta pushed Margaret away, and Jack picked up the limp body of Ruez and carried him into the bedroom.

"He didn't watch. His head was full of tunes," Jack said helplessly, then after a second he seemed to come suddenly alive. "Quick, Loreta, what shall we do? What herbs? You must know!"

"Crushed sage from the hills." Loreta didn't look up. She was undressing the boy as fast as her fingers could work. "Bring water, for the Niño's head."

It was well that the boy was still senseless while they bound the raw flesh of his arms and hands with crushed sage—but Loreta grew frightened when the late afternoon sun came into the room and still Ruez hadn't opened his eyes.

Margaret never left the bed. She was sitting quietly in the dusk when Ruez moved ever so little and opened his eyes.

"Margaret," he whispered. "You won't let them take my fiddle away from me until after I play the beautiful song about the hair of our mother?"

"No, Ruez. They won't take the fiddle away."

"Where is it? I can't see it hanging on the wall."

Margaret reached up and lifted the turkey-red bag from the nail. "Here, Ruez. Right here in the bag."

But the pain had come on, and Ruez groaned and turned his head away. His eyes were bright, and his body hot. Loreta walked in and stood beside the bed. The boy saw her and screamed for Margaret. He wouldn't be quiet until Margaret's head was close to his own over the bed. "Don't let Mother come," he cried. "She doesn't want to hear the music from my fiddle. Margaret, don't leave Ruez and the fiddle."

"Oh, Ruez, I do want to hear the music," Loreta managed through the strangled feeling in her throat. "You must lie quiet so that you will get better and can play the sweet chants." She had prayed all day as she worked, to the Virgin who watched over the young; prayed that the poor hands of Ruez would heal and be able to move over the strings once more.

"No—no—you don't. You wouldn't hear the song about your hair!" Ruez groaned and feebly shook the head that was plastered with tallow. "Go away—go away—"

Loreta looked a moment at her young son, and then her eyes met Margaret's.

"Perhaps some willow tea," Margaret said softly. "The boy has fever and doesn't know what he says."

"He *does* know what he says," Ruez groaned. "Margaret—keep Mother away—, and Father too. The songs go when *he* comes!"

Jack Preble stood in the doorway looking helpless and miserable as Loreta passed him. "Shall I ride to town for the doctor?" he asked. "I can't bear just standing here doing nothing. I can't! I can't!" He followed her out to the kitchen, and stood like a child while she lighted the lamp. Then he sat by the fire and held his head in his hands. "Ruez is a good little chap," he said softly, "never bothers—never impudent—" He rubbed his head and tousled the hair that was shot with silver. "Why did I ever let him hold the hot iron?"

Loreta went over and put her hand on Jack's shoulder. She stood quietly by his side for a minute, thinking her marinero was only a boy too, a boy filled with sudden anger and then remorse. The years hadn't changed him much—

"We will send Vincente for the doctor if it will make you feel better," she said softly. "I will brew willow for the fever."

Jack jumped up. "Not Vincente! He'll be too damned long on the way. I'll go myself. No one in Carmelo can ride as fast as Jack Preble when he's a mind to."

373

"But your hip—" Loreta started.

"Do you think I care about my puny old bones when Ruez lies there suffering from burns?" His eyes were angry, and the limp pitiful as he tried to hurry across the floor toward the door. "I should not have trusted to Indian herbs. I should have gone this morning for a doctor!"

Ruez was delirious, but he knew Margaret, and screamed every time she was out of his sight, afraid that the fiddle would be taken. As the girl sat in the dark, soothing her brother, she thought of Pedro—waiting at the Mission.

"This is sea waves moaning a song for lost sailors on foggy nights—" Ruez told her and hummed a low tune. "Are you listening, Margaret?"

"Yes—a beautiful tune—" the words came without thinking— Perhaps she could send a message to Pedro by Vincente, the old Indian.

"And here's the sea lions roaring at Point Lobos—"

"Ruez, try and sleep. Margaret must go to the kitchen and eat a bite—"

"No—no—they will take the fiddle!" The black eyes moved restlessly and were too bright. Even willow tea hadn't helped the fever.

"But I'll watch the door while I eat. No one will come in, and you can make a funny song about bread and cheese and the clatter of dishes," she suggested hopefully.

There was a smile. Ruez nodded ever so slightly. "But don't let your eyes go from the door or they will take grandfather's fiddle away— You are the only one who loves my music, Margaret."

"I will watch," Loreta whispered. "I'll stand here where he can't see me, poor Niño. I am afraid for him."

Margaret stood under the winter stars not far from the door of the adobe. She took a great breath, and thought of Pedro—waiting for her. His arms were eager to hold her; they were warm and caressing with comfort. She could saddle a pony and be off. Clothes—nothing mattered; Pedro loved her.

374

And yet inside the house lay Ruez—terribly burned. There was a frightened look in the eyes of her mother! The saints would never forgive Margaret Preble if she left her mother alone. No, Pedro would have to wait. Later she could tell him. Vincente was too devoted to her father to be trusted with a note—. Margaret looked a long time at the red dog star and sent a prayer that Pedro would understand, then turned back into the house.

Ruez was wild with delirium when the doctor arrived. The old man dressed the hands, poured quieting medicine down the dry throat, and then sat in the kitchen by the fire to wait. Jack limped out to feed and wipe down the horses. Margaret sat by the boy, and Loreta made some food for the tired doctor.

"This has been a busy week," he told her as he scraped some dried food from his vest with a horny black-rimmed fingernail. "Don Feliciano Soberanes died this morning and Francisco is taking it very hard."

"Soberanes was a good man," Loreta said as she cut bread. "He tried to help Indians and often had fights with Alvarado and Vallejo because they tried to get land—long ago."

"Those two certainly changed after the Americans took over. I'm told Vallejo was a great help to the state and the administration. He has worked hard to bring peace under American rule."

Loreta poked the fire. She didn't look at the old doctor.

"An Indian woman does not forget the troubles he brought to the Padres at the Missions. People who have been to Sonoma tell that Vallejo now has thousands of acres of Mission lands."

"He isn't the only one with pueblo lands! Monterey has just lost the suit against the Scotchman who bought pueblo lands at auction for a song!" the doctor said. "What can anybody do when boundaries are marked by wells and trees—and the trees have been cut down, and wells filled up to gain the ends of crafty ones?"

"It would be nice to go back to old days when Indians and

375

Padres were here alone to till and knit and hunt—" Loreta sighed. "The days when Don Feliciano Soberanes, and Don Hartnell, and Don Carlos Espinosa used to bring meat and fiesta to the Mission. They are all dead now, and Americanos and Scotchmen on the land." She pulled herself up. "But an Indian woman with a sick boy must not dream of what is gone. Food is ready. Pull up your chair, Doctor."

Chapter XXI

THE FORGOTTEN TOBACCO POUCH: 1870. 1873

MONTHS went by, and still Ruez could not use his hands without opening up the sores that were so slow in healing. Loreta's heart ached for her son who looked so helplessly at the fiddle, hanging in its turkey-red bag against the white adobe wall. The boy never spoke to her of his music. Margaret's face was sad too. Loreta wondered if this was because Pedro Gonzales never came to church now, or because Margaret was afraid of the same thing her mother feared; that Ruez would never play his grandfather's fiddle again.

How could Loreta know that the prayer her daughter sent to Pedro as she watched the red dog star had been lost in a fog of misunderstanding? Pedro crossed over to the other side of the street now when Margaret saw him in Monterey.

Once when her father sent her to Hardsell's for a paper she met Pedro face to face.

"Pedro, I couldn't help what happened, Ruez was burned," she began in a low voice—

"I'll have you know that no Indian squaw keeps me cooling my heels all night in a deserted Mission for nothing," Pedro said under his breath. "There's too many other women." His eyes gleamed with anger as he shoved her aside and strode out of the shop before Margaret could say a word. He didn't care enough to hear what had happened.

That angry black look of Pedro's cut into Margaret. Was this the way a man treated the woman he loved? Surely Satan had crept into the gentle-voiced Pedro whose arms had caressed her so tenderly. Her lover would remember the warm kisses of his Margaret after hurt and anger burned out. She

377

would wait patiently and pray to the saints for Pedro. Love was not a thing that went from people so quickly!

Life on the Preble rancho settled down into month after month of cheese making and churning; of cooking for vaqueros and hearing about the tremendous loads of tan bark that went from Monterey by schooner. There was not even the music from the fiddle. Ruez didn't look now toward the turkey-red bag. He went at his work of mending fences and herding cattle, and seemed to grow suddenly into a little old man. Only once did he go with his father and Escobar, the famous bear hunter, after a grizzly that stole calves.

People dropped in for a meal now and then, and to get irons made at the smithy when Jack was home from the tan bark camp. Loreta noticed that Dick Sanger, the Irishman, had many excuses for coming to the adobe. The young blood had an uncanny way of knowing when Jack was away, so that it was necessary to wait in order to have a horse shod or a wheel mended. Then he would smile at Margaret and talk to her. But even an Indian woman saw that there was no answering shine in the eyes of her daughter.

Loreta found out what bothered Margaret the day Jack came home from Monterey and told them that he had seen Pedro sitting on the beach with his arms around a girl.

"You see, I told you! That Gonzales boy was only after the land that will be coming to you some day. With Jack's share divided between you and Ruez, as well as your own share, any man would be glad to marry you!"

Loreta watched Margaret for a minute. The words went hard with the girl, but she was brave. Loreta was proud of the way her daughter held her head high.

"There's no reason why Pedro Gonzales should not have his arms around a girl," Margaret said quietly. "He most likely wants to marry and have sons of his own."

But Margaret's eyes were sad when they looked into the eyes of her mother, and the girl worked harder than ever at her cheese making.

378

When Jack left to ride the range, Loreta tried to comfort Margaret. "San Carlos Day is only two days away. Perhaps Pedro will be at the Mission for fiesta to honor the Saint. Pedro Gonzales is not yet married, Margaret, and many things can change before the moon is dark again."

Loreta thought she saw Margaret's eyes brighten, but the muscles of her face didn't change.

They worked together preparing beans and tortillas for the fiesta, and making meat ready to toast over the coals. "We must save tender bits of meat to take for old Romero," Loreta said. "His teeth are gone and he cannot chew tough meat."

"I suppose you'll put the tough meat into the stew you leave behind for me and the vaqueros," came from the door. "Indians, Mexicans, everyone, comes first before the master of Rancho Preble." Jack strode into the room and reached for his forgotten tobacco pouch.

Loreta smiled at her man who was such a spoiled little boy. "Marinero Jack, Loreta has already put by the nicest piece of the lot for her man to toast at the fiesta on San Carlos Day. The master of Rancho Preble has all the attention his woman knows how to give him!"

She looked at him and saw his face lose its hard look; into his eyes there came a kindliness. He walked over and put his hand under her chin, so that her face was tipped up to his; he kissed her.

"You are good to me, Loreta, but I am good to you. That is the way a man and wife should live together." Then he turned away from her and looked into the great pot of beans that cooked at the side of the fire.

"Who is going to eat so many beans?"

"All of us—November is here and the hills are green," Loreta said. "Fiesta for San Carlos comes tomorrow."

"Not all of us, for I am not going, and Vincente, the Indian, is too old," Jack told her. "What is the use of a fiesta in a ruined church? No one will come to fiesta San Carlos but a bull and a few cows. They will be there only because their

379

master owns the land, and there is good pasture around the Mission. It would be better for you to stay home, Loreta."

Loreta drew up her stooped shoulders as well as she could. "I have never missed once the day that the Saint is honored," she said. "I am a sister of San Carlos, and made vows before the altar. Loreta O-nes-e-mo will be at the Mission on San Carlos Day."

"But the trip will tire you," Marinero Jack insisted.

Loreta sighed. "To stay at home and work will tire me more."

"Oh, have your own way then," Jack said impatiently and moved toward the door. "But leave the children home to help with the work."

"Jack, why does Satan tempt you so much? Once you gave your heart and hands to God—and now you ask me to leave your children home on a Saint's day that comes but once a year!"

Jack stopped in the low doorway. "I go to church over in Monterey, don't I? I give my share of money to keep the priest. Jack Preble does what is expected of him toward the church, but he is not fool enough to take a day off to sit around in a ruined church that is forgotten. There is too much work to do. See that Margaret stays to fix up the food for vaqueros. They work hard and need proper food or they will leave us when we need them the most."

"You told Pedro Gonzales that Margaret must not marry him because she was to help her mother. Margaret goes to the Mission with me tomorrow, to honor the Saint and help her mother. The food will be ready for vaqueros, when they want it," Loreta said, and stirred the beans in the big pot. She did not even turn when the door banged after her man.

Ruez only shook his head when Loreta asked him to go along to the fiesta.

The two women did a whole day's work before they set out for the Mission at sun-up the next morning. Loreta took a stiff brush made of sedges to clean the statue of "Our Lady," and there were homemade candles and roses from her garden tied in the cloth back of Margaret's saddle.

Doña Petra Allen would be represented at the Mission fiesta day, even if the poor little lady was too weak to come over the hill from Monterey, for the roses were grown from slips of her best moss rose bush.

Loreta and Margaret were first ones there, as they had planned to be. They took off coats and rolled up the sleeves of their best dresses, and put on aprons, to keep them clean. With stones, they propped up the rotted boards that once formed the beautiful altar, and then they spread Loreta's best drawn-work cover to hide the warped places. Margaret scattered roses, and put up her own little crucifix, that Don Manuel Boronda had given her on Christmas day.

It was hard to reach the face of "Our Lady" so high up in her niche, but Loreta tied a stick to the sedge brush, and they wiped off the Saint as best they could. Then Margaret placed the candles and roses at her feet, while Loreta went up on the hillside to leave a rose for remembrance, where Antonio Prealta slept alone.

Twice Loreta herded cattle out of the ruins where they were taking shelter from the sun, but some of the more curious cows wandered back and stood at the doors. They chewed their cuds and looked at the women with their great brown eyes, and the sweet milky warmth of their breath came to Loreta through the dank mouldy air in the church.

The sun moved higher; lizards came out to warm themselves, but no one had arrived for the fiesta San Carlos.

"We will wait. Those who must work, and come from far away might be late," Loreta said, and sat down on a bit of adobe wall that had been part of the Indian quarters where she had slept as a little girl. Now that wall was only knee high; soon it would melt once more into the earth. Crows cawed from the gnarled branches of pear trees planted long

381

ago by the Padres. The faraway whinny of a horse came to them through the clear morning air.

Loreta pointed to the flat below the Mission. "When your Grandfather O-nes-e-mo was young, and the Padres first came, they taught Indians to plant corn in that flat by the river. Indians of Carmelo had never tilled the soil, and didn't understand. They would plant the corn as the Padres taught them, so they could have Mission food. Then at night they dug it up and put the earth through a coarse sieve made from willow twigs. They took the corn to their rancherias. But the patient Padres were not discouraged. Each morning they walked to the rancheria after the Indians and the corn—until at last they were able to make Indians know that there would be more corn if the grains were left in the soil to grow." She looked at Margaret, and saw that the girl was not listening; her ears were strained for the beat of horse's hoofs. The young were only interested in the heart beats of young, and not tales from other days, told by lips that were rarely kissed.

The sun was overhead, and still no one came to honor the Padres, and the Patron Saint of the Mission. Loreta took off her apron and put on her hat.

"We have no statue of the Saint to carry in the procession, but we can march around the church and sing every word of the song to him, so that San Carlos will hear, and know that two Indian women of Carmelo have not forgotten him."

She took her Rosary from the little leather bag Jack had brought her from Monterey, and then walked over to the church. Margaret's face was sad, and it was better for an Indian woman not to notice her daughter.

It was hard walking in the weeds, and the head must be turned to look at the earth to keep from stumbling, but the Saint would understand that they could not look up and send their voices to the sky, when weeds grew so thick on the path.

Loreta went first; as she turned the corner of the church, her voice rang out through the silence; and Margaret, walking behind her, soon joined in the Hymn to San Carlos:

382

"Thy purity has won for thee
A crown of fadeless light.
Oh, may its radiance shine on us
And cheer the gloom of night.

Oh, pray for us, San Carlos
For dangers hover near;
Oh, pray that God may give us strength
To conquer every fear."

But when they turned the last corner, Loreta was singing alone—

"And when we've triumphed over sin
And death's dread hour is nigh,
Oh, pray that God may angels send
To bear our souls on high."

They reached the door, and entered the church. Margaret lighted the candles, and then mother and daughter knelt before the altar to pray, and to receive the blessing of the Saint. Margaret's Rosary clicked against the wood where her grandfather and her mother long ago had said their prayers. Loreta was sure that San Carlos sent them a blessing even if there was no Padre to say the words—. She heard footsteps behind her in the church, and was thankful that another had come to honor the Saint.

When Loreta got up from her knees, she looked into the kindly brown eyes of a cow—and remembered that Jesus was born in a manger among the cows.

For fiesta music there was only the far-away boom of waves pounding on the beach below the Mission, and the cry of gulls as they winged their way toward fresh-water bathing places along the river. Loreta didn't bother with a fire for meat, but instead they ate the beans and tortillas cold, for women alone do not fuss over food.

"We must be getting back," Loreta said to break the silence.

383

"There will be the milk to take care of, and a hot supper to make ready." She packed the horse for the return. San Carlos Day was over, and the cross on top of the tower was catching the late afternoon sun. Two Indian women said a prayer at the feet of "Our Lady" and left her to her lonely vigil.

There were so many sorrows for an Indian woman on the Carmelo as the years went on. Her man's face grew set when Jack's name was mentioned. Twice Loreta had seen young Jack on the street in Monterey and begged him to come home to the rancho, but her great, husky, son only sneered and put on the stubborn airs of his father.

"I'm bossing Chinamen who are laying tracks for a new railroad that is coming to Monterey from San Francisco," he told her. "I can earn enough to live and have a few drinks too, without licking my father's boots!" He stepped off the wooden sidewalk into the mud of Alvarado Street to keep his mother from touching him.

Loreta stayed longer than usual at the ruined Mission on the way home that day. She asked "Our Lady" to bring peace and happiness once more to the children of an Indian woman who was still faithful to the memory of Padres. She lighted a candle for each son and her daughter, and placed them in the niche beside the faded, weatherworn statue that had been carved by her father. "Our Lady" was not beautiful like the ones in the church in Monterey, but she was much dearer to a Sister of San Carlos. This Saint made by O-nes-e-mo understood the heart of an Indian.

Chapter XXII

CONSCIENCE MONEY: 1875. 1879

RUEZ was twenty-two, the day he sat on the roadside watching sheep and singing a tune that would not go from his head; a song created about the fluffy white clouds that were riding high like great horses plunging into the blue sea. He saw a rickety wagon drawn by two lean horses come meandering around the bend of the road, but his own fine stallions of song could not be stopped. He sang on, and kept his eyes toward the clouds as the wagon came nearer.

"That's good music you're singing," a dark man called from the wagon seat, and he pulled his horses to a stop. "Mind if I listen while the horses rest? I've never heard that tune before."

Ruez was pleased that a stranger had taken notice of his song. The man was kindly looking, with great dark eyes that smiled a little, but there was sadness behind the smile. His face was very pale.

"You've never heard the song, because I was just making it up about those clouds over there," Ruez said and nodded toward the south. "They're horses plunging—" But he didn't have a chance to finish.

"Sing it again, will you?" the man asked eagerly, "I want to hear—" He got off the wagon and came to sit on the yellow earth beside Ruez.

When the song was finished, the man was silent. He just watched the sky for a while.

"Did you like it?" Ruez asked, and waited anxiously to hear what the stranger had to say.

"No, I didn't, because your song wasn't long enough." The dark-eyed man looked into the very insides of Ruez and made

385

a great hurt come in the boy's stomach. "The clouds go on and on like the affairs of life. We never know what shape they'll take next!"

"If you want more, I have other tunes," Ruez suggested. "I've tried to keep from thinking of them since I was burned —but there's fiesta music and bear-baitings, and the chant I made to 'Our Lady' who watches alone in the Mission, and is sad because Indians have forgotten her and the Padres. Indians drink instead of going to church on Sundays."

"Please sing on," the man said eagerly. "Your music is good. It keeps me from thinking of night sweats and bad dreams, and the troubles of my dear Fanny."

"I used to play tunes on the fiddle a few years ago—but my hands were burned on the forge. I'll do the best I can at humming." Ruez began the song about his mother's hair which had never been finished on the fiddle. Somehow the eager dark-eyed man brought a feeling of peace. For an hour Ruez sang, and then his throat was dry and he stopped.

The man had tears in his eyes. He didn't talk.

"Are you a vaquero?" the boy asked. "You don't have a saddle in your wagon. Our vaqueros always bring their own saddles."

"I'm not a vaquero—I'm a bit like yourself," the stranger murmured. "I look at clouds, and trees, and waves, but instead of singing about them, I write words on paper, so that other people far away will see things through my eyes, when they read the words."

"Mr. Berwick showed me about reading at school. I wish other people could hear the songs I hear." Ruez kicked at a bunch of wild grass.

"Ye gods, they can, if you write notes for other people to play! Your songs will go on and on, long after you're dead, instead of fading away on a hillside. Haven't you heard of notes? Haven't you ever seen music notes on white paper?" The man's eyes shone with feverish excitement, and red came

386

into his cheeks as he looked at Ruez. His brown hair was damp and curly now.

Ruez shook his head. "I just know music that comes from inside me, and what my mother sings, and chants I hear in church and when people play."

The man took an envelope from his pocket and wrote something on it. "I'm staying the night on the Berwick rancho, but I'll look around, and try to find someone to show you how to clap the beautiful music from inside you onto paper. God knows—perhaps a penniless consumptive can show his gratitude to these parts, by making it possible for all the world to hear music from the hillsides of Carmelo!"

He handed Ruez the paper. "You'll find me most any time of day at Jules Simoneau's restaurant in Monterey—or the saloon of Sanchez. If I'm not either place they'll tell you where I am. Sometimes I stay in bed to keep warm." His great eyes looked straight at Ruez. "And sing on, boy! Sing of sand pipers running along the beach; sing of tall dark pines, and surf rolling white on the crescent of Monterey Bay in the moonlight —and God bless you." He turned quickly, climbed into the wagon, and clucked at the lean bay horses.

On the back of the envelope, written in a scrawling hand, was the name, Robert Louis Stevenson.

That night under the stars when they were walking from the barn, Ruez told Margaret about the man, and what he had said about writing music notes for other people to read.

"I went into the privy with the fiddle to try and play while father was in the house tonight," Ruez confessed. "My fingers are stiff, but I managed a tune."

"Ruez! Then you've started to play again." Margaret's voice sounded relieved and pleased.

"The stranger said to sing on. Perhaps my songs will live even after I'm dead, because they will be written on paper. The first thing I'll do when I learn, will be to put down the

387

notes of Padre Amores' chant, that you sang to me so long ago. Ruez will not let *that* die on the hillside—"

Margaret stopped him before they reached the house. "Tell Mother your news. She is sad because you never speak to her of music. She is so proud of the songs you make. If she knows you can play again, even one little tune, she will be happy, and it will make her forget for a minute or two her worry about Jack."

"No," Ruez shook his head. "She didn't want me to play the song that morning. *She* didn't care."

"But if you hadn't played as she tried to tell us—then father would not have been angry and perhaps the accident to your hands would never have happened. Mother prays to the saints for you every day, Ruez. Perhaps this man Robert Louis Stevenson was sent to you because of her prayers—"

"No," Ruez said. "She never asks me about songs."

"Sit down here." Margaret's voice was harsh. "I want to tell you something!" She pulled him beside her on the edge of the watering trough. "Don't you know that a mother lives on in her children? If they are bad it hurts her. If they are fine and good it makes her proud. Mothers are like that. Our mother has sorrows. It is your chance to make her happy and young again, living through Ruez and his songs. Tell her your news or maybe the saints will not let your songs live on. You are a part of your mother—just as your songs are a part of you!"

"Oh, all right, but a man's better keeping his mouth shut," Ruez told her crossly.

Disappointment came hard on the heels of happiness. Ruez was not able to get away to Monterey for several weeks. The rains came on, and cattle must be attended to. The fences were old and did not hold well. There was much patching of wires and propping of posts to keep in the strong yearlings that stretched their necks to nibble at grass just outside the fences. The wet weather made his father's hip stiff and lame, and an aching joint didn't improve the disposition of a man who must sit by the fire in the Preble adobe!

Robert Louis Stevenson was not at Monterey, when Ruez finally had a chance to make the trip. Jules Simoneau who kept the restaurant shook his head sadly, and straightened the red and white table cloth. "The poor soul lies sick at the goat ranch up in Robinson Canyon. Johnathan Wright, the bear hunter, is doing for him. You see half the time he didn't have enough to eat, and wet weather goes hard with consumptives."

All the world seemed to end in that moment, for Ruez. He had been living these weeks to see Stevenson again.

"What's the matter?" Jules Simoneau asked. "Is there anything I can do?"

"Señor Stevenson liked my music. He promised to try and find someone to show me how to put the notes on paper so that my songs wouldn't fade away on the hillside. . . ."

"There's no composer here now, lad." Simoneau shook his head. "But who can tell? Things are changing fast. A big new hotel called the Del Monte is going up the other side of El Estero. A hotel that will bed down two or three hundred people and bring money into Monterey. Maybe a man who writes music will come there sometime." His eyes were bright and he walked up to Ruez with quick steps. "If Stevenson liked your music, you are not to be pitied. Young folks are impatient. Writing the notes will come to you at the proper time."

The first person Ruez saw when he went along the street was marinero Swan. The poor old man looked haggard, and carried a slate and a tin cup. A long tin ear trumpet hung from a dirty string around his neck. His face lighted in a smile when he saw Ruez.

"Well, how's the fiddler?" he asked. "I've thought many a time how quick you milked me of what I knew of fiddling." He held the trumpet to his ear.

"A man named Stevenson told me that my notes could be written on paper like words. He was going to help me but he's sick," Ruez said. "Do you know about notes on paper?"

"Only by ear," Swan cackled from a mouth empty of teeth. "Never was much on notes, and now my ears are shut tight

389

from sound. I reckon there's some folks around here that's glad Jack Swan can hear no longer. Most likely wish his mouth was dumb too."

"What do you mean?" Ruez shouted through the trumpet, while a yellow dog sniffed at his legs.

"You sucked the tits too recently to understand, boy," the old man grinned. "You tell your father that Gore and the Scotchman still fight over the land that María Berreto sold three times, but the Scotchman's just sold Pescadero Rancho and part of La Lagunita to some highty-tighty rich railroad folks for five dollars an acre—and him not even having a clear title to it. These gold rush fellers, Stanford and Huntington, and Crocker and some more, figures on building a hotel resort for rich folks from San Francisco. The cellar's dug already and lots of men working out there."

"Come home with me for a few days and tell Father your news," Ruez shouted into the horn. "He's laid up, and you'll cheer him."

The old man shook his head. "There's lots of new folks in town. We haven't had a town meeting for nine years and there's to be one soon. I want to be here." He smiled. "I may be deaf, but I'm not dumb. Besides, I tell folks yarns about the old days in Monterey before the Americanos sailed in, and then they jingle a little into my tin mug to keep me going. Don't know but what it's more fun yarning, and scaring some folks that's got guilty consciences, than it is working in gold mines. You see them that changes boundary lines and does other shady itims, don't know exactly how much old Swan is telling the new-comers about them. So it pays the guilty ones to drop a jingle or two in the cup as a sweetener for safety's sake. I pick up quite a bit of conscience money." He patted Ruez on the back, and, cackling to himself, the old man went on his way.

Robert Louis Stevenson did not forget his promise. One day Ruez came into town with a load of potatoes. He was just going into the shop of Trujillo the jeweler to get the gold pin that his father had ordered for Loreta's forty-third wedding anniversary, when the pale, dark, man caught him by the arm.

"I'm sorry to have let you down," Stevenson told Ruez. "But you see I couldn't help it—the hemorrhages won't wait and neither will the cough! But I'm happy, lad—and I've often thought of you since Jules Simoneau told me you came to see me. I'm going to marry Fanny Osburne! Do you hear that? She's free from her philandering husband and well now. She's told a musical friend about you, who lives in San Francisco. Your notes will see paper yet!"

Ruez looked into the bright eyes that no longer had sadness looking out from behind the smile. "I'm glad you are to be married," he said. "I hope it stops your cough."

Stevenson threw back his head and roared with laughter. "I'm afraid it'll take more than love to do that. But the writing business looks up. I've finished 'Amateur Emigrant,' and 'Vendetta in the West,' and here's hoping a pocketful of money will come my way." He held out a paper and began searching in his black coat for a pencil. "Write your name and how we can reach you on this, and sing on in your wilderness. Someday the right person is *bound* to hear your song! That's all that has kept me weaving tales. We dreamers must live on hope when the food runs low."

Ruez wrote on the rumpled paper. This man had not forgotten the songs he had hummed on the hillside. When Ruez finished, he handed the paper back. "Music is coming to me now about this Fanny who has taken away the sadness from your eyes," he told Stevenson. "Maybe some day I can send it to you on paper. I'll call it 'A Song to Fanny.' That is all I can do for you, except wish the saints will smile on you, and I'll light a candle now and then on feast days."

"I'll be waiting for 'A Song to Fanny,'" Stevenson said quietly, and put out his hand. "Goodbye, fellow-dreamer on the hillside. I'll probably never see you again."

Chapter XXIII

GOLD FOR MONTEREY: 1880

JACK PREBLE was excited over the great new Hotel Del Monte that was bringing money and business into sleepy old Monterey. The streets had a decent number of people walking on them again. Rusty keys turned in rusty locks, and adobe buildings were aired and made ready once more for shops. There was even talk of putting in street lights, so strangers wouldn't break their necks where wooden sidewalks ended suddenly in a mud puddle. Natives knew just who had ripped up the sidewalk to burn on foggy nights, but strangers couldn't be expected to know this. It looked bad for the town.

Mr. Berwick was making money selling big strawberries packed in fresh green leaves to the Del Monte, and Jack went with him to see the chief steward. After that, Preble potatoes, and Preble fine steer meat brought good prices from the hotel.

"It's too bad Don José Abrego couldn't have lived to see the grand ball-room of Del Monte," Jack told Loreta. "How he would have loved the gold and glitter of it—so would David Spence! They died just a little too soon. Only Jack Preble and a few tougher ones remain to see the old capital wake up and stretch again."

"The Americanos don't serenade and have cascarone fiestas on the streets. The ball-room is only for rich ones," Ruez said. "And there are no more grizzlies to fight bulls in the weedy place behind the Pacific House."

"But these Crockers and Huntingtons and Hopkins, will bring more money than Monterey has seen!" Jack cried. "Look at us all selling our produce. Monterey is having her taste of gold dug from the mines! These men who own the Del Monte

belong to the Southern Pacific Railroad. They only call themselves the Pacific Improvement Company."

Loreta sighed. "With money coming into Monterey again,
there will be only fights and trouble that it brings."

"I suppose you'd rather starve and see weeds and grass growing in gardens of the adobes in Monterey. But there's something the rich people are doing for you, Loreta, something
that should make your heart sing. Even your old Jack is happy
about it." He put his arm around her.

"Rich people can do little for an Indian woman, Marinero
Jack."

"But folks from Del Monte have been coming over the hill
to Carmelo in carryalls to see the San Carlos Mission. They
make pilgrimages to it, and Father Casanova ordered Machado
to clean out all the rubbish and sand from the church, and
fence it so that cattle do not wander in. Machado and his
daughter were hauling rubbish out with a wooden sled as I
passed this morning."

Loreta could hardly believe the good news. A priest taking
an interest in the abandoned Mission that Indians loved!
Maybe the statue of "Our Lady," who had watched during the
years, would smile on these people, and bring them a message
from Juan O-nes-e-mo who had built the church. Only a few
Indians were left now to sing the song of San Carlos on feast
days. The rest had died, or moved away—or forgotten the
vows they had once made to the saint. Indians couldn't do
anything but keep the roof over the sacristy, and Cristiano
Machado, the Portuguese custodian, had helped with even
that bit of work!

The next day Francisco Soberanes rode into the rancho on
his way up the Carmelo to Los Laureles rancho. The hind left
shoe on his horse was loose and the metal clinked on the hard
adobe as he came up to the smithy.

"What would we do without the ranchero who pounds
metal?" he called. ":Carmelo can't get along without Preble,
and his irons and hammer." He waved at Loreta who stood

393

at the door of the adobe winding wool for knitting socks.

"That makes me think of the days when we were both youngsters attending Mass at the Mission, Loreta. The first time I really noticed you, you were knitting, and the Padres were adjusting the great grinding stones that eventually did away with the metates that Indian women used. And now you still knit—but we buy flour and no longer have Spanish fiestas with races and games. You were very little then, and so was I." He laughed. "Doña Petra Allen is ailing, Loreta. She said if I managed to see you, to tell you it would be nice if you dropped in when you came to Monterey next time."

Loreta didn't wait. She rode into Monterey with Ruez that very morning, on the wagon that took produce to the Hotel Del Monte. She wanted to see Doña Petra—and to look at the newly cleaned Mission with her own eyes!

"I'll be waiting at the plaza for you," she told Ruez when he stopped on the road to let her off below the adobe where Doña Allen lived.

Doña Petra had a cold on her chest. She looked pale and worn. Umesia, the Indian woman who came often, fussed over the fire brewing herb tea for the cold.

"I'm not really sick," the gentle old lady told Loreta, "I stayed up too late with Rosalia Leese who has been sick. But an aunt must do what she can for her niece."

"Not so much that the aunt gets sick," Umesia grunted. "Let General Vallejo, her brother, do something about having people stay with Rosalia."

When Umesia had gone out, Doña Petra made a face over the hot concoction in the china cup, and then held it out to Loreta. "Have a little," she laughed. "It will cure you of anything and everything. I'm sure Umesia put a pinch of every herb she's ever gathered into this pot full of tea."

Loreta laughed then, for she too had brought herbs to dose Doña Petra! Umesia had hurried down from Stork Creek with her bare leather-hard feet and arrived first!

394

An hour later Loreta was waiting for Ruez in the Plaza, when Father Casanova raced up on his sorrel horse. He was very much excited, and called out, as he jumped to the ground:
"Come—I have news!"

Women stopped gossiping in the shade, and old men who sat in the sun and dozed and then waked up again to talk of other days, moved their stiff joints. Vaqueros and caballeros came out of nearby shops; fancy dressed Del Monte visitors hurried over to where the priest was standing. Loreta saw Ruez stop the horses over by Don Cooper's and tie the reins to a tree. She hurried to join the crowd.

"We have uncovered graves in Mission San Carlos de Borromeo on the Carmelo," the priest cried. "The grave of Padre Junipero Serra, founder of the Missions in California, and Padre Crespi and the Padre Lopez. The slabs were buried under the sand and rubbish! Everybody is invited to come and see the tombs opened. All come tomorrow for the ceremony! We will have music. You will want to see what's in the graves."

A beautifully dressed woman turned to Loreta. "I don't understand Spanish. What does the priest say?"

"Tomorrow there will be a ceremony at the Mission San Carlos—to open the graves they have just found," Loreta told her. "Everybody is invited. They will open the graves and have music."

"Oh, how wonderful! We'll tell our whole crowd over at the hotel, and take a tally-ho and make a picnic afterward." She went off with the others, full of chatter that came so fast Loreta could not understand it.

An off-key cackling voice came from the corner by Alvarado Street. "Father Junipero Serra isn't there at all. His bones do not lie in Americano soil—Te-lam-o knows. Te-lam-o's father helped them carry away the bones in a rawhide stretcher when the Spanish Padres left the Mission," an old Indian woman laughed mirthlessly. "Do you think Spaniards would leave

395

their favorite Padre's bones to rest among dirty Mexicans, when they could not be there to guard them?"

"Hush," a señorita said, and crossed herself. "You will disturb souls with such talk."

"Hush, yourself," the woman hissed. "Te-lam-o knows. She was there. Te-lam-o's father helped carry Serra's bones over to Monterey and put them on the boat for Spain. The tomb of Serra is empty."

The crowd watched the Indian woman for a minute and then began to talk excitedly.

"It is only the raving of a crack-pot Indian," a tall Mexican said. "Never listen to her. Te-lam-o knows nothing about bones of Padres. She is old and a fool!"

"No bones in the tomb. See for yourself tomorrow!" the old woman shrieked.

Father Casanova came to where Loreta stood beside Ruez. "Do you know anything of this?" he asked. "I have heard the Indian legend that Serra was taken away, but if that is true, why weren't the records changed? You are a Sister of San Carlos, Loreta; tell me."

"I know nothing about the bones," Loreta said. "My father, Juan O-nes-e-mo, and I went up the hill in an ox cart and saw Padres away when they left the Mission long ago. I remember Te-lam-o well."

"It was done in the night," Te-lam-o said, looking with beady black eyes and pressing her nut-cracker jaws together in such determination that her nose was less than an inch away from her pointed chin. "The bones were carried away in the night, for they didn't want the Mexicans to know! Serra was a great Spaniard. They would not leave his bones to waste away in Mexican soil, with no Spanish friar to watch over them."

"Shut up—" a tall Americano in dark clothes growled, and kicked the old woman away. "What time are the ceremonies, Father Casanova? There are many visitors at Del Monte for the Fourth of July holiday. St. Patrick's Cadets are here. No doubt most of the people would like to come. I'll put up a notice."

"The Cadets of St. Patrick shall be our guard of honor at the ceremonies! It will bring color and beauty."

Ruez helped Te-lam-o up from where she had fallen on the hard yellow clay, and Loreta brushed off her rusty black dress. As she adjusted the shawl, Loreta pressed a coin into the old woman's hand. "It is well to be silent," she whispered. "Indians know many things, but talking only makes white people call them fools."

"May the Spirit of Serra in far away Spain bless you, Sister Loreta, of San Carlos, and may all your children have shining faces when they meet Gabriel and Saint Peter," the old woman cackled. "But you shall see tomorrow. The tomb will be empty. Te-lam-o knows." She shuffled along the creaky board sidewalk.

"Poor Te-lam-o," Father Casanova said, looking after the woman. "She never misses a Mass, and yet one wonders, Loreta, if there is anything going on behind those bright eyes."

"Perhaps San Carlos understands the minds as well as the hearts of Indians who built a church to his memory—" Loreta said.

On the way home Ruez was silent, but he stopped with his mother to say a prayer to "Our Lady" in her niche. No longer did they walk among broken tiles from the roof, for the church was cleaned now, and Machado stood by the door to receive praises for his hard work.

"Americans in silk dresses come into the ruins and look at the statue your father carved," he told Loreta. "The dresses swish—and their cloaks are rich and heavy to keep out cold fog. Sometimes they drop a coin in my hand when they leave. Twice lovers who are happy and feel the charm, have put gold pieces in this hand! The statue brings good luck to lovers. I tell lovers that."

Loreta thought of the wet, cold night that she had knelt

397

with Margaret, and asked the saint to bless the girl and her lover Pedro Gonzales. The saint had smiled just the same that night as she did now on happy Americano lovers who dropped gold pieces into the hand of Cristiano Machado the Portuguese. But no happiness had come to the grand-daughter of Juan O-nes-e-mo who had carved the saint.

"I can't bear to think of Americanos rushing over to Carmel in their carryalls and making fiesta," Ruez said, his face pulled into a frown. "Those silly girls on the Plaza giggling, and laughing, and talking of picnics—." He switched the horses and looked off toward the hills where his grandfather O-nes-e-mo's Room-se-en tribe had lived before the Americano ranchero had turned them off.

"God knows," Loreta said. "Perhaps Americanos will be different about the Mission after a while,—"

"I'll make them feel different, damn them!" Ruez cried hotly.

For the first time Loreta realized that her dreamer of songs had inherited some of his father's fight. She had never seen him so resentful; so black and scowling.

"But they have been good people," Loreta said in a soothing voice. "Better than bad Spanish and Mexicans. There are bad as well as good folks in all people—even Indians. Te-mo, an Indian, was the cause of Antonio's death—. José died because of Tiburcio Vasquez, who was hanged four years ago in San José."

Ruez ate his supper that night and disappeared. Loreta didn't see him again before she went to bed. Margaret looked worried, but the women didn't speak of the boy as they sat around the fire that warmed bones chilled by July fog.

Long after they were in bed, Jack touched Loreta tenderly. "I hope Ruez is not fighting or drinking, Loreta. He worries me, not being home. Did you see him leave? At supper he looked black and full of fight."

Loreta moved close. "Marinero Jack, you know now, how many times when you were young and full of fight, I lay here thinking just such thoughts as you have about Ruez tonight. When I worried and asked you not to go, you only pulled away, and said it was toughening for a man. Perhaps you too must learn to wait—"

"But that was different. I *had* to go. There were things to do," he said quickly. "You don't understand, Loreta. I wouldn't want a single cloud for you on the day that San Carlos de Borromeo Mission is to bloom once more. The Mission gave me you, Loreta." Then he held her close as in the old days so long past when they were young, and gray hairs were in the future.

Chapter XXIV

WOMAN PLAYS HER PART: 1881. 1882

THERE was a cold, wet fog July 3, 1882. Loreta was afraid visitors would not come to the grave-opening ceremony at San Carlos. But after breakfast was cooked, and the milk attended to, the sun came out. Lunch was packed and all made ready for the day.

Loreta could not help thinking of fiesta days before this one when only a handful came to the Mission, and her own family had been so different. Little María, Benito, José, and his father Antonio! All these people were only memories now for an old Indian woman.

"Are you ready?" Jack was impatient. "I have the horses hitched!"

"Where's Ruez?" Loreta asked Margaret. "He had no breakfast."

Ruez was nowhere to be found. They called him—and Margaret ran along the hills searching until she was warm and moist.

"We'll leave him here then. He's old enough to look out for himself, and there's plenty of horses to ride," Jack said crossly. "Let's be going. I want to see the crowd and have a word or two with old friends. Soberanes says that Don Cooper is coming to the Mission. I want to talk to him about the bean crop over at Watsonville."

When they turned the last bend in the road by the Padres' pear orchard, Loreta saw there was a big crowd gathered at the Mission. Popcorn men and an ice cream cart were set up in the stubble field that had once been the patio where Mission Indians worked and played and ate their meals. Horses of rigs

400

and carryalls were tied to the pear trees. Loreta sent a prayer for Padre Payeras who had stayed alone in the orchard to bid the old gnarled trees farewell before he left in 1836.

Some fancy young soldiers with white braid across their chests talked and laughed in a group by the church door. A band with plumed hats was getting ready to play. Fine ladies with bunches of silk sticking out behind on their dresses, and white laces at their throats, were walking around with their men folks to look at the ruins. There were young men, middle-aged men with well-trimmed beards, and old men in black frock coats, and women with shawls over their heads—and señoritas. Children darted through the crowd playing hide and seek among the ruined walls. A pair of lovers scratched hearts and their names on the wall of the Mission while they waited. The whole place was filled with people who talked excitedly.

Old Romero, whose father had helped build the Mission, came over to where Loreta stood in the shade by the door. "Will they take it away from us, now they like the Mission?" he asked. "It is still only a ruin belonging to Indians, even if the Padres' bones are found."

"Father Casanova is a good priest," Loreta told him. "All we can do is trust him."

Jack came from tying the horses. Margaret walked beside him in her best black silk dress with hand-drawn cuffs and collar. She wore the hat bought only last year, and it shaded her face and made her look beautiful. Loreta was proud of them both as she saw them come toward her. But she wished an Indian sister of San Carlos could have her sons standing beside her. Where was Jackie today? Somewhere in a bunk-house of a railroad crew? Where had Ruez gone so secretly, with such dark looks?

The band struck up and drowned out the calls from the popcorn vendors and then Father Casanova, in his black coat and stiff collar, said a prayer.

Loreta missed the patched and faded brown habits and

sandals of Padre Abella and Padre Payeras. She remembered
so well seeing the Padres standing where Father Casanova
stood now. But times were changed. Grass grew between great
stone slabs that had fallen, and men sat on the ruined altar!

Father Casanova told these people about the building of
the Mission and the struggle Padres had to bring the Indians
to work and to prayers, and then, while he read the records de-
scribing the burial place of the Padres, Machado opened the
graves. There was a silence and the crowd moved closer as
each body was identified by the vestments in the grave and a
few bones. One tomb contained only dirt and vestments so
far as Loreta could see. Te-lam-o must be right about the bones
being taken away, but the priest said nothing. A soldier reached
down to pick up a bit of cloth . . . it crumbled in his hands.

Father Casanova took a bit of the vestments from each
tomb, as holy relics; then the graves were closed and sealed
and a marble slab placed over each mound.

After the priest finished saying a prayer, the band struck up
a hymn and everybody sang. But when the last notes of Americano band music died away, a violin called clear and sweet
from high up in the bell tower. The beautiful chant of Padre
Amores rang once more through the Mission San Carlos on
the Carmelo.

No one in the crowd moved. Loreta thought she would die
from happiness. Surely the good San Carlos heard the son of
an Indian woman playing the chant his grandfather had played
so long ago. The faith in San Carlos had been carried through
the years in the hearts and minds of faithful Indians, when
they could no longer keep the building they had made with
their hands. But the tower of Juan O-nes-e-mo stood with its
cross high in the sky, and the music a Spanish Padre had given
to Indians still rang through the air.

Loreta turned and smiled at "Our Lady" crudely carved
by her father, and faded by rains and sun. The Saint smiled
back from the niche where she had been placed by loving
hands.

Loreta wondered if now the Mother of Sorrows would send some happiness to mix with the sadness that was in the heart of Margaret, who stood straight and beautiful beside her mother. Long ago, the blue robed saint had smiled on Loreta and Antonio and she had brought love and happiness to Don Allen and the dainty Petra Boronda, when they had confessed their love and lighted candles to her. Surely she would not forget the patient Margaret who had carried the chant of her grandfather in her heart when there was no one to play the fiddle at Mission San Carlos. O, Holy Mother, a bit of ease for the heart of Margaret, and all would be well on the Carmelo.

Father Casanova put up a hand.

"You have heard the song of a Padre, played by the grandson of an Indian who labored with his heart and his hands to build this crumbling Mission. The boy wanted you all to know and understand what this church that crumbles away, means to the faithful Indians who still worship inside these abandoned walls. Are we going to break faith with the Padres who blazed the trail for us, so that we might reap the harvest? Is San Carlos on the Carmelo to crumble and disappear from the earth because Indians can no longer keep a roof over the ruins? That, my friends, is the message that comes to your hearts from the fiddle of a Padre long ago turned to dust."

Loreta stood by the door as people moved around in the ruined church. She saw Ruez come down from the tower carrying the fiddle that had belonged to her father, and she heard her man brag to people nearby, that Ruez, the fiddle player, was his son!

Money from purses of the richly dressed clinked onto the turkey red bag she had made so long ago for Juan's fiddle on San Carlos Day.

"For a shingle roof to save what is left," a man in a frock coat called to the crowd. "Drop your money and checks onto the fiddle bag, and keep faith with the Fiddler of Carmel. It

403

takes so little to save so much! Mrs. Leland Stanford has started the fund."

Loreta saw Margaret look lovingly at Pedro Gonzales, over the head of a señorita who strolled by his side. "Come," she murmured, "let us get nearer the wall, where we will be out of the way."

Shouts of popcorn vendors came from outside. They had moved their wagons to the place where Loreta had often seen Juan O-nes-e-mo in the shade making shoes for Spanish señoritas. Loud laughter of the young soldiers came from north of the Mission, where Antonio slept on the hillside. A man in a silk top hat shoved Loreta and Margaret aside, as he rushed toward a group of laughing men and women.

"The show's over, and we've a party on. We'll never get back to Del Monte, if we don't start soon. The tally-ho is ready," he called to them.

Margaret's eyes still followed Pedro.

"Now you are sad in the heart, Margaret, because Pedro walks with another, but many things can change, and men change too. At the right time the saints will send you the blessings you deserve," Loreta told her daughter, and saw that there were tears in Margaret's eyes. "After Americanos have gone, we will light candles for 'Our Lady' and maybe she will bring the day for your happiness closer."

"Drop your money and checks on the fiddle bag!" The words, shouted out by a man in a frock coat, rang through the church where once, not long before, only two women had lifted their voices in the song to San Carlos so that the Saint would know that he was not forgotten on the Carmelo. Now that the Mission was fashionable, Americano men were so anxious to raise money that they cried out like vendors in a market place.

Without Margaret, people would not be dropping money onto the fiddle bag for the Mission, Loreta thought. Ruez with his fiddle playing was only the *outside* man part, that put into doing the things that women felt in their hearts. But now,

404

women must stand silent, and let men shine and shake their feathers in the sun like roosters. Long ago Marinero Jack had wanted an Indian Sister of Carmelo to do away with her baby Ruez, before he was born. But today Ruez was shining out proudly because his mother had brought him into the world, and his sister had been patient through the years and taught him the chant of his grandfather. That was the way women must serve God and the saints, with only a song and the red fiddle bag to show to the world.

"Put your money here," called the man, "save the Mission."

Loreta took Margaret's arm and they walked toward the door. As they came up close, Jack Preble dropped five gold pieces on the pile, and then glanced proudly toward Loreta and his daughter.

Loreta looked up at "Our Lady" in her niche. Juan O-nes-e-mo, her father, had saved the statue from savages of pirates on the very day Loreta was born, and now the Saint was smiling back at the daughter of Juan, through lips that were faded and weather worn. Two women understood the ways of men and were silent.

THE END

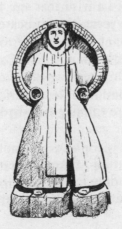

405

AFTERWORD

WITHOUT a fine old lady this book could not have been written. She was Isabella Meadows, and she was born July 7th, 1846, the day the American flag went up over the Mexican Custom-House in Monterey, California. Isabella's mother was a Carmel Mission Indian, and her father an English cabin boy on a whaling ship.

Isabella Meadows was a great lady in every sense of the word; she had dignity and poise, and her clear brown eyes reflected inner peace and a workable philosophy of life.

When I first met her in 1932 she welcomed me into the kitchen of her two roomed cabin, and gave me a plain kitchen chair. There was no apology, no resentment. This was her home and I was welcome. Many times after that, I was invited to share the one dish of beans cooked Spanish style, or tortillas, or jerked meat, or fresh pears brought from Carmel Valley orchards. This old lady, who had once been the daughter of a rich ranchero, had no hatred in her heart because of lost luxuries; instead, she took a great interest in new things that were going on, and often expressed a wish that she might fly.

Down through the years, she had carried in her keen mind intimate details of life at the Mission during her grandfather's day; things her mother knew and had heard, and in time passed on to her daughter. On checking the historical dates that were possible to check, I found Isabella was extremely accurate. She would not only tell me the day and date, but often what kind of a day it was sixty or seventy years ago when something happened.

Many times we went into the country in a car and she showed me the herbs that Padres had taught Indians to use for sicknesses. She would point to a gnarled old oak tree, and say, "That

406

is where Indian bodies stayed until Padres came out from the Mission to bless them," or "A man was hanged there," and she would give the details.

After several years of note-taking came the historical research necessary for a book of this kind, and during this time, I became acquainted with the grandsons and granddaughters and great-grandchildren of the Spanish Dons, who had known Isabella's grandfather and her mother, and who attended Mass at Carmel Mission. Among these gracious people, who spared no time or effort to help me re-create the life of the time, was the Boronda family, descendants of Don José Manuel Boronda, and of Petra in the book. They showed me many family heirlooms that are described.

Mr. Benito Soberanes and his son Nathaniel opened their treasure chests to let me examine old Spanish documents, letters, clippings, pictures and objects used in the old Spanish days of Monterey.

I am indebted to Mr. Thomas Meadows, younger brother of Isabella Meadows, for many details of Carmel Valley days during the seventies and eighties.

Good friends were generous in the loaning of many valuable and rare books and pamphlets, especially one about the earthquakes from the time the first record was printed.*

For several years, Miss Isabella helped me to piece together details of family life on the Carmelo, until scientists from

* BIBLIOGRAPHY:
BANCROFT, HERBERT HOWE, *History of California*
DAMON, CHARLES RIPLEY, *Damon's American Dictionary of Dates*
ENGELHARDT, FR. ZEPHYRIN, O.F.M., *Franciscans in California*
HITTELL, THEODORE, *History of California*
HOLDEN, EDWARD S., L.L.D., List of Recorded Earthquakes in California, Lower California, Oregon and Washington Territory
HUNT & SANCHEZ, *Short History of California*
MACFARLAND, GRACE, *Monterey, Cradle of California Romance*
POWERS, LAURA BRIDE, *Old Monterey*
QUINN, J. M., *Monterey and San Benito County History and Biographical Record*
WATKINS, MAJOR ROLLIN, *Monterey and Santa Cruz*

AFTERWORD

Washington discovered her and found her to be a clever linguist and the last of the Carmel Indians to speak the Room-se-en language. They took her, tortilla pans, dried herbs and all, by automobile to Washington, where she spent several years, vitally interested in her new work—started at the age of 89.

Miss Isabella was generous, and gave me all she had to give, and it was with great sadness and a distinct feeling of loss that I, along with members of the Boronda family, attended final services for her at Carmel Mission. She had simply grown tired one day in Washington, and decided, at 94, to "rest." She didn't wake up from that sleep. It was fitting that the granddaughter of a Mission builder should be brought back to stay, for a little while, under the tower her grandfather had helped to build, before she was put beside her ancestors.

Thank you, Isabella Meadows.
Hasta la vista.

Anne B. Fisher
Carmel Valley
California

Carmel Mission
in the early 1800's